SOMEWHERE SUMMER

26 KISSES AND *HOW MY SUMMER WENT UP IN FLAMES*

ANNA MICHELS AND JENNIFER SALVATO DOKTORSKI

Somewhere SUMMER

SIMON PULSE

New York   London   Toronto   Sydney   New Delhi

SIMON PULSE

An imprint of Simon & Schuster Children's Publishing Division

1230 Avenue of the Americas, New York, New York 10020

This Simon Pulse paperback edition May 2020

26 Kisses copyright © 2016 by Simon & Schuster, Inc.

How My Summer Went Up in Flames copyright © 2013 by Jennifer Salvato Doktorski

Cover photograph copyright © 2020 by Getty Images

All rights reserved, including the right of reproduction in whole or in part in any form.

SIMON PULSE and colophon are registered trademarks of Simon & Schuster, Inc.

For information about special discounts for bulk purchases, please contact Simon & Schuster Special Sales at 1-866-506-1949 or business@simonandschuster.com.

The Simon & Schuster Speakers Bureau can bring authors to your live event. For more information or to book an event contact the Simon & Schuster Speakers Bureau at 1-866-248-3049 or visit our website at www.simonspeakers.com.

Book designed by Jess LaGreca

The text of this book was set in Adobe Garamond Pro.

Manufactured in the United States of America

2 4 6 8 10 9 7 5 3 1

Library of Congress Control Number 2020930415

ISBN 978-1-5344-7378-2 (pbk)

ISBN 978-1-4814-5248-9 (*26 Kisses* eBook)

ISBN 978-1-4424-5941-0 (*How My Summer Went Up in Flames* eBook)

These titles were previously published individually.

For my bestie

CHAPTER 1

SETH LOVED ME FIRST.

And maybe it was wrong of me, but I think I really did believe that, deep down, he would always love me best. Even when I started dating someone else, even as school and life and other friends got in the way, for some reason I assumed that because of everything that had happened between us, I would always come first for him. But now, as we're ducking through the crowd lining the street for the Dune Days parade, I see him look at Melinda the way he used to look at me. That look where his eyes go soft and his jaw relaxes, where the tension that's usually wound up inside him like a spring driving him forward, always on to the next thing, the next adventure, just . . . evaporates. The look that always made me pull away from him and turn my back because it was too intense. He gives her that look, and instead of being happy for him, all I can think is *Oh shit*. Because if my two best friends hook up this summer, where does that leave me?

A microsecond later Seth pulls himself together and takes a giant bite out of his churro, sending a cloud of powdered sugar floating into the air.

"Come on," he says over his shoulder, plunging straight into the thickest part of the crowd packing the street for the parade, his trademark dark clothes making him stand out from the tourists dressed in brightly colored T-shirts and hats. "We're not going to be able to see from here."

Mel hooks a finger around my belt loop as the crush of people engulfs us, and I fight the urge to shake her off, to disappear into the chaos. But Seth reaches back to grab my wrist, and the three of us end up sitting shoulder to shoulder on the curb, in a prime location to catch any freebies that might get thrown from the floats.

"Do you want some?" Seth offers his half-eaten churro to Mel, who shakes her head and turns away in disgust.

"Too much sugar," she says, running a hand through her short black hair, fingers tangling in her curls.

"It's Dune Days," I say. "What's the point of life if you can't have a churro or some ice cream?" I try to keep any tinge of annoyance out of my voice—it's none of my business if Mel has recently decided that sugar is basically poison.

She shrugs and leans back on her hands, stretching her feet out into the street, the laces of her untied Converse dragging in the dust.

I try to catch Seth's eye over Mel's head, but he's giving her that look again and totally ignoring me. Someone standing behind us knees me in the back, and I flinch.

"Do you want me to go get you some roasted Brussels sprouts from the organic truck?" Seth asks Mel, his voice light and teasing. "Maybe some wheatgrass juice? A kale salad? You know, something really parade appropriate."

Mel smiles and bumps her shoulder against Seth's. "Oh, shut up," she says, and leans against him for a moment longer than is strictly necessary.

I pop the last bit of waffle cone into my mouth and try to think of a new topic of conversation—something that will make the two of them stop looking at each other like a couple of freshmen at their first homecoming dance. How long has this been going on, and why didn't I notice it before? I must have been blind to miss seeing the tension between them—although I have been a little preoccupied lately.

I sweep my hair up into a ponytail, able to focus on only two things: how miserable I am right now, and how much more miserable I'm going to be for the rest of the summer if Mel and Seth disappear to do the boyfriend-girlfriend thing. Not that I don't deserve it after having practically abandoned them for the past two years.

Seth finally tears his gaze away from Mel and looks across the street. His eyes widen. "Veda, is that . . . ?"

"What?" I squint into the sun.

"Um . . . nothing. Never mind." Seth wraps the remainder of his churro in a napkin and sets it aside. "I think I hear the marching band."

"Really? I can't hear—" My voice falters as I realize what—who—Seth has spotted. "Oh God. We have to move." I struggle to my feet.

"No!" Mel grabs my arm and pulls me back down. "What are you talking about? We've got great seats."

I turn my head and put my hand in front of my face, shielding it. Seth frowns, his green eyes now locked on mine. I feel trapped inside the group of giddy, churro-eating tourists surrounding us. "Please, guys. Let's get out of here."

"It's Mark," Seth explains to Mel. "He's sitting right over there."

She cringes and leans forward, searching the crowd.

"Don't look!" I duck my head down farther, but I also risk a glance to the other side of the street. My eyes are drawn right to the faded blue baseball cap I know so well. Mark is camped out with his parents and two younger brothers, all of them leaning back in lawn chairs. A large, wheeled cooler sits at their feet, probably packed with the amazing sandwiches his mom is famous for. My stomach flips. A year ago I tagged along with them to watch this same parade, and Mark fed me potato chips as the mayor of Butterfield cruised by in an open-top convertible. The memory is close enough to touch, and I shudder as I remember the way Mark's eyes widened when I gently licked salt off his fingertips.

"Hey." Mel grabs my hand and laces her fingers through mine, her silver rings warm against my skin. "Screw Mark. It's totally his loss, right?"

"Right," I agree automatically. But that doesn't mean I can handle sitting within sight of him for the next hour without having some kind of public meltdown.

I close my eyes. It has been ten days since Mark told me he didn't want to "be attached" when he went off to college. That no one stays with their high school girlfriend forever.

No one stays with their high school girlfriend. It sounds like something that would be true. After all, what is high school but cross-country meets and three-minute passing periods and drinking Mountain Dew at midnight so you can stay awake to finish your pre-calc homework? High school doesn't matter. And high school girlfriends probably don't either.

Too bad my high school boyfriend meant everything to me.

I open my eyes. I cannot, under any circumstances, face Mark today. I'll just have to lie low, pretend to watch the parade, and then escape as soon as it's over.

"Uh-oh," Seth says.

Mark's mom is pointing at us and whispering in his ear. He tilts the brim of his baseball cap with one hand and raises the other in a tentative wave.

"God damn it." I drop my head and stare into the gutter, which is already filled with candy wrappers and ticket stubs, the universal debris of summer festivals.

"He's coming over," Mel warns, squeezing my hand tighter. "You're going to have to interact in three . . . two . . ."

"Hey, Vee."

I take a deep breath and look up into my favorite face on the planet. "Hi, Mark."

He looms over the three of us, blocking out the sun. The leather bracelet I got him in February for his eighteenth birthday circles his wrist. Why is he still wearing it?

"How's it going?" Mark's totally at ease, thumbs hooked around his belt loops, posture relaxed. As if we're friends—when in reality we're something so much more and also, now, so much *less* than friends.

"Okay."

Mel lets go of my hand and leans over to Seth, whispering something in his ear. They both ignore the fact that Mark is standing two feet in front of them.

"My mom wanted me to say hi for her. And Kyle and Oliver were wondering why Jeffrey couldn't come today."

I wave at Mark's mom, who gives me an enthusiastic two-handed wave back, and feel another pang of regret that I won't be going over to Mark's house for weekend bonfires or Ping-Pong tournaments anymore. "It's my dad's weekend, so my mom took him over there last night."

Mark nods. "That sucks. Your dad didn't want to come to Dune Days?"

I shrug. "You know my stepmom's not really into crowds."

Mark looks down and fiddles with his bracelet. Faint drumbeats float through the crowd, signaling the start of the parade.

"So . . . are you okay, Vee?" he asks, glancing uncomfortably at Mel. "About everything?"

I nearly laugh. It's so like Mark to check up on me, even now that we're not together. He hated it when we occasionally fought, could never drop me off at my house and go home until he felt like everything was okay between us. Even as I turned away from him in tears ten days ago, he reached out to comfort me, his fingers burning like a hot iron on my arm. "Sure," I say, my voice cracking. "I'm fine."

"Great. That's good." He looks like he wants to say more, but the sound of the marching band is getting closer. "Well, I better go sit down," he says. "See you later. Maybe at work?"

"I quit," I call to his back as he jogs across the street and collapses into his lawn chair, the only sign that seeing me here has rattled him at all. I'm surprised no one has mentioned it to him yet. The only reason I even got a job at the Butterfield Big 6 Cinema was so Mark and I could feed each other popcorn and make out in empty movie theaters while getting paid $8.25 an hour. Now I'm pretty sure I'm never going to be able to even watch a movie there ever again, much less work right alongside Mark in the same building where he first told me he loved me.

"Asshole." Seth says it loudly enough to get a few looks from the people standing around us. It's not the first time Seth has used that particular word to describe Mark, but it *is* the first time I've kind of agreed with him.

"Good job, Vee." Melinda high-fives me and leans forward, shoving her thick black glasses up on her nose. "You were totally cool. That wasn't so bad for a first post-breakup encounter, right?"

"No," I say as the Cheeky Cherry Basket float glides by, blocking my view of Mark. Mel puts her arm around my shoulders, leaning her head briefly against mine, and I almost believe my own lie. "Not bad at all."

Seth is teaching a piano lesson this afternoon, so he disappears into Ellman's Music while Mel and I walk to the car in silence.

"I hate parades," she says once we're in her old Buick, inching down Main Street. With the constant beach traffic from Chicagoans fleeing to Michigan for the weekend and five different festivals between Memorial Day and Labor Day, it's pretty much impossible to drive anywhere in Butterfield during the summer.

"I know." I close my eyes and crank the seat back so I'm practically horizontal. "Why did you come?"

She shrugs. "Seth wanted to."

I remember the way he looked at her earlier, and I have to stop myself from reminding Mel that the only reason she and Seth even got to know each other is because I introduced them. I may be heartbroken, but I'm not a jerk.

It didn't take long for Mel and me to become friends after she moved to our tiny Michigan town from New York City. When she showed up in my math class on the first day of seventh grade, with her chunky bracelets and awkward smile, everyone else thought she was a little weird. I thought she was the coolest person I'd ever seen. It wasn't long before she started coming over to hang out at my house, and then I introduced her to Seth, who lives across the street and was basically my lifeline when my parents were getting divorced.

Together the three of us survived middle school and nervously edged our way into Butterfield High, but then I spent the better part of the past two years ditching Seth and Mel to spend time with Mark and his cross-country team friends. I can't count the number of inside jokes, Instagram photos, homecoming dinners, and movie nights I missed with my friends because I was too busy with Mark. I guess I didn't even realize how close the two of them had become, but it wouldn't be fair to resent their bond now.

Mel turns on the radio and hums along to the guitar riffs as I reach into my pocket and feel for my leather bracelet, the twin of the one Mark is inexplicably still wearing. It's worn smooth from nearly a year of use. I never took it off, not even to shower or swim—until the day he broke up with me. Now it stays hidden away, tucked into my pocket or bag but still always nearby. Mel would kill me if she knew.

I raise my arm to block my eyes as the tears start to flow, and it takes Mel a few moments to notice I've lost it again.

"Hey, whoa," she says, turning off the music and resting her hand on my knee. "You okay?"

I shake my head. I'm not okay—not okay with the fact that Mark dumped me approximately eight minutes after receiving his high school diploma, not okay with the overwhelming feeling that my life has suddenly veered off course in a potentially devastating way, and, worst of all, because it is entirely unfair of me, I am not okay with the possibility that Seth now loves Mel more than he loves me.

"Vee, you did great. We shouldn't have gone to the parade. We should have known Mark would be there."

I rub my eyes and swallow hard, trying to hold it together. "I just feel really stupid."

"I know, babe. But you shouldn't. He's the one who—" She sighs and drums her fingers on the steering wheel. "Never mind. There's no point in rehashing what a complete, total, utter *asshat* Mark is." She takes a deep breath. "I have to get over to work the Big Float. You still want to come?"

I don't respond, suddenly exhausted. Mel's dad owns Flaherty's Float & Boat, the biggest boat rental company in the area, and he sponsors a free inner tube float down the river every year for Dune Days. Working the Big Float is a nightmare of yelling at kids who haven't put their life jackets on properly, seeing all the people from high school I'd rather avoid during the summer, and splashing fully clothed into the river to chase after errant tubes. It is not on my list of favorite things to do, but I always go and help out to keep Mel company—and the fifty dollars her dad throws in doesn't hurt. But today, just thinking about the chaos of the float makes my eyes well up again.

"You don't have to," Mel says. She lets go of the steering wheel and grabs my hand, shaking it until I open my eyes again. "Seriously, Vee. I'll just take you home."

With my brother over at my dad's house for the weekend, my mom will go into overdrive on chores, then abandon the tidying and dusting halfway through when she gets bored. I'll probably lie on the couch all afternoon, watching TV and repeatedly pushing Fat Snacks, my overweight cat, off my chest. Throw in some shameless stalking of Mark's Instagram account, and it sounds like the most depressing day ever.

I clear my throat. "It's fine," I say. "I'm not going to abandon you."

Mel glances over at me. "I don't want to be responsible for you having a complete breakdown," she says.

"I promise not to let the Big Float snap my fragile psyche."

Mel grins and bounces in her seat. "Good. And you'll get to meet Killian."

I stare out the window at the post-parade traffic, unable to muster up any enthusiasm for the newest male summer help at Flaherty's Float & Boat. Knowing Mel, she'll have him smitten within two weeks and then will just play mind games with him all summer— something she does with boys more often than she'd like to admit, and which she blames on her fear of commitment. A group of people darts out into the street in front of us, and Mel swears and slams on the brakes.

"Stupid idiots!" She honks the horn and rolls down the window. "Go home, fudgies!" Mel's intolerance for the vacationers who overrun our town every summer is legendary, but she secretly loves giving the tourists shit and would miss them if they were gone. She has even been known to intentionally give them bad directions or warn them about the sharks in Lake Michigan. Leaning on the horn, she swears under her breath and rolls her eyes at a family jaywalking through the intersection.

Despite myself, I smile.

CHAPTER 2

THE PARKING LOT AT THE FLOAT & BOAT IS ALREADY HALF full of minivans and SUVs, as well as families in their swimsuits and T-shirts, standing outside their vehicles, greasing up with sunscreen, and doling out beach towels. Mel pulls her car into a grassy area behind the office, bouncing over exposed tree roots and rutted dirt.

"I swear, this stupid float gets more crowded and ridiculous every year," she says, pushing her sunglasses back into her tangle of dark hair. "Let's go see what Dad wants us to do."

Mel is on office duty since she's the only one who knows how to use the credit card machine if people want to buy snacks or bottled water from the mini concession stand. After a heated game of Rock, Paper, Scissors with Mitchell and Heather, two of the seasonal employees, I'm relegated to the inner tube brigade. There's no way I'm wearing my favorite shorts to go into the river, so Mel grabs the backpack full of old clothes she always keeps in the car and tosses it at me. I duck into the dark, spider-infested bathroom to change into her middle-school gym shorts and a Powerpuff Girls T-shirt, shoving my bare feet into a pair of crusty tennis shoes that have spent too many hours squelching through river mud.

"Beautiful," Mel pronounces when I emerge, and grabs a very tall, solid-looking guy by the elbow as he walks past. "Killian! This is my best friend, Vee."

Killian, as Mel has repeatedly mentioned over the past week, is pretty cute, with shaggy blond hair escaping from underneath a baseball cap and bright blue eyes. And, perhaps most important to Mel, he's from Trawley, the next town over, so we don't know anything about him, which I guess automatically makes him fascinating. I force a smile, already dreading the hours of discussion my best friend is undoubtedly going to want to devote this summer to the dissection and analysis of her every interaction with this guy.

"I am so happy to meet you," Killian says, holding out his hand. I go to shake it, but he folds his fingers into a fist and bumps it against mine, giving me a goofy grin that reveals a small space between his front teeth.

"Um, yeah. Me too," I say, shaking my head in bewilderment.

Mr. Flaherty hurries past, a clipboard held in the crook of his elbow. "People are lining up. Mel, get to the life jacket shed. You two"—he wiggles his fingers at me and Killian—"down to the water."

Killian nods. "Yes, sir." As Mr. Flaherty turns away, he winks at me. "Looks like it's crunch time," Killian says, taking off his baseball cap and setting it backward on his head. "Ready to get wet?"

"Heads up, Vee!"

A black inner tube rolls down the steep riverbank and slams into my chest, nearly knocking me over. I catch my balance and grab for the tube before it floats away.

"Okay," I say, gesturing to three tween-age girls in tiny bikinis. "You're next." They pick their way over to me, squealing every time a weed brushes their feet, taking pictures with iPhones sealed inside Ziploc bags. They sit gingerly in their inner tubes, and I shove them out toward the middle of the river, wincing as one of the girls shrieks right in my ear.

"Have a good float," I mutter as the current catches them. I pause for a second, hands on my hips, and try to figure out how many more people could possibly be waiting in line up by the life jacket station. It feels like I have seen nearly everyone from Butterfield in their bathing suits today—*not* necessarily a good thing.

"Vee!" Killian stands on the shore, shirtless. A hint of sunburn is starting to spread across his shoulders. "Sorry about that last one. My muscles got the best of me."

"Whatever." I kick some water at him. "Those girls might have been impressed, but I don't go for gym rats."

Killian pulls a ridiculous pose, his muscles popping in a way you generally don't see on teenage guys. "Would you believe me if I told you I've never lifted weights in my life? I'm too lazy for that nonsense."

"So how do you explain *that*?" I point at his bulging bicep.

Killian shrugs. "Genes. Luck. The fact that I grew six inches this year and am apparently turning into the Hulk." He taps his chest. "Trust me, I'm a scrawny little pipsqueak at heart."

I have to admit, he looks good—and not at all scrawny. But after a full afternoon of tossing sticky inner tubes at each other and trading good-natured insults, I think it's safe to say I'll probably never be able to set eyes on Killian without flashing back to the uniquely sickening smell of hot rubber and sunscreen. Mel can have him.

A couple of teenage guys jog over and splash into the river. "Killian Hughes! Dude, what's up?" One of them holds out his hand for a high five but then pulls it away just before Killian's palm meets his. "Gotcha."

"Good one, Drew," Killian says, his voice patient and measured. He pulls a couple inner tubes down from the rack and hands them to Drew and his friend. "Have fun."

The other guy, a beanpole whose swim trunks are barely clinging to his bony hips, flashes a braces-filled grin. "Sweet gig, Kill. Getting to see who's out and about in Butterfield? Any hot chicks?" He raises his eyebrows.

"Sure." Killian turns his back on them and crosses his arms, squinting back toward the life jacket shed. "See you guys."

Drew elbows his buddy in the ribs, and they toss their inner tubes into the river, hurling themselves on top of them and sending a spray of water over my shirt.

"Friends of yours?" I ask once they've floated out of earshot.

Killian snorts. "Just a couple of Trawley lowlifes." He sighs and takes off his baseball cap, bending down to cup some river water into his hand and splashing it over his hair. "I don't see anyone else coming. Want a break?"

"Yes, please." I slosh my way over to the bank and flop onto the thick carpet of pine needles.

Killian joins me, slipping in the mud and splashing water everywhere as he tries to sit down.

I raise one eyebrow. "You're like an elephant."

"Nah." He pushes his hair out of his eyes. "Elephants are more graceful."

I close my eyes and try to ignore the shrieks and laughter from the people out floating on the river, concentrating on the birds in the trees and the branches rustling in the light wind. My body relaxes as a cool breeze caresses my face. This isn't so bad.

"So, Mel said you guys are going to be seniors?" Killian busts my Zen moment wide open.

I take a breath and sit up. "Yeah. You?"

Killian nods. "Same. Me and the twenty others in my graduating class."

"Wow, small school. Is that how you know those two?" I gesture toward the river.

Killian nods. "Unfortunately. And, if you can believe it, there are more just like them. That's why I decided to get out for the summer and work in Butterfield."

"I hate to break it to you, but I think there are guys like that everywhere."

"Trust me." Killian's startlingly blue eyes lock on me. "Anywhere has got to be better than Trawley." He looks away again and cracks his knuckles. "It's total backwoods. Everyone only listens to country music. We don't even have a movie theater."

Ugh. Another reminder that I'm fresh out of a job for the summer. "I used to work at the Butterfield Big 6."

"Oh yeah?" Killian leans back on his hands. "So you like movies?"

I stare out over the river, embarrassed to admit I only applied there because of my then-boyfriend, who turned out not to be that into me in the end. "Sure. You?"

"Totally. I'm in the drama club at Trawley. Not that that's saying much, but . . . acting, plays, movies, improv, debate. It's all awesome."

I shoot him a look. "You do debate?"

"Is the sky blue?"

I pause, a little stunned. "Answering my question with another question—and one that requires an objective answer. Classic," I say. "I'm on debate too." I wrack my brain, trying to remember if I've ever seen him at a competition before. I would not have pegged Killian as a debater, but knowing he must be at least a little bit of a nerd automatically puts me at ease. I'm not like Mel, who can strike up a conversation with virtually anyone about anything and turn on her charm so that fifteen minutes later they're best friends for life. But give me a topic to investigate, an argument to make, and I will run with it until I prove my point or die trying. That's what I love so much about debate—it's black-and-white. There's a right side (the one you're arguing for) and a wrong side (your opponents'). Not like real life, where everything is so much more complicated.

Killian laughs. "No way. Is the debate team as nerdtastic at Butterfield as it is at Trawley?"

I smirk at him. "That depends. Has your team ever thrown you a Constitution-themed birthday party?"

"Is this a cross-examination?"

"Are we only speaking in questions?" I smile, and Killian kicks some water at me. "Seriously, it's a total nerd alert over at Butterfield. We're always collecting obscure facts we can use in our cases. You would not believe the stuff that comes in handy—like, we were once debating whether Santa Claus is real, and I won the argument because of something I remembered from science class about the Arctic's polarity."

Killian looks at me and raises his eyebrows. "You proved Santa Claus exists? You are officially my hero."

I duck my head. "It was probably my best argument to date. Too bad it took place in the library during practice after school instead of during a competition."

"So, do you want to be an actor or a lawyer?" he asks. "Seems like everyone who's into this kind of stuff is either one or the other."

"Lawyer." I swish my feet through the water. Looking up information and arguing about it for a living . . . What could be better?

"Then I'll be sure to address you with proper respect, counselor." He dips his head toward me in a mock bow.

"Stop it. What about you?"

"Both," Killian says, deadpan. "I want to be an actor who plays a lawyer on *Law & Order*."

Before I can respond, a shrill whistle rises up from behind us, and I turn to see Bob, Melinda's dad, waving at us, his face almost as red as his hair. A lifeguard whistle dangles from a string around his neck. "You guys are done!" he shouts. "Slowing down up here."

"Thank God," I groan, wiggling my toes inside Mel's sneakers. My feet feel bloated and cold, and I try not to think about all the things that could potentially be in the river water that's soaked into my skin over the past few hours.

Killian clasps my hand and hauls me to my feet with one swift tug. We struggle up the riverbank, our tennis shoes making disgusting squishing noises as we walk. Mel stands over by the life jacket shed, out-fitting a few late-coming floaters. I can't help but feel a little resentful— she's completely dry, all popped-collar polo shirt and untied Converse, while I look like I just crawled out of a mud pit.

"Wow, I'm really glad I learned how to use the stupid credit card machine," Mel says as she comes over to us, dusting her hands off on her spotless shorts. "You're definitely going to need to shower before tonight, Vee."

"What's happening tonight?" I wring some water out of my T-shirt.

Mel holds up her phone. "Brianna and Landon want to hang out.

And Seth's free. We should all do something." She flashes a smile at Killian. "Want to?"

"Sure," he says, pulling his T-shirt back over his head and interrupting Mel's not-so-covert inspection of his abs.

Mel grabs our arms and pulls us closer. "Awesome. I have the best idea." She peers over my shoulder and whispers, "Let's come back here tonight, when it gets dark. We can watch the fireworks from the dock."

"Mel! What are you trying to do, get us arrested?"

"Chill out, Vee. It's my dad's place; it's not like we'd be trespassing."

It's all I can do to suppress my inner attorney. "Uh, actually, it totally would be trespassing if—"

Mel grabs my hand and squeezes hard, silencing me. "Are you in, Killian?"

He shifts his weight from foot to foot. "I don't know. . . ."

"Oh, come on." She sighs impatiently. "What's with you two? Relax. It'll be fun." She crosses her arms and waits.

Killian looks at me, his eyebrows raised in a silent question. I hesitate for a second and then nod.

"Okay," he says finally, taking his baseball cap off and running a hand through his hair. "I'm in."

CHAPTER 3

"THIS IS A BAD IDEA," I SAY. MEL AND I ARE BACK IN THE BUICK, lurking in the corner of the Float & Boat parking lot, waiting for everyone else to arrive, and I can barely breathe through the cloud of perfume wafting off her body. The sun is just about to go down, and clouds are racing in from the west to cover the stars. Soon the sky will be pitch-black—perfect for watching fireworks.

"Shhh," she says. "It'll be fine. You'll have fun—maybe even meet someone."

"What? Who am I going to meet?"

She turns to me, her brown eyes huge in the dark. "You need a guy this summer, Vee. So I invited a few."

I stare at her in disbelief.

Mel shrugs and looks away. "What? I took initiative. And it's not like a setup; it's just hanging out with some guys, and if you hit it off, great. If you don't, you can continue to mourn Mark."

I slam back against the passenger seat, shocked at the magnitude by which Mel has misjudged where I'm at mentally in the whole breakup process. "You invited Seth, Killian, and Landon. Landon is dating Brianna, you've already staked your claim on Killian, and Seth is . . . Seth. Who am I supposedly going to hook up with?"

"First of all, I have not *staked my claim* on Killian. I'm perfectly happy for you to jump his ripped bod this summer. But I also invited Vince and Adam. They're both single. And hot."

Vince and Adam. I flip through the pages of the yearbook in my mind, trying to put faces with those names. The only people I really hung out with over the past couple of years were Mark's cross-country friends and my teammates during the debate season—and Mel and Seth, of course, when I could find the time. But Mel seems to know everyone at Butterfield High—especially the guys, despite the fact that she has never been in a real relationship.

I rub my temples. "Mel, I am so, so not ready to think about moving on. I'm barely functioning as it is. I still cry every morning when I wake up. I don't have a job. I do not need a guy this summer."

She sighs. "Look, don't take this the wrong way. I know you think you're totally devastated about Mark—"

I snort.

"But let's face it, Vee: you don't even know what it would be like to date someone else."

I'm tempted to get out of the car and hitch a ride home rather than walk into what is apparently just a weird three-way blind date. "Yeah, yeah," I say. "I've only slept with one guy—"

"You've only *kissed* one guy."

I glare at her. Hearing it out loud makes it sound more pathetic than it actually is, and it's not like she has that much more experience than I do. I've only kissed one guy because once Mark came along, I didn't need anyone else, not because I'm a prude or challenged in the art of seduction. And anyway, Seth would have kissed me if I had let him—but that was all a million years ago, and Mel certainly doesn't need to know about it. Especially now.

Mel grabs my hand as headlights wash over us. "Someone's here."

We watch as a dark pickup truck pulls into the gravel lot, followed quickly by an old white Jeep. We climb out and gather with Killian, Brianna, and Landon.

Mel gives Brianna and Landon huge hugs, carrying on as if she hasn't seen them in years rather than just the couple of weeks since school got out. I wave awkwardly and try to think of something to say so they won't ask me about Mark.

Killian nudges me. "What are the chances of us getting caught?" he whispers.

"Slim to none. No one comes down this road at night, and I told Mel we were absolutely not having a bonfire, so I don't think anyone will see us."

"Good. I really don't want to get fired in my first week."

I glance up at him. Mel sure seems to have gotten her claws into him quickly. "So why did you come?"

"I'm dying to hear you prove that Santa Claus exists. I've been thinking about it all day." He knocks my shoulder lightly with his fist.

Alarm bells go off in my head. Is Killian *flirting* with me?

I'm saved from having to respond by Brianna shoving a can of bug spray into my hands. I spray myself down—always necessary in the Michigan woods at night—as more cars pull into the parking lot. Vince and Adam arrive only a few seconds apart, as if they coordinated when they would leave, and are wearing comically similar outfits—baggy khaki shorts and tight T-shirts, baseball caps perched on top of carefully gelled hair. Mel introduces us, beaming over me like a proud mother.

"Nice to meet you," I say, regretting the words as soon as they're out of my mouth. We've been going to school together for three years—we must have met at some point, and I just didn't bother to remember.

Seth is the last to arrive, dressed in his customary outfit of black clothes and outrageous, eye-catching shoes. Tonight he's wearing his go-to, everyday red high-top Converse. He steps out of his mom's minivan and jogs over to us, bouncing nervously on the balls of his feet. I'm surprised he actually showed up; he doesn't go to a lot of parties. Not because people don't want him there—everyone is fascinated by Seth—but because he finds them boring and predictable, and would rather be home practicing the piano like the antisocial musical genius he is. At least, that's the explanation he gives.

"Hey, Vee." He touches my elbow softly and turns to Mel. "Let's get this over with."

Mel leads us through the woods, past the life jacket shed, and down to the dock. It's not too hot out, but the nighttime humidity is starting to set in, making my whole body feel sticky. I trip over a tree root, and Adam catches my arm, leaning in close to help me up.

"Careful," he says, his teeth flashing white in the dark, his hand hot on my elbow.

"Thanks." I pull away as soon as I find my footing.

Landon and Vince are carrying a big cooler between them, and they start handing out beers as we settle onto the dock. I take one, steeling myself for an hour of pretending to enjoy the foul liquid, and immediately wish I hadn't when Seth coolly turns his down.

Brianna and Landon wander off to the end of the dock, hand in hand. Mel leans over to Killian. "Isn't it gorgeous out here?" The last rays of sun are just visible on the horizon, pink and orange among the clouds. It's a typical Lake Michigan sunset, the kind I watched a million times while snuggling with Mark. I take a giant swig of my beer.

"Absolutely." Killian hands Mel a can. "When do the fireworks start?"

Mel checks her phone. "Ten minutes."

Seth slaps at a mosquito on his arm and scowls. "We're going to get eaten alive. I don't think the bug spray is working."

Mel lays a hand on his arm. "Poor baby. A little mosquito bite isn't going to kill you."

Seth pulls away and crosses his arms.

"Okay." Mel sighs. "Seth, if you didn't want to have fun tonight, you should have just stayed home." She cracks her knuckles and turns to Killian. "Want to go sit down there? We'll be able to see better."

She motions to the end of the dock, where Brianna and Landon are already making out.

"Uh . . ." Killian glances over at me, and I pull my phone out of my pocket, pretending to read a text. "Sure," he says, following her.

Seth stares after them and lets out his breath in a huff, sinking down onto the dock and staring out at the water. Adam motions for me to sit next to him, and I give him a tight smile before settling myself gingerly onto the smooth boards. Vince flops down nearby, cracking open his can with a flourish.

"Cheers," Adam says, tapping his beer against mine. "Happy Dune Days."

"Same to you," I say, trying to ignore the aftertaste on my tongue.

My eyes lock on Adam's, and he raises one eyebrow, a slow smile spreading across his face. I look away, my breath coming faster than normal, every cell in my body aware that I'm sitting very close to a guy who isn't Mark. Where should I put my hands? Should I scoot closer? Am I supposed to be talking to Vince, too? Maybe he and Adam are going to battle it out to prove their dominance, like bucks do during mating season. I silently curse Mel for inviting so many people tonight. If I make a fool of myself, there will be plenty of witnesses.

The first fireworks explode over the tops of the trees, giving me an excuse not to talk to anyone. I sip my drink nervously and monitor Adam's every movement out of the corner of my eye, making my way through two cans of beer before the show is even half over. Eventually, the alcohol kicks in, and my body relaxes. I toss my beer can aside and lean back on my hands. It's a gorgeous night, I'm out with friends, and Mark is (hopefully) sitting at home, alone, wishing he hadn't been so quick to dump me. Or . . . he's over at the fireworks with his arm around some other girl. I push the thought out of my head and let my hand brush against Adam's.

After what seems like hours, the grand finale begins, and it is spectacular—huge fireworks erupting one after the other with booms that make my heart pound fast in my chest, the ghostly imprints they leave behind in the sky crossing over each other and blurring into gray smog. The air smells like a combination of fresh pine and acrid smoke.

I turn to say something to Adam just as his arm swings up and drapes across my shoulders. He pulls me closer and whispers in my ear, "Cool, huh?"

I nod, my palms sweating. Everyone else is getting up and stretching, discussing which fireworks were their favorites, but I am frozen in place with the weight of this guy's arm holding me down. He is shorter, more solid, than Mark. His deodorant smells different, his profile is sharper, he has an earring—but when I close my eyes and let the alcohol fuzz my brain, none of that seems to matter. When Adam turns my face toward his and kisses me, it feels almost natural. And as our kiss deepens and his hands move down to my hips, I realize I'm not nervous anymore. Mark is no longer the only guy I've ever been close to. I'm single—I can do what I want, kiss who I want. All summer long.

I'm free.

CHAPTER 4

I MAY BE A LITTLE TIPSY AND TOTALLY GIDDY FROM MAKING out with Adam, but Mel is completely wrecked. Killian practically has to carry her back to the parking lot as she shrieks and giggles the whole way. The rest of the guys follow behind us.

"Shhh," I say, stumbling along, my hand in Adam's. "Mel, shut up. Someone's going to hear you."

"Who's going to hear me?" She pulls away from Killian and runs ahead, flinging her arms out wide and shouting nonsense. Seth sighs impatiently and takes off after her, his red shoes the only thing visible as the rest of him melts into the darkness.

Killian glances at me but looks away as Adam's arm slides around my waist. We walk to the cars, footsteps crunching over the gravel, and stop.

"Well, this is a problem," I announce as my brain cranks through the calculations of who is sober enough to drive and how many vehicles we have.

Mel leans against the Buick and bends over, hands on her knees.

"You okay?" Seth asks, placing a hand on her back. She breathes heavily for a few moments, nods, and straightens up.

"We can't leave any cars here," she says, an edge of panic creeping into her voice. "My dad will be back first thing in the morning."

Seth sighs and crosses his arms. "Who's okay to drive?"

Mel and I glance at each other, and I nonchalantly link my hands behind my back. Killian slowly raises his hand, as does Landon.

"That's fine. You can take Brianna and your buddies home," Seth says to Landon. "I'll take Mel and Vee."

"I can take them," Killian jumps in.

Seth gives him a long look. "Don't you have to drive all the way back to Trawley?" he asks. "I live right across the street from Vee. *I'll* drive them home."

Killian holds his gaze for a moment, then turns away. "See you later, then," he says. "Thanks for the invite, Mel." He nods at me. "Vee." He walks across the parking lot to the white Jeep and swings up into it without opening the door.

"Well, that's great," Seth says as Killian pulls out of the parking lot. "It would have been nice to have his help moving the cars."

"I can help, Seth," Mel says, stumbling toward him and catching his arm. "I'm not that drunk."

"Mel"—Seth blows air out through his cheeks—"just stay over here with Veda."

Mel leans against me, and I nearly topple over. "Okay, but make sure you hide mine. There's a field. . . ." Her head drops onto my shoulder. "Vee, I have to stay at your house tonight. My mom will know I'm drunk."

"Okay," I say, pulling her over to a tree stump and setting her down. I watch Seth and Landon collect car keys from the other guys and drive their cars down the road so Mel's dad won't be suspicious in the morning. Mel slumps over on the stump, her head dropping down toward her knees every few moments, and then snapping back up as she jerks awake. Adam stands behind me, rubbing my shoulder in a way that starts out sweet but, five minutes later, gets kind of annoying. By the time Seth and Landon are done moving the cars, I feel nearly sober—and am quietly freaking out about the fact that I kissed Adam and I don't even know his last name.

"My guitar," Mel murmurs, staggering to her feet. "In the trunk. Shit."

"Okay, okay," I say, catching her elbow as she stumbles. "We'll get it." I walk her over to Seth's minivan and give him an imploring look. "Please, Seth?"

He clenches and unclenches his hands slowly. "It would have been great to know about the guitar before I parked her car a quarter mile down the road." He doesn't wait for a reply, but turns and walks away.

"Let's go," Landon calls. Adam pulls me away from Mel and dives in for another long, lingering kiss. Things are starting to get a little slobbery.

"I'll call you," he whispers in my ear, squeezing me tight before he jogs across the parking lot.

Mel crawls into the backseat of Seth's minivan and curls up into a ball. Once the roar of Landon's diesel engine has faded, the sounds of the woods at night take over—all the chirps, sighs, and creaks you never pay attention to during the daytime but that seem to become amplified as soon as the sun goes down. Seth returns a few minutes later, his footsteps crunching over the gravel, guitar in hand.

We ride home in silence, Mel passed out in the back. The headlights cut a narrow path through the blank darkness of the country roads, making it feel like we're the only people around for miles. Frustration rolls off Seth in waves, each turn of the steering wheel a bit sharper than necessary, each pause at a stop sign a bit shorter than it might usually be. I know he's waiting for me to commiserate with him about what a lame, stereotypical teenage party we just suffered through—but I stay silent, letting it all sink in. What would Mark say if he knew I had already kissed someone else? I feel a little stab of satisfaction. He asked if I was okay, and I am. I swallow hard and close my eyes, the sharp taste of cheap beer on my tongue. At least, I will be.

CHAPTER 5

A SOUR CHORD JERKS ME AWAKE. MEL'S SITTING ON THE END of my bed, her back to me and her left hand dancing across the fretboard of her guitar as she hums along to whatever music is playing in her head. The heavy curtains draped across my windows block out most of the morning light, but a few rays of sun sneak around the edges and fall across her shoulders.

I stare at the clock, struggling to focus my eyes. It's only seven thirty—way too early to be awake with a Bud Light hangover and a mouth that feels like cotton balls. I stretch and nudge her with my toes. "Mel."

She turns around to grin at me and launches into the opening chords of "Beach Day," a song I helped her and Seth write a few years ago back when I was the official lyricist (code for "She can't carry a tune but she's our friend so we have to include her") for their band. "Seth and I are working on some new stuff," she says. "Feel like doing some writing?"

I shrug. Mel likes upbeat songs about late-night rides in pickup trucks, hot summer days, and first loves that never end. Seth doesn't shy away from a touch of melancholy—he's had enough of it in his life, after all—but I think the only lyrics I'm capable of writing right now would be appropriate for a sappy eighties love ballad. Not exactly their style.

I sit up and groan. Some people, like Mel, can power through hangovers with their sheer adorableness and insistence on being young and invincible. I, on the other hand, feel like I've been hit by a truck—and probably look like it too. Poor Fat Snacks takes one look at me as I lumber to my feet, and scurries underneath the bed.

Mel reluctantly puts the guitar down and rolls into the space I've just vacated, snuggling down into the sheets. "So, what do you remember about last night?" she asks, smiling so widely that her nose scrunches up and pushes her glasses askew.

My stomach tightens as flashes of memory come back in a rush: Adam's arm around my waist. His mouth on mine. My fingers in his hair. I close my eyes. "Not much."

"Not much?" Mel's voice rises. "You guys were all over each other! It was adorable."

I force my eyes open and drop back down onto the bed, nearly squashing Mel's legs. "I feel really weird, Mel. Like, bad weird."

In the harsh light of morning, I can barely even remember what Adam looks like. I try to think back through the beer fog to figure out why in the world I thought it would be a good idea to make out with him.

"Vee, it's fine," Mel says, propping herself up on one elbow. "He's the first guy you've kissed since Mark. And only the second guy since . . . well, ever. No big deal if it feels a little strange."

I meet my own gaze in the mirror on the back of my closet door, dark circles under my eyes, limp brown hair rumpled and static-y, and regret rolls over me in waves. The first time I kissed Mark, I didn't sleep for the next twenty-four hours, reliving the moment in my mind, literally unable to think about anything else. With Adam, all I want to do is push him out of my brain and forget last night ever happened.

"So now I have to deal with the follow-up, right?"

Mel grins and holds up my cell phone. "Your phone is dead, but I texted you his number. You going to use it later?"

This is the kind of stuff I've always watched my friends agonize over, going all the way back to middle school—deciding whether to text a guy, watching the clock to see how quickly he responds, trying to interpret the real meaning behind the shorthand and emoji—until they get bored and move on to someone else. With Mark, it was easy right from the beginning. We were together. We were in love. No games, no uncertainty. I loved knowing exactly where we stood—two halves of a team.

Adam said he would call me . . . but will he? And what will I say to him if he does?

I lie back down, squashing Mel's legs again, and pull a pillow over my face. "I don't think I can do this."

Mel struggles out from underneath me and rustles through her backpack. "Do what?"

"Texting. Flirting. *Dating*." My voice is muffled, and Mel pulls the pillow away.

"Who said anything about dating?"

I raise an eyebrow at her. "Um, you did? You said I needed a guy this summer, and then you brought, like, a whole smorgasbord of them out for me to choose from last night. Remember?"

She shakes her head. "Oh no, Vee. *Dating* is the last thing you need. Did you think you were just going to jump right into another relationship, turn into Vee and Mark 2.0, insert Random Guy in the Mark slot?"

I make a face, confused. "I mean, that makes it sound kind of pathetic."

Mel sighs dramatically. "Think about it. You're not going to *date* one guy this summer. You're going to *hook up* with a bunch of guys." She heads across the hall to the bathroom. "Adam was a good start, but he was just an appetizer."

Water runs in the sink, and I concentrate on breathing normally. A throbbing headache edges its way across my temples, and I clench my hands at my sides, trying not to freak out. Kiss *more* guys?

Mel bangs back into the room. "What are you doing?"

"Nothing."

"Bullshit. You're overthinking—I can see it." Her face is washed, her hair artfully tousled.

"No, I'm not." I cross my arms and narrow my eyes, daring her to disagree with me.

Mel purses her lips. "Look, do you want to use this summer"—she pauses dramatically—*"the last summer of our high school careers,* to go a little wild? Or would you rather start wearing Adam's letter jacket and plan your future children's names together?"

"I think we've established I'm not into Adam," I say, my voice sharp.

Mel doesn't even flinch at my tone, and she stands there, hands on her hips, doing what she does best—daring me to come out of my comfort zone.

I hold her gaze, trying not to let the horrible morning-after feeling that is pressing down on me show. Last night was a mistake, and I'm going to deal with it and move on. But I'm not going to let it happen again.

"Okay, fine," Mel says finally, holding her hands up in defeat. "Never mind. Just stop looking at me with that death face."

I crack a smile, relief washing over me. I'll work through the Adam fallout, and then things will go back to normal. I lean over and straighten the framed picture sitting on my desk, the one of me and Mark.

"What is that still doing here?" Mel asks, doing a double take. "In fact, what are all these still doing here?" She gestures around my room, to the homecoming pictures pinned to my bulletin board and the selfies taped to the wall. Mark is in all of them.

I shrug and hug the framed picture against my stomach, ignoring the voice inside me whispering that I'm never going to find someone else who makes me feel like Mark did if I don't at least get out there and look. "Just haven't gotten around to taking them down yet." My voice catches and I clear my throat, hoping Mel doesn't notice. But, being my best friend, of course she does.

"Hey." Mel leans over and grabs my arm, her brown eyes wide. "Last night wasn't a disaster. You're fine."

I nod reluctantly. I don't feel fine. I feel weird and nervous and like things are moving way, way too fast. "Wouldn't it be awesome if we could just be normal?" I say. It's the question we ask each other whenever our lives seem out of control and everyone else seems to have their shit together—which, for me at least, seems to happen about twice a week.

She rolls her eyes. "Totally. You were practically married to one guy for two years, and I've never actually had a boyfriend. Most people shoot for the happy medium." Mel shakes my arm gently until I meet her gaze. "Just think about what I said." She smiles. "Maybe this summer could be your chance."

Before I can respond, someone knocks on my bedroom door.

"Yeah?"

The door flies open, and my mom bounds in, bursting with an annoying amount of energy, as usual. "Seizing the day early, girls?" She's wearing a pair of my athletic shorts, which ride up just a little too far on her thighs, and one of her special hand-painted T-shirts—

this one has a giant parrot on it. An earbud dangles from her shoulder.

"Always," Mel says, turning and flashing my mom a smile. "Are you going running?"

"Oh no, I'm not a runner like Vee," Mom says. I wince. I don't feel like a runner at the moment, standing here with an enormous hangover, clutching a picture of my ex-boyfriend. "I'm doing Prancercise. Have you heard of it? It's like jogging, but with more elation. My friend Cheryl and I just started last week."

"Better get going, then," I say, not letting my gaze drift over to the mound of clothes in the corner of my room, which I piled there specifically to hide my running shoes so I wouldn't have to look at them. I haven't touched them since the morning of Mark's graduation, when we fit in a quick three miles together before he had to get ready for the ceremony. "Don't want to be late."

"That's the thing," Mom says. "Jeffrey wants to be picked up from your dad's early so he can hang out with Kyle and Oliver. I told him you girls could go get him, but then I didn't see your car in the driveway, Mel."

Mel sets her guitar on the floor, and the strings twang. "Seth dropped us off. That's okay, though, Mrs. Bentley. We can grab my car and get Jeffrey."

I groan, but they both ignore me.

"You guys are the best," Mom says. "Time to prance!" She gallops down the hallway, the floor shaking like the house is about to collapse.

Mel hops up and pulls her shorts on. "Okay, I'm ready."

I reach for the glass of water that's been sitting on my nightstand for three days and chug it in one gulp. "We're going to have to get Seth to drive us back to your car, you know. He's probably still asleep."

Mel shakes her head in a tornado of curls. "No way. Seth never sleeps. He's like a rechargeable battery—sit him down at the piano for an hour or two, and he's good to go." She looks at me hopefully. "Do you want to text him?"

I snort. "No way." I haul myself out of my chair and stumble across the hall to the bathroom, turning on the shower as hot as it will go and taking a giant swig from a bottle of mouthwash. Dad and his wife, Lila, are nearly as bad as Mel's mom when it comes to sniffing out teenage shenanigans, and I really don't need a lecture from them on underage drinking today.

The warmth of the shower soothes my hangover headache, and the overpowering mango shampoo ensures that I won't smell like anything other than a fruit basket when Lila swoops in for one of her awkward hugs. I let the water run over my face and into my ears, wishing I could scrub the memory of last night from my brain.

After a quick blow-dry, I run back to my room, where Mel is texting furiously. "Seth will take us," she says. "Although he is being a real butt about it. I guess he *was* sleeping."

I pull a white skirt and navy blue top out of my closet—clothes more appropriate for a morning at church than a random summer day but that will pass Dad's inevitable inspection and prevent any passive-aggressive comments from him. "Is that what you're wearing?"

I ask, gesturing at Mel's ragged denim shorts and the wrinkly T-shirt she slept in.

"Sure." She shoves her phone into her pocket and shrugs. "Your dad already hates me, so who cares?"

"He does not hate you. He just doesn't understand your unique sense of style." I grab my bag off the floor and remember my phone is dead—which means that at least I can put off worrying about texting Adam for the next couple of hours. "Come on. Let's go pick up the preteen terror."

Seth is a dark smudge against his parents' white minivan, sitting on the bumper, his hands shoved into the pockets of his black jeans. Even his shoes are more muted than usual—brown leather work boots that make him look like a lumberjack. He grunts as we walk up, and then he slides into the driver's seat, not bothering to say hello, and practically vibrates with annoyance as Mel chatters on in the front seat about how cool the party was last night and how she hopes we liked Killian because she thinks we'll all be hanging out with him a lot this summer, *wink, wink.*

I see Seth's shoulders tense and I kick the back of Mel's seat. Seth, of course, has no idea Mel means she hopes *I* hook up with Killian. I don't know for sure if Mel has noticed that Seth's feelings toward her seem to have changed, but things are definitely weird between them right now. It's like they're two magnets constantly switching polarity, sometimes irresistibly drawn together and other times forcing themselves apart.

Mel's car is tucked out of sight on the side of the road, still covered in early morning dew. "Thanks, Seth," she says, and leans over to ruffle his hair. "You're the best." He flinches.

"See you later," I say, and slide out of the backseat.

He pulls away the second I close the car door, his tires spitting up gravel as the wheels spin before gaining traction.

"What are you doing, Mel?" I ask, unable to stop myself from saying something even though I'm terrified of hearing the answer. The way Seth looked at her during the parade, the amount of time they've been spending together, the way she flirts with him—it seems like they're right on the edge of getting together. But then she'll make some comment about Killian being the hottest thing since sriracha and treat Seth like he exists only for her amusement. I don't get it.

"What?" She gives me a blank look.

I study her and finally shake my head, unsure how to broach the subject without making it sound like I'm accusing her of leading Seth on. "Never mind."

CHAPTER 6

"OH. HI." JEFFREY TURNS AWAY AS SOON AS HE OPENS THE front door, which is about ten feet tall and sports an enormous brass knocker that could have originally come from a medieval castle. It's like we're breaching a fortress of affluence.

"Nice to see you too," I say, pushing past him into the foyer, Mel trailing behind me. With a five-year age gap between us, Jeffrey has always been just enough younger than I am to be truly annoying without being quite young enough to be cute. I remember watching Seth and his brother, Luke, across the street, building tree forts together and shooting baskets in their driveway, and feeling jealous that Jeffrey and I didn't have that kind of relationship. But Luke was diagnosed with cancer when he was eleven and Seth was ten, and Seth's world collapsed when he died. I don't know if he'll ever get over it. The black clothes, the amount of time he spends home, alone, practicing piano, his creative genius persona—I wonder how much of it is really him, and how much is a tough-guy act.

A pang of guilt hits me as Jeffrey swipes his too-long hair out of his eyes. I'm the big sister—I should try harder, make things better between us.

"Wow," Mel murmurs, taking in the sparkling wood floors, pristine white furniture, and spectacular views of Lake Michigan that my dad is so proud of, although of course it's Lila's money that pays for it all. "This place gets better every time I see it."

"Take a picture if you need to," I say. "We're leaving soon."

"I'll get my stuff." Jeffrey heads down to the finished basement, which is where he prefers to sleep when he stays over here.

I follow the sound of obnoxious game show music to the kitchen, where my dad is leaning over the granite counter, eating a piece of toast with jam. He's almost scarily skinny, his hair clipped and combed neatly, his shirt freshly ironed—still playing the perfect, nice-guy husband role for Lila. I've never heard him raise his voice in this house, which is pretty impressive considering that when he lived with us, it felt like he spent half his time yelling.

My two-year-old half-sister, Kaylee, is coloring at the table, and my stepmother, thankfully, is nowhere to be seen, although I'm sure she's lurking somewhere close-by. Lila works from home in some marketing job that pays a lot of money, and I can count on two hands the number of times I've seen her leave the house. I'm not sure if it's coincidence or if she's just a big homebody or what. But I guess if my house looked like this, I wouldn't have much motivation to leave it either.

My dad spreads more jam on his toast and blinks at me, looking dazed. "Veda!" he says finally, his eyes widening. "Hey! Didn't know you were coming." His eyes sweep over me quickly, head to toe, and I must look acceptable, because he smiles.

Then he wipes his hands on his pants and walks stiffly over to me, looping one arm around me in an awkward side hug and dropping a kiss on top of my head.

"Mom said Jeffrey wanted to be picked up," I say, pulling away and bending over to grab Kaylee's pink crayon as it drops off the table and falls to the floor. "So we're leaving now. Bye."

Kaylee catches my hand and smiles. "Vee!" she crows, drawing some lopsided circles. "Look! Look!"

"Very pretty," I say, grinning down at her. I have a bunch of these scribbled-on papers tacked up over my mirror at home. I lean over and gently tug the elastic band from Kaylee's soft hair, gathering up the strands that have fallen loose and redoing her ponytail. The feel of her tiny head under my fingers makes my breath catch in my throat. I have a ridiculous amount of love for this little pipsqueak.

She's so absorbed in her coloring that she doesn't even hear me when I say, "Bye, Kay. I'll see you soon."

I'm halfway down the hall by the time Dad yells, "Hey! Don't you want to stay for lunch?"

"No, thanks!" I shout back. Mel folds her arms and pouts.

"Veda? Is that you?" Lila's voice floats down the grand staircase.

I brace myself as she jogs down the stairs, her arms wide open for a hug before she even hits the landing. "Hi, Lila."

"Hello!" Lila swoops in for what I call one of her bird hugs—the opposite of a bear hug. She leans in close to me and pats my back, her shoulder blades moving under her cardigan, her thin red hair in my face. How my dad fell for timid Lila after being married to my tall, strong, creative mother for thirteen years, I'll never know.

"And Melinda's here too!" Lila darts over to Mel and gathers her in for another delicate embrace. Dad wanders into the room, cleaning his glasses on the hem of his shirt and holding Kaylee's hand.

Lila turns. "Barry! You didn't tell me the girls were coming over."

"I didn't know," he says, settling his glasses back on his face and giving Lila's elbow a little squeeze. "Good timing, though."

I glance at Mel and cross my arms. "Why good timing?"

Dad shakes his head. "Let's wait for Jeffrey to come up."

"Jeffrey!" I yell at the top of my lungs. Lila winces. "Hurry up!"

"I can't find my DS!" The house is so enormous that I can barely hear his reply.

Mel nudges me and points to the couch, where the little electronic thing Jeffrey spends half his life attached to is sticking out from under a pillow. "It's up here, Jeffrey!"

Lila's eye twitches, and Dad leans over and lifts Kaylee into his arms.

Jeffrey thunders up the stairs, tilting his head back so he can see out from underneath his long bangs. Grabbing the DS off the couch, he shoves it into his backpack and makes a face at Kaylee, who giggles. "Okay, I'm ready. Let's go."

"Hold it," Dad says. "Let's just stop the stampede for one moment." He takes a deep breath, and I can see him start to get annoyed, the edges of the easy-to-anger person he used to be when he lived with us rising up from the carefully sanded veneer of the person he's become with Lila.

"Um, should I go wait in the car?" Mel asks.

"No." Dad waves his hand and takes a deep breath. "You're fine, Melinda. This will only take a second."

"Okay . . ." Mel pulls out her phone and pretends to text, but I know she's covertly taking photos of my dad's mansion to post to Instagram with captions like OMG, MY DREAM HOUZZZ.

"I'll keep it short and sweet," Dad says, clapping his hands together. "We have two family events this summer I'm counting on you guys to attend. The first one is in just a couple of weeks, at the end of June. Lila is throwing a big party for her work friends here at the house. And then we've got the family reunion next month, the day after Kaylee's birthday."

Shit, shit, shit. "I can't go," I blurt out, my mind racing to follow up with a reason I won't be able to go—to both events.

"Oh no?" Dad cocks one eyebrow. "And why is that?"

"I was really hoping you could make the reunion, Veda," Lila says, her eyes wide. She takes Kaylee from my dad and settles her on her hip. "I thought you could introduce me to everyone. It might be a little nerve-wracking." Her tight smile shows exactly how anxious she is about the idea of meeting my dad's entire family for the first time.

"Uh, well, I'll probably be working," I say, avoiding Lila's eyes.

"For the party and the reunion. I'm looking for a job right now. I don't know if I'll be able to get off." I mentally shake myself. It's going to take a better argument than that to get Dad off my back.

I take a deep breath and reach into my well of bullshit, the one I draw on in debate competitions when I have to elaborate on a point I hadn't prepared an argument for. "You know, I wouldn't want my employer to doubt my commitment. Even summer jobs can be important when it comes to résumés and college applications, Dad. My boss this summer could end up writing me a reference for my first real job."

Dad sighs and gives me a look that says he's on to my strategy. "We should think about getting you an internship this summer, not just a minimum-wage chimp gig. Have you asked at the law offices in town? I'm sure they'd love to have an aspiring lawyer in a few days a week to file and answer the phone, maybe do some job shadowing."

Offhandedly mentioning to my dad that I want to go to law school someday was one of the worst decisions I've ever made. He has gotten so attached to the idea that, God forbid I ever change my mind and decide I want to do something else, his brain might explode trying to process it.

"Whatever. We'll see what happens." I cross my arms. "Is that all you wanted to tell us?"

"Yes," Dad says. "And job or no job, I expect you and your brother to be at the party *and* the reunion." He pushes his glasses up on his nose and adds, "And of course you're invited too, Mel."

Before Mel can accept the invitations and get tangled up in the web of passive-aggressiveness being spun between me and my father,

I hold out my hand to Kaylee for a high five and grab Mel's elbow, hustling her out the door. "Okay, bye!" I yell over my shoulder.

Mel sighs and tucks her phone into her pocket as we hurry down the cobblestone path. "I wish we could hang out over here more often. Are your dad and Lila going on vacation this summer? Do they need a house sitter?"

"Yeah, right. They never go anywhere." I check to make sure Jeffrey is following us. "Got those pictures posted yet?"

"Yeah, duh. Seventeen likes so far. It's not possible to take a bad picture in that place."

I stare up at the brick facade of my dad's mansion, the edge of Lake Michigan just visible through the carefully pruned shrubs and trees that crowd the yard. It's a few miles and a world away from my mom's small three-bedroom, one-bath house with the peeling paint and matted carpet.

I shake my head as Jeffrey pushes past me to climb into the car. Dad always made it pretty clear we weren't good enough. Even when I got an A on my report card, he wanted an A+. The dishes were never done to his satisfaction; our rooms were never quite clean. Mom used to tease him, call him Mr. OCD. She thought it was funny that they were total opposites, that he used vacuuming as a stress-relieving activity while she could go for weeks without remembering to make the bed.

Everything he's got looks pretty perfect now. As we're walking past the manicured flower beds, I step off the path, letting my flip-flop come down on one flawless marigold, smashing its golden petals into the dirt.

CHAPTER 7

AS WE PULL INTO THE DRIVEWAY AT HOME, JEFFREY SLIDES out of the car and slams the door too hard behind him.

"Hey!" Mel calls out the window. "Show some respect!"

He rolls his eyes and saunters up the driveway, his shorts barely clinging to his hips and showing off a generous amount of his blue plaid boxers.

"Remind me why guys are supposedly so great?" I say.

Mel waves her hand. "Come on. You know Jeffrey doesn't count. He's not really a *guy* yet. He's still a boy." She glances up into the rearview mirror—checking to see if Seth is home?

I clear my throat, and her eyes flick away. "Hey, do you want to come over to my house?" she asks. "My mom's making tamales for lunch."

"Definitely." It's a sin to turn down Manuela's tamales. "Let me just run in and get my phone off the charger."

I push open the car door and jog up the driveway. Jeffrey has already installed himself on the couch in the living room, the TV blaring and his eyes glued to his phone as his thumbs move over the screen.

"Mom!" I go into the kitchen and find her sitting at the table, still wearing her Prancercise clothes from this morning and eating a bowl of oatmeal.

"Hey," she says, scraping her spoon across the china. "Everything okay?"

"Yeah, fine," I say, unplugging my phone and glancing at the screen. No new texts. I'm relieved and then annoyed. It would have been nice for Adam to at least make the effort, so I could be the one to decide whether to respond. I do, however, have a new friend request on Facebook. From Killian.

Mom pushes the bowl away and reaches for a banana. "Jeffrey was grumbling about something when he came in. He mentioned a party?"

"Oh." I shove my phone into my pocket. "Dad was just telling us all this stuff we have to do with him this summer. Lila's having some dumb work thing at their house, and then there's Kaylee's birthday, which is fine, obviously. And then Dad's family reunion."

"Family reunion?"

"Yep. Next month." As if it's not awkward enough that I don't really get along with my dad as it is, I'll have to go hang out with him in front of all the relatives I barely know and pretend to be a big, happy family.

"Gosh, already? How often do they do those things, every five years? It seems like we were just there, our eyeballs burning when Uncle Eddie took his shirt off to get into the pool."

Mom sounds lighthearted, but she puts the banana down, and her smile dims. Five years ago it was becoming obvious—even to twelve-year-old me—that my parents weren't going to be together for much longer. Dad must have moved out just a couple of months after that family reunion, and then he married Lila a year after that.

"I know." I shift my weight. "Anyway, I'm going over to Mel's, if that's okay."

"Of course!" Mom flashes a bright smile. "Go ahead."

I hesitate for a moment, one foot already out the door. "You sure?"

"Definitely," she says firmly, and I head back out to the car.

Mel's typing furiously on her phone, but she locks it and shoves it into her bra as I open the passenger side door.

"What's up?" I ask.

"Nothing," she says, but her eyes flick back up to the rearview mirror and I could almost swear I see the curtain in Seth's bedroom window twitch.

Mel clears her throat and starts the car, backing quickly down the driveway. "So have you changed your mind yet?" she asks as we're driving through my neighborhood.

I frown and pull out my phone, dragging my finger across the screen. "Changed my mind about what?"

"Vee! Making a summer romance plan. Taking charge of your

future. Scouting out hot guys to hook up with. Whatever you want to call it."

I scratch a mosquito bite on my ankle. "No, I have not changed my mind. And by the way, Adam has not texted, which is not helping to make me feel any better about the situation. I mean, he said he was going to call. So not even texting makes him a total ass, right?"

"Hmmm." Mel furrows her eyebrows. "Maybe he's busy today. Or," she points out, "he could still be asleep. I wish I were."

I sigh. "You know, I just don't see how kissing a million different boys is going to make me feel better about Mark dumping me and triggering my OCD about an uncertain future, and dying alone and unloved."

Mel glances at me. "Didn't you feel awesome last night when Adam kissed you? Like you were maybe ready to start thinking about moving on?"

"Yes," I admit. "But I don't feel ready now. I feel pathetic. And desperate."

"Vee." Mel pounds the steering wheel in exasperation. *"Desperate* is sitting at home for the next three months, regretting the past three years of your life. *Desperate* is stalking Mark's social media and obsessing over what he's doing right this minute. *Desperate* is clinging to the idea he might someday want to get back together with you, and putting everything on hold until that day arrives, except it probably never will, and then you *will* die alone and unloved." She pauses. "Except for me, of course. I'll still love you."

"You know," I say slowly, "someone else actually has kissed me since Adam did last night."

Mel gasps. "What? Are you serious?"

"Yeah." I grin. "You missed it, but my dad gathered up the courage to actually touch me, and I think his lips may have made contact with my head."

"Oh, come on," Mel says. "That doesn't count." She goes quiet for a moment. "But actually . . ."

"What?" I ask.

"Shut up for a minute. I think I have an idea." She turns up the radio and refuses to say anything more, a mischievous smile on her face.

It's not a long drive to Mel's house, but our neighborhoods are so different, we might as well live twenty miles apart. My subdivision is newish, cheap, and cookie-cutter. Hers is old, picturesque, and quirky. Just a few blocks from downtown Butterfield, the Flaherty home is a small cottage with a peaked roof and a yard that's almost entirely filled up with Manuela's vegetable garden. Beans, peas, and even cucumbers grow up giant trellises nailed to the wooden siding, zucchini and squash plants flop their giant leaves over the ground, and lettuce, carrots, and radishes fill the spaces in between.

"Pepper?" Mel grabs a tiny jalapeño off a plant near the front door and holds it out to me, then crushes it between her teeth when I shake my head. I love her mom's food, but I don't have the same kind of heat tolerance Mel's Mexican side has built into her.

"So tell me your big idea." I cross my arms over my chest.

Mel takes another exaggerated bite of jalapeño, grinning. "Actually, I think I'll just keep you in suspense for a while."

I swear she enjoys torturing me. "Mel—"

"*Mija!* And Veda!" Manuela pops out from behind a tall bush, watering can in hand. Dirt is streaked across the front of her white T-shirt, which pulls tight across her chest and stomach, and her smile grows even wider when she sees Mel chomping on the pepper.

"*Tienen hambre?* Do you want something to eat?"

"No, Mamá." Mel pushes open the front door and motions me inside. "We'll eat later, at lunch."

"You sure?" Manuela's eyebrows dip, unwilling to believe we're not starving to death and in desperate need of a full meal at ten thirty in the morning.

"I'm fine, thanks." I wave as Mel yanks my arm and pulls me through the door and into the riot of color that is her living room. Bright yellow walls, a tufted turquoise sofa, and a green-tiled fireplace fill the space, and about a dozen mirrors bounce the color and light streaming in from the giant windows around in a million different ways.

"Come on," I say, hands on my hips. "Spit it out. You've built up the suspense long enough."

Mel shakes her head. "Hang on. First you have to listen to this," she says, pushing me back against the sofa so my knees give way and I fall onto the squashy cushions. "I think it's really good. Like, really."

She drops her guitar strap over one shoulder and sneaks a glance at me, her hair falling over one eye. "Ready?"

I sigh. "Ready."

She hesitates for a moment, her fingers poised over the strings. "I need you to tell me the truth, okay? Don't be afraid to say if it sucks."

"It won't suck," I say automatically, which earns me another long look. "Okay," I finally say, pulling my knees up and tucking my feet under me. "I promise to tell you if it sucks. Even though it won't."

Mel nods and hunches over the guitar, avoiding my eyes as she picks out the first chords. It sounds like the same song she was playing at my house this morning when I woke up, but rounded out and filled in. My annoyance melts away as her fingers fly over the strings. Her head drops lower as she strums, humming a melody over the top of the chords that reminds me of the way sunlight sparkles on Lake Michigan on a perfectly cloudless day, or the sound of Kaylee laughing as I tickle her. Or the way I felt when Mark first held my hand.

I don't realize my eyes are closed until the music stops.

"Well?" Mel's voice is soft.

I open my eyes, and she fixes her gaze on the wall behind me.

"You can tell me if it's terrible. Please tell me."

"Have you played it for Seth?"

Mel's shoulders jerk, and she sets the guitar down quickly. "Why would I play it for Seth?"

I narrow my eyes. "Um, because you and Seth play all your songs for each other."

"And for you," she says.

"I guess."

There's an awkward pause, and Mel stands up, brushing her hands off on her shorts. "Whatever. It's terrible. Just forget about it."

"Hey." I reach over and grab her hand. "It's not terrible. And you should play it for him."

She hesitates for a moment, then shrugs and pulls away. "I actually am kind of hungry. You want something to eat?"

As soon as Mel opens the refrigerator, Manuela's sixth sense kicks in, and she comes bustling in from the yard, wiping her dirty hands on her shorts. "No, no, no, *mija*, let me get it for you." She nudges Mel away from the fridge and begins pulling out plates of food and jars of condiments.

We eat chips and salsa, and then some fruit salad, and Manuela is about to force a plate of homemade cherry bars on us when Bob comes rushing into the kitchen, his arms full of clipboards and folders bursting with paper.

"Here's my favorite one." Manuela plants a kiss on his cheek. "What's going on?"

Bob tosses the papers onto the counter, nearly knocking over a jar of extra hot salsa. "Heather quit." He shoots a look at Mel, who shrugs.

"Told you she would." She picks up a chip and takes an exaggerated bite. "You should have listened to me."

Bob slumps against the counter. "I don't know what I'm going to do. I need someone else out there."

Mel glances at me and opens her mouth, but I kick her leg, and all that comes out is a little yelp.

He rubs his eyes. "You girls don't happen to know anyone looking for work, do you?"

"No," I say firmly, just as Mel says, "Yes."

I glare at her as Bob looks back and forth between us.

"Vee needs a job," Mel says finally.

"Weren't you working at the movie theater?" Manuela asks.

"I quit," I say, pushing my crumb-strewn plate away. "Long story."

"Well . . ." Bob bows his head and laces his fingers together in mock prayer. "If you wanted to, Veda, it would be a huge help. You know the job—driving the canoes back up the river, hauling inner tubes. Killian would be working with you, so he can do the heavy lifting. Nine dollars and fifty cents an hour."

Mel wiggles her eyebrows and mouths, *Killian*, at me. I try to ignore her but feel my cheeks heating up.

"Take a couple of days to think about it," Bob finally says, although I can tell it's costing him everything he has not to keep pressing me to accept then and there.

Mel leans over and gives me a light punch on the shoulder. I shift away from her and rest my chin on my hands. "No, I don't need to think about it. Of course I'll do it, Bob. Thanks so much for the offer."

His whole body deflates as he lets out a sigh of relief. "Thank *you*, Vee. It'll be great. We owe you one." He slings an arm around

Manuela's shoulders, and she gazes up at him. "Consider yourself set up with free tamales for life."

"Hey!" Manuela pulls away and swats his backside with a dish towel. "Beautiful Veda already knows she has free tamales for life."

Bob grins and chases her around the kitchen, finally pressing her up against the counter.

"Okay, gross, we're going to my room now," Mel announces. "See you later." She drags me off my chair and down the hallway. Slamming the door behind her, she turns to me and taps her fingers together, a devious grin spreading over her face. "This is perfect," she says. "We're going to get to work together and hang out all summer, and I've thought of the perfect plan to get you plenty of boy action."

"Oh God," I say, walking across the room and slumping onto her window seat, which overlooks the backyard garden. "I'm scared."

Mel hops up next to me and wraps her arms around her knees. "It just came to me when you said your dad kissed you. First it was *Adam*, then your dad, who I admit is not exactly hot stuff, but I believe his name is *Barry*. . . ." She looks at me expectantly, eyebrows raised.

"And?" I struggle to find the connection between my dad and Slobbery-Kissing, Non-Texting Adam.

"If you could find a guy named Chris and kiss him next, then it would be *A, B, C.* You could get the whole alphabet, Vee!"

The wave of anxiety I woke up to this morning washes over me again, stronger than before. "Right. Very funny."

"I'm not kidding. You'll get to meet a bunch of guys and see that your dating life doesn't have to begin and end with Mark." She crosses her arms and looks at me expectantly. "So?"

I lean back against the window, the heat from outside leaching through the glass. "I don't know."

"Just try it," Mel pleads. "Try to find a *C* kiss and see how it goes. You can always quit if you want to."

My mind automatically starts scanning through my social media accounts, noting all the guys I know whose names begin with *C*. I shake my head, trying to clear my thoughts. "What if Mark finds out?" The words are out of my mouth before I can stop them, and I cringe as Mel's eyes widen.

"Vee! Who cares if Mark finds out? *He broke up with you*, remember?"

"I know, I know." I look away and fiddle with the hem of my shorts, unable to squash the shrill voice in my head screaming that I would be betraying Mark—and that I have, in fact, already effectively cheated on him by kissing Adam.

"You need to do this," Mel says, sliding off the window seat and grabbing a notebook and pen from her desk. "It's nonnegotiable, Vee. Consider this a love life intervention."

I close my eyes as Mel scribbles in the notebook, letting myself imagine what it might feel like if Mark found out I was with someone else. He might be jealous, which, I admit, would be gratifying, but would probably just make me feel awful in the end. Or he might not

care, which would be even worse. Two weeks ago I could have predicted exactly how Mark would react to any given situation, and the
fact that I feel like I don't even know him anymore is its own kind of
pain.

"Here." Mel interrupts my reverie and pushes the notebook into
my hands. "Read it."

Unbreakable Rules for Vee's
Summer Kissing Extravaganza

Must kiss (or be kissed by) twenty-six guys, one for
each letter of the alphabet, by the end of the summer.

Kisses can be on the lips, cheek, hand, and anywhere
else you might want to be kissed. ☺

You can't kiss a guy more than once. No forming
attachments or relationships! ☻

You CAN do more than kissing if you want.

Tell Mel every single detail of every single kiss so she
can live vicariously through your hot, sexy summer.

Don't think about Mark.

Don't tell anyone (especially the guys you're kissing) about the Top Secret Twenty-Six Kisses Challenge.

LIVE IT UP. LIFE IS SHORT—IF IT FEELS RIGHT, YOU CAN'T GO WRONG.

I scan the list and then stuff the notebook under a pillow. Seeing it written down makes it too real—like something that might actually happen.

"I'll think about it," I say, just to get her off my back. "I probably don't even know a guy for each letter of the alphabet, though. Like, whose name begins with an *X*?"

Mel waves my words away like a cloud of secondhand smoke. "Enough tourists come through Butterfield for us to find any letter we want. There has to be an Xavier around here somewhere. I'll start paying attention to the reservation sheet at the Float & Boat."

"Ugh, Mel. That's creepy."

She shrugs. "Trust me, there's not much to keep my mind occupied when I'm working in the office with my dad. He won't even let me check my phone." She sighs dramatically. "You, on the other hand, will be out getting tan with the beautiful Killian."

I frown—if by "getting tan" she means getting a *farmer's* tan.

"Killian friended me on Facebook," I say. "Or he tried. I haven't accepted yet."

Mel claps her hands. "Well, what are you waiting for? I've been friends with him for, like, a week. And I saw you two talking at the Big Float." She bats her eyelashes. "Looks like a slam dunk to me, since Adam's out of the picture."

My face immediately heats up. "Hey," I say, pulling the notebook out and tossing it back at her. "What about this whole alphabet plan you just concocted? It's supposed to be twenty-six kisses with different boys—not twenty-six kisses with Killian."

"Oh, I know," Mel says, rolling over and propping her head up on her arm. "But having him around sure will be convenient when you get to the letter *K*."

Manuela's tamales are delicious, but I'm still full from our giant snack and I find myself pushing my food around on my plate as Mel and her parents chatter away about summer plans and the Float & Boat. All I can think about is the impossibility of kissing twenty-six boys in one summer when I've only ever kissed two before in my life.

"Everything okay, Vee?" Manuela asks as I help clear the table after lunch.

"Yeah, fine," I say, mustering up a smile. She tilts her head and gives me a hard look, but I turn away and grab my bag from the back of my chair. "Thanks for lunch. I better get home."

"Do you want a ride?" Mel grabs her keys from the counter.

"No, that's okay. I'll walk." It's about a mile and a half to my house, but I'm restless and need to stretch my legs.

Mel walks me out and gives me a quick, fierce hug, shoving a folded piece of paper into my hand. "Think about it," she whispers.

I tuck the paper into my pocket and pull away. "Pick me up tomorrow?" The dentist office where my mom works as a receptionist isn't exactly on the way to the Float & Boat, so it will make more sense to ride with Mel.

"Can't wait!" She disappears inside the house, the front door brushing the bright green leaves of a tomato plant as it closes.

I wander through Mel's neighborhood, not bothering to take the most direct route home. It feels good to move. Almost every house I pass has a different kind of flower growing in the yard, erupting out of pots on the front porch or hanging heavy from vines wrapped around wooden trellises. The smells wash over me, almost overwhelmingly strong, dragging out unbidden memories of sitting in Mark's backyard at night, our fingers tangled together as we watched our little brothers kick a soccer ball past his mother's prize rosebushes.

I pull the piece of paper out of my pocket and smooth out the creases, Mel's handwriting laying out the rules for how I'm supposed to get over my heartbreak. At this point, I don't even really know how I feel. Mark and I have only been broken up for a couple of weeks, and already so much has changed—I kissed someone else and got a new job, Mel and Seth seem like they're right on the verge of getting together, and my dad is suddenly demanding we all hang out as a family. What will it be like when Mark goes off to college in the fall? Things will be changing for both of us every day, and even if we hadn't broken up, we wouldn't have been experiencing them together.

If we had kept dating, how would I have even known that the person coming home for Thanksgiving break was the same Mark I kissed good-bye at the end of the summer?

I kick at a chunk of concrete that has come loose from the sidewalk. I don't want to hook up with a bunch of guys just for the sake of some stupid game. But if I don't get out there and meet people, how am I ever going to find someone new? *That's* what I want—to find a guy who makes me feel the way Mark did . . . but who won't break my heart in the end.

I fold the list back up and put it in my pocket, then sit down on my front step and stretch, letting the tension ease out of my muscles and tilting my face up to the hot summer sun. Maybe Mel's idea isn't such a bad one. Maybe all I have to do is take a chance.

CHAPTER 8

THE NEXT WEEK FLIES BY. BOB HAS ME SCHEDULED AT THE
Float & Boat nearly every day, desperate for the extra help. At first
Killian refused to let me lift anything heavy and ran around like a
maniac grabbing inner tubes and canoe paddles out of my hands until
I told him that he and his oversize muscles could shove it if he kept
treating me like an old lady. Now I come home every night sore and
exhausted, purple bruises peppering my knees from too many colli-
sions with aluminum canoes, and annoying pop songs stuck in my
head, since that's the only music Killian will consider listening to.
The Twenty-Six Kisses resolution lies discarded under my bed, and
my running shoes stay buried beneath the pile of laundry I can't seem
to find the time to take care of, even as my legs cramp and twist each
night.

I go online every evening and sift through my social media, trying
and failing to imagine kissing any of the guys I know whose names

start with *C*. And then I stare at Killian's unanswered friend request, which he hasn't said anything at all about at work. He doesn't seem to be the kind of guy who gets all upset about some perceived social media slight, thank God. I don't know what's stopping me from accepting it. Because Killian has never met a moment of silence he didn't want to fill with good-natured chatter, I already know basically everything I would find out from his Facebook profile (plus other things that are less applicable to social media): he's hopelessly addicted to music written for teenage girls, he has starred in every play at his high school since he was a freshman, and he's terrified of outer space and doesn't like thinking about it because the concept of infinity freaks him out.

But once I hit that accept button, I'm going to open up a whole Pandora's box of online interaction that goes way beyond friendly work banter. It's too easy to get sucked into someone's Internet persona, to scan through years' worth of pictures and learn details of his life that may not even be relevant anymore, to forget you haven't actually known him forever, that this person is really a stranger to you. I'm not ready for that, and I'm not ready for the flip side either—for Killian to look back through my photos and see Mark and wonder who he is and why my relationship status now says *Single*.

"God damn it," I mutter, tightening down the last strap that will hold the canoes in place as we drive them up a six-mile dirt road full of potholes the size of kiddie pools. On the ride to work this morning, Mel mentioned how she has never seen Killian without a smile on his face, and now it's all I can think about—how white his teeth are and how awesome it is to work all day with someone who is consistently in a great mood.

"What's wrong?" Killian leans over to inspect the strap, his blond hair curling at the back of his neck. "You okay?"

"Yeah." I look away quickly. "Sorry. Just thinking about something."

He lays his palm on my hair and squeezes gently, his hand large enough to cover the entire top of my head. "No thinking allowed, counselor. It's summer."

I duck away from him, smoothing my hair down. "Have to keep my brain in shape for debate season. I think Butterfield is going up against Trawley, and I really want to kick their asses this year."

Killian pulls a face and steps onto the Float & Boat minibus, which we use to drive customers up the river for the six-mile canoe float. "I'll let you do the honors," he says, tossing me the megaphone we keep behind the driver's seat.

I sigh and lift it to my mouth. "Boarding for the ten thirty six-mile float," I call toward the parking lot. "Boarding now for the ten thirty, departing in ten minutes."

A dozen college-age kids hurry over, lugging heavy coolers and backpacks crammed with beach towels and sunscreen. They store their stuff in the back of the bus and climb aboard. Killian greets them all with high fives and turns up the radio on the local Top 40 station, the thumping bass blasting out the open windows. Once everyone is on board, I slam the back door closed, double-check the straps on the trailer, and hop onto the bus, settling into the seat directly behind Killian. He fires up the engine and pulls slowly out of the parking lot, the trailer rattling along behind us.

The college kids are already tipsy, beers in hand, taking selfies in the backseat. They'll be hungover and sunburned halfway through the float, probably in a state of near civil war by the time their canoes drift the six miles back down to the landing at Flaherty's. But now, before the dehydration and irritability set in, they're giddy and loud, practically bouncing off the ceiling.

"Hey, do you want a beer?" A tall guy with dark hair and a tattoo of a dragon on his arm leans over the back of my seat, holding out a Bud Light.

"Can't." I shrug. "I'm working."

He bounces his palm off his forehead. "Oh, duh. Sorry." He looks at me, his eyes struggling to focus. "So you like working here?"

"It's okay." I practically have to shout over the music Killian has blasting out of the speakers. "It beats flipping burgers at McDonald's."

He nods and takes a sip of his beer. "I work at Chipotle. It's not that much better."

"We don't have a Chipotle around here," I say. "I would kill for one."

"That sucks. I'm down at Ann Arbor; we have everything there."

Of course. The whole group has probably driven up to Butterfield for the weekend, a summer escape for the university crowd.

The bus hits a pothole, and the guy falls forward, practically top-pling onto my seat. "Whoa," he says, pushing himself upright.

Killian swings the bus in a wide arc, following the permanent ruts in the field next to the river.

"Looks like we're here," I say, standing up before the bus has come to a complete stop. "Have a good float."

The guy has already turned away, handing the Bud Light he offered me to a girl wearing a tiny pink bikini top. I follow Killian off the bus and around to the back, each of us working in tandem to loosen the straps enough to slide the canoes off the trailer. Some of the college guys help Killian lift the boats down from the top part of the rack. We carry the canoes to the edge of the river while the group unloads their coolers and argues over who is going to sit in each boat.

I grab a dozen pieces of rope out of the bucket in the back and hand them to the guy with the tattoo. "Here," I say. "Use these to tie all the canoes together like a big raft. That way you won't drift away from each other, and you won't have to paddle so much."

"Thanks," he says, looking genuinely grateful, his fingers brush-ing against mine as he takes the rope. "Hey, would you take a pic-ture of us?"

They gather around their canoes, the guys with their shirts off and the girls with their sunglasses on, beers held high and stomachs sucked in. "One, two, three," I count, and snap the photo on the iPhone the guy handed me. The picture will be posted to Facebook and Instagram before they even reach the middle of the river, everyone tagged and commenting on a memory they haven't even really made yet.

Killian and I help them load up and then we stand on the bank, waving as the group floats away.

"One reservation down, seven to go," he says brightly.

I groan. "Plus however many walk-ins show up."

"Hey, consider yourself lucky," Killian says, raising his arms over his head in a long stretch. "At least no one puked on the bus this time."

It's a long day, and by the end of it my muscles are burning and my face feels like a big grease pit of sunscreen and sweat. But all the canoe floats launched on time, no one lost any paddles or life jackets, and we only had three broken beer bottles to deal with. So, all in all, a success.

"Looks like our friends from this morning are still hanging around," Killian says as we finish loading a final round of canoes onto the trailer so we won't have to do it first thing in the morning. Some of the guys from our first group of the day are in the parking lot, sitting on top of their coolers or in the bed of a pickup truck, sobering up before the drive home.

"I don't know how they can drink all day and not be passed out by now," I say, inspecting a blister on my finger.

"I'm sure alcoholism is like a varsity sport where they come from," Killian says. "Did you know half of college students regularly binge drink?" He rolls his eyes, and my face flushes as I think back to the other night on the dock. I'm not sure how much Killian drank. One beer? Two? Not enough to make a fool of himself, anyway.

"You know, George Bernard Shaw once said, 'Alcohol is the anesthesia by which we endure the operation of life.' That guy had a zinger for every occasion." Killian looks down at me. "You've heard of Shaw, right?"

I fold my arms. "Of course." A typical debate trick is to start your argument off with a quote from someone famous (and preferably dead). George Bernard Shaw, an Irish playwright, was the king of one-liners, so his words of wisdom tend to pop up quite a bit, on everything from politics to the ethics of vegetarianism.

"Awesome. We should totally have a Shaw-Off." Killian tips back the brim of his baseball cap. "You want to go get food or something? I'm starving."

A Shaw-Off? I suppress a smile. "Mel's my ride," I say, tipping my head toward the office.

"I can drive you home." Killian points to his beat-up Jeep. "Despite the dubious appearance, it's really not a deathtrap, I swear."

He's being so nice, I almost say yes. But then I'd have to explain to Mel why I didn't need a ride home, and just the thought of the knowing smile she would give me is exhausting. "Maybe another day," I say. "I'm pretty tired."

The disappointment is gone from his face almost before I can register that it was there at all. "All right. Toodles." Killian bobs his head at me and saunters off, hands in his pockets. I try not to watch him walk away, but he's so tall—I'm fascinated by the way his body moves, the amount of ground he covers with each step.

He spins around, as if he can feel my eyes on him, and raises a fist in the air as he walks backward. "'What you are to do without me I cannot imagine!'"

I shake my head. "Don't flatter yourself." I turn away before he can respond, and sit down at a picnic table, pulling out my phone to check the time.

"Hey." The college guy with the tattoo walks over. He's sunburned and looks tired, but smiles shyly. "Are you off duty?" He holds out another Bud Light. "It's not exactly cold, but you look like you could use a beer."

I cross my arms and cock my head to the side. "You really want me to drink that. Are you a cop or something?"

He looks down at the can, confused, then laughs. "Shit. You're underage."

"Of course I'm underage."

"Well, hey, Underage. I'm Carson." He shoves the beer into his backpack and holds out his hand. I take it and am surprised by how cool his skin feels. "And I'm actually not twenty-one either, so I think you can be reasonably sure I'm not a cop."

His name starts with a C. The thought floats unbidden through my brain. I push it away, raising my eyebrows and pointing at the large sign hanging on the front of the office: NO UNDERAGE DRINKING. "I don't think Mr. Flaherty would be thrilled to hear that."

Carson laughs. "But Mr. Flaherty doesn't check anyone's ID, does he?"

I shrug and then wave at Mel as she hurries out of the office, letting the screen door slam behind her.

"Freedom!" She jogs over and leans up against me, slipping an arm around my waist. "Making friends, Vee?"

"This is Carson," I say, nodding at him and avoiding Mel's eyes.

"*Carson.*" Mel nudges me and shakes Carson's hand enthusiastically. I nudge her back, harder. "You were on a float earlier, right?"

"Yep." He looks over at his friends, who have started to pack up their stuff. "Sorry, you are . . . Vee?"

"Veda," I say. "And this is Mel."

Carson grins. "Veda and Mel, what are you two up to this evening?"

"Um . . ." Honestly, I was planning to make Mel drive me straight home, take an ice-cold shower, and lie in bed for the next twelve or so hours.

"We're not doing anything," Mel chirps. I resist the urge to elbow her in the ribs.

"Well, I think some of us are going to head over to the Dune Days carnival," Carson says. "Do you want to come?"

Mel's eyes meet mine, and I give a quick shake of my head. I have not officially signed on to her Twenty-Six Kisses scheme. I have not even officially signed on to being over Mark. There is no reason for me to go out tonight with a boy I don't know whose name happens (curse you, universe) to begin with *C.*

"Definitely," Mel says, grabbing my hand and pulling me toward her car. "We'll meet you guys down there."

CHAPTER 9

"I CAN'T DO IT," I MOAN, HANGING MY ARM OUT THE passenger-side window and letting my fingers drift in the breeze. "This is so stupid. Of course the first guy who creeps on me at work would be named *Carson*."

"Vee, come on. He's not creepy; he's cute," Mel says decisively, flicking the turn signal and pulling onto the field being used as the carnival's overflow parking lot. "This is a sign. You have to do the Twenty-Six Kisses thing, and you're starting tonight."

"I don't even know him!" I press back against the headrest.

"You can always bail if it gets weird," Mel says, sliding out of the front seat. "Just tell him you have cramps and you have to go home."

I'm speechless at the thought of ever saying that to a strange guy—I didn't even really like to talk about that stuff with Mark—but I follow her to the ticket booth. Even though Dune Days is technically over, the carnival is packed and it's a total sensory overload. Flashing lights from dozens of different rides blaze into my eyes, people shriek in unison as the swinging pirate ship reaches its peak and swings back down in a near free fall, and the overpowering smell of fried dough assaults my nose.

We each pay eight dollars for five ride tickets and wander across the grass. "Maybe Carson will win you a stuffed animal," Mel says as we pass the carnival games and a scrawny-looking guy swinging a giant hammer at the high striker. He sends the metal puck screaming up the track.

"Get a life," I say, giving Mel a little shove. She walks over to the prize tent and strokes a giant purple teddy bear. "He wants to come home with you, Vee," she calls.

"If you're hoping I'll win that for you tonight, I think you picked the wrong guy to hang out with," a low voice murmurs into my ear.

I spin around, heat rushing to my face. "I don't— I wasn't—" My voice catches in my throat as I take Carson in. He's changed out of his swim trunks and T-shirt and into a pair of nice flat-front shorts and a short-sleeved button-down, the tail of his tattoo trailing out from underneath one sleeve. His hair is gelled, and he's wearing a pair of thick-rimmed glasses. With the hint of a sunburn spreading across his cheeks, making his smile flash extra-white, he looks absolutely perfect.

"Hey, chill." Carson smiles and reaches out briefly to touch my elbow. "I'm just saying these games are rigged, and I'm not smart enough to figure out how to beat the carnies."

"Oh." I look down at my sandals, mentally willing Mel to get back over here and help move the conversation along.

Two of Carson's friends from the canoe trip come up behind him, also looking considerably more well groomed than they did a few hours ago, and Mel appears at my side.

"I'm Mel," she says, holding out her hand to shake.

Cody and Nick introduce themselves, and Mel flashes me a quick look. *You want to trade Carson for Cody?* I respond with a quick shake of my head that will just look like a hair toss to the guys. Carson looks—I have to say it—unexpectedly hot. And if everything goes well, I am going to kiss him tonight. My stomach flips.

The evening starts, as all the best evenings do, with cotton candy. Mel shudders as I pinch off a blue piece of Carson's sugary cloud and pop it in my mouth.

"I'm going into a diabetic coma just watching you," she says, shaking her head.

"But it's sooo good," I say, the sugar zapping straight to my bloodstream and shocking my system.

Carson hands the mostly full cotton candy wand to me. "I'm going to need both my hands," he says. Cody and Nick are looking around the picnic area, deep in discussion. "I probably should have warned you—we're kind of carnival connoisseurs. We go to basically every festival we can and buy a bunch of the most ridiculous fair food and pig out before we go on the rides."

"*Before* you go on the rides?" I say.

"Yeah." Carson shrugs. "I don't know why we do it in that order, but it usually turns out okay."

I look at Mel, and she raises her eyebrows.

Nick pulls out his phone and types furiously, tipping the screen so Carson can see. "So we've got cheese curds, mini doughnuts, fried cherry pie, chocolate-covered bacon, and Fat Elvis on a Stick. Everyone okay with that line-up?"

"Oh God." Mel closes her eyes, her mascaraed lashes dark against her cheeks. "Mini doughnuts. I totally forgot about mini doughnuts."

Cody raises his hands in the air and bows his head. "All hail the Mini Doughnut God, the high deity of carnivals, festivals, and state fairs everywhere."

I have to say, despite the jittery feeling in my stomach, a mini doughnut (or four) does sound pretty good right now.

We divvy up the list, each of us responsible for buying one of the things on the menu. I'm assigned Fat Elvis on a Stick, and Carson gets fried cherry pie. As we split up to join the lines at our respective booths, Carson grabs my arm.

"Come with me," he says. "The line for cherry pie is so short, we can hit both booths by the time everyone gets back."

The sugary smell of pie filling is overpowering, and I'm starting to feel a little sick from too much cotton candy. "You know, I don't even know what Fat Elvis on a Stick is," I say to Carson. "I haven't been to a carnival in, like, five years, and I don't think they had it back then."

Carson gives an exaggerated gasp. "You live in Butterfield, and you don't go to the Dune Days carnival? What's wrong with you?"

"When you live somewhere that's basically a tourist trap and has a million different festivals each year, it gets kind of old hanging out with carnies and tourists." I cringe and mentally backtrack, reworking my argument. "Not that you're a tourist. You're a college kid, so it's different."

Carson leans in close and plucks a shred of cotton candy off the end of my nose. "And you're an adorable townie," he says, his lips curling into a half smile.

I drop my head and look down at my feet, which, after just a few days of working at the Float & Boat, already sport a tan line at ankle level. How many other "townies" has Carson picked up with that line as he and his friends sample fried food at festivals across Michigan?

Doesn't matter, I tell myself as Carson asks the guy in the booth for an extra piece of foil to cover the fried pie. *Tonight is just about the kiss.*

"I also can't believe you don't know what Fat Elvis on a Stick is," Carson says as we walk across the grass. "But I think your life is about to change."

Peanut butter, chocolate, and bacon wrapped in banana-flavored batter and fried until it's crispy: that is Fat Elvis on a Stick. We've laid out all the food on a picnic table, and Cody insists on documenting each item with a photo before we're allowed to dig in.

"Oh my God," I gasp after the first bite.

"We have another convert," Nick says.

"It's just . . . exactly what you want food to taste like," I say. "All food should taste like this. Try it." I hold the stick out to Mel.

"No way," she says, batting the fried concoction away. "I'm sticking to cheese curds." But I see her gazing longingly at the mini doughnuts, even though she's too committed to her recent anti-sugar crusade to take even one bite.

After the food come the rides. The guys are buzzing on sugar, darting through the crowd, punching one another, fake-wrestling on the grass. And they want to ride *everything*—the Scrambler, Zero Gravity, the Tilt-a-Whirl, and every other bouncing, spinning, vibrating contraption that makes me dizzy just thinking about getting on it.

While the guys are swinging forty feet above the ground on the Fire Ball, Mel and I buy a couple of bottles of water and collapse onto a bench. I glance at my phone—it's nearly ten o'clock.

"Vee, this is seriously one of the best nights ever," Mel says, holding her water bottle against her forehead. "This is a night we're going to reminisce about when we're old and can't stay awake past nine o'clock. And," she says with a wicked smile, "I have a feeling you're going to end the evening with a bang."

I tip my head back, squinting into the dark sky, but it's impossible to see any stars past the blazing carnival lights. "We'll see."

She turns to me, pouting a little. "Aren't you having fun?"

"Yes," I admit. "Although if you had told me this morning I would be having a great time at the carnival with a bunch of guys I'd never met before, I would have sent you to the psych hospital."

"You can't plan a night like this," Mel says solemnly. "It just has to happen."

We watch the crowd go by—families, couples, groups of friends, and some adorable grandparents who are even more excited about playing Skee-Ball and Bozo Buckets than their grandkids are.

The Fire Ball does one last gut-wrenching revolution and returns to the ground. Carson, Cody, and Nick are the first ones off the ride, shoving one another good-naturedly and laughing as they come down the ramp.

"That. Was. Amazing," Nick says, leaning over to catch his breath. "Are you sure you guys don't want to go? We all have enough ride tickets for one more."

"Oh no," I say, pulling my own tickets out of my pocket. "I've been saving these for the Ferris wheel, and I think it's time to cash in."

Cody groans. "I can't even remember the last time I went on a Ferris wheel. Maybe when I was three."

"Oh, come on." Mel hops up and tosses her water bottle into a recycling bin. "It'll be good for you. You're probably getting brain damage from bouncing around on all those fast rides."

Carson holds out his hand and tugs me up from the bench. I try to pull away as soon as I'm on my feet, but he tightens his grip and laces his fingers through mine, flashing a smile that sends unexpected butterflies swirling through my stomach. "Tell Mel I owe her one. I don't think I could handle another ride that goes more than five miles an hour," he whispers.

"Too much Fat Elvis?" After a second of hesitation I squeeze his hand and he squeezes back, our fingers engaged in a complex conversation that has nothing to do with what we're actually talking about. I had forgotten this—the thrill of touching someone new, try-ing to decipher the meaning of each tiny movement. And with no alcohol involved, I'm even more hyperaware of how strange it feels to be with someone who isn't Mark.

Carson groans. "Way too much." His thumb traces slow circles in my palm.

The Ferris wheel is nearly deserted, the ride operator watching a video on his phone as we walk up. He waves our tickets away as he opens the gate and lets us board the first two cars. "Save 'em for some-thing better, guys."

Mel squishes between Cody and Nick while Carson and I sit in the car behind them.

"Behave yourselves back there," Mel calls, turning and giving me a quick thumbs-up. The Ferris wheel lurches to life, and she squeals, their car swinging as Cody and Nick rock it from side to side.

"I'm so sorry," I say, pulling away from Carson, my face burning. "She doesn't have a filter."

"Hey." He drapes his arm loosely over my shoulders. "It's cool. This is fun. Right?" He tilts my face toward him, fingers light on my chin.

"Right," I whisper. We climb higher and higher, the swirling lights falling away. Carson's hand is warm against my skin, and my shoulder fits perfectly in the space under his arm. C is going to be a good kiss. No gross, watery beer; no Seth watching me with judge-y eyes; no strings attached. Just a fun night, a nice guy, a Ferris wheel ride to the stars. All I have to do is close my eyes.

CHAPTER 10

THE NEXT DAY, I TAKE DOWN ALL MY PICTURES OF MARK AND put them away. I fish the Twenty-Six Kisses rules out from under my bed and tack them to the middle of my bulletin board. And I accept Killian's Facebook friend request. *It's not much*, I think as I shove the cardboard box full of two and a half years' worth of memories with my ex-boyfriend onto the top shelf of my closet, but at least it's something. I catch a glimpse of myself in the mirror and can't stop a smile from spreading over my face, wondering what Carson is thinking about right now on his drive back to Ann Arbor.

Jeffrey walks by my room and sticks his head in. "Why are you cleaning?" he asks, his face scrunched up in confusion.

I sigh. We've never been the kind of family that does the dishes immediately after dinner—much to my dad's chagrin—but it's sad that my twelve-year-old brother literally doesn't understand the concept of cleaning or why it might be necessary.

"I'm turning over a new leaf," I tell him.

"Okay, whatever." He taps his fingers on the doorjamb. "Don't forget Dad and Lila's party is this weekend."

"Ugh." I had forgotten. "You don't want to go, right? We can make up an excuse and skip together."

Jeffrey shrugs. "I have to babysit Kaylee. They're going to pay me forty bucks."

"Forty bucks to watch your own sister?" I raise my eyebrows.

He rolls his eyes and pushes away from the doorframe, backing into the hallway. "Just saying, Dad will be pissed if you don't show up."

I swing my door shut without pointing out the obvious: that I don't really care if Dad gets mad at me. My room looks better than it has in months—maybe years—although there are still dirty clothes on the floor and books and papers I'll have to deal with later heaped on top of the desk. I open the curtains to let more sunlight in and I take a quick picture to send to Mel with the text new start.

My phone rings a few seconds later.

"So this means you're officially in, right? I saw the Twenty-Six Kisses rules on your bulletin board."

At that moment, with a half-cleaned room, no Mark pictures in sight, and *A* through *C* crossed off the alphabet, anything seems possible. I grin. "I guess I'm in."

Once she has gotten her earsplitting shriek of delight out of the way, Mel launches into a detailed analysis of which guys from Butterfield would be the best candidates for each letter. She has obviously put some thought into the matter.

"But wait!" She interrupts her own monologue. "You should write down everyone you kiss, and, like, details about what happened so we can remember."

It seems ridiculous to think I might ever forget the circumstances around kissing someone, but I can see how once you get past the fifteen mark or so, some of the less memorable ones could start to blend together.

"Okay, hang on." I put the phone on speaker and rifle through my desk drawers, looking for a notebook that isn't already filled with scribbly class notes. I find one with a few blank pages near the end and grab a pen. "What should I write?"

"Name," Mel says. "Duh. And where you kissed him."

Adam.

"What's Adam's last name?"

Mel sighs. "Wow, Vee, you really are oblivious. It's Cook."

Adam Cook
On the dock at Flaherty's Float & Boat

"Okay, what else?"

"I don't know. What else do you want to remember?"

I tap my pen on the paper. "This might be too mean, but we could, like, rank the kisses?"

"Yes!" The phone crackles. "That's perfect. Score them out of ten, and then at the end of the summer you'll have to pick which one wins Best Overall Kiss."

"Adam gets a six," I say, writing it down with a flourish.

"Ouch, only six out of ten?"

"It probably would have been a seven if he had called me like he said he would," I admit. I wrinkle my nose, trying to figure out how to score Dad's kiss. It barely even counts.

Barry (Dad)
An awkward dad kiss—duh! At his house.
1/10

"My dad gets a one. Just . . . because."

"Fair enough. And Carson?"
Carson from Ann Arbor
Dune Days carnival Ferris wheel
8.5/10

I lean back, letting myself relive a little bit of last night—the taste of cotton candy on my tongue, the feeling of Carson's warm hand closing around mine, the last revolution of the Ferris wheel, and the feeling of being suspended in space at the top. "Eight and a half."

"Eight and a half?" Mel sighs. "It looked like a pretty freakin' perfect-ten kiss to me."

I push the notebook aside. "Mel, I've experienced a perfect-ten kiss. And, as cool as Carson was, that wasn't it."

She snorts. "Must be nice."

"What is that supposed to mean?"

"Nothing." She clears her throat. "Never mind. But we need to strategize about your next letters. Do you want to go out for breakfast?"

Fat Snacks leaps onto my bed and snuggles into my side, purring loudly. "Maybe lunch?" I say, stroking his soft fur and hating the idea of getting up again.

"Okay, I'll come get you in a couple of hours," Mel says. "In the meantime, do some research. *D* through *Z*."

"Yes, ma'am," I say, and end the call. I lie there, intending to get up and keep cleaning my room but instead getting more drowsy with each passing minute, as I tend to do whenever Fat Snacks graces me with his presence. He's like a warm, furry sleeping pill.

"You're the best boyfriend I've ever had, Fatty," I say, and close my eyes.

"So let's hear it," Mel says, picking at her club sandwich. We're sitting at an outdoor table at our favorite café on Main Street, watching the tourists flock past. "Who's on your To Kiss list?"

"Shhh," I say, glancing around. "Don't tell all of Butterfield what I'm up to."

Mel waves her hand dismissively. "They're too busy buying souvenirs to pay attention to what a couple of townies are talking about."

I eat a few cucumbers out of my salad. "Am I really going to do this? Pick a guy and go after him just because of the first letter of his name?"

"Yes," Mel says, in her no-nonsense voice. "And it will be totally worth it in the end." She tips an ice cube into her mouth and crunches down on it loudly, making me wince. "There are going to be bonfires and beach parties all summer, plus the usual Butterfield tourist trap festivals, so getting out and seeing guys won't be a problem. And you have *K* all lined up, obviously." She smiles suggestively.

I shake my head, even though something tells me I wouldn't have much trouble getting Killian to kiss me if I wanted him to—but there's no point in obsessing over that right now. "I think I have *J* figured out too." I bat my eyelashes as Mel leans in eagerly. "Jeffrey."

"Ugh, gross, Vee." She wads up her napkin and throws it at me. "That doesn't count."

"My dad counted for *B*. And *F* can be Fat Snacks. . . ."

"No!" She laughs. "You're not allowed to just kiss all the male members of your family."

"Well, what about—" I'm about to bring up Seth for letter *S*, but I catch myself just in time.

"What about what?" Mel narrows her eyes at me, almost as if she knows what I was about to say.

"Um, what about my stepmom's big party my dad told us about? It's this weekend. Maybe I can get a kiss or two there." The transition is pretty seamless.

Her expression clears. "That's a great idea. I'll ask around and see if anyone we know has been invited. It's supposed to be for her work friends, right?"

"Yeah, and I think they mostly live in Grand Rapids."

Mel shrugs. "Someone we know has to be there. And if not . . . you're getting good at making new friends."

"Why does Vee need new friends?" Seth appears from nowhere, a black shadow against the colorful small-town backdrop. He leans over the railing separating the café patio from the sidewalk and grabs a fry from Mel's plate.

"I don't," I say, giving Mel a warning look. There is absolutely no reason Seth needs to know about the Twenty-Six Kisses thing.

"What are you doing down here?" Mel asks, guarding her remaining fries with her hand.

"Lesson." Seth pulls out his phone. "I'm late. But do you want to work on the album later?"

I smile blandly, trying to ignore the twinge of jealousy that shows up whenever Mel and Seth talk about "the album." They've been writing and recording songs for a couple of years and will spend hours at a time locked away in Seth's basement, working on them. If Mark was at a cross-country meet or something, I used to occasionally tag along and pretend to read a magazine or whatever while they talked about chord progressions and fiddled with the temperamental knobs on Seth's ancient four-track recorder, but there was nothing lonelier than watching the two of them get totally in the zone and forget I was even there.

"Sure." Mel swirls a fry through the puddle of ketchup on her plate. "I'm not working tomorrow. Text me."

"See you later." Seth bops me on the head as he turns to leave.

Mel watches him go and then focuses her eyes on me, the devious look returning to her face.

"You're not working tomorrow?" I stick out my lower lip. "I thought we were supposed to have all the same days off."

"Yeah, Dad messed up the schedule. Can you get a ride with your mom?"

"Probably." I sigh and put on an exaggerated sad face. "But the Float & Boat just won't be the same without you there."

Mel laughs. "Stop trying to distract me. Let's focus on letter *D*. We have options." She waves her phone at me and taps the screen, studying what I can only presume is a list of her nine hundred Facebook friends. "Danny Bridges . . . he has a girlfriend. Darren Peters . . . I think he's working as a camp counselor this summer." She scrolls, her eyes whipping back and forth as she scans the screen. "Dexter Claybourne?"

"Dexter?" We've been going to school together since second grade. He's nice. The oldest of five siblings. Kind of short. "I don't know. That would be weird."

"It will not be weird." Mel puts her phone down on the table, and to my horror I see she's calling Dexter.

"No, wait—" I reach for the phone, but it's too late.

"Hello?" He's on speakerphone. I look around at the other café patrons, praying no one I know decided to come out for a nice lunch.

"Hey, Dex. It's Mel Flaherty."

"Oh. Hey, Mel." Dexter's voice is deep and gravelly, and, understandably, he sounds a little confused. "What's up?"

"What are you doing right now?"

"Uh . . . nothing, really. My cousin and I are watching my little sisters."

Mel looks at me and grins. "At your house?"

I tip sideways in my chair and put my hands over my face. I can't believe this is happening—Dexter must think she's a freak.

"Yeah."

"Okay, don't go anywhere. See you in a few minutes."

"Wait, what—"

Mel ends the call and leaps up, pumping her fist. "Okay, let's go!"

The only place I want to go is home, so I can disappear inside and never come out. "I hope this is one of those things I'll be able to look back on someday and laugh," I say, tossing some money onto the table.

"I love your attitude." Mel grabs my hand and pulls me to the door. "Poor Dexter's not going to know what hit him."

By the time Mel pulls up to the curb in front of Dexter's house, which is right by our old elementary school, my hands are shaking.

"Okay, quick strategy meeting," Mel says, turning off the ignition. "I think—"

"No." I open my door and get out of the car, knowing if I put too much thought into what's about to happen, I won't be able to go through with it. "Let's just do this."

I stride up the sidewalk, Mel racing along after me, and follow the sound of kids shouting to the backyard. A sprinkler and Slip 'N Slide are set up on the grass, and three little girls prance around in their swimsuits, squealing as they run through the sprays of water.

Dexter's leaning against the deck, talking to a guy who must be his cousin, and he looks up in surprise as we come around the corner of the house. He's wearing oversize sunglasses and swim trunks. No shirt. I stop short, and Mel crashes into me, gripping my arms as she struggles to keep her balance.

"Hey," Dexter says. The other guy turns around, and my heart sinks. I don't know how I could have forgotten, but Dexter is related to Ryan Kelly, one of the guys on Mark's cross-country team. "What's going on?"

I freeze, my mind racing, the sick feeling that washes over me in a debate when I'm getting my ass handed to me now settling in my stomach.

"Go!" Mel whispers in my ear and pushes me forward.

I'm fixated on Dexter's mouth, which I've never noticed before. His lips are a little chapped, probably getting sunburned. He should put a hat on.

"Hey, Dexter. Ryan." I nod, frantically trying to come up with an excuse for why we're here. I cannot kiss Dexter in front of Ryan—if

I do, Mark will find out about it in the time it takes to send one shocked text. But my brain is failing me. I have no notes, no prepared arguments. I have not practiced for hours in front of a mirror envisioning a situation in which I have backed myself into a corner and must kiss my way out of it.

"Vee wanted to give you something," Mel says. She grabs my elbow and propels me forward until I'm just a few feet from Dexter. "Right, Vee?"

"Right," I say.

"Okay . . ." Dexter raises one eyebrow. "What is it?"

Screw Ryan. There's no backing out now. I step forward and grab Dexter's arm, suffering a millisecond of panic about the placement of our noses before I mash my lips against his. We're frozen there for a few seconds, and then I pull away.

"What the . . . ?" Ryan's jaw drops.

"Run!" Mel says, and takes off across the lawn, me right behind her. As we race toward the car, I hear Dexter's little sisters start up a gleeful chant. "Dexter and that girl, sitting in a tree. *K-I-S-S-I-N-G*."

We start laughing as Mel pulls away from the curb, tires squealing in protest on the asphalt.

"I . . . can't believe . . . I just did that." I gasp for air as the Buick whips around the corner.

"You were awesome, Vee!" Mel tips back her head and howls. "His face was priceless! I should have videoed it."

We turn up the radio and drive back to my house, dancing to

every dumb song that comes on. My heart is racing, and adrenaline pumps through my body.

"That was a total kiss ambush," Mel says. "You need, like, a superhero name. The Kamikaze Kisser. The Smooth Smoocher."

"The Magnificent Macker." I giggle.

"Who is Dexter's cousin? Ryan somebody, right?" Mel says.

"Yeah." I tip my head back against the seat. "He's on the cross-country team."

"Oh." Mel shoots me a worried look. "Does that mean . . . ?"

I nod. "Yeah. Mark probably already knows by now." For some reason that seems to matter much less than it did fifteen minutes ago. "But it's fine."

She cheers. "Vee, I'm so proud of you. You're back! My girl is back!"

"I'm back." I linger over the words, savoring the way they roll off my tongue. "And I have a lot of boys to kiss."

I hurry into the house after Mel drops me off, still buzzing on adrenaline, and take the stairs two at a time to my room.

"Okay, time for more cleaning," I say to myself. If I can walk up to a boy and kiss him, I can keep my room looking like a normal living space and not a bizarre, oversize bird's nest. My dad did contribute to at least half of my gene pool, so the Cleaning Chromosome must be in there somewhere.

I pull the plastic laundry basket out of my closet and start tossing clothes into it. My hand hits the familiar mesh of my running shoe hiding underneath the dirty clothes, and I freeze, closing my eyes against a wave of emotion, trying to hold on to the crazy feeling of triumph from just a few minutes ago. I pull the bright blue shoes out from underneath the pile, and toy with the frayed ends of the shoelaces, my chest tightening as I think back to three weeks ago, when Mark walked me over to a deserted corner of the high school gym after his graduation ceremony, took his black mortarboard off his head, and told me he wanted to break up.

He had to drive me home afterward because I didn't have another ride. All I remember about those excruciating fifteen minutes is how I concentrated on staying completely silent, afraid if Mark could even hear me breathing, it would somehow make me more vulnerable to him, that he would be able to hurt me more than he already had. When he dropped me off, I flung myself into bed and didn't get out for two days. After that, I didn't even think about going running because I was moping and wanted the excuse to be lazy for once, but also because running was something we did together, and I just couldn't face lacing up my shoes and heading out into the world alone.

I glance out the window. It's past noon, sunny and hot, and I always run first thing in the morning, before the humidity sets in and the sun gets too ruthless. The adrenaline rush from kissing Dexter is gone, my body suddenly achy and tired. Maybe tomorrow, I tell myself. *Maybe tomorrow* I'll be ready to get out there again.

CHAPTER 11

I SET MY ALARM TO GO OFF EXTRA EARLY THE NEXT MORNING with the idea that I'll go for a run before work, but for some reason it doesn't ring at all. Mom bangs on my door at eight thirty, startling me out of a dream where I'm running and running but not getting anywhere. It's a relief to wake up.

"Why didn't you get me up earlier?" I yell, dashing into the bathroom to brush my teeth. "I'm going to be late!"

"So am I!" Mom joins me at the sink and applies her mascara so quickly, I'm afraid she'll stab herself in the eye. "I overslept too." She's wearing her favorite pair of scrubs, bright purple with little llamas dancing all over them.

I spit and rinse, grab my backpack from the floor of the hallway, and pound down the stairs, frustrated I didn't even get the chance to decide whether I wanted to go running this morning. "I'll be in the car."

Mom only speeds a little bit while we're still in town, but as soon as we hit the country road, she floors the accelerator, gravel spraying from beneath our tires and clanging against the car's undercarriage. The Float & Boat parking lot is already half full when we pull in.

"Thanks, bye." I slam the door and look around for Mel's dad. He must still be in the office—maybe he didn't notice I was late. I dash over to Killian, who has just pulled the minibus around for boarding.

"Sorry. Bad morning." I toss my backpack inside the bus and bend over to retie one shoe.

"You okay?" Killian gives me a funny look, and as I straighten up, I realize my hair is still in the ponytail I slept in, and I didn't wash my face.

"Yeah. Just overslept."

"That sucks." He tosses me the keys to the bus. "Why don't you drive today, and I'll help load everything up?" He turns away before I can even thank him, and I climb onto the bus and collapse gratefully into the driver's seat.

Killian turns. "Do me a favor and don't change the radio station, okay?"

"Of course not," I say. "I wouldn't dare."

He shimmies his shoulders. "Thanks. Not sure I could make it through a whole day without my girls Rihanna and Taylor Swift."

The day passes quickly. There are a ton of reservations, so Killian and I drive to and from the canoe launch a dozen times, grooving to his music and loading up as fast as we can before heading up the river again. We barely even have time to eat lunch.

"So, I just have to ask . . . What is up with your musical tastes?" I say while we're loading more canoes and getting ready to drive a birthday party reservation up to the boat launch. Eight-year-old boys in neon swim trunks scatter in every direction, shouting and chasing after one another, and a shaggy golden retriever joins the fray as well, barking happily.

Killian gives me a quizzical look. "What do you mean?"

"Pop music. It's what thirteen-year-old girls listen to. And you listen to it all day, every day. At first I thought you just played that stuff on the bus because it puts the crowds in a good mood, but you actually seem like you're addicted to it."

"'If you cannot get rid of the family skeleton, you may as well make it dance.'"

I raise one eyebrow. "Shaw again?"

He nods. "Of course. My way of admitting that, yes, it's a little weird that I have a deep, lasting love for Beyoncé, but at least I'm owning it."

"I don't think most guys would admit to that. Like my friend Seth, who watched the fireworks with us. He hates pop music." I hold out my hand, and Killian shakes a couple of chips into my open palm.

He wrinkles his nose. "And I'm guessing Seth thinks his taste in music is better than everyone else's?"

"Well . . . yes," I say. "But he's not as pretentious as that makes him sound. He's a really talented musician." I stuff the chips into my mouth and chew slowly.

Killian shrugs. "I love pop music because it's easy to love. It sounds good and I can dance to it and our brains are programmed to enjoy the repetitive patterns and chord progressions. Anyone who says they hate pop music because of the way it sounds is lying."

"Elmo!" One of the dads chaperoning the group calls after the golden retriever dashing across the grass, brandishing a leash. "Elmo, come!"

I react before I've even really processed what's happening, an image of the alphabet poster that used to hang in our elementary school library flashing through my mind. E *comes after* D. "Hang on a sec," I say to Killian, grabbing some more chips out of his hand as the dog trots by. "Good boy, Elmo." I hold out a chip, and Elmo hesitates, his nose quivering. "Come on," I say. "Want a potato chip?"

"Hey!" Elmo's owner yells. "Elmo, get over here."

"It's okay!" I wave and smile—*no problem here, sir, just coercing your dog into giving me some love.* Elmo trots over and noses my hand. I slip him one potato chip and crouch down, hesitating for just a second before I let the elated golden retriever slobber all over my face in gratitude for the treat.

Killian wrinkles his nose and looks down at me. "What are you doing?"

I straighten up, and Elmo gazes longingly at the rest of the chips clutched in my hand before he bounds off toward his owner, tongue lolling. "Um, nothing. Can't resist puppy kisses." And now *E* is crossed off the list, although I'm sure Mel won't be too happy to hear about my canine conquest.

"Oookay." Killian cocks his head to one side. "Anyway. I was going to say there's a great TED Talk— Do you watch TED talks?"

I wipe my damp chin on the sleeve of my T-shirt. "Uh, just for, like, school."

"You should watch them. They're like mini-studies in how to give an effective, informative speech, really useful for when you're practicing for debate. Anyway, there's a really great one that's basically about why classical music is something any human can enjoy. The same principles apply to pop."

"Okay." I pop the last chips into my mouth and lean against the side of the trailer. "You've obviously put some thought into this."

Killian shrugs. "I'll tell you more about it later."

"Later?"

"Yeah, later. After we're released from this never-ending loop of torture. Do you want to do the Shaw-Off? Or go watch some informative-but-entertaining TED talks?"

I stuff the chips into my mouth and chew slowly. Mel and Seth are working on the album today and will probably be wrapped up in it all afternoon, and I don't really feel like tagging along. Since Mr. Flaherty has finally arranged the schedule to give me a few days off in a row, I have nothing going on for the next two days until Dad and Lila's party.

"Uh, I don't have any plans."

"So, do you want to hang out?"

I wonder for a moment if Mel is totally wrong about Killian liking me. He stands there, his arms at his sides, his eyes trained on me. If he wanted to be more than friends, wouldn't he be more nervous about asking me out?

That's when I realize *I'm* nervous—my palms are sweating, and I'm having a hard time meeting Killian's gaze. What the hell is going on?

"Sure," I say, cringing at the fake-casualness of my voice.

Killian nods and gives a beat-up red canoe a friendly pat. "Cool," he says, and climbs onto the bus, motioning for the people lined up by the waiting area to go ahead and start boarding. I help carry a few coolers, suddenly self-conscious about the sweat stains under my armpits, and my frayed shorts.

I slide into my usual seat directly behind Killian, avoiding his eyes in the rearview mirror, and send a panicked text to Mel. Of course, the day Killian asks me out and I stupidly say yes would be the day she isn't here to talk me down from my hysteria.

go, vee!!! but do not kiss him yet. you're only on e!

actually, i'm on f now ;-)

But it doesn't matter, I tell myself, because there's no way Killian will try to kiss me. We're just going to hang out, like friends do. And, besides, I'm pretty sure no one ever used their common interest in George Bernard Shaw quotes as a pickup line.

CHAPTER 12

Elmo the Dog
Puppy kisses
1 million/10
(all dogs automatically get 1 million
for everything)

FOUR O'CLOCK COMES FASTER THAN IT EVER HAS BEFORE,
and then Killian and I are grabbing our backpacks out of the life
jacket shed and walking to his Jeep.

"Where are we going?" I ask, hoping that wherever it is, it involves
food. The only thing that makes me hungrier than working at the
Float & Boat is running.

"It's a surprise." He hops up into the Jeep and leans out the top,
arms dangling over the roll cage. "Does that work?"

I only hesitate for a second. "Okay," I agree, tossing my bag into the back. "But just a heads-up that I'm starving and will probably get grumpy soon if I'm not fed."

My joke is rewarded with a glimpse of his gapped front teeth as he drops back into his seat. "Got it. Let's go."

I open the passenger-side door and get into the car like a civilized person. I buckle my seat belt, trying to ignore the fact that my hands are shaking, and only belatedly notice there's a blue plastic tarp covering the dashboard and steering wheel, anchored by a complex system of ties and heavy rocks holding down the edges.

"Sorry," Killian says, leaning over to untie the corner in the passenger-side footwell, his chest brushing my knee. "I usually cover all this up before I go into work in case it rains, and to stop any idiots from messing with it."

I'm about to ask why anyone would mess with his car when he pulls the tarp away. I gasp. Written all over the dashboard in gold and silver metallic marker are . . . words. Phrases, really.

TODAY I DON'T FEEL LIKE DOING ANYTHING
BAND-AIDS DON'T FIX BULLET HOLES
MMMBOP

I run my hand over the dashboard and turn to Killian, who is watching me closely. "These are song lyrics."

"Good observation." He grins and starts the car.

I read more.

CAN'T STOP 'CAUSE WE'RE SO HIGH
IMAGINE THERE'S NO HEAVEN
SHAKE IT OFF

"What are they for?"

He shrugs. "I was listening to the radio one day a year or so ago, and I heard a song I really liked, but I knew I wasn't going to remember it. I had one of these." He picks up a gold Sharpie out of the center console. "It was from a school project, so I just scribbled the song's hook down on the dashboard. I liked how it looked, and I kept going. Voilà."

"Wow." The contrast of metallic gold and silver against the dusty black of the dashboard is messy and beautiful. I recognize most of the lyrics, but not all of them. I fight the urge to pull out my phone and start googling the unfamiliar words, to hear the melodies that must elevate these broken phrases from flat nonsense to something profound.

Killian ducks his head and glances at me. "It's just another way my quote obsession manifests itself. If I hear a lyric I like, I write it down. If I'm upset or sad and I know the perfect lyric to express what I'm feeling, I write it down and then listen to the song to get all my angst out."

"I love this," I say, running my hands over the words again, my fingers narrowly missing Killian's as he reaches to adjust the stereo volume. I love it, and I would have never thought to do it in a million years. Writing on your dashboard is the kind of thing people who don't believe in regrets do. You can't go back. You can't wipe it away. Everything Killian felt while he was writing each lyric is right here on display for anyone to walk past and see.

Killian turns on the radio, already tuned to the ubiquitous Top 40 station. "I love it too. But it means I'll never be able to sell this damn thing."

WHAT THE HELL AM I DOING HERE?
SOMETIMES WHEN I MISS YOU, I PUT THOSE RECORDS ON
AND IN THE END, THE LOVE YOU TAKE IS EQUAL TO THE
LOVE YOU MAKE
TAKE ME TO CHURCH

"What's the last one you wrote?" I ask.

He ducks his head a little. "Um . . . I don't remember."

"You're lying!" Without thinking, I smack him lightly on the shoulder, but then I quickly fold my hands in my lap.

Killian shakes his head as the Jeep accelerates. "I'm not just going to tell you. Try to guess."

SEEMS TO ME IF YOU CAN'T TRUST, YOU CAN'T BE
TRUSTED
I'M BRINGING SEXY BACK

"I have no idea." I lean forward and look more closely. Some of the words run into each other, lines crisscrossing back and forth across the hard plastic. "I can't even tell which ones were written first."

"Then I guess you'll never know."

"Come on, Killian!" My hair whips against my face as we barrel down the road. "Just tell me."

"Okay, fine." He reaches over and points to short lyrics written right above the glove box: **YOU REALLY GOT ME**

"The Kinks!" I say. "I love that song. Who did you write that about?" I ask, teasing him. "Beyoncé?"

Killian turns to me, not saying anything. His gaze lingers so long, I grab the wheel. "Whoa, eyes on the road."

We drive toward Trawley, the radio turned up loudly enough that we don't have to talk. Killian pulls into the parking lot of a small hot dog stand off the side of the road. "We're going to need food we can walk with. Hot dog or grilled cheese?"

"A hot dog is fine," I say. I can't remember the last time I ate one, but pretty much anything with mustard and a pickle on it tastes delicious.

Killian is back in moments, two hot dogs and a giant box of fries balanced in a cardboard takeout holder. He hands it to me and hops back into the Jeep. "Onward!"

We blow right through Trawley, three green lights in a row letting us pass the entire downtown in less than a minute, and soon we are back in the country. Killian drives north, through deep swathes of pine forest and over roads that get increasingly rougher. If I were with any other guy, I would be seriously worried about getting abducted, but it's hard to be scared of Killian, who bops along to the radio, the wind making his blond hair stand up in a soft little mohawk.

"Almost there," Killian mutters a couple of times, glancing down at the clock and then over at me. I smile and shrug. I've got nowhere better to be.

Killian takes a left into a driveway I didn't even see, and the Jeep crunches down a gravel road that's only wide enough for one car, low-hanging tree branches scratching against the roll cage. Finally we pull into a clearing, and my head spins as I reorient myself and realize we're right next to the lake. Rocky cliffs reach out into the vast expanse of blue, and the wind is blowing in from the west. I shiver.

Killian cuts the engine and leans forward on the steering wheel, looking sheepish. "So, I'm going to be honest," he says. "I haven't been here for a while, and that drive is a lot longer than I remembered."

I shrug and hold up the hot dogs, which by now must be stone cold. "Bon appétit?"

Killian reaches for a limp fry and tosses it into his mouth, then catches sight of his disheveled hair in the rearview mirror and hastily reaches up to flatten it. Our eyes meet, and I try to hold back the laughter that's building in my stomach, but Killian snorts, and then we've lost it. I set down the food and brace myself against the dashboard, a little confused about what exactly is so damn funny but almost unable to breathe because I'm laughing so hard.

"Stop laughing," Killian finally says between gasps. He starts giggling again and shakes his head. "Stop it."

"I'm trying!" I try to think of very serious things: global warming, SAT tests, heartbreak. But even conjuring Mark's image doesn't completely wipe the smile off my face.

We finally recover. Killian helps me out of the Jeep and leads me over rocky shoreline. There's absolutely no one around—for all I know, we could be the only people for miles. A seagull cries at it dips down and flies past us, no doubt eyeing the food Killian is carrying. "Can you at least tell me where we're going?" I ask.

"It's right around the corner," he says, pointing with his free hand. "Look."

A small lighthouse stands at the edge of the rocks, only about twenty feet tall, old and in disrepair. The original navy and white stripes painted on it have faded and peeled, all the windows are broken, and its door hangs from one rusty hinge. It's tragic and beautiful, and totally worth a dinner of cold hot dog.

Killian takes off his sweatshirt and drops it to the ground, gesturing for me to sit down on it. "I always told myself I'd bring a girl here someday," he says, flopping down next to me. "But I think maybe I should have put a little more planning in on the front end."

I flush and grab one of the hot dogs. "This is great," I say. "Really. How did you find this place?"

Killian reaches over and takes the hot dog from me, his fingers brushing mine. I tense up, watching his face come closer. I should back away, but for some reason I don't.

"Sorry," he says, flashing an apologetic gap-toothed smile. "This is the tofu dog. I'm a vegetarian." He raises it to his mouth and takes a big bite. "You know what George Bernard Shaw said about eating meat, right?" Killian asks, regarding me over his hot dog, which is oozing mustard.

"Oh." My face flushes, and I tear my eyes away from his. "I do know this one," I say, unreasonably proud to finally be able to feed Killian's Shaw obsession and grateful to feel my heart rate returning to normal. "'Animals are my friends, and I don't eat my friends.'"

"Exactly." He finishes the tofu dog in two more bites. "Although, I have to admit, these don't fill you up quite the same way meat does."

I'm way too nervous to eat now. "So, you've always wanted to bring a girl here?" Probably the last words I should be saying, but they're literally the only thing I can think of at the moment.

Killian grins and crosses his long legs, trying to find a comfortable position on the hard ground. "Yep. Sometimes I just get in the Jeep and drive. I don't have anywhere to go, but it just feels good to go *somewhere*, you know? And I found the lighthouse, which I think has been totally forgotten. I can't find anything in books or online about it or anything." He shrugs. "But I could never convince a girl—or anyone, actually—to come on any of my adventures with me. Until now."

My mind is all over the place, trying to think of something witty to say and simultaneously stuck on the fact that I'm apparently on a date. An out-of-alphabetical-order, unrelated-to-the-kissing-challenge, real-feelings-might-be-involved, honest-to-God *date*.

"So what's the deal with that bro-looking guy?" Killian turns his gaze away from me, playing with the hem of his shorts.

For a moment I think he's talking about Mark, and then I remember the illicit night at the Float & Boat. "Oh. Adam?"

Killian shrugs. "I guess. The dude from the fireworks."

I shift uncomfortably. "There's no deal with him. I don't even know him."

He looks at me, eyebrows raised. "Really?"

"It was a weird night," I say. "I had literally never done anything like that before." *Although I have done something similar a few times since.* I push the guilty feeling away—the Twenty-Six Kisses Challenge has nothing to do with Killian.

He nods and looks out toward the lighthouse, cracking his knuckles with short, sharp pops. "Can I ask you a question?"

I blink. "Yeah."

He props his chin in his hand and says thoughtfully, "This might sound stupid, but have you ever felt like you were born in the wrong place at the wrong time? Like you're not supposed to be wherever you are?" He turns his piercing blue eyes on me.

"I don't know." I think back to when my parents first decided they were getting divorced. It was the worst time in my life, but I didn't really feel like it had anything to do with me. They were the ones who just couldn't seem to figure anything out.

"Oh." He seems disappointed.

"I mean," I say hastily, "I'm sure everyone feels that way sometimes. Out of place. Thinking everyone else has it all figured out and you're just making it up as you go along."

Killian nods thoughtfully. "Trawley really sucks," he says. "Thank

God, I only have one year left. I'm glad I've switched allegiance to Butterfield for the summer." He grins and nudges my shoulder.

"What exactly is so bad about it?" I ask. This isn't the first time Killian has made grumpy comments about his hometown.

He shrugs. "Remember those guys who showed up at the Big Float?"

"How could I forget Drew and his string bean friend?"

Killian smirks. "Well, they were on their best behavior that day." He reaches down to retie one of his shoes. "I've lived in Trawley my whole life, but I've never really fit in, at least with the guys. It's weird. You'd think they would have gotten used to me by now. But they haven't."

"What is there to get used to?" I can't imagine someone having a problem with Killian. He's friendly, outgoing, easy to like. *Very* easy to like, actually, as I'm finding out.

Killian shrugs. "They just don't get me. And I don't get them either, I guess. I actually like learning things, while they'd rather just play video games. My music, the drama club stuff. George Bernard Shaw. Literally everything I care about is something they think is weird or stupid." He looks at me and smiles. "People in Butterfield seem to be much more enlightened."

I smile back. "Now all you have to do is move and make it official so you can join our debate team. We'd be unstoppable."

Killian picks up a limp French fry and makes a face. "Thanks for not freaking out about the food or the longest car ride ever down deserted country roads with a guy you barely know. I promise next time we can do something normal. Like watch TED talks."

I get to my feet and stand at the edge of the rocks, watching the waves crash against them and trying to ignore the flutter that went through my stomach when he said the words *Next time*.

"You know, now that you mention it, lately I have kind of felt like I don't really belong either," I say.

Killian comes to stand next to me, his shoulder nearly touching mine. "Yeah?" he says.

"Yeah." I can feel him looking at me, but I keep my eyes on the horizon, too scared of what might happen if I turn my head to meet his gaze. "But right now I feel okay."

"Me too," Killian says, and the relief in his voice is palpable. "Me too."

CHAPTER 13

THE NEXT MORNING, I WAKE UP SO EARLY THAT IT'S STILL almost dark outside—which in the middle of summer in northern Michigan is saying something. It's not quite five a.m., but I am completely awake, and I know as soon as my feet hit that floor that I am going to run and it will be glorious.

I pull my hair up into a ponytail and tie my shoes quietly, leaving a note on the kitchen table in case Mom gets up early and notices I'm gone. It feels so good to step out into the cool, fresh air, and I breathe deeply, my whole body relaxing as muscle memory takes over and I sink into a deep stretch, feeling my breath move easily in and out of my lungs as my body warms up. Everything about this feels right, even the fact that I'm running alone.

Mark used to pick me up early in the morning and drive me to the beach. We'd stretch in the deserted parking lot, the sun streaming over water, the sound of the waves on the shore somehow quieter in the morning calm. And then we'd run, usually along the hard-packed sand at the edge of the lake but sometimes up into the dunes for a harder workout, our muscles pushing against the unbending forces of gravity and shifting sand, too breathless to talk. When we reached the top, we'd fall to the ground, and Mark would pull me against his chest, our hearts practically slamming into each other from beneath our T-shirts—mostly because of the exercise, of course. But I always liked to think that we were just that much in love, that even when my heart was going a hundred miles an hour, it would speed up just a little more whenever he put his mouth on mine.

I stay far away from the beach this morning and run through my neighborhood, directly away from the lake, taking refuge in the cool forest trails carpeted by pine needles and fallen leaves. My phone bombards my ears with music so I don't miss the sound of Mark's breath next to me, and I keep my eyes trained straight ahead, not allowing my peripheral vision to search for a flash of his blue baseball cap. And soon enough, it's Killian who my mind drifts to—Killian with his goofy grin and giant hands and pathetic, romantic, beautiful attempt at a first date that made me feel like I was finally turning back into myself.

I round a corner and startle a doe grazing at the side of the trail. She disappears into the trees in a flash of white and brown, and I stop, bending at the waist, lungs heaving with the most satisfying pain.

Something moving through the trees alerts me to the fact that I'm not the only early morning runner up and about. I automatically reach into my pocket and curl my fingers around the tiny can of pepper spray my mom insists I carry.

I move off to the side of the trail as the other runner comes closer, making room to pass. I bend over and stretch, pretending I've purposely decided to stop and rest here rather than being forced to slow down because I'm grotesquely out of shape after only a few weeks of laziness.

The runner sprints past, and I catch only a glimpse of navy blue shorts and a white T-shirt before he's gone again. But then the footsteps slow down and stop. "Veda?"

I straighten up and peer through the trees. "Oh. Hey, Ryan." The shocked look on his face when I kissed Dexter flashes into my mind. If my cheeks weren't already burning from exertion, I'd be turning red.

"Hi." He puts his hands on his hips, his chest rising with each deep breath, looking like he regrets stopping. "So." He looks at me, then away again. "What the hell was that with Dexter the other day?"

I pretend to think for a moment, as if showing up in people's backyards and kissing them is a normal enough occurrence in my life that I could possibly have forgotten what Ryan is talking about. "Oh. That. Yeah, that was a dare."

As the words come out of my mouth, I realize it's a great cover, and not even necessarily that much of a lie. The Twenty-Six Kisses Challenge *is* kind of a big, extended, summer-long dare. A dare that's designed to allow me to take back my life.

Ryan rolls his eyes. "Real mature, Vee."

"I know." I shrug.

"I hope you weren't doing dares like that when you were still dating Mark."

I study him, the beads of sweat sliding down the dark brown skin at his temples, the suspicion in his eyes. "Um, no," I say, crossing my arms over my chest, my voice hard.

He holds my gaze. I stare back, and finally he blinks and glances away.

"Ryan, I never would have done anything like that while I was with Mark. Okay?"

He nods, and I let my arms fall to my sides. "Did you tell him?" I ask.

The beat of silence that elapses before he speaks is the only answer I need. "I had to," Ryan says, his chin jutting out. "I thought maybe you had been cheating on him, and that's why you broke up."

"Well, it wouldn't have mattered at this point, would it?" I turn away from him and break into a slow jog, trying to avoid thinking about how hurt Mark must have been to hear about the Dexter kiss. *Not as hurt as I was when he dumped me.*

"Veda, wait!" Ryan's footsteps crunch over the path behind me, and I slow down again. There's no use trying to outrun him—he's much faster than I am and has more endurance. "Look, I'm sorry," he says. "It was none of my business."

"You're right," I say, spinning to face him. "It wasn't. And I'm actually trying to finish my run here, so if you could just leave me alone, that would be great."

He doesn't leave, but he doesn't keep talking either, just falls into step beside me, easily matching my pace. I shove my earbuds back in and turn up the music, trying to forget he's there. We run three miles together, all the way into town, before I'm totally exhausted. I slow down to a walk, my chest heaving, struggling to remember exactly what I ever loved about running.

"It's not safe for you to run alone," Ryan says. Annoyingly, he's barely even breathing hard.

I look up at him and raise my eyebrows. "Ryan, we live in Butterfield, Michigan. How is it not safe to do anything here?" I slip my hand into my pocket and shove the pepper spray farther down, hoping he can't see the outline of it through my thin athletic shorts.

He doesn't respond but just stands there, smirking at me.

"Anyway, I'm training for a race, so I really need to get going." Of course I'm not training for anything, and I couldn't run another step even if there was a bear chasing after me, but it's all I can think of to say to get him to leave me alone.

"You're training for the half?" Ryan brightens. "Me too."

I close my eyes briefly. The Butterfield Half Marathon takes place at the end of every summer. Just another reminder of something Mark and I used to do together.

I sigh and cast a withering look at Ryan's antelope-like body. "Do you even need to train?"

"Of course I need to train." He looks insulted. "Look, I'm sorry for giving you crap about Dexter. It was just weird."

I nod reluctantly. "I'm with you on that."

He stretches his arms above his head and yawns. "So, you're pretty good. Do you want to run together sometimes? We can keep each other on track."

Great. Now I have a running buddy for the half marathon I wasn't even planning to do. I cock my head to the side, not sure whether he's being serious or not. "Why?"

Ryan looks uncomfortable. "I don't know. Sometimes it's more fun to train with someone. Especially on the long runs." He holds up his right hand. "I swear I won't give you any more crap about Dex. And I'm not trying to hit on you or anything." He lets his breath out in a rush. "What do you say?"

"Sure," I say, mostly to get him off my back so I can go home and weep over the two new blisters on my ankles. I give him a sarcastic smile. "Text me. You can get my number from Mark."

CHAPTER 14

BEFORE I BUMPED INTO RYAN OUT ON THE TRAIL, I HAD NO intention of running the half marathon. But for the rest of the day, as I bum around the house with Jeffrey and look up George Bernard Shaw quotes on the Internet (with occasional breaks to click through Killian's Facebook pictures), I can't stop thinking about it. If I am going to do the race, I definitely need new running shoes. And one of those CamelBak water bottles would be nice. The next day, as I'm indulging myself by online window shopping for running clothes I can't afford, Jeffrey barges into my room.

"What the hell?" I yank the sheet up to my neck. I'm wearing sleep shorts and a tank top, but still.

"Can you take me over to Dad's?" Jeffrey's hair is still wet from the shower, and he smells like he was involved in an explosion of the men's fragrance department at Macy's.

"Now?" Lila's dreaded party isn't until tomorrow night.

Jeffrey blows air out through puffed cheeks. "Yeah, I decided I want to go now and stay over."

"Mom's at work, isn't she? I don't have a car."

"Can't you get Seth or Mel or someone to drive me?"

I shake my head, totally confused. Jeffrey hates going over to Dad's house, the same way I hated going over to Dad's house before I turned sixteen and opted out of the whole stupid custody arrangement. "Why do you want to go over there early?"

Jeffrey shrugs. "I don't know. It's boring here."

I roll over, turning my back to him. "Give me a break, Jeffrey. You're twelve and you're on summer vacation. You're supposed to be bored."

He doesn't move for a few seconds, and then he walks out of the room. "Shut the door!" I yell, but he doesn't. I hear rustling in his room, the squeak of the drawers in his old dresser. Footsteps coming down the hallway, passing by my open door.

"I'm going to Seth's to ask him to drive me," Jeffrey calls, already pounding down the stairs.

"What? Jeffrey, don't you dare!" The front door slams.

I leap out of bed and sprint down the hallway, using the handrails on either side of the stairs to swing down and jump the last four. Peering out the window, I see Jeffrey is already halfway across the street, his backpack slung over his shoulder, his skateboard tucked under his arm.

"God damn it." I shove my feet into a pair of old flip-flops and go outside, standing on the cement front step.

"Jeffrey!" I call, beckoning for him to come back. "Get over here!"

He turns around and waves, a cocky grin spreading over his face. "Sorry, I can't hear you!"

By the time I shuffle across the street, Jeffrey is standing at Seth's door. "I already rang the doorbell," he says calmly as I come up behind him and grab his elbow, squeezing as hard as I can.

"Get back inside," I say between gritted teeth. I pull on Jeffrey's arm, but he brushes me aside easily. When did he get to be so strong?

"Get off me!" Jeffrey says as I pull on his backpack, leaning all my weight onto it so he staggers backward. Just as I'm about to tip him off the step and onto the sidewalk, Seth opens the door.

"Hey," he says, his eyes widening. I let go of Jeffrey and cross my arms over my chest.

"Hi, Seth," Jeffrey says. "My sister wanted to ask you if you could drive me over to my dad's house since our mom's not home and we don't have a car."

Seth turns his green eyes on me, and I shake my head. "You don't have to," I say. I poke Jeffrey in his side. "He can wait until Mom brings the car back."

Jeffrey gives me an evil look. "Actually, it's kind of important that I go now."

I sigh and push my hair out of my face, remembering only as I'm doing it that I need to keep my arms over my chest to hide the fact that I'm not wearing a bra. "Seriously, Seth, he's being a total brat. Don't drive him anywhere."

Seth looks back and forth between the two of us and shrugs. "Sure, I guess I can take him."

Jeffrey smiles and elbows me in the ribs. I swat his arm away. "Well, I'm coming too," I say, putting as much authority into my voice as I can. "Just give me five minutes to get changed."

I turn away and pull my shorts down over my thighs, feeling Seth's eyes on me as I hurry back to our house.

"Thanks for making me look like an idiot, Jeffrey," I mutter as I dig through my mostly empty drawers. With the majority of my clothes still in the laundry from my cleaning binge the other day, the best I can come up with is a too-small sports bra, a paint-spattered T-shirt I used to wear to do crafts with Mom, and long basketball shorts that might actually belong to my brother. I can already imagine the stink-eye I'm going to get from Dad for showing up at his palace looking like an artistically challenged middle-school boy.

you are in deep shit, I text to Jeffrey. He sends back a poop emoji.

When I get outside, Jeffrey is showing off for Seth on his skateboard, doing the only two tricks he knows over and over again in the street while Seth sits on the minivan's bumper, elbows on his knees.

"That's sweet, dude," Seth says as I walk over. "Ready to go?"

"Shotgun!" Jeffrey yells. I flip him off and wrench open the passenger-side door, settling onto the faded fabric seat before he has a chance to start squawking about injustice.

Once Jeffrey's settled in the back, Seth fires up the van and pushes a piano concerto CD into the CD player, turning the volume up loud enough that we don't have to talk. Jeffrey sighs and pops his earbuds in. I kind of wish I could do the same, unexpectedly missing the energy and strong beat of Killian's music. With the sole exception of the songs he and Mel write together, Seth is not a big fan of music with any lyrics at all. He says words get in the way of what music should actually be doing. But now, having seen Killian's amazing dashboard and the way those words have tied him to the emotions of the songs he loves, I might disagree with Seth on that point.

I watch the shabbiness of our neighborhood fade into the cute charm of downtown Butterfield, then open up to grassy fields and miles of clear sky before we turn onto Dad's tree-lined waterfront road.

When we pull into the driveway, I spot Lila in the yard, an enormous straw hat perched on top of her head and tied underneath her chin with a wide ribbon. She seems to be doing some kind of gardening in the elaborate flower bed underneath the giant picture window, but there's not a speck of dirt on her polka-dot gardening gloves or her white linen pants.

"Vee!" Kaylee appears from behind a bush and makes a beeline for me as we climb out of the van. "Hi!"

"Hey, you." I catch her under the armpits and swing her up into a big hug. She has mud on her shoes and her knees, and I squeeze her tight against me, so happy to be reminded that, despite the fact she is growing up in a mansion with two housekeepers, she is still just a normal little kid.

"What's going on?" Lila hurries over, her face pinched underneath the hat. "Is everything okay?"

I look at Jeffrey, who drops his gaze to the ground and scuffs his shoe against the grass. "I, uh, thought I'd come early this weekend," he says, his voice cracking painfully. "To hang out with Kaylee."

"Well!" Lila has the grace to turn her surprise into delight. "Isn't that nice?" She leans over and squeezes Kaylee's arm. "Your brother came over early to see you, baby!" Kaylee looks at Jeffrey and hides her face in my shoulder.

Lila pulls off her gardening gloves and sticks them in her back pocket. "But your room isn't ready," she says, turning toward the house and beckoning for us to follow. "Claudette was supposed to put fresh sheets on the bed this afternoon, but I'm sure we can get it taken care of now."

Kaylee squirms in my arms, and I put her down so she can race after Lila.

"We actually have to get going," I call, raising my hand in a wave. "Just dropping Jeffrey off."

Lila waves back and disappears into the house, and Jeffrey sighs and starts after her.

"Hey." I grab his arm. "You want to tell me why you were so excited to get over here?"

"Nope." He slips away. "Thanks for the ride, Seth."

"No problem."

We watch Jeffrey trudge across the lawn and up the steps to the front door, dragging his feet like he's on his way to the electric chair. I shake my head. Something is up with him, but I have no idea what it could be.

"Maybe he has a thing for your stepmom." Instead of heading back into downtown, Seth drives us toward the beach.

My jaw literally drops. "Are you serious?" I say. "Is that possible?"

He shrugs. "Maybe. She's all right, I guess."

I shudder. "You obviously don't know Lila. She's like the human equivalent of"—I think for a second—"a box of chalk. Dry, plain, boring. Also, where are we going?"

"I haven't been to the beach once yet this summer," Seth says.

"No kidding." I glance down at his freckled arm, the skin so pale, it's nearly translucent.

The parking lot is already half full, even though it's not even lunchtime on a Friday. Lots of families are out and about, staggering up the dunes with cameras in hand or running out onto the beach with towels, shovels, and buckets. Seth always looks a little ridiculous at the beach, especially once the iconic shoes come off. His bare feet are long, thin, and blindingly white, and when he rolls up the bottoms of his dark jeans, he looks like a punk rocker trying to escape a flood. He picks his way across the sand, wincing at every little rock and twig he steps on.

"Let's go walk by the water," I say, pointing to the overgrown shortcut that bypasses the dune climb and takes you directly to the beach. My feet are still tough and calloused from running, but the miles I did yesterday have me limping along nearly as badly as Seth.

Seth walks on his tiptoes, practically leaping from step to step. "I remembered why it's better to just stay inside," he says, sighing with relief as we hurry to the cool, wet sand at the edge of the lake. "You're going to have to carry me back to the parking lot."

I fall into step beside him. "Your nose is already turning pink," I say, handing him the mini bottle of sunscreen I keep in my purse during the summer.

Seth takes it gratefully and slathers it over every bit of exposed skin. He doesn't rub it into his ears all the way, and little white blobs cling to the ends of his hair. The beach is crowded today: towels, umbrellas, and kids' toys litter the bleached sand. The lake reflects the deep blue of the sky, and tiny waves lap at our feet as we follow the curved path of the shoreline.

My phone vibrates with a new text. It's from Killian. i liked yesterday. you?

I flush and shove the phone back into my pocket. Seth glances over at me, raising his eyebrows. "I feel like I've barely seen you lately," I say quickly, reaching over to give his hand a quick squeeze.

Seth squeezes back and then releases his grip, shoving his hands into his pockets. "You've been busy. And heartbroken."

"Yeah," I say, ducking as a squawking seagull swoops over our heads to investigate an abandoned bag of chips. "That does take up a surprising amount of time."

Seth grins. "I can imagine. You have to listen to sad songs and cry along with them, write letters to your ex that you'll never send . . ."

"Eat lots of ice cream," I supply. "Read trashy magazines."

"Get a drastic haircut."

"Dang! I knew I forgot something." I tug on the ends of my hair, which is exactly the same as it's always been. I wish I had taken advantage of the breakup to do some of those things. They sound a lot more interesting than what I actually did—lie in bed and cry my way through two boxes of Kleenex and an entire season of *The Bachelor* illegally streamed online.

A familiar-looking guy trudges toward us, shoes dangling from one hand. I shade my eyes. "Hey, Zane?"

He looks around, not able to place my voice. I wave, finally catching his attention, and he jogs over the sand to us. Two years younger than I am and as jumpy as they come, Zane is also the most talented kid on our debate team. The dude is some kind of rhetoric genius, albeit slightly awkward.

"Hi, Vee." Zane's dressed in a long-sleeved T-shirt and jeans. He looks nearly as out of place here on the beach as Seth does.

"Hey. What's going on?"

Zane shrugs and steps aside as a couple of kids with floating noodles race by, splashing into the water. "I was going to meet Tracy here, but I think I must have gotten the wrong time or something, and I lost my phone, so I can't call her."

I pull my phone out of my pocket and scroll through, not sure whether I have Tracy's number, squashing the temptation to read Killian's text again. "You're in luck." I hold out my phone. "Go ahead."

Zane hesitates. "Really?"

"Absolutely."

He takes my phone, a shy smile on his face, and turns away. Seth gives me a questioning look, and I mouth, *Freshman*, at him, only belatedly realizing Zane isn't technically a freshman anymore. The thought makes me unreasonably sad—everything is changing, even the things that shouldn't really matter, yet somehow do.

Zane's on the phone for only a minute. "I got the wrong day," he says, shrugging and handing the phone back to me. "I guess I really can't function without my planner."

I laugh. We always gave Zane crap about his dedication to his stupid school-issued schedule planner, filling in his homework assignments and debate practices like his life depended on it.

"By the way," he says, holding out his hand to Seth, "I should introduce myself. I'm Zane Haywood."

Seth hesitates for a moment but recovers quickly and gamely takes Zane's hand. "Seth."

There's a beat of awkward silence as Zane grins at Seth and pumps his hand up and down, basking in the glory of getting to meet the elusive musical genius Seth Moore, who everybody at Butterfield High knows but few know much about. "Sorry," I say, shaking my head. "I wasn't sure if you guys knew each other."

Zane waves away my apology. "Thanks for letting me use your phone," he says.

"No problem. See you around."

He takes a few steps but then spins back toward us. "Hey, Vee? Some of us from the team were thinking about hanging out. You in?"

I glance at Seth, whose face twitches as he suppresses a smile.

"Uh, sure," I say, looking up at Zane. "Who's coming?"

He shrugs. "Oh, you know. Pretty much everyone. Jason, Callie, Jenn, Tracy."

So by *everyone*, he means the underclassmen, not the juniors and seniors I hung out with during the school year.

"And, uh, you can come too, if you want." Zane glances at Seth.

"Sweet. Cool." Seth clearly has no idea what to say.

"Awesome. Well, I'll see you guys." Zane basically runs away.

As soon as he's out of earshot, Seth sighs and shakes out his limbs, as if that conversation literally set into his muscles and caused him pain. "So awkward."

"Awkward but nice." I glare at Seth, reminding him not to judge everyone around him.

He nods. "Yeah, I guess." He stretches his arms over his head, his shirt lifting to reveal a sliver of skin at his stomach that is even paler than the rest of him. "Want to go back? I think I've had enough of the beach for the summer."

"Let's at least wade in a little bit." With the sun beating down on my head and the waves so cool against my toes, I can't walk away from the lake without getting a little wet.

Seth wrinkles his nose at the thought of actually stepping into the water, and I snatch his shoes out of his hand, dropping them near the line where the wet, packed sand starts to dry out. "Can't I just wait here for you?" he says.

"Roll your pants up higher," I say. "This will be good for you."

He sighs and bends over, struggling to force the stiff denim of his jeans up over his knees. "I'm only going in for a minute. I hate it when my feet get all pruney."

"Okay, Grandpa."

The water is heaven. Clear, cool, soft. I take giant steps, pushing myself in deeper and deeper, ignoring the occasional piece of seaweed brushing against my skin. When I'm knee deep, I turn back to find Seth hesitating near the shore, the tiny waves lapping somewhere around his ankles.

"Come on!" I call.

His shoulders slump, but he inches forward, his face tipped down as he searches for anything that might be lurking under a couple inches of crystal-clear lake water. I look back out over the horizon and hold my hands up to my face to block the view of the beach and the people swimming. All I can see is the water and the sun and the sky, the light reflecting a million different ways as the lake moves with the wind and whatever deep, unfathomable forces that lie beneath it. I close my eyes and, just for a second, everything is perfect.

"Okay, this is as far as I go," Seth announces from behind me. "My pants are already wet."

I drop my hands to my sides. I could do it, if I thought I could handle the truth. I could ask him about Mel right now and get the whole issue cleared up.

"Vee?" Seth says. "I said I'm not going any farther." The grumpy tone I haven't heard for a while starts to edge back into his voice. He rarely talks like that when Mel is around, I realize.

I take a deep breath. "Seth, I have to ask you something."

"Yeah?" He sounds distracted, ready to get off the beach and move on with his day.

My mouth is dry, and I'm afraid I won't be able to force the question out loud enough to rise over the sound of waves lapping against the shore. "Are you in love with Mel?" I ask, still looking out over the never-ending stretch of water, unable to tell where the lake stops and the sky begins.

The beat of silence that hangs in the air before Seth answers tells me everything I need to know.

"I'm not in love with anybody," he says finally.

"It's okay," I say, reaching down to cup some water into my hand and splash it over my face, shivering as cold droplets slide down my neck and inside my shirt. "It won't bother me if you two get together." This is the first time I've ever lied to Seth, and my skin grows colder. Even with everything that happened between us before Mel moved to Butterfield, I always told him the truth. He knew I didn't like him the same way he liked me, and although I'm sure that didn't make it any easier for him, at least I was honest.

"That's not going to happen," he says with such finality, I turn around to stare at him. Seth looks out of place in the water, the same way he looks out of place in the hallways at school or sitting at a desk in a classroom. The only time I ever see him blend in seamlessly with his environment is when he's sitting behind the piano—or when he's with me and Mel.

"Why not?" My heart lifts for a moment because I'm selfish. Maybe Seth is going to suppress his feelings for Mel so that the balance of our three-way friendship won't be thrown off. Maybe he would do that for me.

But the look he gives me is dark and complicated, the half smile on his mouth not reaching his eyes. "I don't want to ruin it," he says. And I know he's not talking about ruining what the three of us have—he's talking about ruining whatever's going on between him and Mel right now. He's afraid to tell her how he feels because she might shut him down, the same way I did five years ago.

"Seth . . ."

He shakes his head. "It's fine, Vee. Really, it's fine now. But I just . . . don't want to have to go through it again." The wind ruffles his hair, and a long curl falls over his eyes.

"Okay." I nod.

I turn back and run my hands over my arms, goose bumps rising up on my skin. It's not a surprise, obviously. But sometimes, even if you already know something, hearing it out loud makes it real in a way that's hard to deal with. *You have no reason to be jealous*, I say to myself. *None at all.*

We eventually get out of the water and walk back to the car, Seth grumbling about getting sand everywhere, and things feel almost normal again. But the sun doesn't seem as bright as it did an hour earlier, and the crowded parking lot grates on my nerves. Once again, I'm winning the Worst Friend Award, because I don't do the one thing that would make up for everything I've put Seth through over the years.

I don't tell him I'm pretty sure Mel loves him, too.

CHAPTER 15

I WALK INTO THE HOUSE TO THE SOUND OF THE VACUUM cleaner, which is an unusual enough occurrence that I have to go check it out. Mom is standing on a chair in the middle of the living room, vacuuming dust off the top of the ceiling fan blades.

I hit the power button, and the ancient Electrolux sputters to a stop. Mom looks down at me, dirt streaked across her face.

"Have you been reading *Good Housekeeping* again?" I ask. "Because I don't believe you thought of doing that all by yourself."

Mom gives me a wry smile. "Guilty." She steps down off the chair and collapses onto the couch. "Being a grown-up is exhausting."

I lie down at the other end and put my feet in her lap. "Tell me about it." Seth and I didn't talk about anything important after we left the beach, but his feelings for Mel hung in the air between us the whole ride home, like a dripping faucet you can't quite bring yourself to fix but is just loud enough to be impossible to ignore.

"Lila invited me to her party tomorrow," Mom says.

I sit up and look at her. "Are you going?"

Mom looks alarmed. "Are you kidding me? It wasn't a real invitation. I'm sure she just felt like she should ask me to come."

"Oh." I lie back down. "I wish you could go instead of me."

"That makes one of us."

I reach down and turn on the vacuum, waving the brush over her feet. She squeals and pushes me away, pulling the plug out of the wall.

"Mel has this whole summer romance plan cooked up for me," I say, making it sound like a big joke. "You could come watch me crash and burn while trying to flirt with guys at this stupid party."

Mom sits up and hugs a throw pillow, her tan arms dark against the white fabric. "Vee, are you doing okay without Mark?"

I shrug, glancing away from her. "I guess." Even though it was only a few weeks ago, I'm a little embarrassed about how I reacted to the breakup. I probably could have been a little less dramatic. "It still sucks. It seems like the Bentley women are always getting left behind, huh?"

I feel the wrongness of my words as soon as they leave my mouth, and Mom's eyes widen in surprise. "I'm sorry," I blurt, reaching out to her. "That was a stupid thing to say."

Mom grabs my hand and holds on tight, her eyes locking on mine. "Vee, you know things didn't work out between your dad and me for a lot of reasons. He didn't just—" She swallows. "He didn't just leave me. And I don't want you to worry that the same thing is going to happen to you, because it's not."

Her eyes are watering, and I hate myself. No matter how many times she tells me and Jeffrey that the divorce was amicable, I remember the way her face crumpled when Dad walked out the door that last time. "I know," I say, gently pulling my hand away and brushing my bangs out of my face. "I'm sorry."

Mom turns away, and I sink back into the couch cushions, wondering how someone who is so good at saying the right thing during a debate can get pretty much everything else so totally wrong.

i just found out that gabriel latimore is going to be at your stepmom's party tonight!!!

I sigh and rifle through the clothes hanging in my closet one more time, hoping I'll find a dress or a skirt I had forgotten about, something that would be at least slightly more interesting than my usual conservative, Old Navy-esque style. Mel and I never got a chance to discuss our wardrobe options for the party. Maybe it's for the best, though. I'm sure Dad wouldn't appreciate me showing up to his and Lila's big event, wearing anything that might hint at me having a life outside my family.

I don't respond to the text, but Mel is insistent. My phone dings again.

and he just broke up with ashley.

that's great, I text back. but i'm still on f. *And I went on something that might qualify as a semi-date with Killian, and I kind of liked it. Even though I'm afraid to text him and admit it.*

I turn back to my closet, finally picking out a navy blue dress. It's tight and daringly short, but it has long sleeves. Hopefully Dad will only notice my upper half.

that's okay. we'll find an f for you, and then you can move on to gabriel.

I sigh and strip off my shorts and tank top, wriggling into the dress. Gabriel and I have always gotten along—he's someone I say hi to in the halls and will partner with on group projects in class. I've known him practically my whole life and never once considered the possibility of kissing him. But he's cute and nice and, assuming Mel can wrangle me a guy named Finn or Fletcher to start off the night, I suppose it wouldn't be the worst thing in the world to kiss Gabriel Latimore.

"This place isn't real."

I didn't think I was capable of being impressed anymore. My dad's house is enormous, on the beach, and has always looked like it could pop out of a magazine. But tonight the trees sparkle with a million fairy lights, and there are airy white cabanas set up all over the back-yard. Waiters in crisp black suits glide between groups of guests passing off tiny hors d'oeuvres, and a jazz trio is set up on a small stage, the rich notes of a saxophone drifting across the grass.

"So, is Taylor Swift also going to be at this party?" Mel asks me as we trip up the flagstone path in our heels. "Because this totally looks like her scene."

"Shhh." I stumble and grab her arm. "Please do not let my dad hear you say anything like that. I'm sure he's really loving how fabulously wealthy and sophisticated throwing this thing makes him look."

Mel and I walk under a wrought-iron arch dripping with roses and stop for a moment, admiring the view. It's immediately obvious we're out of our league here, although Mel, at least, looks gorgeous. Her hair is pinned on top of her head, and she's wearing a long, flowing skirt and a coral camisole underneath a fitted black jacket. She went heavy on the eye makeup, dramatic swoops of thick black eyeliner and a bright pop of eye shadow luminous against her golden skin. In comparison, I look like a fifth-grader on school picture day, with my long-sleeved dress and low heels. But we're both outclassed by nearly everyone we pass as we make our way toward the towering buffet table. My eyes bounce from diamond bracelets to flowing hair extensions to killer manicures and back to more diamonds. My dad and Lila are nowhere in sight.

"I don't know any of these people," I say, loading up a china plate with cocktail shrimp, mini quiches, and as many little cheesecake squares as I can squeeze onto its surface. "And I don't want to spend all night asking around to find someone whose name starts with *F*." I scan the crowd, which is mostly made up of middle-aged men in suits. "We need to say hi to my dad to prove we showed up, get these kisses, and get out of here before I break something totally expensive and irreplaceable."

"Relax," Mel says, plucking two glasses of champagne from a tray offered by a smiling waiter. "Part of this Twenty-Six Kisses thing is the journey, not just the destination." She sets our drinks on a tall bar table and grabs a shrimp off my plate. "And so far," she says, "the journey is delicious. Cheers."

"Cheers," I say, grudgingly clinking my glass against hers.

Jeffrey wanders over to us, leading Kaylee by the hand. She looks totally adorable in a little white dress, her hair braided and tied back with a flowered headband.

"Here." Jeffrey unceremoniously passes Kaylee's hand to me. "You can watch her for a little while."

"Jeffrey!" I pick Kaylee up, settling her on my hip, and she inspects the food on my plate. "You're getting paid to babysit, aren't you? Where are Dad and Lila?"

He rolls his eyes. "I don't know. Just give me two minutes to go get some food." He slouches over to the buffet table, his shirt already coming untucked and his shoes untied.

"Hungry," Kaylee says, reaching for my plate.

"Want one of these?" I offer her a mini quiche, and she scrunches up her nose and points at the fruit salad.

"Oh no," Mel says, taking Kaylee from me. "You're not allowed to get strawberry juice on your dress." She hands Kaylee a grape and picks up my plate. "We're going to sit down. You go scout around."

Standing in the backyard of my dad's mansion, I feel like a complete imposter. I don't belong here, and neither do Mel or Jeffrey or Kaylee. I grab my champagne glass, just to have something to hold on to, and make my way to the periphery of the party, hoping I can forget about *F*, spot Gabriel Latimore, swoop in to kiss him on the cheek or something, and go home to watch Netflix in my pajamas.

"Vee!" Thin fingers dig into my shoulder, and I jump.

"Oh, hi, Lila." She looks radiant, her hair in loose waves, a giant necklace sparkling above the plunging neckline of her dress. I wonder if my dad gave it to her, and think about the thin, battered gold wedding band my mom tucked away in her jewelry box the day she signed the divorce papers.

"Isn't this such a wonderful party? Are you having fun?" She leans harder on me, champagne on her breath.

"Definitely," I say. We watch a waiter, surrounded by a group of adults I don't know, pop open a new bottle of champagne, the cork sailing off toward the beach. Everyone laughs as the bottle overflows, pushing their glasses forward to catch the foamy wine. "Are you having a good time seeing your work friends?"

Lila grips my shoulder tighter and leans in. Her pupils are dilated, her eyeliner slightly smudged. "I'm a little stressed," she confesses. "All these people. I took a pill."

"Oh." I've seen pill bottles lined up in the master bedroom medicine cabinet. Lila obviously has some quirks, but I've never asked what her deal was. I'm about to ask her if she should be drinking with her medication, but she spots someone in the crowd and totters off to say hello.

Jeffrey is standing under a cabana, talking to a cute girl with extremely long brown hair who looks to be around his age. I come up behind him and sling my arm around his shoulder.

"Hey, bud. Aren't you supposed to be on babysitting duty?"

Jeffrey pushes me away and levels me with a look of pure fury. "Okay, chill out. I'll be right there."

After a brief pause the girl holds out her hand. "Hi," she says. "I'm Chaundre." Her hair swings forward, and she tucks it back behind her ear.

"Veda," I say, shaking her hand, which is so small, I feel like I could crush it with one good squeeze. "I'm Jeffrey's sister."

"Oh," Chaundre says, her smile brightening. "Nice to meet you. Your dad has a beautiful house."

"Chaundre lives next door," Jeffrey says, shoving his hands into his pockets. "I better go find my little sister," he says to her. "See you later."

Before she can respond, Jeffrey digs his shoulder into my arm and hustles me toward the table where Mel and Kaylee are gleefully dunking every food item imaginable into a chocolate fountain.

"So when did you meet *Chaundre*?" I ask. Jeffrey is only twelve, and he has always been such a guy—video games, skateboarding, farting contests with his friends. As far as I know, he has never even looked at a girl, much less struck up a conversation with one who looks like she fell off the *Game of Thrones* set. It's dawning on me why Jeffrey has wanted to spend more time over at Dad and Lila's lately. . . .

He pushes me away. "I don't know. A couple of months ago when I was over here for the weekend." He pulls out the chair next to Kaylee and flops into it. "Okay, I'm watching her. Now go away."

"I just saw Gabriel Latimore over by the DJ," Mel cuts in, dunking a pineapple slice into the chocolate fountain and placing it on Kaylee's plate.

"Who is Gabriel Latimore?" Jeffrey asks, popping the pineapple into his mouth and batting his eyelashes at me. "Your new boyfriend?"

I shake my head in exasperation and grab Mel's arm, pulling her up from the table. "This whole night is getting weird fast," I murmur as I pull her away from Jeffrey and Kaylee. "Lila is zonked out on drugs, and Jeffrey was talking to some mysterious girl like they're best friends."

"Drugs?" Mel hurries along next to me. "Like, *drugs* drugs?"

"I don't think so. More like medication drugs. But still."

"Still." She nods in agreement. "Are you going to tell your dad?"

I catch sight of Gabriel, who looks incredibly hipster-cute in suspenders and a bow tie, chatting with the DJ. I stop, turning my back to him. "I don't know. She was acting so bizarre, he's got to notice it himself." I take a deep breath.

Mel waves her hand. "Not your problem right now. We need to find you an *F*, stat, before Gabriel leaves."

"Well, what do you want to do? It's not like people here are wearing name tags."

"Follow me." Mel grabs my arms and steers me toward a group of rich-looking adults.

"Mel, what are you doing? Those guys are old!"

She ignores me and keeps pulling me along. "Hello," she says, interrupting the group's conversation. "I don't believe we've met. I'm Melinda, and this is Veda, Lila's stepdaughter."

The group falls silent for a moment, and one older lady with green eye shadow raises her eyebrows slightly, but then everyone starts to fawn over me, asking what it's like to be a big sister to Kaylee, and isn't it wonderful that my dad and Lila found each other. We chat with Denise, Richard, Linda, Patty, and Jack for a few minutes before Mel elbows me in the side. If nothing else, this Twenty-Six Kisses thing is going to make me really good at remembering people's names.

"So lovely to meet you," I chirp in a voice I barely recognize as my own. We scurry away, scouting out the next group.

"Look, there're six men all standing together over there," Mel whispers. "Probably commenting on how everyone's boobs look in their dresses. Let's go."

"This is going to take all night," I say. "There has to be a faster way."

"Well, unless you want to ask Lila who—"

A waiter hurries past us, champagne bottles in hand, and calls out to the bartender. "Hey, Frank, we're going to need some more of these pretty quick."

I'm striding across the lawn before Mel even has a chance to open her mouth, sneaking around behind the bar, which is stocked with every type of liquor you could imagine, bottles of wine and beer, and tubs full of cut lemons, limes, and oranges. I stay in a low crouch, and Frank backs into me as he turns to scoop ice into a glass. I let my mouth make contact with his suit jacket, which smells like fabric softener.

"What the hell?" he says, spinning around.

"Sorry!" I say, straightening up and hurrying away so I don't have to come up with an excuse about why I was back there in the first place.

"I don't know if that counts," Mel says, a note of admiration in her voice. "You didn't actually touch his skin."

I roll my eyes. "You're getting awfully technical. Where's Gabriel? Let's get this over with and get out of here."

"Remember, you're not allowed to tell him you're doing a kissing challenge," Mel says.

"I know, I know." I take a deep breath and close my eyes. "God, this could get totally awkward. What's going to happen when we go back to school in the fall?"

Mel grins. "Vee, don't you know the code? What happens on summer vacation stays on summer vacation."

"Yeah, but I can't just walk up to him and smash my mouth onto him like I did with Frank the bartender."

Mel narrows her eyes, thinking. "You've had some champagne," she says finally. "You're probably tipsy. You might be a little friendlier than usual."

"What?" I stare at her for a moment before it finally clicks. "Oh!"

I look around for a waiter, but they all seem to have disappeared. I grab a half-full champagne glass off the nearest table and hesitate for only a moment before taking a swig, swishing the liquid around in my mouth to coat my teeth and tongue.

"Wow," Mel says, raising her eyebrows. "I'm impressed. And a little grossed out."

"Go big or go home," I say, then run my hand through my hair, pull my dress to the side so one of my bra straps is visible, and half-close my eyes. "How do I look?"

"Trashed," Mel says, grinning. "Go get 'em."

It doesn't take much to get someone to assume you're drunk. A little stumble as you approach them, a quick hug when usually you would only wave, a sip from the champagne glass in your hand. I'm intending to smack a kiss on Gabriel's cheek, but the hug is over nearly before it began, and I miss my chance.

"Hey." I pull back and flash him a wide smile. "I didn't know you were going to be here."

He lays a hand on my wrist, steadying me as I list to once side. "Ditto." His top front teeth are slightly crooked, but he told me once he didn't want to get braces because he's terrified of going to the orthodontist. "Feeling good, Veda?"

I feign embarrassment and set the glass down. "Oh God. Is it that obvious?"

He shrugs. "A little. But not in a bad way."

I glance over my shoulder, but Mel has melted away into the crowd. "I can't let my dad find out. He'll totally freak." I grab Gabriel's wrist and pull him toward an empty cabana. "Come on. Hang out with me while I sober up."

Gabriel stumbles after me, laughing as I pull him along. The draping white fabric mostly shields us from view, and the fairy lights strung across the canopy give off a cozy, romantic glow. It's like Lila's party planners intended for people to sneak in here and make out.

"So, what are you up to this summer?" Gabriel asks, sinking onto a bench and patting the space beside him. "Brushing up on your legal terminology?"

I wince. Being a debate term nerd really is my only claim to fame at Butterfield High. I guess that's what I get for hiding behind my older, more outgoing boyfriend for two years. I toss my head, flicking my hair over my shoulder. "I'm kind of taking a break from all that right now," I say, looking up at Gabriel with wide eyes. "Just hanging out. Training for a half marathon." I smirk. "I'm sure you heard Mark and I broke up." I look away, bracing against the brief flash of pain that still comes with saying those words out loud.

"Yeah." Gabriel lays a comforting hand on my arm. "That must have been rough."

I shrug and lock eyes with him. "It's probably for the best. I'm ready to move on."

There's a beat of silence, and I consider going for the kiss right then. My lips part, and I tip my head up toward Gabriel's. His grip tightens on my arm.

"Well, Mark doesn't know what he's missing," Gabriel says,

brushing his hair off his forehead. "You look great tonight, Veda."

"Thanks." This is the part where he's supposed to lean over and kiss me. *Come on*, I silently urge him. *Do it.* "I'm really glad you're here," I say, trying to give him an in.

Gabriel hesitates and catches his bottom lip between his teeth, which is unexpectedly sexy. I'm practically vibrating with anticipation and nerves. I want him to do it so I can cross the letter *G* off my list and leave this bizarrely upscale party, but I realize I actually also really want senior class president Gabriel Latimore to kiss me in this gorgeous, dimly lit cabana, the happy chatter of party guests and the waves of Lake Michigan in the background.

For whatever reason, though, he's not getting the hint. We're sitting so close to each other, I can feel the heat of his body through my dress, and we're gazing into each other's eyes, totally alone and shielded from view. He can't be that oblivious to the tension building up between us—why won't he make a move?

"You know what? I'm just going to go for it," I announce, enjoying the split second of shock that registers on Gabriel's face before I close my eyes and lean in, my mouth finding his. At first I'm afraid I've just made a huge fool of myself and this will be the most awkward kiss of all time. But then he kisses me back, more forcefully than I expected, his mouth opening slightly and his arm wrapping around my shoulders, bringing me closer. He smells like warm laundry and chocolate, and his hands are so hot, they feel like they're burning my skin as he runs them down my arms.

I finally have to pull away to catch my breath, my heart hammering. Gabriel Latimore is a seriously good kisser. "Wow," I say, tipping my head back and smiling. "I drank too much champagne, and that was amazing."

He laughs and pulls my face back to his, beginning another scorching kiss that sends lightning bolts all the way down to my toes. My head is spinning so fast, I almost believe my own lie about being drunk. Gabriel's lips move away from my face and to my neck, dipping down to my collarbone and then making their way back up. If he starts nibbling on my ear, I'm done for.

"I have to go," I say, gasping and pulling away, very aware that what was supposed to be a quick drunk kiss is going way further than I had intended. "Even though I don't want to." I lean in one more time and kiss him, my hands finding his suspenders and holding him tight against me before wrenching myself away and running out of the cabana.

"What happened to you?" Mel comes out of nowhere and intercepts me as I flee Gabriel's incredibly hot kisses. "You look"—she studies me—"disheveled."

I grab her arm and pull her along with me, detouring toward the swing set, where Jeffrey and Chaundre are pushing Kaylee in the baby swing. "I'm leaving. Get a ride home with Dad if you don't want to sleep over," I call to Jeffrey.

"Gabriel Latimore is a kissing god," I say to Mel, nodding and smiling at people I vaguely recognize as Dad's friends as we pass. "And I was on the verge of letting myself be ravished in the cabana, so I ran."

Mel lets out a low whistle, dropping back momentarily to kick off her stilettos, and trails after me in her bare feet. "I'm not surprised," she says as we pile into the Buick. "He's good at everything else . . . Why not that, too?"

"He did take forever to kiss me, though," I say, pulling my shoes off and tugging my skirt down. "I actually had to start it. But once he got going . . . Wow."

Mel grins at me as she starts the car. "Better than Mark?"

I close my eyes. That's the million-dollar question, isn't it? The question I'm still not ready to face, seven kisses into my summer experiment. Was kissing Gabriel Latimore better than kissing the guy who I considered, up until a few weeks ago, the love of my life?

My first kiss with Mark wasn't scorching hot. It didn't melt me down into a little puddle of hormones, and it wasn't the kind of kiss you could write to a teen magazine about, because it didn't take place under a waterfall or on the football field in front of the entire school. There wasn't anything particularly special or interesting about that kiss, except it was our first one—and as soon as Mark pulled away and looked into my eyes, I felt like I had come home. We never looked back from that moment. From that kiss forward, it was Mark and me, me and Mark. Until the day it wasn't.

"No," I say finally. My eyes are still closed, but I can feel Mel watching me, and I know she's going to be disappointed with my answer. "It wasn't better than Mark."

CHAPTER 16

Frank the Bartender
Dad and Lila's party
I kissed the back of his jacket
2/10 (an extra point because he smelled good)

Gabriel Latimore
Also Dad and Lila's party
We made out in the cabana!
9/10

MOM HAS THE NEXT DAY OFF, SO I GET TO DRIVE THE CAR TO work. I turn on Killian's radio station and sing along to the songs I know by heart now, going over last night's kiss with Gabriel in my head. I almost can't believe I went through with it.

"Hey!" I say, jogging over to Killian after I've stashed my backpack in the office.

"Hey." He holds out his hand for a high five, making me jump up to smack my palm against his, but his smile is subdued. I realize with a jolt that I never texted him back yesterday. "Let's get going." There is already a crowd of people waiting impatiently to board the bus.

Killian barely says a word as we drive the first reservation up to the river. The ride back is completely silent except for the bounces and creaks the old minibus makes as it jars over the ruts in the dirt road. The quiet is unnerving—no meandering conversation, no music. It feels wrong, but I don't know what to say to break the silence. Would it be awkward just to admit I got his text but forgot to reply? I wonder if Killian somehow heard something about me and Gabriel, but then I push the thought out of my head. There's no way he could know, and even if he did, there's no way he could be mad about it. We're friends. That's it. Right?

Finally I can't take it anymore, and I stick my head around the front seat. "What's up?"

Killian jumps, like he was a million miles away. "Um, nothing," he says, flashing me a smile in the rearview mirror. "Just counting down the weeks until we don't have to worry about drunken drowning and the hazardous combination of glass containers and recreational boating."

"And how much longer do we have?" I ask, even though I know perfectly well. We have eight weeks of summer left, and I have nineteen kisses to go.

"Only eight weeks." His face falls. "I'm dreading it."

"Because of school?"

"Because of everything." He waves his hand. "I keep telling myself it's only one more year, and then I'm going to get out of here and never come back."

I rest my chin on my hand. "Did something happen?" I ask cautiously.

Killian shrugs. "Just the same shit that always happens. I can't go anywhere in Trawley without running into some asshole who has plenty to say—about my hair, my car, the way I talk."

"The way you talk?" I think Killian talks like a normal human being—nothing to make fun of there.

He laughs bitterly. "You'd be surprised at the number of people at my high school who are afraid of three-syllable words." He shakes his head in frustration, glancing at me in the smudged rearview mirror. "Nothing is ever going to change for me there, and I'm sick of it."

I stand up as Killian guides the minibus back into its spot at the Float & Boat. "Well, you can look forward to watching me kill myself running a half marathon at the end of the summer," I say, desperate to get the smile to come back to his face, the words tumbling out of my mouth before I have a chance to consider the fact that if I tell someone I'm running the half marathon, I might actually have to make up my mind and do it.

"Wait, what?" Killian follows me off the bus. "You're a scholar and an athlete? I think my brain just exploded."

"Please." I blush. "It's not a big deal."

"Um, *au contraire*, counselor. A half marathon is 13.1 miles, 23,056 yards, or 69,168 feet. Or one giant heart attack, if you're me."

"You are so full of useless knowledge, I'm amazed you can remember your own name." I grab the end of a canoe that's still wet from the river, and Killian helps me lift it onto the trailer.

"In my free time, when I'm not angsting over how much my hometown sucks, I've been reading a bunch of those Uncle John's Bathroom Readers to bone up on my random facts. I need to prepare to go up against my archnemesis from Butterfield this year." He smiles, and although it's not quite as bright as usual, I'm happy to see it.

I raise one eyebrow. "Wow, bathroom readers. I see you're focusing purely on academic resources for your information."

We battle good-naturedly for the rest of the afternoon, Killian's bad mood forgotten, spinning off into tangents about the history of the cherry industry in Michigan and why celebrities look so scary without any makeup on (a subject Killian has obviously put a lot of thought into). Killian is the only person I've met with whom having a conversation is like a competitive sport. He weaves his words together with the practiced ease of a runner in a warm-up jog. I almost can't believe it when I glance down at my phone and see the day is almost over.

Our last reservation launched at two, and theoretically they should land back at the Float & Boat around five thirty, but after we finish shutting everything down for the day, it's a quarter to six and there is no sign of them. Clouds are sweeping in from the west, and the weather app on my phone shows a thunderstorm heading straight toward us.

Bob and Mel come out of the office and walk out onto the dock where Killian and I are sitting, dipping our feet in the water. "Still nothing, huh?" Bob says, shading his eyes with his hands and looking out over the river.

"Not yet," Killian says.

Bob scratches his head. "I'm sure I have a contact phone number in their reservation, but I know service can be spotty out on the water."

"This is when we need GPS trackers installed on each canoe," Mel says.

"I hope they have enough sense to get off the river if it starts raining." Bob scans the sky, his face lined with worry.

"I'm sure they'll be back soon." Killian stretches. "They had to notice the storm coming."

Bob looks at his watch and sighs. "So much for my date with Mrs. Flaherty."

"You should go," Killian says. "We'll stay here and wait for them."

He hesitates. "I don't know. I should be here in case anything happens."

"Dad." Mel nudges him. "Mom will be really mad if you're late."

Indecision plays over Bob's face. He glances up at the sky again. The storm is definitely on its way, but it could be another half hour or more before it gets here. "Are you sure?" he asks Killian and me. "I can absolutely stay if you feel like you need me to. I *should* stay."

"Go," I say, trying to sound convincing, although I have no idea what we'll do if the group doesn't show up before it starts storming and Bob isn't here.

Bob hesitates, then smiles and theatrically wipes the back of his hand over his forehead. "Whew. You two are lifesavers." He pulls a lanyard heavy with keys out of his pocket and hands it to me. "Just lock the keys inside the bus when you're done, and I'll get them tomorrow morning."

"I have to go with him—I'm his ride," Mel says, shrugging apologetically.

We wave as they walk to shore, Bob with his shoulders back, whistling happily, on his way to a date with his wife. Even before things went totally south with my parents, I can't imagine a time when they would have been so blatantly overjoyed to be spending time together.

After I hear Bob's car door slam, I tell Killian, "You can get going if you want. You have a longer drive home than I do." I cross my fingers and hope he refuses to leave.

Killian gives me a strange look, as if it's completely out of the question for him to leave me at the Float & Boat alone, for which I'm secretly grateful. "You know the insurance doesn't let Mr. Flaherty have part-time employees working out here alone. Too risky—you might fall into the river and drown."

I push my foot deeper into the river, feeling for the colder water that lies a few inches beneath the sun-warmed surface. "I promise to wear my floaties."

"No way." Killian takes his hat off and lies down on his back on the dock, dropping the hat over his face to block the sun. "This is a two-person operation, counselor. Team Us."

I hope the canoers are just taking their time coming down the river, maybe stopping at one of the tiny islands to explore. I'm not sure what we'll do if something is actually wrong.

Killian's only able to suffer through a few minutes of silence before he gets the conversation going again. I've never met anyone so interested in life that they can't bear to stop talking about it. "So," he says.

I look down at his broad body spread across the dock, his fingers drumming nervously on the weathered boards, and my stomach tightens. "So."

"You didn't text me back."

I wince. "No, I didn't. I'm sorry."

He taps his fingers on the dock, waiting for more. I kick my feet, watching water droplets fly into the air, my mouth clamped shut. I should have texted him back. I know exactly what I would have said: i liked yesterday, too. But how can I go from texting a guy one minute to kissing someone else the next?

Killian sighs. "Okay . . . new topic of conversation. Remember that night we came out here with Mel and those other guys?"

My face heats up. He just dives right into the awkward conversations. "Yes. Didn't we talk about this already?"

Killian's fingers stop their frantic dance. "Sorry. I don't mean to keep bringing it up. But I was just curious . . . Pop-music–hater Seth seemed kind of into Mel. Are they together?"

I shrug. I don't want to think about Seth and Mel right now. "It's complicated. They're best friends."

"I think Mel was trying to use me to make him jealous." Killian's voice is calm and flat, just stating the facts.

I stay quiet. That is definitely what Mel was doing, but it sounds extra-terrible when Killian says it out loud. "I don't think she does it consciously. She's not awesome at relationships. Flirting, yes. Actually being committed to someone, not so much."

Then it hits me—*this* is the main reason it's so upsetting to think of Mel and Seth getting together. Not because I irrationally want to keep Seth for myself even though I don't like him that way, or because I want them both to love me more than they love each other, but because their relationship has an expiration date. They'll be happy for a few months before Mel gets distracted and finds some other guy to chase, and Seth will be devastated. And that will be the end of the three of us.

Killian sits up quickly, his hat dropping into his lap. His face is only a few inches from mine, and all I can see is slightly sunburned cheeks and clear blue eyes. "What about you, Vee? Are you any good at relationships?"

I tear my gaze away from Killian's and struggle not to laugh. I used to think I was an expert at being in a relationship. If you had asked me six months ago, I would have said I was an A+, honor-roll,

Dean's-list-quality-relationship partner. But the fact that I was completely blindsided when my boyfriend broke up with me suggests I still have some things to learn in that department.

"I—" A loud whoop cuts me off, and four canoes float into sight. "Thank God, there they are," I say, scrambling to my feet. The crowd in the canoes waves their paddles in the air and sing along to the strains of "Sweet Home Alabama" coming from iPod speakers set up on one of the seats.

"Great. They're totally hammered." Killian rises to his feet. "But I do love this song. I'll put the canoes away if you can get them to the parking lot so we can close the gate behind them."

"Deal." I stare at the approaching canoers, feeling Killian's eyes on me but afraid to meet his gaze. "I bet we can be out of here in half an hour."

The canoers greet us with big hugs and slaps on the back, and half-coherent stories about their beer-soaked day as they stumble through the shallow water at the edge of the river, unloading coolers, empty bottles, and sopping wet towels. It takes a little longer than half an hour, but we're finally able to get them herded over to their cars as the sky darkens with the coming storm. Killian locks Bob's keys inside the bus, and I push the rusted iron gate closed. The drunkies can stay in the parking lot all night if they want to.

The wind picks up suddenly, and we hear the rain before we feel it, the soft pitter-patter of drops falling down through the pine branches growing louder with each passing moment.

"Here we go," Killian says, and holds out his arm, his tan skin speckled with raindrops. Thunder booms overhead as the rain picks up. "Come on!" Killian yells, running for the parking lot.

I tear after him, feet crunching over the gravel, the sharp smell of rain in my nose.

"Where's your car?" he yells.

I point, unlocking the doors remotely as we run. We duck inside as the shower of rain falling through the trees turns into a roar. I brush at the raindrops clinging to my legs and shake out my hair. Killian's T-shirt is polka-dotted with dozens of dark circles, and his hair is matted and hanging down into his face.

"Any chance you could give me a ride home?" he asks. "The Jeep is good for many things, but driving in the rain is not one of them."

"Oh my God," I say, craning my neck to look out the window. "Will it be okay?"

Killian shrugs. "It's kind of at the point where nothing can hurt it anymore. It's parked under the trees, and I put the tarp on this morning."

I fasten my seat belt and start the car, kicking the windshield wipers into high gear as the rain crashes down, splashing through rapidly forming puddles as I turn left onto the country road, heading away from Butterfield. Lightning flashes in the sky, a great forked strike that seems to freeze time for a split second, searing into my eyeballs.

I grip the steering wheel, suddenly nervous. "Maybe it's not the best idea to be driving around in this storm," I say. "I think it's getting worse."

"There's a bridge with a pullout underneath in a few miles," Killian says. "We can stay there until it's over—twenty minutes, tops." He reaches over and gives my arm a quick shake. "It'll be okay. Promise."

I nod and hunch forward to stare out the windshield, but the rain is coming down faster than the wipers can whip it away. I don't even see the bridge until we're practically underneath it. "Pull over here," Killian says, and slides out of the car as soon as it comes to a stop.

I push open my door and step out, goose bumps rising on my skin as a cool wind sweeps under the bridge, bringing a spray of water with it.

"Do you have some towels or anything?" he asks.

"Sure." I pop the trunk and pull out a couple of beach towels and a blanket.

Killian wipes down the hood of the car, offering me a place to sit.

"Hop up." He drapes the blanket around my shoulders as I step onto the bumper and settle myself on the hood. "Now, watch."

From underneath the bridge, we can see out across a few acres of cherry fields, right into the heart of the storm. Lightning strikes nearly every minute, each flash brighter than the last, and the air is sharp with the smell of rain.

Killian sits next to me and leans back on his hands, swinging his feet. I pull the blanket more tightly around me, shivering as another gust of wind sprinkles cold rain on my face.

"I'm so glad those idiots didn't get caught out in this storm."

Killian nods. "I don't know if they would have made it, and I would not be looking forward to explaining to Mr. Flaherty how some of his customers sank their canoes and drowned."

He leans back, his hand landing close to mine. I stiffen. Maybe it's the thunderstorm and being stuck under the bridge and feeling like we're the only people in the world right now, but every cell in my body is aching to reach out and touch him. But I can't. I still have *H*, *I*, and *J* to get through first. And even then, will I be able to kiss Killian? For the first time, I'm not sure if I even want him to be my *K* kiss. Getting him involved in the game seems . . . wrong.

"So, do you have any brothers or sisters?" I go for literally the most boring topic of conversation possible, hoping to squelch the feelings rising up in me like floodwaters.

He gives me a long look. "Nope. Just me and my parents. What about you? Do you have a million brothers and sisters? Or a giant python in a cage underneath your bed?"

I laugh. "Trust me, I'm not that interesting. I have a mom and a brother and cat named Fat Snacks. And a half sister who lives with my dad and his wife." It sounds so complicated when I lay it all out like that. Usually I don't think of Dad and Lila as my family—it's really just me and my mom and Jeffrey. "My dad's relatives mostly live far away, but we're having a stupid reunion in a couple of weeks."

"I was testing you on that python thing, you know." Killian looks at me and raises one eyebrow. "If you had screamed or looked at me like I was a psycho, then our friendship would be over. Because I definitely have a giant python in a cage under my bed."

I make a show of scooting away from him. "Okay, that is kind of disgusting."

"Dang." Killian snaps his fingers. "And I thought we had a good thing going."

We do have a good thing going. As Killian said, we're Team Us. My stomach flutters at the thought.

The rain is starting to lighten up, and the sky is turning light blue at the edges. The storm is moving east. I hug myself against the cold. Killian hesitates for a second and then drops his arm around my shoulders. I stiffen.

"Ah. Okay." He pulls away. "Sorry."

"No, it's fine. I mean, it's not really fine. I don't want—"

He holds up a hand to stop me, his smile not completely covering the hurt in his eyes. "It's okay, Vee. You don't have to explain."

"I'm just going through some stuff right now," I say, because Killian is awesome, and he does deserve an explanation, even if it's not the whole truth. I hate myself a little bit now for even getting wrapped up in the Twenty-Six Kisses thing in the first place. "I went through a bad breakup at the beginning of the summer, and I'm just trying to figure things out."

He nods and stares straight ahead. "I didn't mean to force you into having this conversation." I open my mouth to protest, but he plows ahead. "But since we're having it, I just want to say I knew I was going to like you from the minute we met. And I was right."

I clasp my hands together in my lap. "Thanks." I don't know what else to say. *I think you're pretty cool too, but I'm taking the summer off from real relationships to smooch my way across Northern*

Michigan? Give me a week or so to get to K *and we'll see how it goes?*

"I better get you home," I say, letting the blanket drop from my shoulders even though it's so warm, I'd be happy to stay curled up underneath it all day.

Killian gives me another long look. "Okay," he says finally, sliding off the hood of the car and offering his hand to help me down.

Awkwardness hangs thick in the air on the rest of the drive to Trawley. Killian bops along to the radio like usual, but the normal happy, uncomplicated atmosphere that exists when we're together has been replaced by something much more emotionally charged. I can't imagine what is going through his head. Mine is filled with a never-ending loop of regret: *You screwed up. You screwed up. You screwed up, and you're never going to get another chance with him even if you decide you want one.*

I pull up to his house, a plain two-story, and he punches me lightly on the shoulder before getting out of the car. "If I ruined things between us, I'm going to hate myself," he says, running a hand absently over his stubbly jaw. "So let's just rewind to a couple of hours ago and start over from there tomorrow, okay?"

"Okay," I say, doing my best to smile. I'm not surprised he doesn't invite me in, but I am disappointed. I would have loved to meet his parents and see his bedroom, to get a glimpse into the inner workings of Killian Hughes. But he disappears inside the house without looking back, and I drive home to Butterfield, knowing something has gone wrong between us and being totally unsure of how to make it right.

CHAPTER 17

THE NEXT COUPLE OF WEEKS AT WORK ARE EXCRUCIATING.
Killian and I do our job, and, despite the fact that we're trying to pretend nothing has changed between us, the job is all we talk about—how many reservations we have for the day, what to do if someone left their phone on the bus, how many little kids we're allowed to fit into one canoe. It sucks. I miss Killian's ramblings and theories, and the way we could start a conversation about something mundane, like canoe paddles, and end up laughing so hard we nearly pee our pants.

I take out my frustration on the running trail, going out nearly every morning. Ryan does get my number and starts pestering me to run with him. I meet him out on the trail a couple of times a week, and try to keep up with him as he lopes along. As I start racking up the miles, I feel like I might actually have a shot at running the half marathon in August.

"So you've kind of stalled out on Twenty-Six Kisses," Mel says, letting the credits roll on the movie we've just finished watching on her laptop in her bedroom. "You're still on H, right?"

"I'm on *I*, actually," I say. "I forgot to tell you. Remember that little kid who had a birthday party at the Float & Boat last week? Hugo?"

Mel nods.

"Well, he ran over and kissed my wrist at the end of the day."

Mel giggles. "That is adorable. I hope you gave him a ten."

"Still saving the ten. Hugo gets a 9.999, so he's the highest scorer so far. Except for Elmo the dog, who got a million."

Mel rolls her eyes, clearly not pleased with some of my tactics for accumulating kisses. "So why haven't you gone for I yet?"

I grab the computer and start scrolling through more movie options in hopes of finding something else to distract her with. I haven't told her about my conversation with Killian or my mixed feelings about continuing on with the challenge.

"I just needed a break for a little while," I say.

"Well, are you ready to get started again?" She takes the laptop away from me. "Because I have some great ideas."

I shrug, and Mel sighs. "Okay, let's forget about Twenty-Six Kisses for a minute. If you could ask any boy out on a date, who would it be?" Mel props her chin in her hands. "Leaving the alphabet out of it."

"I don't know." I don't allow myself to answer the question, even in my head.

She pushes her hair out of her face. "Come on, Vee. The summer is half over, but it's still a blank check for you. If you could ask any guy out—*any* guy—and just have one incredible night with him, who would it be?"

I mentally turn the pages of our yearbook in my mind. There are a lot of good-looking guys at Butterfield High—I have to admit. It's tough to choose. Maybe Brandon Lewis, the all-state swim team champion with ridiculous abs. Or Dave Martinez, who graduated in May and won some incredible scholarship to Princeton.

"Kevin Nardone," I say finally.

Mel wrinkles her nose. "Kevin Nardone? Who's that?"

"Seriously?" I cross my arms. "You don't know who Kevin Nardone is?"

Mel shrugs.

"He's a year behind us. He was in my Modern History class last year." I roll off the window seat and look out the window onto the backyard garden. "I don't know. He just seems like a really nice guy, like he'd be fun to hang out with. He kind of reminds me of Phil on *Modern Family*." Kevin's a nice, generic guy. Boring. Not particularly smart. The opposite of Killian.

Mel groans. "Phil, like the *dad* on *Modern Family*?" I nod, and she sighs in exasperation. "Vee, I don't think you're focusing on the right things here. And you can't pick Kevin. You're saving your *K* kiss for Killian, right?"

I turn away from her, not trusting myself to talk about Killian without my face giving something away. "I thought the point of the exercise was that I didn't have to consider the alphabet?" I check the time on my phone and rise to my feet. My mom will be home from work soon, and Jeffrey insisted on spending the next few days at Dad's house, so I need to hang out with her and remind her at least one of her children loves her. "I have to go," I say, waving. "I'll see you later."

"What about Killian?" Mel calls, but I'm already around the corner and out of sight.

What about Killian? I have no idea. But I only have *I* and *J* left before I have to figure it out.

Ian Swanson.

Mel's text arrives just as I'm about to go to bed that night.

??? I text back.

you never bothered finding out who i would ask out if i could choose any guy. and that's who it would be: ian swanson.

so?

so he's the only person i have in my phone whose name starts with I. you should go on a hot date with him because 1. you'll get your I kiss and 2. i can live vicariously through you.

I brush my teeth and let her wait for a response. Of course, I already know I'm going to do it. I've been wracking my brain and looking through the yearbook, and the only people whose names start with *I* are Ian and Isabella Elias, an intimidating cheerleader to whom I've never spoken in my life.

oh, and 3. maybe afterward you can introduce us & he'll fall madly in love w/ me & we'll have lots of beautiful babies. i'm not too proud to take your leftovers.

I snort and toss the phone aside, digging out the yearbook and flipping to Ian's picture. I honestly don't know much about him. He plays basketball, isn't in any honors classes but isn't flunking out of school either, and has dated his way through most of the cheerleading squad, including a short stint with Isabella Elias herself. Hopefully, he's taking the summer off from cheerleaders, though. The last thing I need is to pick a catfight with one of the scariest girls in school.

I get ready for bed and then turn off the light, making sure the alarm on my phone is set. I have to get up early tomorrow to run before work. Shoving my pillow over my head, I go to sleep, dreaming of miles of pavement disappearing underneath my feet.

Mel's dad has a bad cold and can't come to the Float & Boat the next day, so he tells Mel to have me work in the office with her, answering phones, checking people in for their reservations, and taking payments. It's nice to be inside in the air-conditioning for once, although a twinge of guilt runs through me whenever I glance out the window and see Killian struggling to load the canoes onto the trailer by himself. He turns, as if he can feel me watching him, and catches my eye through the window, flashing me a quick smile that makes my stomach flip over. Mel has the radio playing softly in the office, and I find myself listening more carefully to the lyrics than usual, wondering if I can find anything worth writing down on Killian's dashboard.

The phone rings and I jump, taking a moment to clear my head before answering it with a perky, "Flaherty's Float & Boat! This is

Veda speaking. How may I help you?" The customer wants to make a reservation for twenty-two people (yikes) for a class reunion in two weeks. I mark it down on the calendar and make a mental note to request that day off.

As soon as I put the phone down, Mel sidles up and pokes me. "I did your Ian research for you, since I knew you wouldn't do it yourself," she says. I mentioned to her my concerns about going on a date with a guy who is recognized property of the cheerleading team, hoping that would put an end to it, and I could have a few more low-key, kissless days to myself while she strategized another plan. But no luck. "He's not dating anyone right now," she says. "Apparently, he's tired of blowing all his money on girls and is saving up to buy a car."

"Great," I say, scooting my chair closer to the window air conditioner so it's blowing deliciously cold air directly onto my shoulders. "Then he's definitely not going to want to take me out."

Mel shakes his head. "No, no, no. You're going to take *him* out. You're calling the shots on this one, Vee. That means you pay."

My stomach tightens, and I immediately hate myself a little bit. It's the twenty-first century, for God's sakes. Women can be doctors, engineers, physicists, astronauts . . . anything men can be. Law schools across the country are graduating nearly as many female students as male students, and the number of women who are the primary breadwinners in American households is constantly on the rise. And, apparently, reciting feminist facts to myself is my default reaction to feeling nervous. So why do I feel the need to wait for a guy to ask me out, and assume he will pay for everything?

That's not the real issue, though. The real issue is the fact that even though things are weird between us right now, I can't stop thinking about Killian. How is it right to ask a guy out when I'm obsessing over someone else? Even if I basically already told that someone else I wasn't interested.

"I can see your brain working through something," Mel says, watching me closely. "And I have a feeling I don't really want to know what it is. But will you do it?"

"Let me think about it."

Mel sighs.

"What?"

"Nothing." She tosses her phone aside and flips through a stack of papers, avoiding my eyes.

"Mel, come on. Are you mad?"

She closes her eyes briefly. "I just want you to have fun, Vee. You were with Mark for so long, and now you have this awesome chance to just forget about commitment and relationships and have a summer you'll never forget."

I cross my arms and stare out the window. How can I tell her part of the reason I'm hesitating on the kissing challenge is because I might have feelings for Killian, but I'm not even totally sure what's going on in my own head? "Fine," I say. "I'll ask Ian out." The phone rings again and I pick it up, chirping out the Float & Boat greeting.

Mel claps her hands in delight and pulls out her phone to text me Ian's number. I turn away from her to write down the next reservation, hoping the cheerleaders won't come after me when they find out I'm after their number-one favorite basketball player—and I'm not making a huge mistake by not putting a stop to the alphabet challenge right now and just going after Killian instead.

I have Ian's phone number. I know he doesn't currently have a girlfriend. And I'm pretty sure he'll be up for scoring a free meal. There's only one problem left: I'm not positive Ian Swanson even knows who I am. Luckily, that's what Facebook is for.

Two hours after I send a friend request, Ian has accepted it and appears to be online. I take a deep breath, open the messenger app, and dive right in.

hey, ian. :)

hey, what's up?

I pause, my fingers poised over the keyboard. This is going to be so humiliating if he turns me down.

i was just wondering if you wanted to hang out sometime?

It takes him a while to respond, although he doesn't go offline. I wonder if he's trying to figure out a way to say no without being a complete asshole about it. Or, an even more humiliating possibility, maybe he's scanning my pictures to see if I'm cute enough for him to bother going out with.

Finally Ian types back: sure, hit me up.

He gives me his phone number, which of course I already have, and I tell him I'll text him before signing out of Facebook as quickly as possible, my heart racing. I just asked a guy out! And he didn't say no.

I grab my phone and send a new text to Mel. okay, he said he'll go. now, where the hell am i supposed to take ian swanson out on a date?

CHAPTER 18

IF THERE'S ANYTHING I'VE LEARNED FROM LIVING WITH THE human tornado that calls itself my brother, it's that guys like to eat. And since Ian is an actual athlete instead of a skinny little skateboarder wannabe like Jeffrey, I can only assume his life revolves almost completely around food. So that's what this date is going to be: food, a little physical activity to give me a chance to burn off some calories, some more food, and then we'll round the evening out with a nice big helping of . . . food.

I study myself in the bathroom mirror, trying to gauge how much the burned-out light bulb in the two-bulb fixture above the sink has affected my makeup-applying process. I wonder if Ian will think I'm pretty. I'm no cheerleader, that's for sure. I don't smile enough, and the hair around my temples tends to get kind of weird and halfway curly in the humidity, rather than lying long and flat and straight like theirs does. But I'm strong and lean from running, I plucked my eyebrows yesterday, and as long as nothing gets stuck in my teeth during our two-and-a-half meals tonight, my smile looks nice. This is as good as it's going to get.

"Mom, I'm taking the car, remember?" I stick my head into my mom's bedroom, where she has a large piece of plywood and several yards of bright purple fabric laid out on the carpet.

"Go ahead." She sighs and sits back on her heels, a hammer in one hand and a hot-glue gun in the other. "I'm going to be here all night."

"What are you doing?" Whatever it is, it doesn't look like it's going to be worth it in the end.

"I saw a tutorial on a blog about how to make your own uphol-stered headboard for thirty dollars," Mom says wearily. "But that was assuming you already had a big piece of plywood hanging around and your fabric was on clearance. So mine is more like fifty dollars. And I can't screw up because I don't have any extra fabric."

"Well, maybe Jeffrey can help you with it," I say.

"He's at your dad's again," Mom says, laying the hammer down in disgust.

"What?" Jeffrey finally came back from Dad's yesterday and stormed into the house in such a terrible mood that I thought he'd finally realized being here with Mom is way better. "When did you take him over there?"

"While you were in the shower. He said he was bored here and it was more fun over there." Mom bites her lip.

"Oh my God." I walk over and kneel down next to her, slipping an arm around her shoulders, mentally shaking my fist at Jeffrey. "I'm sure he didn't mean that, Mom. He's twelve. He's a jerk."

"I know." Mom's voice shakes, and to my horror a tear slides down her cheek. "I just want him to be happy."

I'm going to kill Jeffrey. After Dad abandoned us and took all his high standards and important rules with him, there was only one rule left here: Don't upset Mom. There have been so many times when I was stressed and annoyed and would have loved to take my feelings out on her, but instead I just stuffed them away and put on a smile. My mom has already lived through one of the most heartbreaking, life-ruining things that can happen to someone, and there is no reason she should have to put up with that kind of bullshit from her children. Even if Jeffrey somehow thinks it's more fun to be over at Dad's house, he should know better than to tell Mom that to her face.

"I'll talk to him," I promise, giving her another squeeze. "He's just being a boy, Mom. Don't worry about it." I draw back and look at her. There are no more tears, but her eyes are red. "Do you want me to stay home tonight? We can finish this up and then binge watch some HGTV."

"No." Mom shakes her head and pushes me away. "Absolutely not. Go out and have fun."

I argue with her for a few more minutes, even offering to give her a foot rub. She hesitates for a moment, then smiles and says, "Rain check on the foot rub. And don't try to get out of it later. But you should go." By the time I grab her car keys and head toward the front door, she's whistling to herself and happily pounding tacks into the plywood.

Ian lives about a mile from me, in a modern ranch with an attached garage that is nearly as big as the house. He comes out the front door as soon as I pull into the driveway, dressed in basketball shorts and a gray T-shirt. I grimace and congratulate myself on not making a reservation at a fancy restaurant.

"Hey, Veda." He folds himself into the passenger seat and slouches down a little to stop the top of his head from brushing against the car's roof. "What's up?"

"Not much." I try to match his ultra-casual tone, which just makes me sound like I'm drunk and/or half asleep. I clear my throat and try again. "Ready?"

"Sure." He bounces his leg at high speed as I back the car out of the driveway. "So, this is kind of weird," he says as we're heading toward the lake. "I've never gotten picked up by a girl before."

"There's a first time for everything," I say.

"Yeah." He leans the seat back a little and stretches. "It's kind of nice. Mind if I change the radio?"

I shrug, and Ian scrolls through the stations until he happens upon a sports talk show. "This one is my favorite," he says. He gives me a quick update on the host's background and explains why the heyday of sports radio is over. I tune out, nodding or making little noises of approval every now and then, enjoying the murmur of the radio in the background and the way the air rushing past the open window slides across my skin.

Twenty minutes later we pull into the parking lot at Touchdown, a sports-themed restaurant that also has arcade games, bowling, and darts. It's known for blaring sports games on giant TVs turned up loud enough that they're impossible to talk over, fifty-cent wings, and elaborate poker tournaments. An enormous American flag flies out front, and the whole place is still decked out in red, white, and blue bunting from Fourth of July weekend.

Ian looks at me, his brown eyes wide. A slow grin spreads across his face. "No *way!*" he says. "I haven't been here in forever. Veda, you are officially the coolest girl I've ever met." He reaches over for a fist bump.

"Here's the plan," I say, before he can escape from the car and go inside to run up a huge tab at the Skee-Ball machine. "It's still kind of early, so I thought we could have some snacks at the bar, then play darts or bowling or whatever you want, then have dinner. And we can have dessert here or get ice cream on the way back."

Ian tents his fingers together and nods seriously. "Okay. Best. Date. Ever."

Ian and I rip through a basket of wings with garlic sauce, a chicken quesadilla, and soft pretzels with melted cheese, pausing only to grin at each other over our food-filled plates, before heading to the bowling lanes. I feel self-conscious as I change into my red-and-white bowling shoes, which totally clash with my shirt, but Ian helps me up from my seat, smiling, and spends ten minutes hunting all over the place for an eight-pound ball for me.

Watching him bowl is like observing a panther stalking its prey, all rippling muscles and measured movements. Even with his white athletic socks peeking out of the stupid bowling shoes and his ugly basketball shorts, Ian looks like he should be on TV somewhere, getting mobbed by adoring fans wearing jerseys with his last name printed across the back.

"Your turn." His score is nearly double mine, but he's not being a jerk about it, and he actually seems interested when I tell him a little bit about debate team and how I've started running again after taking a few weeks off.

"I hate running," Ian says, passing his fourteen-pound ball from hand to hand like it weighs nothing. "I mean, obviously you run a lot in basketball, but there's a point to it. Like, there's the ball, go get it. But I hate just running for no reason."

"It sucks at first," I agree, hitting a gutter ball on my tenth frame and sinking into my seat in defeat. "But once you get into it, it's kind of addictive."

"Maybe," he says, shrugging. He glances at his phone. "I'm starving. You ready to eat?"

"Sure," I say, although I'm still totally full of wings and pretzels. As we're walking back to the sit-down restaurant area of the building, I feel a slight pressure on my lower back and realize Ian's hand is there, guiding me through the maze of tables and chairs. I glance up at him, but he seems totally unconscious of the fact that he's touching me.

We're farther away from the blasting TVs than I had hoped—I

have no idea what to say if I have to make conversation. I ask Ian if he wants to move.

"Nah," he says, sliding into the cozy corner booth. "This is perfect."

I order a small salad because I'm still so full, but Ian goes for a giant cheeseburger with onion rings instead of fries. "I'm totally going to have to steal some of your onion rings," I say without thinking. "I always get them instead of fries, too."

"Totally," Ian says, shifting a little closer to me. "Have as many as you want."

And then he grabs my hand.

In what universe did I ever imagine myself sitting in a dark booth at Touchdown, holding hands with Ian Swanson, the star of Butterfield's basketball team and one of the most popular guys in school? None. No possible universe. I could never have imagined this in my wildest dreams. But here I am, and Ian's big fingers are entwined with mine, and it feels strange but also pretty okay.

Ian again seems unconcerned with the physical contact he has initiated. He toys with the saltshaker absentmindedly and peers over at the nearest TV to check the score on the game. "I'm having a really good time," he says, not looking at me.

"Oh." His thumb bumps over my knuckles as he rubs my hand. "That's good. That was kind of the point."

Now he meets my gaze, those soft brown eyes weirdly compelling in the blue light of the TVs. "No, I mean, usually I don't have a good time when I go places with girls. They always want to go to, like, fancy restaurants where you can't pronounce half the shit on the menu, and all they want to do is sit around and talk, instead of bowling or whatever." He swallows, and his hand tightens around mine. "But you're different."

I shrug, guilt building in the pit of my stomach. "I just thought you might like to come here."

Ian nods thoughtfully. "Yeah, that's what I'm saying. You get me."

Our food arrives, borne by a twenty-something waitress who obviously thinks we're the cutest things she's seen all night. Ian is forced to let go of my hand to concentrate on his burger while I pick at my salad, wondering how I am going to live with myself after I kiss this cute, simple, good-natured guy and then have to tell him I actually didn't like him that much after all.

By the time we finish dessert and make our way back through the crowded parking lot, it's getting late. The sports talk show has switched over to classic rock, and we drive home in the dark, humming along to Aerosmith. While I'm waiting for a stoplight to change, Ian leans over and brushes his lips against my neck, his hand hot on my thigh. "Want to go to the dunes?" he whispers.

I stiffen. "Going to the dunes" is the local euphemism for finding a secluded spot in the parking lot and letting things go as far as you want them to go. The summer Mark got his driver's license, he and I parked out by the dunes nearly every night.

"I don't know." My voice comes out soft and strangled as Ian nuzzles my neck. He may not be a rocket scientist, but he definitely knows what he's doing with his body.

"Come on." He nips at my ear and slips a warm tongue inside, tracing the tender skin at the edge of my hairline. "We don't have to do anything you don't want to do."

I want to. Oh God, I want to. I've been so tied up in my emotions all summer that I haven't had a chance to miss the physical part of my relationship with Mark. But now it all comes back in a rush—the feeling of being wrapped up in someone's arms, your bodies intertwined. I ache for that feeling now. But what if we go to the dunes, and Ian falls in love with me? I still have more than half the alphabet to get through. And then there's Killian.

Killian.

"I'm sorry." I push Ian away and smooth down my hair. "You're awesome, Ian, but I really don't think we should."

He stares at me disbelievingly. I'm sure no girl has ever turned him down before. Finally he lets all his breath out in a huff and shrugs. "Okay, whatever you want."

I drive him home and let him kiss me again as we sit in his driveway. "This was the best date I've ever been on," he says. "Call me if you want to do it again. For real." And the romance of the moment is only a little bit ruined by the enthusiastic high five he gives me as he gets out of the car.

CHAPTER 19

Ian Swanson
In the car after the weirdest date ever
9/10

RYAN SPINS AROUND AND STARTS RUNNING BACKWARD,
coaxing me along. "Come on, Bentley!" he yells.

I glare at him and clench my fists, willing my aching legs to push forward just a little harder, a little faster. My heart hammers in my ears, and each breath burns my lungs. We're supposed to run seven miles this morning, but I'm having a bad day and am probably going to have to stop and walk it out before we even hit five.

"Can't." I gasp, slowing down so I'm barely jogging, my feet dragging over the dirt path.

Ryan stops and waits for me to catch up to him, handing me a water bottle. I gulp gratefully, water spilling out over my lips and trailing down my chin. "Thanks."

He takes the bottle back and neatly squirts a jet of water into his mouth. "You've got to step it up, man," he says. "We're four weeks away from the race."

"I know," I say, a little more forcefully than I had intended. "I'm trying."

Ryan claps a hand on my shoulder. "I know you are," he says. "You're doing a great job."

I shake my head and turn around. "I have to go back now if I'm going to walk most of the way. I don't want to be late for work."

Ryan looks longingly down the trail, his fingers tapping his thigh. I can see how much he wants to keep running, and I feel bad for slowing him down. "Go ahead," I say. "I'll be fine."

He shakes his head. "No way. I'll walk with you."

"No, seriously." I give him a little shove, and he pretends to fall, stumbling dramatically.

"God, careful," he says, rubbing his shoulder.

"Run." I point down the trail, and he hesitates for just a second more before obediently ducking his head and loping away like a caged animal finally free.

I'm halfway home before the stitch in my side disappears, and I stop at a gas station at the edge of town to buy a bottle of water. As I walk out, a familiar figure unfolds from the front seat of a giant SUV. I freeze, wondering if I can just step back inside and wait until he leaves, but it's too late.

"Hey there, Veda." He beckons me over.

"Hi, Dad." I take a giant swig from my water bottle as he runs his credit card through the machine and selects the option for premium gas.

"How's it going? Are you ready for the reunion?"

Is that this weekend? I try to visualize the calendar on the kitchen wall where I know I wrote the dates of Dad's all-important family events. But now that I think about it, the stupid thing might still be turned to June, even though we're well into July.

"Uh, yeah. Totally ready." I wipe my forehead. "When is it, exactly?"

Dad sighs and gives me a little bit of a death glare. "Well, Kaylee's birthday is the day before, so you and Jeffrey were going to come over for dinner. We have to leave for the reunion pretty early the next morning, so it would be best if you two could spend the night."

"Um, no thanks." I haven't slept over at Dad and Lila's house since I got the right to decide who I spend my weekends with. I have my own room there, decorated in white and deep pink, but I don't think I've set foot in it since I cleared all my "Dad's weekend" clothes out of the closet and slammed the door behind me the day after my sixteenth birthday. "Can't you just pick us up in the morning?"

Dad turns away and pulls the nozzle out of the gas tank, replacing it with a clang. "I guess." He prints the receipt and checks it over closely. "Where are you going now? Do you need a ride?" he asks.

"No, I'm good." We look at each other, and the awkward silence

ticks on for a few more seconds than necessary. "Well, see you later."
I turn and walk toward the road.

"Friday," Dad calls. "Six o'clock."

I barely have time to shower and get ready before Mel picks me up
for work. She's practically bouncing in her seat as I climb into the car,
wincing with every movement.

"Guess what," she says.

"What?" I nibble on a half-defrosted bagel.

"There's a beach party this weekend. It's apparently going to be,
like, the biggest thing ever. Total kiss potential."

"Oh, dang." I make an effort to sound disappointed. "I have to do
all this stuff with my dad this weekend. I probably won't be able to
make it."

Mel gasps dramatically, as if I had just told her I was moving away
to Alaska. "What? Vee! No! You have to go to this party."

I groan. "Mel, honestly, I'm kind of burned out on kisses. I can't
help but creep on every guy I see to find out what letter his name
starts with. It's disturbing."

She waves her hand dismissively. "Whatever. You're almost at *K*!
You can't stop before then."

I shade my eyes with my hand. "Did you ever consider maybe
Killian doesn't *want* to be kissed?" I say, my voice flat.

"What?" Mel sounds shocked. "Does he have a girlfriend?"

"No."

"Well." She laughs. "Then he wants you to kiss him. Trust me."

She sounds so confident, I almost tell her about how Killian already made a move but I shot him down, and that things have been weird ever since. But I don't, because I'm still not sure how I feel about the whole thing, and lately whenever Mel sticks her nose into my relationship business, things just seem to get an awful lot more complicated.

Killian and I work in silence for most of the morning, communicating primarily in grunts and hand signals. We've been working together long enough to get a routine down, going through the motions on autopilot. I feel Mel watching us out the office window and avoid making eye contact with her.

Finally, after our third trip back from the canoe launch, Killian runs his hand through his hair and takes a deep breath. "Okay, Vee. I can't take it anymore." He hops off the trailer and falls dramatically to his knees, clasping his hands. "I'm sorry for trying to put my arm around you and making things awkward, and I promise I'll never do it again if we can just go back to the way we were."

Relief floods through me, mixed with just a tiny bit of disappointment. All he wants to do is go back to the way things *were*?

"How were we?"

His eyebrows arch in surprise. "We were friends."

I nod and reach down to pull him to his feet. "We're still friends."

"Okay, good." He heaves an exaggerated sigh of relief, his whole body relaxing. "Because I read this fascinating article about all the different varieties of really intensely hot chili peppers a couple of days ago, and I've been dying to tell you about it."

I smile and motion down to the water, where a group of people has just landed at the end of their float. Killian's voice washes over me as we each grab the end of a canoe and tip it upside down to dump out the murky river water, then carry it back up to the trailer and load it on. It's like the floodgates have opened up inside him, and he can't stop the flow of conversation. Killian strides happily across the pine needle–covered ground for the rest of the afternoon. I'm happy to be wrapped back up in the cocoon of his words.

Mel runs outside at the end of the day and grabs my hand. "You two look like you've been having fun," she whispers in my ear. "I told you so. Invite him to the party."

"What's the point of inviting him to a party I'm not going to?" I look around to make sure Killian isn't within earshot.

"It doesn't even start until, like, ten on Friday night, Vee. What are you going to be doing with your dad then?" Mel nudges me, watching as Killian reaches up to secure a canoe strapped on the top rack of the trailer. His shirt rises, revealing the tan abs I've been trying to ignore all summer, and I feel my resolve weaken.

"Well, maybe I can come," I say. "But that day is Kaylee's birthday. I still have to get her a present, and I'm definitely going to have to go over to my dad's house for dinner that night—"

"Just figure it out." Mel pokes me in the side. "I'm heading to Seth's now, but I'm refusing to take you with me, so you have to ask

Killian for a ride. It'll be the perfect chance to invite him."

"Mel—" I reach for her, but she dances away and hurries toward the parking lot, taunting me by jingling her keys as she goes.

"Looks like your ride is leaving," Killian calls.

"Yep." I shoot Mel a death glare before turning back to him. "Can I catch one with you?"

"Of course." He brushes off his hands. "Ready?"

"Let's go."

I try not to let the dashboard lyrics distract me, but when Killian pulls off the tarp, I find myself reading through them again, mesmerized by the disjointed phrases and metallic ink.

"Do you want to add something?" His voice jolts me out of my reverie, and he tosses a silver Sharpie into my lap.

"Uh, no. I'm good." What would I write?

"Yeah, it's a lot of pressure," he says, nodding solemnly. "Your words immortalized forever on the dashboard of a shitty Jeep."

"Oh, shut up." I drop the Sharpie into a cup holder. "I just don't have the lyrics to hundreds of songs filed away in my head like some people. Give me a few days to think it over, do some research."

"Nope." Killian flips down the sun visor as we turn into Butterfield. "That was your one and only chance, and now it's gone forever. Sorry, counselor. Sometimes you have to think on your feet."

Main Street is clogged with traffic once again, and we crawl along, stopping at nearly every crosswalk to let clumps of tourists hurry across the street. As we near the edge of downtown, an SUV backs out from its street parking space, holding us up for another few seconds.

"Hey, pull in there," I say as the SUV rumbles away.

Killian doesn't even blink, just spins the steering wheel and glides the Jeep smoothly into the narrow spot. I'm halfway out of the car before he even throws the gearshift into park. "Come on," I say, one hand on my hip. "Let's see how good you are at thinking fast."

Half an hour later Killian is down on his hands and knees, inspecting an old dollhouse that's missing half the roof and could use a new paint job. "Okay," he says, wiping his forehead theatrically. "I give up. I have no idea what three-year-old girls want for their birthdays." He looks pointedly at the dollhouse. "But I'm pretty sure it's not this."

"Come on." I reach out and help him to his feet, peering around at the mounds of clothes, furniture, toys, and books inside Second Chance, Butterfield's antique store. Penelope, the owner, pops out from behind the counter, her bright red hair piled into a messy bun on top of her head.

"Can I help you now?" she asks, practically sprinting over to us. "You're looking in all the wrong places. You'll never find anything over here."

"That would be great," I say, tipping my face up toward Killian's and smiling sweetly. "*If* someone admits he's not quite as much of a genius as he sometimes likes to think."

Killian's face scrunches up in an exaggerated pout. "I didn't do anything to deserve this," he says to Penelope. "She's picking on me."

Penelope laughs, and the keys on the giant ring clipped to her belt loop jingle. "Somehow," she says, looking Killian up and down, "I doubt that. You look like a troublemaker."

She leads us across the room to a tall wooden chest and throws it open, revealing a collection of beautiful antique dolls and dozens of exquisite miniature outfits. "You're looking for something for your little sister, right?" Penelope asks.

"Yes." I pick up one of the dolls, which has silky blond hair just like Kaylee's. "She would love this."

"They're gorgeous," Penelope says with the air of a satisfied collector. "I keep them hidden away so the tourist kids won't come in here and mess them all up."

I turn the doll over and catch a glimpse of the price tag attached to her foot, and my breath catches in my throat. "Actually," I say, carefully setting her down on the shelf. "These might be a little out of my price range."

"Oh." Penelope blinks, as if she never even considered that a couple hundred dollars might be a bit much for an old doll, no matter how gorgeous it is. "Well, no problem." She lovingly rearranges the skirt on one of the dolls and closes the cabinet.

"Maybe a board game?" she says, tapping her finger against her chin and surveying the crowded room. "I have some lovely vintage Monopoly sets. Or perhaps a jigsaw puzzle?"

"She's a little young for Monopoly," I say.

"What about this?" Killian rummages around behind an old ironing board and pulls a tiny rocking chair out from underneath some quilts.

Penelope claps her hands and rushes over to him. "There it is!" she says, lifting the rocking chair up to the light and inspecting it. "I was wondering where this had gone."

Killian turns over the price tag and looks at me, eyebrows raised. "Twenty dollars," he says.

"Whew." Much more manageable on a summer job budget.

Penelope sets the rocking chair on the ground, and I crouch down to look at it. It's absolutely adorable—painted a light pink and identical to the rocking chairs that a lot of people in Butterfield keep out on their front porches for kicking back and relaxing in the evening. I can already imagine Kaylee rocking away on my dad's deck, grinning from behind her heart-shaped sunglasses, a sippy cup in one hand.

"Gosh darn it," I say, straightening up and giving Killian a light shove. "You really are too smart for your own good."

He smirks and mimes brushing off his shoulders. "Sign me up as a personal shopper for little girls."

"What do you say?" Penelope asks. She toys with the price tag, her bright green nails garish against the soft pink of the rocking chair. "I raised the price on a lot of things a couple of months ago, but this one was hiding and escaped."

"How much more should it be?" I ask, bracing myself.

Penelope glances at me and then up at Killian. "Twenty dollars is fine," she says. "I hope your sister loves it."

I smile. "She will." We wind our way through the overloaded shelves and towering stacks of furniture, and I hand over twenty dollars at the counter. "Thanks so much, Penelope."

"No problem. Come back soon!"

"We will," I say automatically, and glance up at Killian as he holds the door for me. He's not paying attention, his eyes are unfocused, and he's whistling a tune under his breath.

The street is getting less crowded as shops start closing down for the night, but we pass a café bustling with activity and a wine bar with a line out the door. "This is crazy," Killian says, nodding at the brightly lit sign. "Everything in Trawley shuts down at six o'clock. It turns into a ghost town."

I shrug. "Tourists have to eat."

He takes the rocking chair from me, even though it isn't very heavy, and carries it to the Jeep, stowing it in the back and tucking some old towels around it so it won't move around while we drive.

"Any other problems you'd like me to solve for you tonight?" Killian asks with a grin.

"Nope, I think that's it." I wait until he's distracted with backing out of the parking space before I lean over and grab the Sharpie out of the cup holder. "But now I know what I'm going to write."

"What? No!" He grabs my hand and then immediately drops it, as if it's hot. "You missed your chance earlier."

"Try to stop me," I tease. I lean over and scrawl three words on the dashboard, not too big, but large enough that they're definitely legible. Now I'm a believer

"Hmmm." Killian glances at what I've written, and a smile tugs at the corners of his mouth. "I suppose that's acceptable."

I look out the window, my face turned away from Killian so he's not able to see that I can't stop smiling.

CHAPTER 20

I SEE MEL'S CAR PARKED AT THE CURB OUTSIDE SETH'S HOUSE as soon as Killian turns onto my street, and I realize I had completely forgotten they were going to work on the album—and that I am supposed to ask Killian to come to the beach party tomorrow night. I clench my fists and think frantically about how to bring it up as he pulls into my driveway and insists on carrying the rocking chair up to my house.

"Thanks," I say, trying to block the screen door with my body just in case the front hallway is even messier than usual. "For carrying this, and for finding it in the first place. Kaylee would be stuck with a dumb stuffed animal from Target if it weren't for you."

"No problem." He runs a hand through his shaggy hair, making it stick up in front. "So." He shuffles his feet, seemingly at a loss for words. "I'll see you later?"

"Definitely."

He reaches for me in a way that looks like he's going for a hug, but he turns it into a fist bump halfway through, slamming his knuckles into mine. "Cool," he says, backing away and nearly falling off the front step. "Well, later."

"Hey," I say, my heart hammering in my chest. "Wait a second."

He stops and shoves his hands into his pockets. "Yeah?"

I take a deep breath. "Mel and I are going to this beach party tomorrow night. Do you want to come?"

Killian tips his head to the side, and a slow smile spreads across his face. "Sure," he says. "I'll come. As long as . . ."

"As long as what?"

He clears his throat and looks down at his shoes. "Uh, I was just going to say as long as I don't have to watch you kiss any other guys this time."

All the blood rushes to my face. I actually get a little dizzy and have to reach for the iron railing.

"Actually, forget I said that," Killian says, a red flush creeping up his neck. "But, yes. I'd love to come. I'll see you tomorrow."

I lean against the house and watch him lope down the driveway, all long legs, big hands, and floppy hair. I stash the rocking chair inside and come back out, sinking down onto the concrete step and sending Mel and Seth a quick text to see what they're up to.

My whole body tingles, like I've been up all night drinking Mountain Dew, and I can't seem to get Killian's smile out of my head. A few minutes later, my phone pings, but the text isn't from Mel or

Seth. It's from Killian, a picture of something black and silver and gold. I open up the message and squint down at the screen. I can make out the words I wrote on his dashboard just half an hour ago, but something else is written above it.

THEN I SAW HER FACE
Now I'm a believer

I fly out the front door and jog across the street, struggling to catch my breath as I ring the doorbell. Seth opens the door nearly a minute later, squinting against the outdoor light even though the sky is still filled with low-hanging clouds. "Vee," he says, pushing his hair out of his face. "Hey."

He swings the door open to reveal Mel, who's standing right behind him, feet bare, long-sleeved Henley pushed up to her elbows. They both look slightly dazed, the way they often do when they've been working on new songs, each of them locked away in their inner world but somehow still connecting on the same creative frequency. The corners of Mel's mouth turn down, and I know I've shattered whatever energy they had woven between the guitar and the piano.

"Everything okay?" Mel asks, pulling her hair back and securing it into a stubby ponytail.

I step inside, edging past Seth, and kick off my shoes. "Um, yeah." I give her a meaningful look. "I did the thing you wanted me to do. For Friday."

Mel looks puzzled for a moment and then she beams. "Oh! And?"

"Yes," I say.

Mel nods, but she still looks distracted, like she can't quite remember what it is we're supposed to be talking about. Seth looks at both of us and shakes his head, turning and beckoning for us to follow him down the basement stairs. The shag carpet and wicker furniture always makes me feel like Seth's basement is a wormhole back to the 1980s. Mel's guitar is propped up against the giant beanbag chair, her water bottle and a Tupperware container filled with carrot sticks sitting nearby. Seth's iPad and laptop sit on an end table next to the piano, ready to record.

"Can I hear what you've been working on?" I ask, flopping onto the gray sectional.

"Uh," Seth says, looking at Mel.

"No," Mel says firmly, flipping the laptop closed. "It's really rough. Not even really a song—just some chords and stuff we're trying to fit together."

"Is it the song you played for me at your house a few weeks ago? Because that was good."

"Oh . . . no." Mel bends over her guitar and fiddles with the tuning pegs, her face unreadable. "That was totally different."

Seth drops onto the piano bench and crosses his ankles. "What song?"

"Nothing." Mel clears her throat. "Just forget it."

An awkward silence fills the room. "Come on, you guys," I say, still buzzing with nervous energy and desperate to find something else to pay attention to so I don't have time to obsess over Killian. "Let me hear something. I don't care if it's finished or not."

They glance at each other, and Mel finally shrugs. "Okay."

I burrow into the couch and close my eyes as Seth plays a lilting piano intro. Mel joins him on the guitar, and the notes dance around me, a soundtrack for my thoughts as my mind drifts back to earlier today, poking around in the antique store with Killian and feeling, for once, like I belonged somewhere.

Mel misses a note and swears quietly, then brings her hand down hard across the strings. "That's about it for now."

"I like it," I say. "But not as much as the one you played for me the other day."

"Now you have to play that one, Mel," Seth says, leaning back on the piano bench. "I want to hear it."

Mel goes completely still for a second. "Nah," she says, lifting the strap from her shoulder and pushing the guitar aside. "I'm kind of done for now." Her glasses slide down her nose, and she regards me over the thick black frames. "Seth, did you hear about Vee's summer resolution?"

Seth raises his eyebrows. "I don't think so."

I stare at Mel, confused. Seth is the last person in the world who would see the humor in the Twenty-Six Kisses Challenge, and not just because he used to have a thing for me—although Mel doesn't know that, of course. The kissing challenge is exactly the kind of teenage shenanigans he hates. Why is she bringing it up?

She rambles on, ignoring me. "We decided Vee needed some motivation to move on from Mark, so she's going to kiss a bunch of guys this summer—one from *A* to *Z*. And you're already through . . . What letter, Vee?"

I open my mouth and shut it again, desperately trying to figure out a way to change the subject—but I'm stuck. Mel has thrown me under the bus. "*I*," I say finally, watching Seth's knee bounce up and down rhythmically. "I'm through *I*."

"She's had these fantastic kisses . . . on a Ferris wheel, at this really swanky party at her dad's house. I'm superjealous."

In my head, I'm screaming at Mel to shut up. Seth's face has gone completely blank, the way it does whenever he gets so upset with the people around him that he literally can't bear to associate with them anymore.

"Well," he finally says, his voice flat. "That's fun."

I stand up, too angry to even look at Mel. I don't understand what just happened—she basically forced me to ask Killian out and then she spilled the beans about the kissing challenge to Seth. And for what? "I'd better go home."

Seth puts his hands over his face and rubs his eyes. "Yeah. I'm pretty wiped too," he says. "I don't think I can work on this any more today."

"Okay." Mel yawns and stretches, pushing herself deeper into the beanbag. "Do you want to watch a movie or something?"

"No." Seth drops his hands. "I might take a nap."

"Oh." Mel looks at Seth, who stares down at his fingers twisted together in his lap. "Okay. I guess I'll head out, then." She stands up and grabs her guitar.

I unfold myself from the deep sectional and follow her up the stairs. "See you later, Seth." He doesn't respond.

Mel and I walk through the spotless kitchen and down the hallway lined with old family pictures. I always feel slightly creeped out in Seth's house when he's not right beside me. It's immaculate and silent, like no one really lives there. I stop briefly to study the largest picture on the wall, a snapshot of Seth, his parents, and Luke. Seth once told me it was the last picture taken of all four of them before Luke died.

The screen door slams as Mel goes outside, making me jump. I hurry after.

"What the hell, Mel?" I don't bother keeping my voice down. "Why would you tell him about the kissing thing?"

She stows her guitar in the trunk and leans against the Buick, inspecting her fingernails. "Sorry. It just slipped out."

"Bullshit." I put my hands on my hips.

She sighs and tips her head back. "Why is it such a big deal?"

"It's just . . ." I don't know what I can say without having to admit to her there's this giant thing I haven't told her about Seth and me. "I didn't want him to know."

"Look," she says, reaching up and pulling the elastic band out of her hair with one sharp tug. "It was just . . . We were really making progress on the album, and then you came over and threw everything off." Her eyes widen, and she claps her hands over her mouth. "Oh God. Vee, I'm so sorry. I did not mean it to come out like that."

I shrug, clenching my fists and digging my fingernails into my palms to have something to concentrate on other than the pain of hearing my worst fears validated—Mel and Seth really don't want me around anymore. They've got each other now.

"It's fine," I say, using every ounce of willpower I have to keep my voice from breaking. "I'll leave you to it, then." I walk across the street, barely able to see where I'm going, and Mel doesn't call me back.

The first time Seth told me he loved me, I laughed at him. It was about a month after my parents broke the news about the divorce to Jeffrey and me, and I had started spending a lot of time over at Seth's house because watching them tiptoe around each other as my dad prepared to move out was more than I could handle. Seth's brother had been dead for a year, and his family was still riding the shock waves of grief that resonated long after the grass had grown over Luke's grave at the Butterfield cemetery. Basically, Seth was my island . . . and I think I was his.

We were sitting on his front step, sharing a can of lukewarm root beer, and he looked down at his blue Doc Martens and said, "I love you, you know." And I was twelve years old and stupid, and after the laugh slipped out, I clapped my hand over my mouth.

I don't remember exactly what happened after. I'm sure he made some excuse and disappeared inside his house. But I kept going over. I couldn't stay away from Seth. Everything about him fascinated me—his broodiness, the way he'd sit in his dark basement and play piano for hours, the way he seemed captivated by me. And he kept telling me he loved me nearly every day, whispering it into my hair, tracing the words on my back. It became part of my landscape. The grass was green, the sky was blue, and Seth loved me. But I never said it back. Watching my parents struggle their way through a divorce had taught me something about love: that it didn't last.

We went back to school in the fall, started hanging out with Mel when she moved to town, and I kind of forgot the intensity of whatever it was Seth and I had had that summer. We never kissed, didn't even hold hands. Middle school turned into high school, I started dating Mark, and I never told Mel about that summer, or about Seth and me.

I guess he finally got over me, though. Maybe while I was missing his piano recitals to watch Mark run a cross-country meet or hanging out at a bonfire while Seth and Mel wrote songs together in his basement, Seth decided he didn't want to wait around for me anymore. Or maybe it happened gradually, the love leaching away a little bit at a time, until one day he woke up and realized he was over me. I should be happy for Seth—for him *and* Mel. And if I were still with Mark, I know I would be. But my head's all over the place, bouncing between Killian and Mark and Seth, as well as the alphabet *A* through *I*. I've never been closer to more people in my life, and I've never felt so alone.

CHAPTER 21

dinner tmrw @ six, k's bday. don't be late.

I never thought my hyperarticulate, OCD, grammar Nazi father would ever stoop low enough to send a shorthand text message, but I guess he finally got tired of spelling out every word and battling autocorrect on his phone.

i know, I text back. Does he really think I'd be able to forget just a couple of days after seeing him at the gas station?

I already have Kaylee's present wrapped and ready to go. I can't wait for her to open it and laugh the way she does whenever she gets too excited to talk. Too bad celebrating Kaylee's third birthday also means spending an evening with Dad and Lila.

I pound on the wall next to my bed. "Do you have a birthday present for Kaylee?" I shout to Jeffrey.

A pause. "No!" he yells back.

I sigh. "Okay, I guess you can share mine. But you have to at least get her a card."

A minute later Jeffrey stomps into my room. "She's three, Vee. She's not going to care if I get her a birthday card." His voice is sharp.

"Whoa, chill out," I say. "It's not that big a deal."

"I don't care. I don't want to."

"Do you want to be a good big brother or not?" I cross my arms and look at him.

He rolls his eyes and stares at the floor. "I bet you didn't get me a birthday card when I was three."

"That's because I was only eight. You're twelve years old and perfectly capable of buying your baby sister a card. Step it up, Jeffrey."

He sighs and drags himself back down the hallway. "*Okay.* I'll get her a stupid card. Just shut up and stop talking to me."

Mom calls down the hallway, "Jeffrey, I can help you make a card if you want!"

"No, it's fine!" he yells back, slamming his door shut. "Don't worry about it."

I smile, not completely blaming him for deflecting that one. Mom's card-making skills fall somewhere below her T-shirt–painting abilities. She comes down the hallway and sticks her head into my room. "What are you doing after Kaylee's party tomorrow night?"

"Um, Mel and I are going to a thing," I say. At least, I think we're still going. I haven't heard from Mel, and I'm sure as hell not going to be the one to text her first.

"A 'thing'?" Mom curls her fingers in air quotation marks. "Is that a work 'thing' or a social 'thing'?"

"A social thing." I open up Google and type in *George Bernard*

Shaw, just to look busy. The less my mom knows about the beach party (which isn't technically legal and has a 100 percent chance of involving underage drinking), the better.

"I'm kind of in the mood to marathon something on Netflix," she says, leaning against the doorway. "Jeffrey, do you want to overdose on bad TV with me tomorrow after the party?"

"Sure," he says, his voice muffled. I'm willing to bet he's staring at his phone or DS and doesn't even know what he has just agreed to.

Mom claps her hands in delight and grins at me. "Got him," she says, lowering her voice. "I think I've finally figured out the art of getting middle-school boys to agree to things: ask them when they're distracted and lock them in early. Then lay on the guilt if they try to back out of it later."

I smile. "Well, don't keep him up too late. We have the family reunion the next day."

Mom shakes her head. "Biggest upside of getting divorced: not having to go to those things anymore."

"Lucky you," I say. "Can I divorce Dad?"

She snorts and shakes her head. "Someday you'll be glad you still have a relationship with him," she says, one hand on her hip. "It might just take a while."

"Yeah, like, twenty or thirty years."

"Vee, come on." She gives me a disapproving look, and I flop over onto my stomach. I don't know why she cares that Jeffrey and I even see Dad anymore. I sure wouldn't if I were her.

The next night, Mom drives Jeffrey and me over to Dad's house and comes inside with us for a moment, opening her arms wide to give Kaylee a hug. "There's the birthday girl!" she says, tickling Kaylee and making her scream with delight. "How old are you, sweetie?"

"Three!" Kaylee squeals, hopping up and down in the most adorable way possible.

"I got her a little something," Mom says to Lila, handing her a gift-wrapped package. "But I'll let you all get to celebrating and see myself out."

"Thanks so much, Pamela," Lila says, her eyes widening with surprise. I don't know why my mom is so nice to her. If Mark had left me for some other girl, you can bet I wouldn't be showing up at her house with presents for the child they had together.

"Hi, guys!" As soon as the door closes behind my mom, Lila's shoulders relax and her smile broadens. "Dinner's almost ready. Hungry?"

"Starving," Jeffrey says, making a beeline for the kitchen.

Kaylee tugs on my hand, and I kneel down so she can climb onto my back and ride into the dining room.

"Love you," she says happily, pulling on my ponytail.

"Love you too, Miss Kaylee." She wiggles off my back, and I turn around to lift her up into her high chair. The table is set for five with Lila's fancy china, pristine white linen napkins, and gleaming silverware as meticulously placed as if we were in the middle of a magazine photo shoot. Dad, Lila, and Kaylee look like the perfect little family. I'm sure Dad wishes he didn't have to include his two sullen teenagers in the equation.

Lila serves up homemade macaroni and cheese, broccoli, and applesauce—all of Kaylee's favorites. I pick at my food, grumpy with myself about how good it feels to actually eat a regular meal cooked by someone else rather than scrounging for my dinner in the fridge. Jeffrey must feel the same way, because he eats three bowls of macaroni before crawling off to the living room to lie down on the couch in a food coma.

"I guess we'll wait a bit for cake," Lila says, the corner of her mouth twitching as Jeffrey groans loudly from the other room. Kaylee's still absorbed in her dinner, carefully stacking macaroni noodles into a tower that threatens to topple onto the white tablecloth.

"So let's talk about the reunion," Dad says. "Remember we're leaving pretty early in the morning."

I set my fork down and stare at him. "We'll be ready. Don't worry."

"I'm staying here tonight," Jeffrey calls from the living room.

"Excuse me," I mutter, sliding my chair away from the table and striding into the living room. "Jeffrey, what do you mean you're staying here?"

He slides his phone into his pocket and shrugs, splayed across the couch like he owns the place. "I'm tired. I've got clothes and stuff. I'll just sleep here, and we can pick you up in the morning."

"What about Mom? I thought you said you were going to hang out with her tonight."

Jeffrey sighs. "Why do I have to go? You're going out with your friends. I just want to stay here and watch TV or whatever."

I collapse onto the couch and lean in, catching a whiff of that god-awful body spray he uses. "Yeah, because I have legitimate plans. Do you know how hurt Mom is going to be if you decide to stay here with *them* rather than hanging out with her when you already told her you would? And you'd just be watching TV with her anyway—go home and do it."

He shrugs, and the couch vibrates slightly as his phone goes off in his pocket. "It's stupid to go home and then have Dad pick us up again in the morning. Mom won't care."

"God!" I stand up. "What is with you, Jeffrey? You've been acting like a total tool all summer."

"Look." He's on his feet too, and I realize with a jolt he's exactly as tall as I am now. "Seriously, just leave me alone, Vee. You're such a hypocrite."

"What is that supposed to mean?"

"Nothing." He pulls his phone out and looks at it again.

"Will you put your stupid phone away?" I lean forward and give him a little shove. "What do you mean, I'm a hypocrite?"

Jeffrey tosses the phone onto the couch and shoves me back. "Don't pretend like you don't know. Everyone is talking about you and your new boyfriends."

I gasp. "What are you—"

"All right, that's enough." Dad looms in the doorway, arms crossed, his face turning red. He glances back toward the dining room and lowers his voice. "What the hell is going on in here?"

Jeffrey and I look at each other. "Nothing," I say finally, staring at Jeffrey as his gaze drops down to his feet.

"Goddamn right it had better be nothing. It's your sister's birthday. So get back in here and have some cake and be happy about it." He glares at both of us and turns away, his footsteps thudding down the hallway.

"We're not done," I say, grabbing Jeffrey's arm as he walks past me. He shrugs me off like I'm Kaylee's size.

Everyone's talking about you and your new boyfriends. I wrap my arms around my stomach and stare at the pictures of Dad, Lila, and Kaylee perched on the marble fireplace mantel. Is that what people are saying? I think back over the summer, mentally cataloging the guys I *actually* kissed (not counting the nonromantic ones, obviously). How many is that? Five? That's not enough to be labeled the town slut, is it?

"Vee!" Dad roars from the dining room. "We're waiting."

"Coming," I say, trying to slow my racing heart. It can't be true. Jeffrey has to be wrong.

After we sing "Happy Birthday" to Kaylee and eat Funfetti cake with pink frosting, it's time for presents. She rips through a dozen packages from Dad and Lila before reaching for the rocking chair, but as soon as she opens it, her eyes light up. "My chair!" she says in wonder, standing up and carefully lowering herself onto it, her feet flying up off the floor when the chair rocks back.

"Say thank you to Vee and Jeffrey," Lila reminds her.

"Tank you!" Kaylee shouts, running her tiny hands over the armrests. I grin, noticing not even Jeffrey can completely hold back a smile, and silently thank Killian for helping me find the perfect present.

The eastern edge of the sky is just beginning to darken when Lila hustles Kaylee off to her room for bath and bedtime. Kaylee doesn't want her birthday to end, and she clings to me, her fingers sticky with frosting and her little heart beating madly.

"Happy birthday," I whisper into her hair, and she starts to cry.

"I think someone's a little tired," Lila says, untangling Kaylee's fists from my hair and lifting her away.

"No!" Kaylee sobs, and my heart wrenches as she reaches her arms out to me. "No!"

"Night, Kay." I smile brightly and wave. "Time to go to bed."

As soon as Lila and Kaylee are upstairs, Jeffrey bolts for the basement. I chase after him, thundering down the carpeted stairs. I haven't been in the basement in months, and I had forgotten how huge it is—a never-ending expanse of plush carpet dotted with the biggest sectional sofa I've ever seen, a pool table, an air-hockey table, and anything else a preteen boy could wish for.

Jeffrey sprints into the bathroom and locks the door behind him. "Come on, Jeffrey," I say, keeping my voice low enough that Dad won't come down here and ream us out again. "Come out for a second."

"I don't want to talk to you," he says. "Just leave me alone." He flips on the bathroom fan and water runs in the shower. I sink down to sit on the floor and lean against the door. He'll have to come out eventually.

jeffrey said people are talking about me and the guys i've kissed, I text Mel. is it true?

I hope she's not still mad about what happened at Seth's yesterday. I need her to be on my side right now. Luckily, her response is almost immediate. whaaaaat?!? no. i have not heard anything like that.

i don't know if i want to come tonight.

I can imagine Mel standing at her bathroom sink, holding the flatiron to her hair with one hand and typing madly with the other as samba music blares from her iPod. A department store's worth of makeup is scattered across the counter, and she's wearing one of her dad's old button-down shirts so she can get ready without spilling eye shadow on her outfit. Maybe she's even pregaming with some rum mixed into her Diet Coke or vodka-soaked gummy bears.

you have to. tonight is everything. you could cross off a bunch of letters all at once!!! and you know who is coming, right?!

Yep. Definitely pregaming. I close my eyes, suddenly nervous about seeing Killian tonight. There's only one letter standing between me and K—and I realize with a jolt that the one remaining letter is J.

i need to talk to jeffrey and find out what he knows.

Mel doesn't respond. Inside the bathroom, the shower shuts off, and I quietly move away from the door, hoping Jeffrey will think I've given up and gone away. He spends twenty minutes humming to himself and banging around in there. I hear the distinctive hiss of an aerosol body spray can and wrinkle my nose. Finally the door opens and Jeffrey steps out, a towel wrapped around his waist.

I'm on my feet and next to him in a flash, my shoulder pressing against his damp arm. He smells like the love child of Hollister and an overripe banana. "If you don't tell me what the hell is going on, I'm going to rip this towel off, take a picture, and send it to everyone in school," I say, the tone of my voice calm and conversational. I hook one finger under the towel and give it a gentle tug. "So I suggest you just do what I say."

Jeffrey stiffens but doesn't pull away. "You wouldn't do it," he says, but the hesitation in his voice tells me I've got him right where I want him.

"Try me."

He lets his breath out in a huff. "Fine, but get away from me. You're freaking me out."

"Come over here." I tug him across the room and force him to sit down in a corner of the sectional. I stand over him, hands on my hips. "Spill."

Jeffrey squirms, goose bumps rising on his chest as water drips from the ends of his hair. "I've just heard some stuff," he mutters, avoiding my gaze.

"What stuff?" I brandish my phone at him, camera app at the ready.

He cringes. "Kyle and Oliver told me Mark had some people over last weekend for a bonfire at his house." I stop breathing for a moment, the smell of woodsmoke and the feeling of one of Mark's giant hoodies pulled around my shoulders flashing through my mind. "And Gabriel Latimore was talking about how you were all over him at Lila's party."

A flash of anger rips through me. Paired with Ryan's eyewitness account of how I kamikaze-kissed Dexter early this summer, I could see where some people might start to see a pattern. But Mark knows me. He knows I would never actually sleep around. *But is what you've been doing any better?* an annoying voice inside me asks. I choose not to answer.

"All I did was *kiss* Gabriel." I close my eyes briefly, unable to believe I'm having this conversation with my little brother, who apparently is not so little anymore.

Jeffrey takes the opportunity to try to bolt, but I grab the edge of his towel and he quickly sits back down as it begins to slide. "Stop. I don't want to hear about it."

I fall onto the couch, letting the squishy cushions surround me. "Who else knows?"

Jeffrey shrugs. "Beats me." He stands up, clutching the towel to his waist with both hands. "There, I told you everything. Happy? I'm leaving now." He stomps into his bedroom and slams the door.

Shit. I clutch my phone, my hands trembling. Everyone from school must know by now. It's too good of a story—*goody-two-shoes Vee gone wild.* I'm a slut—me, Vee Bentley, debate team nerd, half-marathon trainer, the girl who wanted nothing more than to keep dating her high school boyfriend.

My phone buzzes in my hand, and I jump.

i'm ready, biotch. coming to pick u up.

I'm wearing my Dad-appropriate clothes, hair up in a boring ponytail. Cute and traditional. The same old Vee.

I take a deep breath and stand up, my fingers moving automatically over my phone's screen.

k. but we need to go back to your house first.

They think I'm a slut? Fine. If they want to give me the label, I'm going to look the part. They haven't seen anything yet.

CHAPTER 22

THE GIRL STARING BACK AT ME FROM THE MIRROR IS WEARING more eyeliner than I've ever seen on anyone in my life. Her eyes are huge, her cheekbones sharp, her lips red. She looks like she's going to kick the world's ass.

"You. Look. Incredible." Mel stands next to me, staring at my reflection. "I'm superjealous."

"Mark knows," I say to her, touching the ends of my hair, full and wavy from Mel's curling iron. "Everybody knows."

"They don't know anything," she says, raising her Diet Coke bottle and toasting my reflection. "And they can just go to hell."

It's nearly dark by the time we leave Mel's house, stumbling in our stilettos and folding ourselves carefully into the Buick so we don't flash the whole neighborhood with our impossibly short skirts. I have to drive since Mel ended up pregaming a little bit more than she planned to while I was getting ready, and my hands are slippery on the steering wheel. My senses are heightened under the awareness I'm likely the number one topic of conversation among the teenage population of Butterfield right now—the deep purple shadows of dusk seem sharper, the lake-scented air more crisp.

"I'm done with the kissing thing," I say to Mel. My pulse is racing, imagining what it's going to be like to walk into the middle of a crowd, knowing everyone there thinks I sleep around. "I can't walk into that party and just start kissing more random people. And I was so pissed at Jeffrey when I left that I forgot to kiss him, so I'm not even on *K* yet."

"Vee! How could you forget?"

I shrug and turn on the air-conditioning, trying to keep the windshield from fogging up. Maybe I didn't exactly forget—but if I still have to cross *J* off my list, then there's no risk of having to make the decision about Killian tonight.

Mel shrugs and then rolls the window up a bit so the wind doesn't mess up her perfectly straightened hair. "Well, screw it. Just skip *J*."

I swallow hard. "Is that allowed?"

Mel's smile is dangerous as we pass under a streetlight. "Vee, have you looked at yourself lately? Tonight everything is allowed."

It seems to take about half the usual time to get to the dunes, and when we pull up the parking lot is nearly half full with cars. "Excellent," Mel says, using her phone's flashlight to check her makeup in the rearview mirror. "This is going to be an insane party."

As soon as we climb out of the car, I start shaking and feel like I have to pee. "Mel," I say, leaning against the Buick, the metal warm against my thighs. "I'm scared."

She walks over and puts her hands under my elbows, steadying me. "You don't have anything to be scared of," she tells me, anchoring her dark eyes on mine. "They suck. You are awesome. What else matters?"

She grabs my hand and leads me to the beach path. Laughter and shouts float through the trees, and it sounds like half the school must be here. We pull off our shoes when we reach the sand and step out onto the beach, and I hold my breath as I wait for someone to spot me and shout, *Hey! The slut is here!*

Of course, that doesn't happen. Everyone is already two or three beers into the night, preoccupied with their own drama, hitting on whomever they want to make out with later. There aren't nearly as many people here as I thought, and one quick glance over the crowd tells me Killian hasn't arrived yet—if he's even coming.

I grab Mel's arm. "Let's just go."

"No way. Killian will be here, right?"

"He said he would."

She tosses her hair. "Well, you have to at least wait until he shows up."

We grab drinks from one of the many coolers scattered across the sand and join Brianna and Landon at the edge of the bonfire. Mel flits around, talking to everyone, using animated hand gestures and exaggerated laughter, and I trail after her, trying to drink my foul-tasting beer as quickly as possible to dull the sense that everyone is staring at me.

I stay close to Mel, avoiding the eyes of people I don't know, and keep drinking. I find some wine coolers, which speeds up the process a bit since they don't taste like the bottom of a garbage can, unlike the cheap beer.

"Text him!" Mel says, holding her drink aloft while she dances.

I look down at my phone but can't quite figure out how to type a coherent message. My fingers keep hitting the wrong keys and writing strings of nonsense. Sighing with exasperation, I look up. And there he is. Killian is standing in front of me, his hands on my shoulders as I lean precariously to the side. Suddenly he's the only person in the world who I want to see.

"Are you okay?" he asks, studying me.

"Your hands are so *warm*!" I grab them and lace my fingers with his, a rush of happiness shooting through me now that he's finally here. "Come dance with me."

"Vee—" he says, but then one of his favorite songs starts blasting over the speakers and he grins, his shoulders already twitching to the beat of the song he can't resist.

Whoever made the playlist tonight must have had a direct line into Killian's head. Every song is one we've listened to together at work, one I know he loves and has scribbled lyrics from across the Jeep's dashboard. We dance together, but his eyes aren't really focused on me. He keeps a respectable distance between us, never letting me pull him in close. He's hesitant, wary. I don't blame him, but I also don't care that he wants his space. I move closer, pulling his hands to my hips, letting the neckline of my shirt slip too low.

I've lost track of Mel's trajectory through the night—one moment she's dancing right beside me with a guy I've never seen before; the next she's over by the coolers, laughing with some girls from school. The only light comes from the fire and from the stars, giving everyone a flickering, impermanent quality. I dance most of the alcohol out of my system, and then, suddenly, I'm exhausted.

Another song starts up, and Killian launches into the most ridiculous dance moves yet, his long legs and arms everywhere as he does something that might be the six-foot-three white male version of twerking. He moves farther into the gyrating mass of dancing teenagers, and I let my fingers slip through his, retreating to the outer edge of the circle, sucking the cool lake air into my lungs.

The sand shifts under my feet as I climb the dunes, and the light from the fire recedes, allowing me to see the millions of stars that shine out over Lake Michigan at night. I find a big stick I can use to keep my balance and keep pushing myself farther, faster, away from everyone and everything. Finally, when I can't hear anything but my own gasping breaths, I stop.

The Big Dipper rises up in front of me, and I remember the night Mark and I put glow-in-the-dark stars on my bedroom ceiling, spelling out the constellation LOVE above my bed. My mom and brother were out at a movie, and Mark and I had the house to ourselves for the first time. I'll never be able to describe the feeling that washed over me when he shut my bedroom door and turned to look at me—it was like we were the only people in the world. The only point of existence in the universe. We had been dating for nearly six months, but when he kissed me that night, it was like I had never been kissed before. Everything felt so new. And as we climbed into my bed and did things we'd been waiting so long to do— I push the memory out of my head. It doesn't matter now.

I sink into the sand and cover my face with my hands. The kissing challenge worked. I barely think about Mark anymore, and when I do, the regret and sadness just skim over me, not sinking in and lodging in my soul the way it did just a few weeks ago. I've still got Mel and Seth, I've got a half-marathon training plan and a running buddy, and an upcoming senior year of high school that will likely be totally kick-ass. And I've got Killian, even though, despite all the talking we do, I'm still not quite sure exactly what's going on between us—or even what I want to happen. But deep down, I know I'm not ready to dive into another relationship quite yet, especially in the middle of a very confusing kissing challenge. I'm not ready to trust myself with someone else's heart.

"Vee?" Killian's voice floats over the sand, soft and powerful, the kind of voice that can change the world if it wants to.

"I'm here."

Killian staggers over the rise of the dune and slides down to where

I'm sitting, clutching his side. "Man"—he gasps—"I really need to work on my cardio. That was brutal."

I shake my head. "I think you're probably more exhausted from the dancing than walking the dunes."

Killian frowns. "I can't believe you left during that last song. It was epic."

I shrug, picking up a stick and tracing designs in the sand. "I needed a breather."

"Are you okay?" He leans in, studying me. "You seem . . . different tonight."

I laugh and throw the stick as hard as I can, watching it fly through the moonlight. "Killian, we've talked about a lot of things this summer," I say. "Santa Claus. Music. Lighthouses."

"Shaw," he adds.

"Yes, always Shaw." I nod and turn to him. "But I think I forgot to mention I'm a huge slut. Maybe you heard it from someone tonight, though."

Killian cocks his head to the side. "One, I haven't heard anything like that about you. Two, I wouldn't believe it if I did."

"That's because you don't have any evidence." I look away. "But what if I gave you proof? That I've basically been on a mission to kiss every guy in Butterfield this summer?"

Killian lies back on the sand, his hands behind his head. "Then I would say that doesn't sound like something the Vee I know would do."

"Well, it's the truth," I say.

He gazes thoughtfully up at the sky. "Is this the part where you tell me what's really going on with you?" Killian asks. "Because if not, let's fast-forward through everything else you were going to say and just get there."

I sigh. "It's kind of a long story. A long, tragic, pathetic story with no happy ending in sight."

"Well." Killian shifts his weight, burrowing down into the sand. "I'm just going to look at these ridiculously beautiful stars for a while. And if you were to tell your long, tragic, pathetic story, I wouldn't mind."

It's so quiet. If I listen hard, I can hear the wash of the waves on the beach a few hundred yards away, but other than that, it's just the sound of our breathing and the soft rush of sand flowing through my fingers. I close my eyes, but I immediately start to feel sick, so I keep them trained on the Big Dipper. And it takes a long time—most guys would have given up and left—but finally, one halting word at a time, I tell Killian about Mark and how much I loved him. I tell him about being so happy watching Mark graduate, feeling like things between us were just getting better and better, and having all my dreams smashed just minutes later. I tell him about the kissing challenge, the way I've been chasing after guys all summer, and my little brother calling me a slut. I tell him—only realizing how true it is as the words come out of my mouth—how kissing has stopped meaning anything to me, and how I'm afraid I'm never going to be ready to love anyone again.

Killian reaches for me and squeezes my fingers, then runs his hands up and down my arms, smoothing the goose bumps away. I close my eyes, rooted to the spot, completely unable to move even though I want to pull away, to tell Killian to run as far from me as he can because I'm not sure I'm going to be able to do anything but hurt him. But his touch feels so good, I can't quite make myself do it.

"Is this okay?" he asks, and I nod. He moves closer, bringing one arm around my shoulders and pulling me to him. When I open my eyes, his face is right there, those blue eyes that are always looking for answers staring right into my own. I had never noticed the light freckles scattered across his nose, or the thin scar that runs just beneath his eyebrow.

"It's more than okay." I can barely breathe, but I manage to get the words out, and I bring my hand up to trace that faint scar. "I want to kiss you."

He smiles and leans closer, his breath warm on my ear as he whispers into it. "So do it."

"But I'm not on *K* yet. I still have one more letter to go."

His shoulders shake, and I realize he's laughing. "Vee." He pulls back and tucks my hair behind my ear. "Tell me the truth—do you really care about that right now?"

I want to know what it would feel like to kiss him while he's smiling. I want to lie back in the sand and have his weight on top of me. "No."

"Well, then."

That's all he has to say, and the last of my self-control totally crumbles. Killian's mouth is so soft, and he deepens the kiss just enough to leave me wanting more. We fall sideways onto the sand, and it's in my hair and up my shirt, but I really couldn't care less.

It's over too soon, and then we're looking at each other, the shifting dunes below us and the stars up above.

"That kiss," he whispers, "meant something."

And I nod, because Killian isn't just a random guy I picked because the first letter of his name happened to fall in line with the next letter in the alphabet. Because he can quote George Bernard Shaw all day, and needs reasons, evidence, and logic to back up everything he knows. But that's the problem—there's nothing to show me or him that this kiss was anything more than two drunk people acting on their biological urges. I can't prove to him that I want us to be together, that I really want to abandon the game and kiss only him for the rest of the summer. I can't even prove it to myself.

CHAPTER 23

"YOU KISSED HIM, DIDN'T YOU?" MEL'S FINALLY SOBER enough to drive me home around one a.m., just as the party starts to wind down.

"How did you know?" I roll down the window and breathe in the fresh air.

She shoots me a sidelong look. "You guys were out there for, like, two hours, your hair has a totally new thing going on in back, and you're covered in sand. In fact, if I didn't know better, I'd say you were doing a lot more than kissing."

My breath catches in my throat. "Great. So that's probably what everyone else is going to say too."

"Hey, if anyone wants to call you a slut, they're going to have to go through me first." The protectiveness in her voice makes me smile. "But first—spill. How. Was. That. Kiss?!"

"Oh." I kick my shoes off and curl up in Mel's car, belatedly noticing the sand that's now dusting the passenger seat. "It was good."

"I knew it!" She reaches over and tousles my hair. "I knew you two would get together. So are you, like, going out now?"

"Um." I shake my head, the grin fading from my face. "I don't know. I don't think so."

"What do you mean, *you don't think so*? You like him. It's totally obvious, even though you've been trying to hide it from me."

I should have known she would figure it out. I shake my head, trying to clear the fog that seems to have settled over my brain. "I mean, yes. I think I do. But the point of this summer was to *not* get into another relationship, right?"

"Whoa." Mel slows the car down as we come into town. "The point was for you to get over Mark, and I think you're good there. So now you can do whatever you want."

I fiddle with my seat belt as Mel drives toward my house. "I don't really know what I want to do."

She pulls into my driveway. "What do you mean?"

I take a deep breath. What do I mean? "Hypothetically, what would happen if I decided I did want to finish Twenty-Six Kisses?"

Mel turns and stares at me, her dark eyes reflecting light from the streetlamp. "Excuse me? I thought you wanted to quit."

"I did." I run my hand over my face. "I do. But I also don't. You know?"

"Girl, I hope you're still drunk, because you are not making any sense."

I shift in the seat and pull my knees up to my chin. "Eight weeks ago I was lying in bed, crying myself to death. Now I'm way better. So it must have worked, right?"

"Yes . . ."

"And maybe for me to get the full benefit, I need to finish. Like when you're on antibiotics and they tell you to take them for the whole two weeks even though you feel better after four days."

Mel's eyes widen. "Hey, Vee, you don't have to convince me. I'm all for you finishing Twenty-Six Kisses if that's what you want to do."

I stare out the windshield. My house is dark, except for a soft light glowing in the living room window. "I mean, it seems kind of stupid to give up now when I'm already halfway through."

Mel closes her eyes and sighs. "And what about Killian?"

Great question. Killian is so unbelievably awesome, and that is what scares me. He's awesome enough that I could see myself getting in way too deep again. I need more time. Maybe he'll understand.

Mel knows me so well, she knows what I'm going to say even before I'm sure about it myself. "He is going to be pissed," she says. "He's not going to get it, Vee. You know that, right? You might lose him."

I nod. She's right. Of course she's right. But Killian is different from any other guy—any other person, really—I've ever met. Maybe he'll understand I just can't afford to get hurt again. And, more important, maybe he'll be willing to wait for me until I get my head straight.

"You also have to think about what Jeffrey said." Mel sounds worried. "If you keep going with this thing, people might start talking even more."

I shrug and stare out the window at the woods flashing by. I'm so tired, I don't even care. "It'll be okay," I say, pushing open the passenger-side door and staggering to my feet. "I'll figure it out."

CHAPTER 24

Killian
The Dunes
???/10

THE NEXT MORNING I PUT ON A VIRGINAL WHITE EYELET
dress I know my dad likes. Today's inspection will be extra-rigorous,
and my head spins as I anticipate the awkward catching-up conversations and small talk I'm going to have to engage in with my relatives
at the family reunion.

I meet my own gaze in the mirror. The pale girl staring back at me
is nearly unrecognizable from the one last night with the sexy hair and
kick-ass makeup. Ready to play just another role.

My phone goes off as I slip my shoes on. It's Killian.

morning. ;-)

hey. :)

My stomach gets fluttery every time his name comes up on my phone. If I were a normal seventeen-year-old girl, I'd be drawing hearts on my notebooks and planning when to change my relationship status on Facebook. But I've been burned before, and right now I need my space.

have to go to a family thing, I type. i'll text you later.

Lila doesn't turn around to smile at me as I climb into the back of Dad's Escalade, and Jeffrey never looks up from his phone as I settle in next to him, but Kaylee reaches from her car seat to pull me in for a hug and a kiss. Dad leans over and puts a hand on Lila's knee, whispering something in her ear. She pushes him away and shakes her head.

"Okay, let's go," I say, worried that if we sit in the driveway any longer, Mom will feel like she has to come out to say hi, and then we'll all have to suffer through an unnecessary amount of awkwardness.

Dad glances back at me and puts the car in reverse. He drives down the street nearly at a crawl, glancing over at Lila the whole time. When we reach the corner, she leans over and places her hands on the dashboard.

"Stop," she says quietly. "I don't think I can go. All those people I don't know, your family. Just take me home, Barry."

The car rolls to a stop, and Jeffrey and I glance at each other, bracing ourselves for the inevitable explosion.

Dad takes a deep breath, and I slide down in my seat. "Li," he says gently. "It'll be fine. You can stick with me the whole time."

She leans forward, bending at the waist so her chin is nearly resting on her knees. "No." Her voice is stronger but shaky. "I can't. I need to go home. I feel sick."

"We were supposed to do this together, Li. If you can't do this, how are we supposed to . . ." He trails off, reaching out to touch Lila's knee. She pulls away and curls into herself, shaking her head.

Dad sighs and turns his head to stare out the driver's-side window. Several long, tense seconds tick by. Kaylee shifts in her car seat, and I reach for her to keep her still. I wait for the explosion that never comes.

"Fine," he says finally. "Let's go."

We drive all the way back to their house in silence. Even Kaylee sits wide-eyed and quiet. Lila has her seat belt unbuckled even before we hit the driveway, and she slides out of the car as soon as Dad puts it into park. She opens the back door and leans in to unbuckle Kaylee's car seat.

"No," Dad says, exasperation lacing his voice. "She's coming with us."

Lila jerks back like she's been stung and gives Dad a hard look. I hold my breath, wondering if we're finally going to witness Dad and Lila fighting, if the cracks in their marriage are starting to show through. But then she nods, runs her hands over Kaylee's head, and bends to kiss her cheek.

"Mama?" Kaylee says, her voice trembling.

"Hi, honey," Lila says, smiling at Kaylee. "You're going to a party with Daddy and Veda and Jeffrey. Mommy's going to stay home."

"No," Kaylee says.

"Yes." Lila glances at me and gives me a tight smile. "But you're going to be a big girl and go with Daddy. Have fun." Her voice breaks and she turns away, tucking her purse under her arm and hurrying up the path to the house.

Dad watches her go inside, then flips down the sun visor and backs out of the driveway again, maybe a little faster than necessary.

I lean back and allow myself to breathe again.

"So that's still a thing for her, huh?" Jeffrey says, sticking his head around Kaylee's seat to look at Dad. "Not leaving the house?"

I grab his shoulder and pull him back into his seat. I'm not exactly president of the Lila Fan Club, but even I stay away from the very sensitive topic of why exactly she stays home so much. And now that Lila's not here, there's nothing to stop Dad from blowing up at us in one of his classic tantrums.

Dad doesn't reply, just turns on the radio and makes a silly face at Kaylee in the rearview mirror, avoiding my eyes.

Our uncle Steve organizes these family reunions every five years, and I swear he must spend all the time in between planning the next one. At the last reunion, when my parents were still (barely) married and I was still (barely) okay with attending family functions, Uncle Steve rented out Total Tides, an outdoor water park about an hour from

Butterfield. I've never really seen the point of water parks when you have Lake Michigan in your backyard, but it was awesome having the whole place to ourselves, with no lines for the slides and just a couple of lifeguards who were all willing to turn a blind eye to someone getting a well-deserved wedgie in the deep end of the pool.

This year the Bentley clan is going for a more high-end feel at Cobblestone Farms, one of those rustic wedding venues complete with a one-hundred-year-old farmhouse and a giant barn. The dress code is "country casual," which means Jeffrey is wearing his only pair of khakis, which ride about half an inch above the tops of his shoes. As we pull up the long driveway, our family spills across the lawn in a long arc of dress pants and sun hats, glasses filled with ice and alcohol, and plates of fancy hors d'oeuvres.

Jeffrey flings himself out of the car and disappears into a group of boy cousins who immediately break into a dead run for the barn. I unbuckle Kaylee and hand her off to my dad, who didn't say another word for the entire drive here. Most of the family hasn't met Kaylee yet, so she's going to draw a whirlwind of attention I can't handle right now.

As a crowd of relatives gathers around Dad and Kaylee, I sneak around the other side of the Escalade and make a beeline for the giant white tent set up on the lawn. My head is pounding from the combination of a slight hangover and the incredibly uncomfortable car ride, and all I want to do is sit somewhere quiet and shady.

The grass is long, and the ground slopes slightly uphill, making me stumble a couple of times. I kick off my sandals and continue on barefoot, walking as fast as I can without making my head spin. I duck into the tent and sigh with relief. There's a whole table spread with food and giant glass dispensers full of water, iced tea, and lemonade. I grab a cup and fill it to the brim, slurping down the water as fast as I can.

I hear a noise behind me and spin around, my breath catching in my throat. My grandpa is sitting off in a corner, a plate of untouched food on the table next to him. And, I realize as I take a step toward him, he's in a wheelchair. When I saw him at Christmas, he was leaning hard on a cane but still walking around just fine on his own. Dad didn't mention anything about a wheelchair.

Grandpa's head is tipped back, his eyes closed, and a soft snore escapes from his open mouth. Dressed in spotless khakis and a short-sleeved checked shirt, he looks the same as he always has. Sharp, intelligent, unyielding. But the wheelchair takes that illusion of power away from him and makes him seem . . . withered.

Just as I'm thinking that, though, his eyes snap open, and I see he's the same old Grandpa Phillip, even if his body is weakening.

"Veda." He beckons me closer and pulls me in for a kiss, bumping my cheek with his chin, and I mentally record *P* in the log. It's going to be harder to keep track of the kisses now that I'm not going in alphabetical order. "Is your father here?"

"Yep." I straighten up and step away. "Want me to wheel you over there?"

Grandpa grunts. "Don't be ridiculous. I'll walk." He grabs his cane, which is leaning up against a nearby table, and hauls himself to his feet.

"But what about the wheelchair?"

"I don't actually ride in that cursed thing." Grandpa gives it a look of pure disgust. "But it's a hell of a lot more comfortable to sit in than those folding chairs."

I follow after him, being sure to walk a half step behind him so he won't notice I'm slowing my pace to avoid passing him. "Nice day," I say, unable to think of anything else to talk about. "I heard something about rain earlier, so we're lucky it held off."

He keeps walking, eyes straight ahead. "About time you all got here," he says. "We've been waiting on you."

Uncle Eddie, my dad's younger brother who lives in Florida, sees Grandpa coming, and hurries over. "I think we're all here, Dad," he says. "Do you want to—"

Grandpa waves a hand dismissively. "Let's get the show on the road," he says.

Uncle Eddie grins at me and pulls me in for a hug. "Hi, Veda," he says. I stiffen, but he smacks a kiss on my cheek anyway. So now I have two *E*s. And still no *J*, or anything in between *K* and *P*. My head spins.

"Hi," I say, smiling through my headache and trying to look happy to be here. "Good to see you."

"You too. You're all grown-up." He pats my arm and nods at

Grandpa, who is striding back toward the tent, leaning hard on his cane. "I better go gather the troops. Can you get your brother and the other boys?"

I nod and hurry over to the barn, keeping my head down and avoiding eye contact with anyone. The barn is dark and cool inside, and I briefly contemplate whether I could sneak off into a corner and just hide out there for the rest of the day. Jeffrey and our cousins are clustered around a game of giant Jenga that stands nearly as tall as I am. I lean against a post and watch as Jeffrey kneels down to wiggle out a piece from the bottom of the stack.

"That's his classic move," I say to Brad, one of the cousins who falls somewhere in the age range between me and Jeffrey. "Take as many out from the bottom as possible and screw the next person over."

"Shut up, Vee," Jeffrey says, his hair falling over his eyes as he tries to extract the piece without toppling the pile. He pulls it out carefully, and we all hold our breaths as the tower sways. For a moment it looks like Jeffrey has gotten away with it, but then the stack of wooden pieces tilts, and one piece slides off the top, sending the rest of the pile tumbling to the floor.

All the boys groan. "Come on. We have to go outside anyway," I say to them. "Grandpa's going to talk."

We file over to the tent, where all the adults have gathered at round tables. Aunt Nancy is helping Grandpa test the microphone. A loud squawk of feedback quiets everyone down, and Grandpa taps the mic. "Is this thing working? Oh, okay. It is."

Everyone laughs, and Aunt Nancy hurries back to her seat, giving Grandpa the floor.

"Well, here we are at another reunion," Grandpa says, looking out over the crowd. "How many of these things have we done, Steve?"

"Five," Steve calls, raising his glass of iced tea in the air, his other arm around his wife, Hannah.

"Five. Goddamn," Grandpa says, and everyone laughs again. "So that's twenty-five years of reunions. Some of us are getting older." He waves his cane. "The kids are growing up. But no matter who comes and goes, we'll always be a family. And I gotta tell you, that means a hell of a lot to me."

He nods, and we applaud politely. "I won't bore you any longer," Grandpa says, "but Barry has an announcement to make."

As Dad stands up and walks toward the front of the tent, my eyes find Jeffrey's. "What is he going to say?" I whisper, and Jeffrey shrugs.

"Hi there." Dad brings the mic too close to his face, and his voice booms through the tent. "Whoa, sorry. Uh, hi there. It's so good to see everyone today. I hope you all have gotten a chance to meet my little girl, Kaylee."

Heads swivel as Dad waves at Kaylee, who is sitting with a group of Dad's cousins I don't know very well. Guilt churns in my stomach—I should have been watching her.

"Unfortunately, my wife, Lila, wasn't feeling well and couldn't make it today. I was looking forward to all of you meeting her, and I was hoping we would make this announcement together."

I catch Jeffrey's eye, confused.

Dad passes the microphone from hand to hand, his excitement palpable even from twenty feet away. "I'm very excited to share that Lila has accepted a new job opportunity in San Francisco, California. We'll be moving out there at the beginning of September. Even though we'll be farther away from our wonderful family, this is a once-in-a-lifetime opportunity for us and for Kaylee, and we couldn't be more thrilled."

I assume there's applause and cheering, congratulations and laughter, but all I hear is the roaring in my ears. Jeffrey's shredding a paper napkin in his hands, his gaze trained on the white tablecloth in front of him. Aunts and uncles surround Dad, patting his shoulders and hugging him. I do something with my face that hopefully approximates a smile, frozen to my chair. Dad pours champagne, and someone shoves a flute into my hand, winking as I try to protest. We toast Lila's new job, and I should be happy because this means I'll barely ever have to see Dad and Lila . . . but my eyes are locked on Kaylee, who has no idea what is going on but beams up at the smiling adults.

The champagne is sour in my mouth. I set the glass down on the table, standing up and hurrying out of the tent. I dash behind the barn and lean over, hands on my knees, willing myself not to throw up.

"Are you okay?" Jeffrey comes around the side of the barn, his hands shoved into the pockets of his khakis.

I nod but don't straighten up. "Just hungover," I say.

He kicks at the ground, sending dust into the air. "I wish they would have told us first."

"Well, we all know how good Dad is at communication. Especially with us."

Jeffrey sinks to the ground and drops his head into his hands. "This is so messed up," he says, and it takes a moment for me to realize he is crying.

"Hey." I drop to my knees next to him, ignoring my white dress, and put an arm around his shoulders. "It'll be okay."

He hesitates for a moment, then pushes me away and stands up, running the back of his hand across his face. His nose is red, his hair matted with sweat. "He already left us once. Why does he have to leave again?" His shoulders heave. "Mom is always busy. And everyone is talking about you, Vee. *Everyone*. I'm going to start middle school soon, and everyone will be telling jokes about you and asking me if you're really a ho."

"Jeffrey." I kneel in front of him. "I'm sorry. I don't know what else you want me to say—"

"Stay away from me." Jeffrey backs up, holding his hands out to stop me from trying to get close to him. "Just leave me alone." He turns and runs, and I stare out over the beautiful Michigan farmland, hating every single thing I see.

CHAPTER 25

I PACE BACK AND FORTH IN THE GRASS BEHIND THE BARN, unable to stop thinking about my little sister flying all the way to the West Coast, gazing out the window of an airplane as Dad and Lila take her about as far away from us as she can get without leaving the country. How often will I see her, every year or two? A year is an eternity when you're that little. She'll grow up without me. She might not even recognize me and Jeffrey the next time we see her.

I have to get out of here.

Mel is at work. I can't call Seth—it would be too weird now that he knows about the Twenty-Six Kisses thing. Killian doesn't need to know any more about how screwed up my life is.

I text Mark.

The last time I rode in Mark's car, my world was falling apart. I never would have thought I could feel worse than I did at that moment.

But—surprise!—life is funny that way. It can always be worse.

"Please don't ask any questions," I say as I climb inside the little blue car I know so well, the one that witnessed so many important moments in my life. "Just drive."

"Okay," Mark says, his hands at ten and two on the steering wheel, and I feel a flash of relief that he's not Killian, that he doesn't need to ask a million questions. He understands that sometimes it's better not to talk.

I send Jeffrey a quick text as we pull onto the road. tell dad i'm leaving. sorry. about everything.

I roll down the window and close my eyes, focusing on the comforting, familiar smell of Mark's car and the feeling of the wind in my hair. I erase everything from my mind and imagine myself running on the beach, not letting anything into my head but the rhythm of my feet over the sand, repetitive, soothing, unending.

I jolt awake when the car stops and forget where I am for a moment. "Mark?"

"Hey," he says, tilting his baseball cap off his forehead. "Sorry. I didn't know where else to go, so . . ." He shrugs.

We're parked on the street in front of the library, our go-to meeting place back before either of us could drive. We'd each have our parents drop us off here under the pretense of doing homework, then hole up in a study carrel together or sit outside on the broad concrete steps if the weather was nice.

"This is fine." I climb out of the car and walk up to the top step, our usual perch. Mark follows slowly behind me and sits down, locking his hands together between his knees. Now that I'm used to Killian's bulk, Mark's legs seem almost comically skinny. He's always been gangly, but he seems even thinner now, maybe going through a late growth spurt. We sit there as clouds gather over the sun, watching people walk by with shopping bags and cameras.

"Thanks for picking me up," I say finally. "I had kind of a rough day. Actually," I say, pushing my hair behind my ears, "I've had kind of a rough summer."

"Yeah." Mark nods. "I know what you mean."

I shoot him a questioning look, but he doesn't elaborate. "Why has it been rough for you?" I ask.

He shrugs and fiddles with his sports watch. The leather bracelet, I notice, is gone. "It's weird at work without you. Everyone kept asking me why we broke up." He rubs the back of his neck. "I don't know. I guess I'm just worried about college, wondering if I made the right choices."

I snort. "Don't talk to me about bad choices." Mark shifts uncomfortably. "I know what Gabriel and Ryan told you," I say, staring straight ahead. "And I know what people are saying. Most of it isn't true."

"I know," Mark says quickly. "Ryan told me later it was all a big joke. But I never believed it anyway. I know you better than that."

I nod. "Thanks."

There are so many things I wanted to say to Mark, things I

rehearsed over and over in my head during the first week after our breakup. I had four or five different conversations all mapped out, each crafted to first make Mark understand what a terrible person he was for breaking up with me and then convince him that all he wanted was for us to get back together. Now I can't remember how a single one of those conversations was supposed to go.

"I'm sorry for breaking up with you," Mark says, reaching over and laying a hand on my knee. "I thought it was going to make me feel less nervous about leaving for college, but it didn't."

"Oh," I say. I wish he had said he was sure he made the right choice, that he was excited to head to college in a few weeks and leave Butterfield—and everyone in it—behind. Has everything I've gone through this summer just been a waste? "It's okay. I mean, it was really hard, but I'm fine now."

"That's good." A dark cloud passes over the sun, throwing the bustling downtown scene rushing past us into shade. I wipe my hands on my shorts and am about to stand up and suggest we get going when Mark clears his throat.

"Can I say something?" he says.

I look at him, puzzled. "Sure."

He bites his lip. "I don't want you to get mad."

I shrug and look away, bracing myself for the day I always knew was coming—the day Mark got a new girlfriend.

"It's just . . . I still miss you," Mark says quietly. "Do you miss me?"

I turn back to stare at him. My mouth opens, but I can't seem to make any words come out. And before I can react to what is happening, Mark slips his arm around my waist and pulls me to him, hesitating for just a moment before bringing his lips to mine.

Kissing Mark is simultaneously the most natural and the most bizarre thing I've ever done. I've kissed him a million times before, and nothing has changed except the fact that there have been several kisses with different guys in between then and now. Nothing, except the most important thing of all—I have changed.

I jerk away and scramble to my feet, scraping my palms on the library steps in my haste.

"Whoa," I say, backing away from him. "What the hell, Mark?"

He doesn't answer and looks down at his feet, cradling his head in his hands. "Sorry," he says, his voice so soft, I can barely hear him. "I shouldn't have done that."

"No," I say, the confusion in his eyes almost more than I can take. "You shouldn't have."

And I walk away.

By the time I get home, it's past noon and my feet are sore from walking more than a mile in sandals. The house is empty and I pound upstairs to my room, pulling my dress over my head as I walk down the hallway, unhooking my bra without bothering to close my bedroom door. I grab a dirty sports bra from the laundry basket, pull a T-shirt and running shorts out of my dresser, and slap a couple Band-Aids over the new blisters on my feet. I barely have enough patience to stretch before I launch off the front porch and start running. I don't care that I'm still hungover, or that my knees are screaming in protest as I hit the ten-mile mark and keep going. I run and run and run until I'm too far out to ever have a hope of running back, and I have to call my mom to pick me up and bail me out of the mess I've gotten myself into.

Grandpa Phillip
Family reunion
1/10

Mark
On the library steps
-10/10

When Dad drops Jeffrey off later that afternoon, he comes inside to talk to Mom about my "embarrassing behavior" at the reunion. I lie on my bed and listen to my own father make it very clear he doesn't particularly like me.

"Veda's nearly an adult," Dad says, his voice tight. "She needs to start acting like one."

Mom murmurs something unintelligible and then says, "Kaylee, sweetheart, would you like some juice?"

Kaylee's squeaky voice tugs at my heart, but I stay where I am. What will happen when Dad and Lila move to California? Will Kaylee even remember me when I come to visit?

"Jeffrey, take your sister outside," Mom instructs. The screen door slams, and I peek out my window to see Jeffrey carrying Kaylee around our small, bare yard, letting her ride on his back like he's a horse.

"Veda told me about your little surprise today," Mom tells Dad, her voice like ice. "I can't believe you sprang it on them like that, Barry. How could you?"

He clears his throat, and I can imagine the way he's leaning away from Mom, getting defensive. "We were going to tell them in the car on the way over," he says. "But then Lila decided not to come, and I just didn't know what to do. I wasn't sure they'd care."

Mom sighs. "Of course they care, Barry."

I roll over and shove my pillow on top of my head, holding it tight to my ears so I can't hear anything else. I stay under the pillow until I feel the vibrations of Jeffrey's feet going to his room, and then the hard slam of his door.

My phone buzzes with a text from Killian. i know you're busy today, but i've been saving this to show you, and i can't wait any longer. I click on the link embedded in the text and am transported to a Pinterest page (why does it not surprise me that Killian uses Pinterest?) dedicated entirely to George Bernard Shaw. I scroll through the pictures and quotes, smiling every time I spot something Killian has clearly created himself in a gesture of fandom to a dead Irish playwright.

One of the quotes in particular catches my eye: "Life isn't about finding yourself. Life is about creating yourself."

I must have read this quote before at some point, but now the words sink in and knock the breath out of me. I send Killian back a quick smiley face and set my phone down. I sit up and look at myself in the mirror across from my bed. I stare at my reflection for a long time, trying to understand what everyone around me sees— the things that might make people believe I'm nothing more than a debate team nerd, or a huge slut.

I walk over to the bulletin board and touch the ragged edge of the Twenty-Six Kisses Challenge, meeting my own gaze in the mirror. It doesn't matter how sad I was at the beginning of the summer, or what people may be saying about me now. All I can do is look ahead and figure out what the hell should happen next.

CHAPTER 26

KILLIAN BOUNDS INTO WORK THE NEXT DAY LIKE A PUPPY, HIS
face breaking into a huge smile as soon as he sees me.

"Vee!" He holds his hand up for a high five and then pulls me to
him, squeezing me tight for a second before letting me go.

I can barely look at him, nearly overcome by the butterflies that
wing their way through my stomach when I remember our kiss at the
dunes.

"Hey," I say, grabbing the clipboard and shoving it into his hands.
"We'd better get going."

His smile dims briefly, but then he salutes me and climbs onto the
bus. "Yes, ma'am."

The hours crawl by. We're past the midsummer rush, so Killian
and I actually have some downtime, which we would normally use to
gab our heads off. But he keeps bringing up new subjects, trying to
get a conversation started, and when I try to respond, the words dry

up before I can spit them out. By the end of the day, he's given up and just blasts the radio.

As soon as everything is put away for the day, Killian grabs his backpack and heads for the Jeep.

"Killian, wait." I hurry after him, catching a glimpse of Mel's concerned face in the office window as I go past. "Hold on."

He tosses his backpack into the backseat and turns to me, his arms folded. "It's okay," he says, not meeting my eyes. "I know what you're going to say, and I'd just rather not hear it."

"What am I going to say?"

He rolls his eyes. "That the other night was a mistake and you were drunk and it shouldn't have happened. 'Sorry, Killian, my bad. I think you're a great guy, but I just want to be friends.'"

I stare down at my beat-up tennis shoes. "That was pretty much the speech I had planned," I admit. "But it's not the truth."

"Oh yeah?" He leans back against the Jeep. "So what is the truth?"

I shrug and take a deep breath. "The truth is, I don't want to be just friends." Killian's head snaps up in surprise, but I keep going, knowing that if I don't say this now I never will. "I like you way too much to be just friends. You're the smartest, most interesting person I know."

Killian runs a hand through his hair. He's not smiling now. "But?"

"But . . ." I drop my arms to my sides. "God, this is hard to say out loud. But I want to finish the twenty-six kisses thing."

He opens his mouth to protest, but I cut him off. "I was a mess at the beginning of the summer, Killian. I could barely function. And it sounds crazy and desperate and I'm not even one hundred percent sure it's the right thing to do, but something about this dumb task of kissing my way through the alphabet has helped me. I just want to finish it, to prove to myself I can do it."

Killian laughs softly and looks down at the ground, scuffing his sneaker in the dirt. "Okay."

"Okay, what?"

"Okay." He shrugs. "If that's what you want to do, then go ahead." He turns away, shutting me out.

"Killian." I reach for him. "Come on. That's all you have to say?"

He shrinks away from my touch as if I have electricity flowing through my fingertips and he's scared of getting shocked. "Don't."

I cross my arms, panic rising inside my chest. This is the worst thing he could do—shutting down, freezing me out. "Please." My voice cracks.

"You were my lifeline, Vee." He stares off into the woods as he talks, his voice low, the words rushed. "You still don't get it. I don't have friends at Trawley. A year ago I was the short, weird guy in drama club. The *only* guy in drama club. This"—he gestures down at his tall, broad body—"all happened in the last six months. I've lived there my whole life, and no matter what I look like or what I go on to do in the future, those guys are only going to see me one way—as someone they can pick on."

I stare at the ground, wondering how anyone could see Killian as less than he is—smart, talented, amazing. "I'm sorry."

"I don't need you to be sorry." He clears his throat. "I need you to be there for me."

"We're friends, Killian. Of course I'm there for you."

"We're more than friends, and you know it!" A couple of people walking by look up at the sound of Killian's voice, and he takes a deep breath, trying to rein himself back in. "I thought this year wouldn't be so bad. School would suck, but then I would get to see you."

I imagine what that would be like—Killian and I each going through our school days, fifteen miles apart, then meeting up afterward for ice cream or just to do our homework together. It sounds great, but it also sounds like another serious relationship. For the first time, I can kind of understand where Mark was coming from when he said he didn't want to go to college still dating his high school girlfriend. "I can't think about that kind of thing right now," I finally say. "I'm just not ready."

"Okay." He turns away and climbs into the Jeep, clearing the tarp away with one angry swipe. He's gone before I even have the chance to apologize.

debate team reunion?!?!?!?

The group text appears on my phone a few days later. I had forgotten about Zane's invitation to the underclassmen debate team get-together but, apparently, he remembered to include me even without the help of his trusty planner. Responses from other team members start blowing up my phone immediately.

yes yes yesyesyesyesyesyes.

this is everything i need in my life right meow.

affirmative.

The plan is to meet tonight at the Dune Buggy, a terribly gimmicky ice-cream parlor near the dunes. I don't really feel like going, but I need to get out of the house. Mel and Seth have been working nonstop on the album, and Killian has called in sick to work the last two days in a row. I'm starting to go crazy stuck inside my own head—even to the point where I asked Jeffrey to show me some tricks on his skateboard just so I would have someone to talk to for half an hour. Besides, I can't pass up the opportunity to restart Twenty-Six Kisses. After all, *Z* is not a terribly common letter. I go for a quick run with Ryan before dinner, barely leaving myself enough time to eat and shower before I have to leave.

Mom even lets me take the car to the Dune Buggy so I don't have to face the humiliation of asking an underclassman for a ride. Most of these kids can't even drive yet, but I recognize Jason Winslow's car, and Becca Fong's. They're already in line, along with a few other people from the team, when I swing open the door and step into the overly bright, sugary-smelling shop.

"Strawberry is clearly the superior flavor," Zane says to Tracy, a small girl with braces that take over her entire face when she smiles. "The frozen strawberry chunks are certain to contain more nutritional value than whatever is in those lumps they call 'cookie dough,' which probably also contain uncooked eggs. If that's not a public health hazard, I don't know what is."

"Hey," I say, poking Zane in the side and making him jump about a foot in the air. "Stop that. It's summer vacation."

"Vee!" He turns to me, but his eyes immediately dart over my shoulder. "Your friend didn't come?"

I think back to weeks ago when Seth and I ran into Zane on the beach. "Seth? No."

"Too bad." Zane turns back toward the counter and peers up at the giant chalkboard that lists all the flavors. "You know, maybe I will go for cookie dough after all."

Tracy gives me a little side hug, giggling when I squeeze her back. "What are you going to get?" she asks.

"One scoop chocolate, one scoop pistachio," I say automatically. Classic and delicious—and the Dune Buggy is the only place you can get pistachio ice cream that doesn't taste like it's overloaded with artificial flavors and chemicals.

The Dune Buggy is filling up with families and tourists. After everyone in our group has an ice cream cone in hand, we file outside and grab one of the few shaded picnic tables. I perch on the edge of a bench, pressed shoulder to shoulder between Zane and Becca, and try not to feel left out as the conversation revolves around who will be elected sophomore class president and which semester everyone is taking driver's ed—everything I was worrying about two years ago. But last week my mom brought home a giant college guide, which I haven't even opened, and soon I'll be filling out applications and FAFSA forms and petitioning for scholarships, getting ready to leave Butterfield behind and start my real life. The thought is terrifying.

I nudge Zane. "One of the guys I'm working with this summer is on the team at Trawley." Guilt flashes through me as Killian's face pops into my mind.

"Oh man." Jason leans in, his ice-cream cone tipping precariously. "You have to get the scoop from him. If we can take Trawley down, we could make regionals."

Callie tosses her hair. "Maybe you could, like, flirt with him? And get some insider information?" She wiggles her eyebrows suggestively and blushes.

My stomach jolts, and I shrug, hoping my face hasn't given anything away. "Worth a shot."

"You have to let us know how it goes." Callie turns to her best friend, Jenn, and whispers in her ear. They both glance at me and break down in giggles.

Zane launches into a monologue about the ethics and conference-mandated guidelines of interacting socially with members of other teams outside the official debate season, which sends the group into a heated theoretical discussion about whether twins who had been separated at birth and reunited only after their debate teams competed against each other should be allowed to live together during the season or if they would have to wait until the championships were over to resume normal sibling relationships.

The sun drops lower and lower over the horizon, and parents start showing up in minivans and SUVs to pick up the kids who can't drive. Soon it's just me, Zane, and Jason left at the long picnic table stained with melted ice cream. I gather up crumpled napkins and the bitten-off ends of waffle cones and toss them into the trash.

"I'm going to take off," Jason finally says. "But we should totally do this again."

"Absolutely," Zane says, and I nod.

"Do you need a ride?" I ask him.

"Nope." He pulls out his phone and sends a quick text. "I think my mom is going to come get me." His phone pings almost immediately, and his face falls. "Actually, I guess I could use a ride. I forgot she has yoga class tonight."

I laugh and punch Zane lightly on the shoulder. "For someone who is so smart, you do forget things an awful lot."

He grins. "Why do you think I carry that planner around all the time? I'm literally useless without it."

"I promise never to give you shit about that again. The whole team would fall apart if you started missing practice." I point across the parking lot. "My car's over there."

Zane stares out the window and hums along to the radio as we drive into downtown Butterfield, and he unselfconsciously drums his hands on his knees.

"I know you live around here somewhere, but you'll have to give me directions," I say as we get close to Mel's neighborhood.

"Take a left here," he says, and I turn onto a wide, tree-lined street that boasts some of Butterfield's oldest and biggest houses. Zane lives in an enormous brick house with blindingly white trim around the windows and a half-circle driveway.

"Thanks for the ride, Vee," he says, his hand on the door handle. "See you around."

My mind goes blank. I have no idea how to make this happen naturally. I assumed Zane wanted to invite me to a mini-reunion because he had a crush on me, but right now he's acting pretty much the way Jeffrey would if I gave him a ride somewhere. "Zane, wait," I blurt.

He turns toward me, the passenger-side door half open. Zane's eyes are a muddy brown-hazel combination, and I notice he has a smudge of chocolate on his shirt.

"Yes?" he says. He looks so young, and doubt flickers through me for just a second before I lean over and press my mouth to his.

I've kissed a fair number of guys by now, and usually when you kiss someone, you get some kind of response. They lean in, they stiffen up, they move away. *Something.* But Zane stays perfectly still, like he's been frozen. I panic, totally unsure of what to do next. Rather than pulling away, I move my lips a little, desperately hoping he'll get the idea and kiss me back so I can save face at least a little bit, but nothing happens. After a few excruciatingly awkward seconds I wrench my face away from his and drop my hands on top of the steering wheel.

"Well, I'll see you around." My voice is high-pitched and breathless, barely squeezing out of my throat as embarrassment closes itself around my vocal cords.

Zane clears his throat, settles back into his seat, and closes the car door.

No, I think. *What are you doing? Get out of the car. Get away from the weird older girl who just assaulted you with her face.*

"Vee . . ." Zane's voice breaks, and he clears his throat again. "I really like you, you know, as a friend . . ."

"Oh God." I drop my forehead onto the steering wheel. I'm about to get a patronizing let's-just-be-friends talk from a fifteen-year-old debate team nerd. "Zane," I say. "That kiss did not mean what you thought it did. Let's just forget this ever happened, and move on with our lives."

He sighs, and I glance over at him. He's leaning back against the seat, eyes closed, face pale. A thought strikes me—has Zane ever kissed anyone before? Did I just steal his first kiss for my own nefarious purposes? I press my forehead harder into the steering wheel. This was such a terrible, terrible idea. *Stupid Twenty-Six Kisses. Stupid alphabet.*

Zane takes a deep breath. "The thing is," he says quietly, "I've never kissed a girl before."

"Shit." I sit back against the seat with a thump. "Zane, I am so, so sorry. I can't even—"

"It's okay," he interrupts. "I've never kissed a girl before because I'm gay."

I stop breathing. How did I not know this? Have I really been so preoccupied with my own life and with Mark that I missed the fact that one of the guys I strategized, practiced, and competed with all of last year is gay?

Zane must see the panic on my face because he says quickly, "No one really knows. Except my parents."

I feel my face turning red. Even worse than stealing someone's first kiss is forcing them to come out before they're ready. "Zane, I am so sorry. I promise I won't tell anyone—"

"Thanks." He glances over at me and smiles. "I'm going to come out at school this year, but until then . . ."

"My lips are sealed." I do the lock-my-lips-and-throw-away-the-key move and immediately feel like an idiot. I am handling this whole thing like a second grader.

"But if I were into girls, I would totally go out with you," he offers, laying a consoling hand on my arm. "I hope we can still be friends."

"Absolutely," I say, trying to fight off the wild laughter that threatens to consume me as Zane pats my arm. "Thanks, Zane."

He gives me a knowing look and slides out of the car, and I pull away practically before the passenger door slams shut, only making it around the corner before I park the car at the curb and lay my head on the steering wheel again. I have no idea what I'm doing.

CHAPTER 27

Zane Haywood
In my car. But turns out he's gay!
5/10 (the kiss was a 2. But he gets 3 extra
points for being honest—and brave)

"SO KILLIAN IS OKAY WITH YOU FINISHING TWENTY-SIX Kisses?" Mel leans over and pulls a weed from between two tomato plants, tossing it onto the pile of greenery slowly turning brown in the sun.

"Ha. No. *Okay* is not the word I would use."

"But you're doing it anyway."

I nod.

"Why?"

I look up at her. "I started it. I feel like I should finish."

She sighs and turns her attention back to the garden, obviously baffled by my commitment to what she sees as just a tool to get over a breakup. But it's become more than that to me.

"And the kiss with Zane was . . . ?"

"Fine." I reach down to retie my shoelace, careful not to meet Mel's gaze. I know Mel wouldn't spread Zane's secret around, but he asked me to keep it to myself, so that's what I'm going to do.

"Hmmm." She eyes me suspiciously. "I feel like you're not telling me something. But you've gotten a lot of kisses. You're doing so good, Vee."

I shrug. "Thirteen if you count both *E*s."

"And you also have *Z*?"

"And *P*."

Mel shakes her head. "It's a lot more complicated when you go out of order. Are you going to be able to finish before school starts?"

"I'm only halfway. What do we have, three weeks left?"

"Ugh." Mel yanks a weed out of the ground and shakes it viciously, sending a shower of dirt onto my legs. "Don't remind me."

I rest my chin on my knee. "I could just keep going through the school year." My voice is light, but my heart sinks at the thought of walking through the halls at school on the prowl for more kisses.

"You know," Mel says, eyeing me. "I never actually thought you would finish."

I raise one eyebrow. "Why?"

"Finishing was never the point," she says, stuffing the pile of weeds she has collected into a brown paper yard bag. "*Starting* was."

"We're hanging out tonight," Killian informs me when I get to work the next morning. He looks younger, somehow, and more vulnerable than usual. "I don't care if you have other plans or feel awkward, or even if you just plain don't want to. We're hanging out anyway."

"Okay." I search his face for a clue to what he's feeling, but he has me completely closed off. "But you're being really bossy." Honestly, I'm so relieved to see Killian back at work and acting like his normal self, I would agree to pretty much anything.

"I think I have to be if I want to get anywhere with you," Killian says, a sharp edge in his voice. "Do you disagree?"

I shrug and pretend to study the clipboard holding today's reservation list, letting a few seconds of silence hang between us.

"You're right." Killian nods seriously and clears his throat. "This is not a very professional conversation we're having. Let's stick to work-related topics, and then we can get into the personal stuff later tonight when we're off the clock."

Killian chatters on for the rest of the day, posing questions and theories about the intricacies of the canoe-manufacturing industry, river ecosystems, and why *The Adventures of Huckleberry Finn* is the best example of the great American novel (only tangentially related to work, but still interesting). He only shuts up during our brief lunch break with Mel—who takes over for him and dominates the conversation with speculation about how awesome our senior year is going to be—and when we're driving up and down the river in the bus, where he cranks up the radio and lets the music do the talking.

After we finish cleaning up at the end of the day, Killian grabs my hand and pulls me to the Jeep. "I don't want you to try to sneak off," he says, opening the passenger-side door and helping me up. Mel appears in the door of the office, hands on her hips, and I mime putting a phone to my ear—*I'll call you later.*

"Where are we going?" I ask, helping Killian clear the tarp off the dashboard. I suck in my breath as the sunlight hits the song lyrics, making them shine.

"This is a strategy session," Killian says. "So we're going to get food, because I can't think when I'm hungry, and then we're going to go to my house and talk through our plan of attack."

"Our plan of attack for . . . ?"

"Finishing out your summer kissing challenge as quickly as possible," Killian says matter-of-factly.

I look at him, stunned, but he just starts the Jeep and pulls out of the parking lot, one hand casually gripping the steering wheel, the other resting on the driver's-side door.

We drive all the way to Trawley without speaking. I read the dashboard lyrics over and over. There's a new one, written in big block letters right in front of my seat: **MAYBE YOU WOULD HAVE BEEN SOMETHING I'D BE GOOD AT**

I wonder if it means that Killian has given up on me.

Killian's house is disappointingly normal, in a neighborhood that looks a lot like mine. He swings open the front door and leads me inside, slipping his shoes off as he goes. To the left is the living room, filled with comfortable-looking furniture, and to the right is a formal dining room that looks like it is probably only used twice a year.

I follow him past a wall of family photos, and down the hallway to a closed door. Then he turns around, hand on the doorknob, and looks at me very seriously. "Are you ready for this?"

I glance around, wondering if I've missed some giant clue about what is about to happen. But the hallway is totally normal—gray carpet, off-white walls. "Sure."

I follow Killian into a large room that, at first glance, looks like a conference room you might find in an office. There's a table with four chairs gathered around it, a whiteboard taking up half of one wall, and shelves packed with hundreds of books. Then I spot the unmade bed in the corner and realize this is Killian's room.

"Have a seat," he says, ushering me over to the table and pulling out a chair. "I should have asked while we were downstairs. Are you thirsty? Can I get you some water?"

I shake my head, my eyes roaming around the room, taking it all in. Now that I'm taking a closer look, the room seems slightly less corporate. Band posters cover the walls, and there's a mountain of dirty laundry spilling out of the closet. In fact, overall the room is pretty messy, just like you'd expect for a teenage boy. But the corner housing the table and whiteboard is spotless, everything in its place.

"This is not what I was expecting your room to look like," I say. "Well, I expected the posters. But not the office furniture." I point at the whiteboard. "Was Office Depot having a clearance sale or something?"

"Our school library kicks everybody out at six o'clock," Killian

says. "The public library, which is barely bigger than this room anyway, closes at eight. Sometimes when we're preparing for a competition, we're up until midnight. This keeps us focused a lot better than
trying to work while sitting on the couch in someone's living room
with the TV blaring in the background." He pulls out a yellow notepad and sits down across me. "So," he says. "Let's strategize."

"Um," I say, tapping my fingers nervously on the table. "Let me just
make sure I understand what's happening here. You want to strategize
with me about how I can finish my summer kissing challenge?"

He nods and twirls a pen in his fingers.

"The summer kissing challenge you're pissed off that I'm doing?"

He nods again.

"Why?"

Killian sits back in his chair and crosses his legs. He thinks for a
moment and then takes a deep, theatrical breath. "Because I like you,
Vee. You're smart and funny and exactly the type of girl I've been hoping to meet but never thought I actually would. Because you let me
talk to you about things that don't matter, and you understand it's not
what we're talking about that's important, but *how* we're talking about
it, and *why*. Because you can be sweaty and covered in river mud, and
I still think you're the most beautiful girl I've ever seen."

Wow. I sit there, stunned into silence. He clearly prepared a speech,
ran through it in front of the bathroom mirror, rehearsed the pauses
and the emphasis. As if he thought I wouldn't see right through all
that. This is the first time Killian hasn't been totally real with me. He's

putting on a show, trying to make me go along with *his* plan. But he's not in charge here. I am.

I roll my eyes. "Right. And so you want to help me figure out how to kiss other guys. That makes total sense. Thanks for clearing it up for me, Killian." I cross my arms over my chest. "You think you can compliment me and use emphasis through repetition to make what you're saying sound more powerful than it actually is, and I'll just fall over and go along with it?" I shake my head. "News flash: I won't."

We stare at each other for a few moments, tension strung like a wire between us. I can practically see his brain whirring behind his eyes, trying to come up with a counterargument that will convince me everything he just said wasn't a total load of bullshit.

Finally he sighs. "Okay. I'm sorry." He tosses the notepad onto the floor, and his pen bounces across the carpet. "No more rhetoric crap." He pauses, and I nod for him to continue. "Look, I do like you, Vee. That should be obvious."

He looks at me questioningly, and after a moment I nod, a sharp jerk of my head.

"Everything I said a minute ago was true. Honestly, I just thought if you could hurry up and finish this Twenty-Six Kisses thing, then there might be a chance of us getting together." He drops his head and stares down at his lap.

I sit there, stunned. "You know, the point of Twenty-Six Kisses was to get over a guy," I say. "Not to find a new one."

"I know." Killian runs his hand over the stubble on his chin, his eyes lowered.

"I feel like you just put on a show. You show up at work and act like nothing has happened, take me up to your house for the first time, and blindside me with a plan that's supposedly about me but is really all about you." My knuckles are white, my fists clenched. I don't realize how angry I am until the words come flying out. For the first time ever, I feel like Killian hasn't been honest with me. "You want to get together, so I'm supposed to hurry up and get over myself so we can make it happen."

"You're right," he says, and the pain in his voice almost breaks me. "You're totally right."

Killian looks up at me, ready to take any more abuse I throw at him. I'd love to keep going—I want to hurt Killian. I'm dying to throw all my lingering frustration about Mark and the stupid Twenty-Six Kisses game and Seth and Mel and my screwed-up family right in his face. But I don't. Instead I stand up and walk to the door, fighting with all my might not to cry. "Could you just take me home now, please?"

CHAPTER 28

"JEFFREY, COME OUT OF THERE. LET'S JUST TALK ABOUT IT a little bit." My mom is sitting cross-legged on the floor in front of Jeffrey's bedroom door. Dad called yesterday to give Mom some details about the moving date, and since then Jeffrey hasn't come out of his room—not even for food or to go to the bathroom.

I stick my head out of my room. *Anything?* I mouth.

Mom shrugs and heaves herself off the floor. "I'm not going anywhere!" she calls, tapping lightly on the door. "I'll just be in Vee's room. I'd still love it if you came out, sweetie."

She comes in and sits down on my bed, lifting Fat Snacks and settling him in her lap. I shut the door and flop down next to her, the beginning of a headache starting to pound at my temples. Killian and I didn't say a word to each other on the half-hour drive back from Trawley, and the tension between us was nearly unbearable.

"Do you have any idea what he's so upset about? I mean, besides the obvious." Mom has dark bags under her eyes. "I know the move is a big shock, but . . ."

I shrug and close my eyes. "There was this girl he was talking to at Lila's party last month who lives next door to Dad and Lila. I think maybe he liked her, and that's why he wanted to go over there all the time."

Mom lets out a long breath. "Ah. And now he doesn't want to go to your dad's because he's upset with them for springing the move on you guys, but that means he can't see his girlfriend."

It's so bizarre to think of my stinky little brother having a girlfriend. "I guess he's growing up, Mom."

"I think you're right." She smiles sadly. "I've known that for a while now, but I've been trying to deny it."

I hold my hand out to Fat Snacks, who sniffs it suspiciously before grudgingly licking my finger. "Well, it looks like neither of your kids handle heartbreak well."

Mom tilts her head and looks at me. "I think you're doing great, Vee. You had a rough couple of weeks at the beginning, but it seems like this summer has been good for you."

"Yeah, well." I lean back and close my eyes. No need for her to know about the guys standing around a bonfire at Mark's house comparing their "experiences" with me or the half dozen creepy Facebook messages I've gotten from people I barely know at school asking if I want to "hang out" (i.e. "hook up"). Or the Killian disaster. I clench my fists, fingernails digging into my palms. "I'm hanging in there."

"That's good. I'm proud of you." She leans into me, and we both freeze as Jeffrey's door opens with a distinctive creak. He shuffles across the hall to the bathroom and slams the door.

"I guess he had to come out sometime," I say.

Mom smiles. "Thank God. I won't bug him, but I think I might run to the store and get stuff to make spaghetti." If there's one food my brother could eat every day and not get sick of, it's pasta. "Thanks for telling me about the girl, Vee."

"Sure." I ignore the twinge of guilt in my stomach. Have I just broken the brother-sister secrecy code? Jeffrey hasn't told Mom about my extracurricular boy activities. *This is different*, I tell myself. *She was really worried.*

"Are you okay?" Mom's eyes are big and concerned. "You seem a little stressed. I know this has all been hard on you."

I wave her away. "I'm fine, Mom. Just tired."

"Hey, why don't you see if Mel and Seth want to come over for dinner too?" she asks. "I feel like I've barely seen them all summer."

I'm stressed out enough as it is—I don't want to have to watch Mel and Seth flirt with each other over dinner, but Mom will definitely interrogate me if I turn down her offer to have my friends over. "Sure." I grab my phone and text Mel and Seth while Mom goes to grab her purse.

definitely, Seth responds. your mom's spaghetti is the best.

i'm at seth's right now, Mel texts. we'll be over in a bit.

I go into Jeffrey's bedroom, which looks out over the front of the

house, and see Mel's car parked across the street. *Don't be jealous.*
They're just working on the album.

The toilet flushes, and Jeffrey comes back in. "What are you
doing?" he says, his face red and his eyes glassy. "Get out!"

"Sorry," I say, picking my way back over the minefield of debris to
get to the door. "I was just looking out the window."

"Well, Mel has been over there practically all afternoon, if that's
what you're wondering about," Jeffrey says, flinging himself onto his
bed, his feet hanging off the side. "Get over it, Vee."

I put my hands on my hips and stare down at him, stifling the
questions that are bubbling up. *Have you seen anything? What are they
doing over there?* I swallow hard. "Look, Jeffrey, if you want me to
drive you somewhere so you can meet up with that girl who lives by
Dad, you can just ask me."

His body tenses, but he doesn't respond.

"Do you want to text her?" I nudge his foot, and he jerks away. "I
saw something online about a battle of the bands tonight in the park.
Maybe she wants to go?"

"No." His voice is muffled. "Go away. I don't want to talk to you."

"I know." I roll the words around in my mouth before saying them,
trying to figure out what I can do to make Jeffrey hate me a little less.
"Look, I'm sorry about what Mark's brothers told you, but it's not my
fault some guys are idiots and spread rumors. I haven't done anything
wrong, Jeffrey." At least, I haven't done anything that qualifies me as a
slut—and even if I had, it's not like it would be anyone's business but

my own. I've done plenty of things wrong this summer, but I hope I'll get a chance to fix them all.

I cross my arms. "So what do you say? Do you want to see if Chaundre wants to go to the battle of the bands?"

Jeffrey flips over and sits up, his shaggy hair matted and dull. "She can't just go and hang out somewhere. Her parents are superstrict, and they have to know exactly where she is and who she's with all the time."

I blink. "Wow. That sucks."

"Yeah." Jeffrey rubs his eyes. "We're only allowed to hang out at her house when her parents are home. She can't even come over to Dad and Lila's. The only reason she was there the night of the party was because her parents were too."

"So . . ." I cringe as the question forms in my mind, not sure I want to know. "When you hang out, what do you . . . do?"

Jeffrey shrugs and looks away, practically squirming under my gaze. "I don't know. Talk. Watch TV. She likes to skateboard too."

I bite my lip, trying not to smile. "Seriously, though, if you can think of a way to see her and need a ride, let me know."

Jeffrey doesn't look at me or respond, but his shoulders relax a little. He knows where I am if he needs me.

"So when do you guys think you'll be done with the album?" I ask, passing the bowl of garlic bread to Seth. With my own thoughts jumbled up inside my head and Jeffrey slumped in his seat, looking like he wants to die, I figure music is the safest topic of conversation tonight.

Mel shrugs and sprinkles some oregano over her spaghetti. "We're getting there," she says.

"You two are so talented," Mom says, beaming at them. "I can hardly believe it."

Seth drops his eyes to his plate, trying to hide his smile. "Thanks, Mrs. Bentley."

"So what are you three up to tonight?" Mom asks. "There're only a few weeks left until school starts. You should take advantage of them."

Mel groans. "Don't remind me."

I nod. "Seriously." For the first time in my life, I'm not looking forward to going back to school. I'm dreading the comments that will inevitably get tossed around in the hallways, the knowing looks, the guys leaning in just a bit too close, trying to figure out if it's really true that Vee Bentley has crossed over to the dark side of slutdom. And, of course, Killian won't be there. He'll be enduring his own private hell fifteen miles away in Trawley.

"Vee was telling me about a free concert tonight," Jeffrey says, winding spaghetti around his fork. "Maybe you guys should go to that."

"Good idea," Mel says. "I'd heard about that too. Seth? Battle of the bands?"

He shrugs noncommittally. "I guess."

"Do you want to go too, Jeffrey?" Mom asks, giving me a look. "I'm sure your sister and her friends would be happy to take you."

"Nah. I think I'll just hang out here with you."

Mom's face lights up. "Well, I'm not going to try to talk you out of that," she says.

We finish dinner and help clean up until Jeffrey and Seth get into a water fight over the kitchen sink, and Mom banishes us.

"Let's go down to the park," Mel says. "We can see what's going on and check out the concert when it starts."

Seth gazes out the window at his house. "Maybe we should just work on the songs some more?" he asks. "I'm up for another couple of hours."

"No, let's go." I'm not really in the mood to sit in Seth's basement and be the third wheel on their musical bicycle tonight.

Seth shoots me a wounded look, and I shrug. "Come on," I say, grabbing my bag from the living room. "Last one to the Buick has to buy sno-cones at the park."

It seems like the entire teenage population of Butterfield is out tonight, trying to soak up as much summer as possible before it's gone for good. Groups of people are setting out blankets and coolers on the lawn surrounding the bandstand, settling in for a long, glorious summer evening.

"Oh, look—there's Brianna and Landon," Mel says, waving frantically at them. "Let's go crash their blanket."

"Hi, guys!" Brianna leaps up and hugs us. "Oh my God, can you believe the summer is almost over?"

Mel shakes her head. "I don't want to think about it. It's too depressing."

They chatter away, and Seth helps Landon unpack what looks like an entire Thanksgiving dinner's worth of food from their cooler. I sit on the edge of the blanket, watching people wander past. It's getting dark earlier and earlier each day, and the sun races toward the horizon.

My phone vibrates. I pull it out and squint at the screen, my breath catching in my throat when I see it's a text from Killian. i'm sorry.

I toss it to the ground, too angry to respond.

"Here, Vee." Mel shoves a bottle of Diet Coke into my hand. "Brianna brought these."

"Thanks." I smile at Brianna and twist off the cap, taking a sip and choking as the rum-filled liquid burns my throat. "Jeez," I say with a gasp, giving Mel a dirty look. "You could have warned me."

"Surprise!" Mel taps her Diet Coke bottle against mine. "To the last summer of our lives."

I roll my eyes and turn to Brianna. "Could you please tell Mel that graduating high school does not equal death?"

She laughs. "I think we'll all still be alive after graduation."

Mel throws herself down next to me. "Yeah, but next summer we'll be getting ready to go to college, so we'll have a million things to do. Then after that, who knows? Some people stay at school all year to work or go on Habitat for Humanity. We might never all be back here at the same time again."

"Stop it," I say. "Seriously, Mel. This is so depressing."

Mel spots someone over my shoulder and gasps. "Oh my God. Vee, it's Noel Callenbaugh."

"So?" I turn around to look.

"So?" She leans in and whispers, "You still need an N, don't you?"

I groan. "Not tonight, Mel. I'm not in the mood."

She pokes me in the side, nearly making me spill my Diet Coke. "Yes, tonight! This is the perfect opportunity. Look at all these people."

"Stop it." I bat her hand away as the first band finishes tuning. "It's about to start."

Mel leaps to her feet and grabs my wrist, tugging me along. "Let's go down there and dance."

I glance at my phone, lying still and silent beside me on the blanket. I can imagine Killian pacing around his bedroom/office, trying to distract himself with books or the Internet for a few minutes before checking his phone again.

"Come *on*, Vee." Mel crosses her arms and lets her lower lip droop in a toddlerlike pout.

"We'll get her up." Brianna and Landon grab my arms and pull, managing to hoist me off the blanket.

"You guys!" I try to twist away, grabbing my phone and shoving it into my pocket. "I don't feel like it."

"Vee." Mel puts her hands on either side of my face and leans in until she's only an inch or two away. "Let's just dance."

And dance we do, in a big screaming mass in front of the stage. Each band that plays is better than the last, and even Seth is down in the crowd with us, a dark shadow leaping and jumping in the flashing strobe lights. Mel keeps pressing more Diet Cokes into my hand, and I drink them, more because I'm thirsty than for any other reason. But the alcohol feels good. I'm buzzing, dancing with Mel and Seth and then twisting off into the crowd to do my own thing, hands up, head back, loving life.

I wiggle my way over to Noel Callenbaugh and lock my eyes on his. I don't know if he has heard the rumors about me, and I don't particularly care. He dances with me, close but not too close, giving me my space when I want it.

What would Killian say if he could see me now?

"Kiss me!" I yell over the noise of the band and the crowd.

"What?" Noel holds a hand up to his head and leans closer. "I can't hear you!"

"I said, kiss me!"

He jerks back in surprise. "Really?"

I smile and pull him closer. "Yes!"

We're still moving to the beat, getting jostled by the crowd around us, and our teeth bump as Noel brings his face to mine.

"Sorry!" he says, shrugging.

I give him a quick hug and turn away. "Good enough!"

There are so many people in the crowd, it takes me a few minutes to find Mel and Seth again. "I kissed Noel," I whisper in her ear.

"No way!" She jumps up and down. "You're amazing."

"I'm going to go sit down," I say, fanning myself. "It's way too hot."

"I'll come with you." Seth's black T-shirt is sticking to his thin chest. "Come on." He grabs my hand and pulls me to the edge of the crowd. I suck in lungfuls of clean, cool air as we weave our way through the coolers and folding chairs scattered across the lawn and back to Brianna and Landon's blanket.

"I can't believe you danced to 'Don't Stop Believin','" I say, nudging his foot as we collapse onto the ground. "What did you call that song once? An unbearable cliché?"

Seth folds his arms behind his head and smiles at the sky. "I guess it didn't bother me as much tonight."

Kyle and Oliver, Mark's brothers, wander past, looking at something on one of their phones. "Hey, Oliver!" I call.

"Yeah?" Oliver says. They walk over.

"Is Mark here?" The twins glance at each other, and I cringe, realizing how it must sound—like I'm still desperate to make up with Mark. Nothing could be further from the truth.

"Yeah, I think he's here somewhere," Kyle says. "He might have left already, though."

"Cool." I grab Oliver's hand, which is dangling right at the level of my face, and give it an exaggerated smooch. "Thanks."

"Uh." Oliver stares at his hand like it has just turned into a spider. "No problem."

Seth rolls over and stares at me as the twins walk away. "What the hell was that?"

"Nothing." I rifle through the cooler, looking for anything to drink that isn't spiked with alcohol. Apparently, Landon didn't think to pack any water bottles.

"You just slobbered all over your ex-boyfriend's little brother's hand for no reason?"

I sigh and pull out my phone, avoiding Seth's eyes. "I'm just a little buzzed, Seth. God. Lay off."

"I hate drunk people," Seth mutters, dropping his arm over his face. The crowd by the stage lets out a cheer as the band launches into a new song. "Can we go home now?"

I watch the crowd roll by, people laughing, talking, fighting over everyday problems. Dexter and Ryan walk by, and I wave, grinning at Ryan as Dexter awkwardly looks away. I close my eyes, and the blanket seems to tilt and rock, like we're floating out on the lake. "Whoa," I say, putting my hands out to steady myself and opening my eyes. "Seth? I don't feel so good."

"Mmmm," he mumbles from underneath his arm.

"Are you asleep?"

No answer. I sigh and struggle to my feet, suddenly having to pee. Maybe if I can go to the bathroom, find a drinking fountain, and walk around a little bit, the world will stop trying to fall out from underneath me.

I stagger to the small building housing the park's public restrooms and duck inside, holding my breath against the smell of urine and bleach. One of the light bulbs in the ladies' room is burned out, and I can barely see well enough to get some toilet paper off the roll. There are spiderwebs in every corner, and the flush of the toilet echoes off the cinder-block walls.

I wash my hands quickly in freezing-cold water and hurry out of the bathroom, feeling sick from the smell.

"Hey." A voice floats out of the shadows, and I jump.

"Hey?" I squint and see the outline of a skinny guy slouching against the wall.

"Do you have a light?" He steps forward.

"Uh, no. Sorry, I don't smoke." I turn away, but the ground spins underneath me, and I stumble.

"Whoa. Are you okay?" The guy has his arms underneath my shoulders, supporting me as I sway. I'm disoriented and can't quite figure out which way I need to walk to get back to Mel and our friends.

"Thank you." I lean into him and let him help me down to a sitting position. "Oh my God. I did not mean to get so drunk."

"Tell me about it." He's beside me on the ground, a warm, comforting weight against my side. "Let's just sit here for a minute. I'll stay with you until you're feeling better and can find your friends."

I let my body relax. "Honestly, I wasn't even going to come out tonight. My friends dragged me."

He laughs. "That's always the way the craziest nights start out. I'm the drummer for Chronic Dehydration. We just finished our set."

"Oh man, you guys were amazing." I lean into him. "Thank you again for taking care of me. I think I'll be okay soon."

"No problem." He puts his arm around me and rocks lightly back and forth in time to the song the band is playing.

I close my eyes and let my head loll onto his shoulder. "This is nice."

"Mmmhmm." It takes me a moment to realize he's nuzzling my neck, his arm dropping from my shoulders to circle my waist. I can smell his tobacco breath, feel the edge of the cigarette box in his pocket against my thigh. His lips are on my jawbone, light and soft.

"Wait," I mumble, my body so heavy, I couldn't move even if I wanted to. "What's your name?"

He brushes the back of his hand against my arm, and I shiver. "It's Thomas."

I lift my head and look at him, his eyes deep and dark. I can't even tell what color they are. My phone vibrates in my pocket. "Thomas," I whisper, leaning closer, my lips nearly brushing his. "That's perfect."

I don't know how long I'm with Thomas, but by the time I break away and stumble back toward the concert, my mouth tastes like old cigarettes.

It's eleven fifteen, more than forty-five minutes since I left to go to the bathroom. I have seven texts, all from Mel.

10:32 P.M. hey, where'd you go?

10:45 P.M. vee?

10:50 P.M. i'm back by landon's blanket. come find me.

10:55 P.M. are you mad? can you at least let me know you're okay?

11:01 P.M. vee??!?! pls call me.

11:04 P.M. i'm really starting to freak out.

11:10 P.M. if i don't hear from you by midnight, i'm calling the cops.

I try to run and text at the same time, but my hands are so unsteady, I almost drop my phone.

I see Mel standing up and scanning the crowd, Brianna next to her.

"Mel!" I call. "Mel!"

She turns and runs toward me, and we crash into each other so hard, I can't breathe for a moment.

"Oh my god, where were you?"

"Sorry." I squeeze her. "I was just over there." I gesture to the bathrooms, already regretting Thomas.

"Stay here," Mel says, pulling away. "Stay right here and don't move." She jogs back over to Brianna and Landon, hugs them quickly, and comes right back to me. "I'm texting Seth to meet us at the car. He's out looking for you."

I'm 100 percent fine, but the way everyone is freaking out and the thought of Seth running around looking for me is too much. I take a deep, shuddery breath and run the back of my hand across my face.

"Vee, are you okay?" Mel grabs my arms.

I nod, suddenly desperate for a breath mint or a stick of gum, anything to get the stale taste of tobacco out of my mouth. At that moment everything hits me at once—the fact that I just made out with a perfect stranger yet am somehow upset about being labeled a slut, the idea of Dad and Kaylee moving halfway across the country, the way I yelled at Killian when all he was trying to do was show me how much he cares. I cling to Mel, my wet face against her shoulder, and she holds me as I cry. Brianna rubs my back soothingly, and Landon stands nearby, hands in his pockets, his eyes trained on the ground.

"Come on," Mel says after a few minutes, slipping her arm around my waist and propelling me forward. "Let's go."

We sit in the dark car until Seth runs up and dives into the backseat. He asks me all the same questions Mel did, grabbing my shoulders and staring at my tear-stained face. I have to tell him I'm okay a dozen times before he believes me. Mel drives us back to my house, which is dark and silent, my mom and Jeffrey in bed. Seth hugs us both before jogging across the street to his house. I see the thin outline of his body silhouetted against his front porch light until Mel and I are safely inside.

Mel walks me upstairs and sits on the closed toilet seat while I take a scalding-hot shower, scrubbing at every inch of my skin. For once I'm glad the mirror fogs over every time someone takes a shower because it means I don't have to face myself once I get out. Then I brush my teeth and rinse with mouthwash until Mel makes me stop.

"Thank you," I whisper as I finally get into bed and Mel pulls the sheet up under my chin, tucking me in tightly. "I don't know what I'm doing, Mel."

"Shhh," she whispers. "It's okay." She sits with me for a while, until the glowing red numbers on the clock next to my bed read: 2:00.

"You should go," I mumble. "Your mom is going to flip out. I'll be all right."

"Okay," Mel says. "I'll call you tomorrow."

I must fall asleep because I don't remember feeling the bed shift as she got up, or the soft click of my bedroom door shutting. I don't dream, and I don't move until nearly ten the next morning when I wake up in a pool of sunlight, my arms pinned to my sides under the tight sheet Mel folded around me.

The night comes rushing back in a flood of regret, and I jump out of bed and hang my head over my wastebasket, dry heaving at the memory of the smell of cigarette smoke.

"You're okay," I whisper to myself, staring down at wads of mascara-stained tissue and the wrapper from a pack of fruit snacks I ate the day before. "You're okay."

CHAPTER 29

Noel Callenbaugh
At Battle of the Bands
3/10

Oliver (Mark's brother)
Also at Battle of the Banks (on the hand)
1/10

Thomas
Again, the fateful night at Battle of the
Bands
-10/10

A FEW DAYS LATER I DRIVE JEFFREY OVER TO DAD AND LILA'S
house. I bought a card for them and made Jeffrey write *Congratulations!* on the inside. Whatever this new job is that Lila's taking, wher-

ever they need to move—it's an opportunity for our family, and we need to be happy for them. Even if the thought of being so far from Kaylee is like a stab in the heart.

"Jeffrey! Veda!" Lila answers the door, and Kaylee comes running when she hears our names, throwing her arms around my knees. "Come in."

Dad's watching TV in the living room, his feet up on the couch. He mutes the TV when we walk in and stands up, hands on his hips. "What's going on?" he asks, his gaze shifting from me to Jeffrey and back again. Lila sidles up next to him and slips an arm around his waist.

I nudge Jeffrey, and he holds out the envelope. "We just wanted to say congratulations on your new job," he says, and I'm proud of how strong his voice sounds. "We're really excited for you. And we'll miss you."

Lila gives a little gasp and turns her face into Dad's chest. He rubs her back in slow circles.

"Thank you so much," Lila says, turning back to us and taking the envelope from Dad's hand, carefully ripping it open. "This really means a lot."

Kaylee tugs on my hand, and I lift her into my arms. "We'll get to go on a plane to visit you sometimes," I tell her. "It'll be an adventure."

She looks at me seriously, her blue eyes wide. "Plane," she says.

Lila wipes her eyes and smiles. "Hey, are you guys hungry? I just made brownies."

Jeffrey pushes his bangs out of his eyes. "Yeah, definitely." He follows Lila back to the kitchen, and Kaylee wiggles out of my arms and races after them.

Dad hasn't moved, his face impassive.

"I'm sorry for running off at the reunion," I say, lowering my voice and bracing myself for his reaction. "I've had a rough summer."

Dad nods. "I think we all have." He clears his throat and awkwardly swings his arms back and forth. "Look, Vee, we should have told you and Jeffrey about the move first. That was a mistake on my part."

"It's okay."

"It's been a stressful decision. Lila is"—he lets out a long breath—"nervous about it."

I glance toward the kitchen. "Is she okay?"

Dad looks at me. "She has some problems, Veda. I'm sure you've noticed a thing or two going on with her."

I nod.

"But I love her." Dad's voice cracks. "She's getting counseling. And this is a big step for her career."

"I know." I play with the hem of my shorts. "But I'm still sad you're leaving. And so is Jeffrey."

"I honestly didn't think you'd care."

I look up at him. "How could we not care? Our baby sister and our . . . our dad are moving halfway across the country."

The look that crosses Dad's face is half joy, half pain. "Well, I'm going to miss you guys," he says. "You know, I didn't ever want to leave you. Everything that happened wasn't because you weren't good enough." He holds his arms out wide. "God knows, Lila and I aren't perfect either. We're just a better fit than your mom and I ever were."

I nod and look down at the floor, not sure where to go from here.

"I could have tried harder," Dad says finally. "To try to work things out with your mom. And to not be so hard on you." His voice is gruff. "I just wanted to say I'm sorry about that."

"It's okay, Dad."

I think the last time I hugged my dad was at his and Lila's wedding, but when he puts his arms around me, it's like I'm a little kid again—like no time has passed at all.

Jeffrey chatters nonstop on the way home about how he and Chaundre might take Kaylee to the beach one last time before summer is over, if Chaundre can get permission from her parents, and speculates about whether he'll be able to go to San Francisco for Christmas break this year. I don't tell him about my conversation with Dad—that's one they should have together too. Jeffrey needs a dad and even if ours isn't perfect, he's all we've got.

As we're driving down the road back to town, we pass a tall guy running along the side of the road, his strides long and even. I honk the horn as we roll past, and raise my hand to wave. Ryan squints and smiles when he sees it's me. Without thinking, I press my palm to my mouth and blow him a kiss. He blows one back.

I can check R *off the list,* I realize with a jolt. I don't even know how many letters I have left, but the end of the summer is right around the corner.

At home I park the car in the driveway and open the garage door for Jeffrey to go inside. "I'm going over to Seth's for a minute," I say. After talking things out with my dad, I feel like anything is possible. I need to talk to Seth about Mel, tell him what's really going on. Seth and Mel are my best friends. If I don't do everything I can to make them happy, what kind of person does that make me?

Seth opens the door just a few seconds after I ring the bell, as if he were expecting someone.

"Hey," I say.

"Hey." He looks surprised to see me but steps outside and pulls the door shut behind him. "Recovered from the other night?"

"Yeah," I say, pushing a strand of hair out my face. "But I think I'm done drinking for a while. I just wanted to talk to you for a minute."

Seth nods and sinks on the doorstep, folding his black denim-clad legs underneath him. I sit down on his right side, my usual spot.

It has been a long time since Seth and I hung out on his doorstep. We used to sit here for hours, not doing anything in particular. We'd watch the occasional car go past, peel the bark off sticks that were lying nearby, scratch little drawings into the concrete with the chalky white rocks that line his mom's flower beds. I can't remember when we stopped doing this. What did we talk about the last time we sat on this step together, and what happened afterward that turned it into the last time?

I take a deep breath, willing my hands not to start shaking. I don't know why I'm so nervous. Maybe because once Seth knows what I'm about to tell him, everything is going to change. "When we were at the beach that day . . . I should have told you Mel likes you."

"What?" Seth looks at me, his green eyes expressionless.

I clasp my hands together. "She doesn't just think of you as a friend anymore, Seth. She hasn't for a while."

He shakes his head slowly. "How do you know? Did she tell you?"

"Not exactly." I shrug. "You're both my best friends. I see the way you look at each other, and also the way you're somehow both completely oblivious to what the other one is thinking. She didn't have to tell me. Just like you didn't have to tell me how you felt about her."

Seth closes his eyes and runs a hand over his face. "Vee . . . I don't know how I feel about her."

"What?" I study him, every detail of his face completely familiar and totally new to me at the same time. "Why don't you know?"

"I thought I did," Seth says. "I thought maybe this year when we went back to school I might finally get up the courage to tell her." He looks embarrassed. "And then when Mel told me about your Twenty-Six Kisses thing, everything from back then between you and me just came rushing back. I thought I was over you. You'd been with Mark for so long, and it didn't even bother me anymore. But thinking of you with someone new did." He swallows hard. "It still does."

"Seth . . ."

Frustrated, he slaps his hands against the concrete, wincing at the pain. "Everything in my life seems to come back to you, Vee. Just tell me—why would you go out and decide to kiss every guy in Butterfield, but not me? How did you think that would make me feel?"

I twist my fingers together and stare out at the street. I'm trembling. "I thought you wanted to be with Mel," I say. "Seth, I didn't think you had feelings for me anymore." I lock my gaze on him, willing him to believe me.

He drops his head into his hands, his fingers tangling in his long hair. "So, how many guys has it been now?"

My mouth goes dry. This was not how this conversation was supposed to go. I was supposed to tell Seth about Mel, he would be happy, and I would wish him all the best and get back to the drama of my own life. "I don't know," I say. I remember all the times Seth reached for my hand and I pulled away, how we never really talked about where things stood between us. I never even tried to give him any kind of explanation about why I didn't like him the same way he liked me.

Seth shakes his head and rubs his temples. "So, what now?"

The whole history of our friendship hangs between us, and I realize—*really* realize for the first time—how shitty it was for me to just ignore the fact that Seth liked me and I didn't like him the same way. How I've probably let him agonize over me for much longer than he would have if we had just talked about it and gotten everything out in the open.

"Seth."

"What?"

"I'm still missing *S*."

His body goes completely still, and his eyes find mine. He grabs my wrist and stares at my face for a long moment, then pulls me to him and cradles my face in his hands. It has been so long since I looked at Seth—really looked at him, the way I used to when my parents were divorcing and he was the only person in the world who I felt understood anything about me. It's amazing how, no matter how old you get, your eyes don't change. The Seth who was in love with me but didn't know what to do about it is staring at me, five years after I pushed him away.

This is a kiss that has been waiting to happen for a very, very long time. And it feels absolutely, completely wrong. I freeze, my mind racing, not sure how to react without hurting Seth's feelings (again) and ruining things between us (again). But I'm yanked back to reality by the sound of a car motor in the street—a very distinctive motor. The Buick.

Mel pulls into Seth's driveway, her face a deceptive mask of calm as she climbs out of the car. She walks over to us, shaking her head, and my heart drops. There's no way to explain this away, no way to convince Mel it was anything less than a betrayal.

"You didn't have to kiss him on the lips," she says to me, her eyes dark. "The cheek, the hand. The elbow, for God's sake. You know any of those would have gotten you your *S*. Or," she goes on, "you could have just found someone else, someone named Sean or Sam, someone who your best friend doesn't—" She stops short as her voice breaks.

Seth stands up. "Mel."

She presses her lips together and shakes her head, refusing to even look at him.

"Seriously, Mel—" I start.

"Don't." She holds up her hand to stop me. "Just don't. You had Mark. You *have* Killian, even though you don't seem to want him. Why do you need Seth, too?" Her voice breaks.

"It didn't mean anything," Seth says, shoving his hands into his pockets. "I swear to God, Mel."

"He's right," I say. "It really, really didn't. I swear."

"I don't care," she says, turning and walking back to the car. "It still makes you a shitty friend, Vee." She spins back around and glares at Seth. "And you . . ." She swallows hard, and devastation flashes across her face. She opens her mouth again to speak, but then she just shakes her head, gets in her car, and drives away.

CHAPTER 30

Ryan Kelly
He blew a kiss from the road
8/10 (for cuteness)

Seth
On his front step
-1 million/10 (for being a huge mistake)

I TELL MEL'S DAD I'M NOT GOING TO BE ABLE TO WORK THE last two weeks of summer, and thank him for giving me the job. He's so nice about it, I feel extra-terrible and wonder if Mel told her parents what a terrible friend I am, or if she and Killian will talk about me when they're at the Float & Boat together, and agree they're glad I'm gone.

After Mel left, Seth and I didn't have much to say to each other.

"I'm sorry," I said finally, staring down at my feet.

"It's not your fault." His voice was soft, almost too soft to hear. "I screwed up." Then he went inside and closed the door firmly behind him, shutting me out.

I haven't heard from him since.

I spend the next two weeks going back-to-school shopping and filling out college applications by myself. Mom is extra-busy at work, with everyone flocking to the dentist for their back-to-school teeth cleanings, and Jeffrey has practically moved into Dad and Lila's house so he can hang out with Chaundre every day, so I'm home alone most of the time. Plus, I keep getting the occasional creepy Facebook message from random guys at school I've never talked to before. Each time I log in and see the message notification, my heart jumps, hoping it's Killian, although I'm not sure what I would expect him to say. But there's radio silence from him as well.

Even though I'm just going through the motions in the other parts of my life, I still meet Ryan near the trail every morning. We run hard, working through the last part of our training schedule, and sometimes I think the only thing keeping me sane is knowing he'll be waiting there for me each day at seven thirty.

"Are you ready?" Ryan asks after our last training run before the half marathon, two days away.

"I guess." I wipe my sweaty face. Honestly, I haven't even really been thinking about the race. Running quiets my mind. If I go for long enough, it kind of makes me numb. Right now that's enough of a reward.

"You're going to do great," Ryan says, clapping me on the shoulder. "Stay hydrated. Carbo load the night before. I'll see you on Wednesday morning."

"Okay." I watch him jog away, envious as always of his easy grace.

Not only will this be the first race I've run without Mark at my side, it will be the first one where Mel and Seth won't be standing on the sidelines, cheering me on as I go by. I sink to the ground by the edge of the trail and wipe my face again, not sure if the moisture I'm blotting away is sweat or tears.

I put together a playlist of all Killian's favorite upbeat songs the night before the race, and good thing I did. I'm going to need it. Ryan's heat was earlier than mine, and I must have missed him in the crowd before he took off.

I stretch, concentrating on keeping my muscles warm and my breathing even. Concentrating on not obsessing over the fact that all of Butterfield has turned up to watch the half marathon and that hundreds of eyes are going to be following me mile after mile, some of them almost certainly believing I'm the world's biggest slut. Double-concentrating on not searching the crowd of runners for Mark's face, or thinking about how I wish with my entire heart that Seth and Mel were going to be here today.

I need to run.

The whistle sending my heat off onto the course is like a get-out-of-jail-free card. I launch forward, not caring about pacing or endurance or stamina—just running as fast as I can, leaving everything

behind. The course winds through downtown and out onto the country roads before looping around and leading back toward town, the
flagpole at the high school the official ending point. I'm four miles
outside of Butterfield before the adrenaline rush starts to wear off, and
I back off the pace a little bit.

People are camped out on lawn chairs, coolers at their sides, all
along the route, holding up signs and screaming as their friends and
family run past. The course passes directly in front of Mel's house, at
11.3 miles, where my family (including Dad, Lila, and Kaylee) will
be hanging out with Mel's parents, oblivious to the fact that Mel and
I haven't spoken in two weeks. I told them not to bother trying to
catch me at an earlier point in the race. I'm not here to smile and have
my picture taken. I'm here to run until I can't feel my feet anymore.

Taylor Swift's "Shake It Off" blasts through my earbuds, and I
match my steps along with the beat, smiling as I remember Killian
laying out his list of facts about how humans are hardwired to enjoy
pop music.

Mile six. Nearly halfway, and I'm feeling good.

I see someone coming up beside me out of the corner of my eye
and veer toward the middle of the road to give them some more room.
But the lanky frame and bobbing gate register deep in my gut before
my mind quite catches up, and my lungs seem to tighten. I start to
cough, cupping my hands over my face even as I keep running.

"Hey." I can see Mark's mouth moving, but I can't hear him over
the music.

"Hang on." I turn down the volume, immediately missing the steady rock beat.

"How're you doing?" Thin trails of sweat snake down from his temples. His skin is flushed from the sun and the exercise, but he looks totally at ease, like running is his natural state of existence.

"Okay." My voice is strained, and not just because I'm in the middle of a thirteen-mile race.

"Look, Vee, can we talk?"

I nearly stop dead. "What do you mean, can we talk? Mark, I'm trying to run right now."

He shrugs. "Yeah, I know, but we used to talk while we were running before."

"Well, things are different now. And this is a race." I would try to sprint ahead and lose him, but it would just tire me out and give him the satisfaction of knowing he's still faster than I am.

"I just want to say sorry again—"

I hold up my hand. "It's fine, Mark. I'm fine. You're fine. Let's just run."

"Vee . . ."

I shake my head and turn up the music, drowning out Mark's voice even as his mouth keeps moving. If there's one thing the kissing challenge has taught me, it's that I don't need him anymore. I don't need anyone.

All I need is to run.

I pass fields of cherry trees heavy with the last fruit of the season, neat white farmhouses with blue shutters, roadside vegetable stands, and entrepreneurial kids who have set up lemonade stands along the race route. Volunteers at mile eight hold out Dixie cups of water for the runners to grab as they pass, and I take one to drink and one to toss over my head. I pass some slower runners, but many more people pass me.

At mile ten I realize my sweat-soaked sock is rubbing against my heel, the beginnings of a blister shooting painful warning signals up through my leg. The playlist has started over, but I'm tired of synthetic beats and synthesizers, and I turn the music off. I wish I had thought to upload Seth and Mel's album to my iPod. I could use the comfort of their voices right now.

As the course meanders back into town, I focus on putting one step in front of the other. My pace has totally bottomed out—I'm barely jogging—but I don't let myself drop all the way down to a walk. Like so many things—school, friendships, kissing challenges—the hardest part is just not letting yourself give up.

As I round the corner onto Mel's street, the sounds of guitar and piano hit me right in the heart. I wipe the sweat out of my eyes and blink, not quite believing the scene in front of me. Mel and Seth are set up on her front lawn, complete with amps and microphones, playing to the crowd that has gathered on the sidewalk in front of them. Mel glances up as I sprint down the street, and she screams into the mic. "Here she comes! Go, Vee!"

She locks eyes with me. "I'm sorry!" I call, using previous air to lift my voice above the noise of the crowd.

It's okay, she mouths back.

My lips are dry and cracked, and the smile that spreads across my face is painful but unstoppable. My family is sitting in chairs on the lawn, and Jeffrey holds Kaylee up so she can wave at me. Even Brianna and Landon are there, splayed out on a plaid blanket.

Mel strums the opening chords to her new song, the song she didn't want to play for Seth. But he's playing along with her, his fingers flying over the keyboard, and they're singing a harmony so beautiful, it breaks my heart.

I want to stop so badly, to join them on the grass, drink a gallon of water, and let the music take me away, but I wave and keep running, wondering what Seth said to finally make Mel forgive me. The music fades and is replaced by the sound of my breathing and the screams of the crowd as they urge us on to the final couple of miles.

"Vee!" Ryan leaps over the curb and matches his step to mine. His sweat-soaked shirt is stuck to his back, and a shiny medal bangs against his chest with every step. He takes it off and shoves it into his pocket. "You're doing great!"

"What are you doing?" I gasp. "You already finished."

"I was just hanging out with my parents. I'll run with you—you just have a mile and a half left. Come on!" Ryan sprints ahead, his lean brown legs seeming to move twice as fast as mine.

"Wait!" I call, but my voice comes out as a soft croak. I force myself to run faster, my eyes on the back of Ryan's shirt as he passes another group of runners. "Ryan!"

He's baiting me, giving me a target to chase after, trying to get me to pick up my pace. I know it's a trick, but I can't help falling for it. The blister on my heel burns, and my knees are screaming in protest at each jarring step I take over the blacktop, but I can see the finish line now. Ryan has crossed it for the second time today and spins around, holding his arms out to me.

"Come on!" he yells. "If you hurry, you can make it in under two and a half!"

The best half marathon time I've ever run was two hours and thirty-three minutes. Sweat is pouring down my face, and my heart is racing so hard, I might throw up the second I start to slow down. I'm less than a block away. Half a block. Fifty feet. Ryan is waiting just beyond the finish line, his dark eyes locked on mine, his arms reaching to pull me in.

Two hours, twenty-nine minutes, and fourteen seconds. Ryan's holding my shoulders, screaming Gatorade breath into my face. "You did it, Vee! You did it!"

"I know!" I'm grinning so hard, my face hurts, and my chest heaves with every breath. "I did it!" He holds up his hand for a high five. "Thank you for running with me."

"No problem." Ryan looks up as a shadow falls over me.

Killian's standing there, a giant GO, VEE sign dangling from one hand, his chest bare and painted with green and blue stripes.

"Oh my god," I say. "You're here. You came!"

Killian rolls his eyes. "Of course I came," he said. "This is how real life works, right? The guy is an asshole and then has to make it up to the girl through some kind of extravagant public gesture." He gestures to his chest. "Voilà."

I laugh, relief flooding my body. I bend over, a little light-headed. "Well, I don't see how I can argue with that logic. Consider me flattered." I wish I could erase everything I said to him the other night. It's true—I didn't expect, or even really want, to end up in a relationship at the end of the summer. But whatever this thing between Killian and me is . . . I can't blame him for wanting to see where it will go.

"You're amazing," he says, shaking his head. "Just when I think you can't possibly be any cooler, you turn around and prove me wrong."

"I just do it to annoy you." I pause, then step closer and stand on tiptoe, my hands on his ridiculous painted chest. All he has to do is tip his head forward and I'll give up the Twenty-Six Kisses Challenge for good. The roar of the crowd cheering the runners on at the finish line recedes into the background as my eyes lock on Killian's.

He pulls me even closer, one hand tangled in the sweat-soaked hair at the base of my ponytail, the other looped around my waist. "Are you sure?" he whispers, his lips tantalizingly close to mine. "Do you want me to?"

I close my eyes and nod, tilting my chin up just a bit. "Yes," I say.

The kiss never comes. I open my eyes to find Killian staring at me with a shit-eating grin on his face. "Too bad," he says, and steps away. "Because unless you've been really busy over the past couple of weeks, you are not done with the alphabet."

~ලැබ~

Fifteen minutes later we're standing on the library steps, overlooking the main hub of the Labor Day festival. Food tents line the street, and the stairs are packed with people chowing down on hot dogs and popcorn. The sound of guitars from a bluegrass band a few blocks away floats through the air, and couples and families walk up and down the street, waving to one another and stopping to talk with friends, celebrating the fact that tourist season is almost over and Butterfield is returning to normal.

"Okay, put this on." Killian drops a giant cardboard sign over my head. Painted on it are the words FREE KISSES FOR ANYONE WHOSE NAME STARTS WITH THE LETTER ___. A square of Velcro marks the spot where the letter should go. "If anyone can finish out an alphabetical summer kissing challenge with a bang, it's Team Us."

"Team Us." I grin up at him. "I'm glad that's still a thing."

"So, what do you have left?" Killian asks, pulling a large manila envelope out of a canvas shopping bag and fishing through it.

"Let me think." I look around at the crowd, incredulous. "You're really okay with watching me kiss a bunch of random strangers?"

"No funny business," Killian says, waving a finger at me. "On the cheek only."

"Got it. You know, this probably isn't going to be as easy as you think. I pretty much only have the weird letters left."

Killian pumps his fist. "Awesome. If you can't find anyone, then you won't have to kiss them, and maybe this won't be so infuriating for me."

"All right, all right. Give me"—I run through the list in my head, not totally sure if I have the letters and kisses straight (they're all blending together)— "Q." I adjust the sign so it's hanging straight. "I don't know if anyone is going to take me up on my very generous free kisses offer, though."

Killian laughs. "Give it about three minutes," he says, and slaps a large paper Q on top of the Velcro. "There's going to be a line out to the street."

I put my hands on my hips and look around, wondering if there's even anyone in Butterfield today whose name begins with Q. No one walking past or sitting on the steps seems to even notice I'm wearing a giant sign advertising free kisses, and the ones who do just give me weird looks and move on.

After a minute or so Killian sighs. "Guess I'm going to have to do some advertising," he says.

"What?" I grab his arm. "Don't you dare."

Killian cups his hands around his mouth and yells at the top of his lungs, "Free kisses! Limited time only! World's most beautiful girl! Come and get 'em!"

The noise of the festival dims for a second as people turn to stare at us.

"Oh my God," I say, pressing my face into Killian's arm. "I can't believe you just did that."

"Free kisses!" he yells again. "What is wrong with you people? Do you not see how gorgeous she is? Are there any red-blooded males out there whose names begin with Q?"

A group of guys I recognize from Jeffrey's class walk up to us, snickering and punching each other. "His name is Quinn," one of them says, pointing to a short kid with spiky hair. "Will you kiss him?"

"Shut up," Quinn says, kicking his friend in the shin.

"Do you want a kiss?" I ask, putting my hands on my hips. "Just on the cheek. It's for a good cause."

"Uh." Poor Quinn stares at the ground, his face bright red. "Sure. I guess."

I step closer and lean in, planting a big old smacker on Quinn's cheek and freezing there for just a second so his friends can get pictures on their phones.

"Okay!" Killian says, snatching the Q off my sign. "What next?"

"Um . . ."

"Hey, pretty lady," a voice says from behind me. I spin around to find Mel and Seth standing on the step below us, holding hands.

"You guys." I clap my hands over my mouth. We stare at one another.

Seth shakes his head and kicks at the ground with his yellow high-top. "Don't, Vee. It's fine. Everything just got kind of screwed up for a while."

"Are you sure?" I lock eyes with Mel. She nods.

"Double sure. What, did you think I would play a concert for you during the race if I were still mad?" She bumps her hip against Seth's. "This loser told me it was all his fault. And he finally realized what he really wanted."

"Which is Mel," Seth clarifies, as if there were any doubt. "This girl, right here, is what I want." He wraps his arm around Mel's waist, pulling her in close. She giggles and nuzzles his neck. My stomach tightens, but in a good way.

I hop down onto their step and throw my arms around them.

"Hey," Seth protests. "You're stabbing me with that sign."

Mel smiles up at Killian. "You're helping her finish it, huh?"

Killian holds his hands out. "I figure the sooner she gets it over with, the sooner I can start convincing her to transfer to Trawley and become my debate partner."

I snort. "Yeah, right. If anybody's transferring, buddy, it's you." I barely recognize my own voice, it sounds so happy. I glance at Seth, unsure if I should stay stuff like that in front of him, but he nods slightly and pulls Mel to him, wrapping his arm securely around her.

"Okay," I say, turning back to Killian. "I know I still need W, X, and Y. Good luck finding those for me."

Killian cracks his knuckles theatrically and hands me the giant X. "Now we need someone whose name starts with an X!" Killian yells to the crowd. Soon Xander, a thirty-something dad with two kids, presents me his stubble-covered cheek while his wife stands by and laughs, holding their daughter in her arms.

"You kids are crazy," Xander says, taking a selfie with me before strolling off with his family.

"W should be easy," Seth says, finally starting to warm up to the game. "Do we have any Ws in the crowd tonight?"

Walter is close to my grandpa's age but still up for a good time.

"Oh, wait!" I say. "I also need a *U*."

It takes a while for us to hunt Ulric down, but we luck out because he's four years old and wearing a name tag in case he gets lost in the crowd. His mom lifts him up to me, and I plant a quick kiss on his baby-soft cheek while he giggles in her arms. *Y* is a tough one, but Mel finally gets the bright idea to call Yeti, a linebacker on Butterfield's football team who has gone by his nickname for so long, no one actually remembers what his real name is. He lifts me up like I weigh nothing and twirls me around until I beg him to put me down.

"I think we only need *J*, *L*, and *V*," I say. "I'll take care of *J* when I see Jeffrey later. I know a sweaty kiss from his big sister is exactly what he wants today."

Mel texts Landon, and he and Brianna jog over. "I hear you're in need of some assistance," Landon says, leaning over to smack an exaggerated kiss on my cheek. "Allow me to be of service."

Brianna giggles and nudges him. "Don't get any ideas," she says.

"Only one letter left," Killian says, leaning down to whisper in my ear. "What on Earth are you going to do once you've worked your way through the entire alphabet?"

"I think I'll figure something out," I murmur, every cell in my body begging for him to sweep me up in his arms and put an end to this torture. "Mel!" I call. She tears herself away from Seth and links elbows with me. "I need a *V*," I say. "Let's get this over with."

Mel bumps my hip with hers. "Vee. Think about it."

"What?"

Her eyes widen meaningfully, and she stares at me.

V. V. *I need a* V. *What am I not getting?*

"Ohhh," I say, the realization dawning.

"There you go," she says. "I knew you'd figure it out eventually."

I untangle my arm from Mel's, and Seth immediately swoops in to take my place next to her, a satisfied grin on his face. Brianna leans into Landon, and Killian just stands there with the envelope full of letters in his hands.

I almost can't believe Twenty-Six Kisses went from being a dumb way to shock myself into getting over Mark to something that actually mattered—that showed me there's no one perfect guy for me, that it's okay for the girl to pay, that you can get your heart broken and come out the other side whole. That the most important thing you can do is love yourself, and other people will follow your lead.

I raise my hands to my mouth, smack a kiss into the center of my palm, and lift my arms over my head. "There's *V*."

Mel whoops and tackles me, nearly knocking me off my feet. The crowd around me cheers, everyone jumping up and down, high-fiving and yelling, as if I've just finished running another race. And in a way, I guess, I have.

I lift the sign over my head and let it fall to the ground. "All done," I say, smiling up at Killian. "Finally."

He twirls the ends of my hair through his fingers. "You sure?" he asks. "You don't want to go back to A and start over again?"

I let my mouth fall open. "Are you kidding?" I say. I loop my arm around his neck and pull his face to mine. "Right now there's only one letter I'm interested in."

"Oh yeah?" His eyes roam over my face, drinking me in. "And what would that be? You'll have to spell it out for me, counselor."

"Oh, shut up," I say, eliminating the last few inches between us. "Just stop talking and kiss me."

Killian
10/10
Team US

Acknowledgments

I've always known that I wanted to write books, but it wasn't until I discovered contemporary YA that I really found a writing home. I first have to thank all the inspiring authors who have paved the way in this space and made it possible for these kinds of stories to reach such a wide audience.

Thanks to everyone at the amazing conference Writers in Paradise and my B&B Mafia crew, especially Ben Pfeiffer, for supporting me from the very beginning.

Buckets of gratitude to my colleagues at Sourcebooks, especially Dominique Raccah, Todd Stocke, and Shana Drehs, for making my day job a dream job.

So many thanks to my unparalleled agent, Pete Knapp, and the teams at New Leaf Literary and The Park Literary Group; also to Sara Sargent, Liesa Abrams, Sarah McCabe, Kaitlin Severini, and everyone who does such incredible work at Simon Pulse.

To my friends, near and far, thank you for putting up with my bookish ways and always being there when I emerge from the reading/writing/editing cave.

Thanks to my family, especially my mom, for raising me right—on poker and books (which, incidentally, is great training for a career in publishing!).

And finally, to Matt—bandmate, roommate, soul mate. Thanks for being you.

For my parents,
Grace and George Salvato.
Thank you for a lifetime of
love, support, and family adventures.
I love you.

CHAPTER 1

I WASN'T ALWAYS THE KIND OF GIRL WHO WAKES UP ON THE first day of summer vacation to find herself on the receiving end of a temporary restraining order. But things got ugly when Joey, my ex, came to an end-of-the-school-year party on Friday night with his new girlfriend—the bleach-blond freshman ho bag he'd been cheating on me with. Until I saw them together, I didn't know he and his indiscretion had become an actual item. It felt like someone had knocked all the air out of my lungs with a blunt object. What can I say? First I lost my heart. Then I lost my mind.

I stare out the screen door and watch as the patrol car drives away, my face burning with embarrassment. What if Mrs. Friedman is watching from across the street? She doesn't miss a thing, ever. What a crappy start to a Monday morning.

"This cannot be happening," I say.

"Rosie, you blew up your boyfriend's car. What did you expect?" says Matty, our next-door neighbor.

"For the last time, I did not blow up Joey's car. It caught fire!"

"What's the difference?"

"Hello, there was no explosion. I was just burning all the stuff he gave me in his driveway." Why doesn't anyone understand this? I've spent all weekend trying to explain it. "The box wasn't even near Joey's car. He was standing right there. I don't know how it happened."

"Lighter fluid and stuffed animals. Bad combination," Matty says.

"Shut up, Matty! I need to think."

"The thinking ship sailed when you lit that match."

"It was a lighter and—what are you doing in my house, anyway?" It's like he doesn't even pretend to go home anymore. When Matty was six, my mother offered to let him come over after school so his mom didn't have to pay for child care. Apparently Matty thought that meant forever.

Matty extricates himself from the couch and walks toward the front door, where I've been rendered immobile by this latest turn of events. "Take it easy, all right? I'm not the problem, your bad temper is."

"I don't have a bad temper." I look down at my purple toenails, away from Matty's beady blue-eyed stare. "I'm passionate."

"Call it whatever makes you feel better. I've grown immune to your acerbic wit and biting sarcasm, but lately it's like you're . . . I don't know, hostile?"

Hostile? Where does he get hostile? Okay. Maybe I'm high-strung. I'll give him that. But at our house, we yell when we're happy, we yell when we're upset, we yell when we want someone to pass the remote. It's what we Catalanos do.

I look down at the paper in my hand. "I guess Joey must've called the cops."

"Ya think?"

I feel like I've just done a belly flop on dry land. My parents are going to freak. They already grounded me, indefinitely, after Joey's mom called Saturday morning to scream about the postparty car fire caused by yours truly. And now there's a restraining order. At this point, my parents will lock me in a tower until I graduate from high school next June. For a brief second I wonder if I can keep the whole thing a secret. Yeah, right, like that'll ever work. I couldn't even burn a box of memories without the police getting involved. I don't know what's happening with me lately.

"Maybe it's a mistake," I say.

Matty grabs the three-page document from me. "Right. This is for the other Rosalita Ariana Catalano Joey dated, who also blew up his car."

I cross my arms and scowl as Matty scans the page. "I've got to talk to him."

"You're to stay away from Joey's house, his job. There's to be no written, personal, or electronic communication with the complaining witness by you or anyone you know." He pauses. "It actually says you are prohibited from returning to the scene of the violence."

"I've got to talk to him," I repeat.

"Have you been listening?" Matty waves the papers in my face. "Restraining order."

"But if I can just explain—"

"Save it for your court date in two weeks."

"What?" Court date? I snatch the papers from him and start flipping through the pages, but my eyes won't settle on any words. Fruity Pebbles rise in my throat and I start to sweat. I suddenly want to throw something at the TV screen. *The View* is on—leave it to Matty. Now I have the urge to throw something at the whiny one's head. Maybe I do have anger issues.

I hand the TRO back to Matty. "I can't find it."

"Right here," he says, pointing to the correct page. "You've been ordered to appear before Superior Court Judge Tomlinson in Essex County, New Jersey, to address the allegations of, let's see, criminal trespass, criminal mischief, harassment, and stalking. Stalking?"

I cover my eyes with both hands. I think I'm either going to vomit or cry. At the moment, I can't decide which would make me feel better. I part my fingers to look at Matty. "It was only a few e-mails and texts."

"A few?"

"And maybe I showed up at ShopRite once or twice when he was getting off work."

"Good way to keep busy after a breakup. Hoping incarceration would fill those empty hours?" Matty says.

He looks as pained as I feel, which is why I need food. I walk into the kitchen and begin opening cabinets in search of the perfect snack to calm me down. Let's see. Temporary restraining order . . . I bypass the pretzels and head straight for the Double Stuf Oreos. I tear open the new package, which rouses Pony, our ninety-pound Lab mix, who'd been sleeping under the kitchen's central-air duct. I smile when he turns his head quizzically as if to say, "Did I hear food?"

"Some watchdog," I say in the baby-talk voice I use when speaking to my pooch and for which Eddie, my brother, always makes fun of me. "Where were you ten minutes ago when the police were at the door? Cookies are a different story, huh?"

Pony saunters over to the counter and nudges my elbow with his big wet nose until I relent. Sugary foods are bad for dogs, but I can't resist his pleading eyes. "Only one, big guy," I say. He gently takes the Oreo and swallows it in a single gulp. Matty comes into the kitchen just as I'm about to pour myself some milk.

"I think I know how to handle this," he says.

Matty is always trying to handle things. Most of the time, it makes me sad that he thinks he has to. I blame his absent father, not that Matty and I ever talk about him. Still, I know one of the reasons Matty likes hanging out at our house so much is that he gets to be a kid here. At sixteen, Matty is a year younger than me, the same age as my brother, and at least a foot taller than us both. When I was in middle school, Eddie and I finally stopped arguing about who Matty "belonged" to. He's our Matty. I love him like a second brother, and unfortunately, sometimes I fight with him like he's one too.

Lately, most of our spats are my fault. I know I've been impossible to be around since just after Memorial Day weekend. That's when I went away with my family and Joey cheated on me with the freshman slut. To his credit, he told me. He begged me to forgive him. He said all they did was kiss. That it was a huge mistake, a onetime thing, blah, blah, blah. As much as I wanted to believe him, I was hurt, angry, and completely shocked. I couldn't get over it and consequently, my entire relationship imploded. Since then, if I didn't know me, I'd think I was a bitch too. And that's why at this moment especially, it's best if Matty leaves. I don't want to cause an argument.

"I'm gonna call my girls," I say. "Wait until they hear this." My best friend, Lilliana, and the rest of our group will understand. I wasn't stalking Joey—right? I honestly don't know what I thought I was doing. Looking for evidence that Joey's fling was a one-night stand? Hoping to find him moping around town wearing an I ♥ ROSIE T-shirt? Whatever it was, I certainly didn't think it was illegal. If only it hadn't culminated in an accidental car fire.

I swallow my last bite of Oreo and start dialing. Matty takes my phone from me.

"I think you need to get out of town for a while," he says.

I grab my phone back. "I think you need to get out of my house for a while."

"I'm serious. I'm leaving for Arizona on Saturday with Spencer and Logan. You should come."

Okay. Here's where my curiosity trumps my need for him to go home. "Who are Spencer and Logan?"

I know some of Matty's friends, but not all. Matty goes to public school, the same school as my ex and his new chicken-head girlfriend.

Oh, and my brother, Eddie, of course. My parents thought it was best for me to attend an all-girls Catholic high school because it's every teenage girl's dream to dress like a Scottish bagpipe player. All because I got busted at an eighth-grade graduation party playing seven minutes in heaven with Armand DelVecchio, who, by the way, kisses like a seal. It wasn't even worth it.

"Spencer Davidson. We're in robotics club together."

"No surprise there."

"Logan's his older brother. He got accepted to ASU."

"Okaay, so why's he leaving now?"

"He has to be there for this special summer session. Logan wants his car in Tempe, so he figured he'd make a road trip out of it. Me and Spence are flying home."

Has Matty told me all this before? Did the information get lost in my I-just-broke-up-with-my-boyfriend haze? I'm feeling a bit guilty.

"So, why did Spencer ask you to go?"

"He's afraid to fly."

Of course he is. So now I'm picturing the scene: me, trapped in a car with three nerds. Doubtful. "And I should go because—"

"It will keep you out of trouble for nine days. You can't stalk anyone in New Jersey while traveling seventy-five miles per hour in a vehicle headed west."

I pretend to think about this for a second. "Right. Sure, I'll go."

"Really?"

"No."

After filling in Lilliana on the whole restraining-order ordeal, I spend the rest of the day trying to distract myself, which is what I've been trying to do every day since Joey and I broke up. Today, it got a lot harder. I take Pony for a long walk before attempting to read one of my romance novels. Usually I plow through them to get to the happy ending, but today, only five pages in, I toss the book aside. Lately, everything—books, song lyrics, movies, even Yankee games—reminds me of Joey.

Eventually, I settle for mindless eating and cable TV. I just want to feel normal again. I love, love, love those shows where they help women find wedding dresses. The gowns are so gorgeous, and I always seem to know which dress the bride-to-be is going to pick. That inspired me to get a part-time summer job at Something New Bridal Boutique downtown. I start next weekend and I cannot wait. I've got a definite knack for knowing what people look good in and think I have untapped potential for designing clothes. I smile as I remember this fashion studio drawing set I had when I was a kid. It had a light board, colored pencils, and all these traceable patterns. I spent hours mixing and matching the templates for tops and bottoms, hairdos and shoes, to create my own sketches. I kept my designs in a folder. My mom, who used to pretend to be a client, wrote ROSIE COUTURE on it for me. I wonder if I still have that folder somewhere.

Around three in the afternoon, I decide to lay out on the deck. The whole world just seems better when I'm tan. I love how my skin smells after I come in from the sun. Pony whines to come outside with me—he always follows me around when I'm home. But after five minutes, he starts panting and stands by the back door.

That's when I remember I forgot to put on sunscreen. I get up to let him in, find a bottle in the kitchen cabinet, and return to the deck. My olive skin is immune to sunburn, but I'm paranoid about skin cancer and premature wrinkling. As soon as I open the bottle, I wish that I had risked it and done without my SPF 50. The tropical scent immediately takes me back to the first time I saw Joey. He was standing on the boardwalk near the pirate-themed mini-golf course. It was September, a warm Indian summer day, and me and Lilliana'd crammed in one last beach day. I was balancing on one foot, dusting the sand off my toes so I could put my flip-flop back on, when I spotted him. He caught me staring, but I never even had a chance to be embarrassed.

"I've seen you before," he said. I couldn't believe this beautiful boy was talking to me. "Your brother goes to Chestnutville High, doesn't he?" I was totally self-conscious because my long hair was all frizzy after a day of sun and salt water. I tried to casually smooth it down while I talked to him, but then he reached over and brushed a stray ringlet away from my eye, like he was already used to invading my personal space, and said: "I love your curls."

A week later, we were a couple.

I think about our first date a lot, remembering how I watched from my bedroom window as he pulled into the driveway. I had been ready for an hour, but I figured I'd let Joey ring the bell and sweat out the first meeting with my family before I went downstairs. If he was going to be a keeper, my family needed to like him and he needed to like my family.

I stood on the upstairs landing, out of sight, and listened to the introductions, followed by easy laughter when my brother said, "There's still time to back out, man. I don't think Rosie knows you're here." When I walked down the stairs a few seconds later wearing a yellow silk tank top that contrasted nicely with my dark eyes and hair (I had worn it curly for him), I could tell he had no intention of bailing. He was all in. Neither of us said a word, but we were both smiling like it was yearbook picture day. People think those time-stands-still moments only happen in movies. They don't. It sounds cheesy, but everyone else just faded away and it felt like we were alone.

"Do you two know each other?" my dad said, breaking the spell. Everyone laughed and then we walked out the door.

As Joey opened the car door for me, he leaned down and whispered in my ear: "You're even prettier than I remembered." A chill rippled from my neck and spread across my body.

Before my date, Matty and Eddie did try to warn me that Joey had a love-'em-and-leave-'em rep around school. But that night, Joey seemed more like an anxious little boy than some arrogant Casanova. He asked me a ton of questions and wanted to know everything about me. It was like I really, really mattered. And he seemed so worried about whether or not I was enjoying myself. I lost count of how many times he asked if my tortellini with pesto sauce was any good. When he spilled his water and his entire face turned red, my heart went out to him. I was making him nervous. Me. I didn't care what Eddie and Matty said about how Joey treated girls in the past. I could tell I was going to be different.

Ha! What a joke. I put the cap back on my sunscreen, lie down, and close my eyes. Forget it. I already got burned.

At five o'clock, I change back into shorts and a tank top and brace myself for what's coming. At dinner, the tiny lift I got from a healthy dose of vitamin D is gone. Probably because we're having pork cutlets and salad with a heated family discussion about criminal mischief on the side.

"Say that again, Rosie," Mom says. "It sounded like you said 'restraining order.'"

"I did. 'Temporary restraining order.'"

I hold out the document halfheartedly. My mother takes it from me, stares at it, closes her eyes, and passes it to my father.

"Oh, *Dios mío*," Mom says. "Are you trying to kill your father and me? This business with Joey keeps getting worse."

Here we go with the Spanglish. Worrying always transforms my mom into George Lopez. Predictably, the veins in my dad's neck bulge out as he reads the restraining order. Let's hope he doesn't transform into the Incredible Hulk.

"I don't know you anymore," Dad says. He's got the papers rolled up and waves them around like a light saber. "My daughter would never do these things."

Well, your daughter did, apparently, says the Rosie in my head. He's right, though. I hate to disappoint my dad. I pick at my food as he gets up and starts pacing. I waited until after he ate to tell everyone. Low blood sugar tends to fuel my father's anger. My mother just rubs her temples. Pony, who had been under the table waiting for scraps, slinks out of the room. Smart dog.

"I'd better not find out you slept with this boy," my father shouts.

"Oh my God, Dad! You did not just say that." I cover my ears. Eddie looks mortified. So does Mom.

That's when Matty materializes at the back door. I spot him first and can tell he's afraid to knock. I'm guessing he's waiting for a pause in my dad's tirade. Finally, Matty taps on the door. His arrival is a welcome diversion—my parents adore Matty.

"Sorry to interrupt," Matty says. "Did Rosie tell you about my plan?"

Wait, what? Why would I? I had practically forgotten until this very second that he'd gone all road trip on me. Okay, maybe Matty isn't a good diversion, but it's too late, he's already pulling up a chair. So, ten minutes later, after he shares his whole getting-out-of-Dodge scheme (he actually calls it that), my parents have fallen into an eerie trance.

"Let me get this straight," Eddie says. "Rosie blows up a car and now she's going on vacation?"

"For the last time, it didn't blow up," I say. "And who says I even want to go?"

"Whatever," Eddie says. "Then I'm going too."

"As much as I'd like to send you along to watch out for your sister, you can't," Mom says. "You have to work."

Eddie is lifeguarding at the town pool club this summer. This is the dream job he's wanted since he was a kid and took swim lessons at the YMCA. There's no way he's giving it up. Furthermore, there's no way I'm giving up my own summer plans. I've got the bridal shop gig on weekends and I was planning on supplementing that money by starting a dog-walking-slash-sitting business. I made up flyers and everything. Plus, at the end of August, I'm supposed to spend two weeks with Lilliana and her family at their beach house.

"Rosie's not going either," Dad says.

"That's a relief," I mumble.

"She's going to work for me at the factory. That way, I can keep an eye on her."

Uh-oh. I spoke too soon. My dad runs the family lampshade business with his brother, my uncle Dominic. Oh, I've done my time at the factory, cutting lampshades into three-by-five rectangular swatches, punching holes in the corners, and grouping the fabrics on binder rings as samples. I have to admit, I've got a gift for arranging certain colors and textures so they're appealing to customers. More than samples, I create palettes.

Still, I am so over it. This summer, I wanted to try something different, even though I feel guilty for not helping Dad more. The business has taken a hit during the last few years with so much stuff being manufactured in countries like China and all, and my mom's salary as an assistant bank manager doesn't exactly make up for it. Now we've got to hire a lawyer. My parents don't need to be shelling out that kind of money right now.

It's official. I suck.

I promise myself I'll be a better daughter, just as soon as I work out this megamess with Joey. Maybe we can both say we're sorry and start over again. Is that what I want? That's part of the problem. I don't think I'll know until I talk to Joey again. What I do know is that I want this conversation to be over. I look at the clock on the microwave. Lilliana and her cousin Marissa are picking me up down the street soon. If I can sneak out, we're going to do a drive-by of Joey's house and job.

"Maybe she should go away," Mom says. She's skimming Matty's trip itinerary.

"What?!" Dad bellows. "We don't even know these boys."

"Well, of course we'll need to call their parents, and Matty will be with her," Mom says. I'm not sure I like where she's going with this.

"Look," Mom continues. "It's not my first choice either. But it will keep Rosie out of trouble until her court date, and she might learn something."

"You're not serious!" Eddie shouts. His nose and forehead are pink, and he has white circles around his eyes in the shape of his sunglasses. He really needs to get some better sunscreen—it's hard to take Raccoon Boy's anger seriously. I stifle the urge to tell him that. I'm already in enough trouble.

"Stay out of this, Eddie," Mom says. "In fact, go outside. All of you. I want to talk to your father."

Outside, I plop my butt on the cushiony chaise lounge on the deck. Matty and Eddie walk down into the yard to shoot hoops. There's a net mounted to our detached garage. It's a good thing that in addition to being Super Dork, Matty is freaking excellent at basketball. He was the only sophomore on varsity. It no doubt saves him from many an ass kicking.

I close my eyes and try to pretend it's a regular summer night. I'm kinda pissed because I'm realizing that blowing up your ex's car and getting a restraining order really robs a person of the sympathy that is her due. I would never say this out loud, but I'm not even that sorry I did it. I'm still angry and hurt. I was in love with Joey, he was my first real boyfriend, and he cheated on me. Ever since we broke up, I've been harboring hope that he was telling the truth when he said that his one-night screwup meant nothing. So when I saw him with his new girl at Kevin's party on Friday, it was like a bikini wax times ten. Even though I knew about her, I didn't think they were dating. I didn't think she could fit under his arm as well as I did. Seeing him with her . . . I came unglued.

But the really screwed-up part of all this is, I still love him. In my head, I had us married with two kids, living right here in town with the rest of my entire extended family. High school sweethearts. Happily ever after. The end. I know I'm supposed to have dreams about college and a career, but the truth is, I dream about my wedding day more. Neither of my parents went to college, and look at the life they built together. Sure, Eddie and I get on each other's nerves sometimes, but for the most part, I'm pretty lucky. My family is close and there's no question we love one another.

A car horn gives two quick beeps as it passes by the front of the house, waking me from my thoughts. I get up from the chaise and peek in through the screen door. My parents are locked in an exchange of intense whispers. I open the door and try to act super casual.

"I'm going upstairs," I say. Neither parent acknowledges me. Cool. I make a point of running loudly upstairs before creeping silently back down, carrying my flip-flops. Luckily, the front door isn't visible from the kitchen. Pony is asleep on the couch. I don't want him waking up, running to the kitchen to grab his leash, and busting me. I turn the doorknob carefully and slip out, vowing to make it the last time I do something like this. For a while, at least.

I round the corner and see Lilliana's car. She fist bumps me when I get in. "A restraining order. Nice."

Lilliana and her younger cousin Marissa go to Sacred Heart with me. We despise plaid and have a shared, but silent, contempt for authority. We've never had detention, and we get along with mostly everyone. I've noticed that girls treat each other pretty good when there are no boys around to impress. All-girl schools still have their cliques, but my friends are the nonjoiners who feel too cool for student council and Spanish club. But the trouble I'm in doesn't feel cool at all. I get light-headed every time I think about what people are saying about me. What's going to happen when school starts again? Am I going to have one of those social outcast nicknames like "Psycho Torch Girl" or something?

"Let's get the drive-by of the dirtbag's house over with," Lilliana says. "Then we're taking you out."

Lilliana is no longer hiding the fact that she never liked Joey. It's only because she missed me. Joey and I were inseparable.

"I can't go out. I'm grounded, remember?" I say. "It's bad enough I'm sneaking out to do this."

"Maybe we shouldn't go," Marissa says.

"Don't be such a wuss," Lilliana snaps.

"A restraining order is serious. Rosie can get in legal trouble if someone sees her near his house," Marissa pleads.

I feel bad for making her nervous. I'm a good girl at heart. A few months ago, I would have felt the same way. Joey cheating on me has caused me to undergo some kind of psychological shift. Sure, I can be loud and dramatic, but flat-out rebellion was never my thing.

"No one will see me. I'll hide back here, I promise," I say, slouching down in the backseat.

I sound confident, but I know I can't keep doing stuff like this. Do I really want to turn out like one of those reality-show freaks? My dad said he doesn't know me anymore. That makes two of us.

We take Farms Road, which starts on my end of town where the older-style homes are only a driveway's width apart, and wind through the small downtown area. We pass the corner deli where the skate kids are hanging out and continue on Farms until it brings us to Joey's neighborhood, where the houses are newer and larger but more cookie cutter, right down to the identical play sets in nearly every yard. A month ago, this was my favorite route. Tonight, it makes me anxious and sick. When we pull into Elm Court, I duck.

"Tell me if you see him," I say. "Is there anyone outside?"

"Nope," Lilliana says.

"Is his car there? Does it look damaged?"

"No cars in the driveway," Lilliana says. "No lights on either. It doesn't look like anyone's home."

"He's probably at work. Let's drive by ShopRite next," I say.

My phone rings while I'm still crouching down in the backseat. Shit! It's my mother. She knows I left the house. She knows I'm up to something. She knows everything. Damn the Catalano sixth sense.

"Hello?"

"Where are you?"

"I'm in Lilliana's car." This is not a lie.

"And where is Lilliana's car, Rosie?"

"It's at the diner. We're about to go inside." Of course, that is a lie.

"That's it," Mom snaps. "You're coming home right now! Your father is furious."

"I know I shouldn't have left the house, but it's just the diner and—"

"Look out the back window," Mom says. I can hear her clenching her teeth.

"Uh-oh," Lilliana says, glancing in her rearview mirror.

Slowly, I rise up off the floor and look out the back car window. Yep. There's my mom in her SUV.

"You followed me?" I shriek into the phone, which is still at my ear.

"I didn't need to. I knew where to find you."

I squint in the low, dusk light. There's someone in the passenger's seat. Dad? Eddie? No effin' way.

"Is that Matty?" It is. Traitor.

"He talked your father into staying home," Mom says. "You should be happy you've got a friend like him."

I should be, but at the moment, I'm not.

CHAPTER 2

I'M LEAVING FOR ARIZONA ON SATURDAY. I COULD GO INTO the details of the Catalano Monday Night Smackdown that led to their decision to send their only daughter on a nine-day cross-county road trip, but it's too exhausting. Suffice it to say, Mom's Ecuadorian temper, I mean passion, trumps Dad's Italian brand. Dad is loud all the time. Mom is loud when she needs to be. We never say it, but we all know Mom wears the pants in this family.

"Call your goofball friends and tell them I'm in," I say when Matty answers the phone. It's late, but I knew he'd still be up.

"Cool. I'm sorry if I got you into trouble, Rosie. I was just trying—"

"No, no. I'm the one who should be sorry. I screwed up. Again. Thanks for having my back."

"Anytime," Matty says. He sounds relieved. We should all aspire to be Mattys.

"But I need my space until Saturday, got it?"

"Got it."

"No watching *The View* on our couch."

"I got it. I got it. You're gonna thank me for this."

"Don't get carried away." I hang up.

I'm drained from the family drama, but I still can't sleep. Pony is sacked out on my twin bed anyway. He has his head on my pillow and he's making these cute mini-yelp noises while his feet twitch. Aw, poor guy. Doggy nightmare. I gently stroke the top of his head between his ears until he settles into a quiet slumber. I sigh. Maybe my dog-walking business will still work out when I get back, but who knows what will happen when I call the bridal shop tomorrow. I can't expect them to hold my job.

I grab my stuffed Clydesdale that I got from Busch Gardens when I was seven and give it a squeeze. When I was little, I had these dreams of learning to ride and begged my parents for a horse every year until my thirteenth birthday, when I got Pony. Luckily, that ten-pound bundle of chocolate-colored fur grew into his name. He was, and is, the best birthday gift ever. Still, I didn't abandon my first "horse," Clyde. How could I? I logged a lot of cuddle time with him before Pony arrived. I've still never been on a horse.

I settle into a spot on the floor between my bed and the open window and sift through my Joey Box outtakes. I didn't burn everything in the fire. There's some stuff I can't part with, like the first card he gave me and the dried, pressed rose from our one-month anniversary. Every month he gave me another. Guess I'll never get my dozen.

Then there's the picture Lilliana took of us at the winter semi-formal. We're slow dancing. Joey is in a suit and tie, looking all male-model-ish with his ice-blue eyes and black hair. I look good too, not that I like to brag. It was just one of those nights when everything fell into place. Perfect hair. No zits or bloating, and I found this amazing metallic silver eyeliner that really made my brown eyes pop. I wore a black lace strapless dress that showed off my cleavage but was classy at the same time. Every inch of me felt good.

What happened to us? That was the night Joey told me he loved me for the first time. He swore I was the first girl he spoke those words to. I believed him. Still do. The Joey Marconi in this photo picked me up every day after school and almost always brought me something that he knew I'd like—an iced coffee, Swedish fish, a Big Gulp. We spent every day together. And he told me everything. Like how he cried in first grade because the kids used to call him Joey Macaroni, how he felt like his older brothers outshined him in everything, from high school sports to the rivalry for their father's attention. My Joey said he'd never push me to take our relationship to the next level. He said he'd wait forever.

When did things change between us, and why didn't I notice? Joey cheats. We break up. He calls the cops. Maybe it was his mom's idea. She never liked me that much. Even after Joey and I had been dating for nine months, she always acted surprised to see me. She was all, "Oh, Rosie. I didn't know you were here." Or, "Oh, Rosie, I didn't realize you and Joey were going to the movies tonight." No one is good enough for her baby boy. Between Joey and his two older brothers, it's like Oedipal overload in that house.

And yet, all I want is to see Joey again. The more I'm told I can't, the more convinced I am that everything will be okay if I can just see his face and tell him why I did what I did. And give him a chance to apologize for being a two-timing snake. Everyone makes mistakes. I can forgive him, right? Then he can forgive me. I never meant for things to go so, so wrong.

I know I can fix this. So that's why, for the second time in one day, I violate the terms of my TRO. The acronym sounds better. In my head, at least. I keep my text short: call me. r. An hour later, I'm ashamed to admit, I send another. we need to talk. please? I fall asleep sometime after three in the morning, still clutching my phone, my heart breaking all over again.

His silence hurts more than his cheating.

The smell of bacon and coffee wakes me early the next morning, despite the fact that I hardly slept, and I feel even more depressed. All I want to do is stay in bed until my court date is over. But my stomach growls. Is there any better smell? There's no real cure for heartache, but bacon comes close. My body feels heavy and my pillow is winning the tug-of-war against those crispy strips until I reach for my phone. It isn't on my comforter. I kick off the covers and search the tangle of sheets and then under my bed. Gone. Stealth mom strikes again. I haul my groggy butt downstairs in my cotton pajamas shorts and matching tee with a picture that looks like a little Pony and says PUPPY LOVE. I'm embarrassed about those messages to Joey and afraid of Mom's reaction.

I stop abruptly at the kitchen doorway when I hear my mom talking on the phone. I know it's Dad. He calls her every morning when he gets to work, even though he left less than an hour ago. I usually admire my parents' close relationship, but this morning, I know they're talking about me. I'm hoping Dad changed his mind and doesn't want me to go to Arizona. I have to admit, the trip might help me get my mind off Joey, but does it have to be so far and with two guys I don't really know?

"Agreed," Mom says just as I step into the kitchen. "Matty's in charge." She's holding my cell. I'm totally screwed yet feeling oddly self-righteous and confrontational. I stand in front of Mom, arms crossed with my grouch face on. She gives me the "one second" motion with her pointer finger. "Uh-huh, yes. Me too. I'll talk to her when she gets up. Love you." Mom clicks off and I start in before she has a chance to.

"What do you mean, 'Matty's in charge'? I seriously hope you're not talking about me!"

"Calm down. Your father and I just don't want to see you get into any more trouble." Mom points my phone at me while she speaks. "Your father is contacting a lawyer today. We need to find out what has to be done before this court date and make sure it's okay for you to leave the state. He's stressed enough about his business; we can't have you calling and texting Joey from here to Arizona."

"So you mean Matty is getting control of my phone?"

"Sweetie, it's for the best. We love you."

"So I'm going to be on house arrest, except in a car." I give Mom my pout face. "Keep my phone. I'll just borrow Matty's."

"You know how much I text you and your brother. I don't want to run up Matty's bill. And anyway—" Mom shakes her head.

"What?"

Her shoulders slump in resignation. "There's a GPS in your phone. Your father will feel better if we track you during this trip."

"Holy mother of . . . are you kidding me? A GPS? Since when?"

"Since always. From the time we got you your first phone."

"Eddie better have one too."

"Watch your tone, young lady. He does. He just doesn't know about it."

I'm certainly not going to tell him. Let him find out the hard way. Then I begin inventorying any other lies I may have told over the years regarding my physical location. It's all too much. My head is spinning.

"I can't take this. I don't want to go. Please don't make me go. Who's gonna walk Pony? You know he only likes to sleep with me."

"The dog will be fine, and you don't have a choice. Look, this isn't easy for us, either, but it's clear that you're not thinking about the consequences of your actions." Mom massages her temple and

I can tell she's not done talking. "Believe it or not, I know what it's like to be obsessed with a boy. Sometimes the best cure is distance. It gives you perspective. Besides, you may even have fun. Did you ever consider that?"

Obsessed? I'm not obsessed. All I can do is scowl as I grab for my Hello Kitty mug. Kitty's polka-dotted purse is fading from too many dishwasher runs, but I still love it. I fix my coffee the way I like it: First, I put in three teaspoons of sugar. Next, a splash of hot coffee to melt the sugar. Then, lots of half-and-half. Finally, I pour the coffee until it's the exact mocha shade that I like. Light and sweet. I help myself to a big plate of bacon and scrambled eggs before thinking twice about it and sliding some back onto the griddle. I'm a big eater and I've been blessed with a metabolism that keeps up, but I've been overdoing it lately. There's a delicate balance between "curvy" and "chubby."

I slip Pony a bacon strip and he gobbles it without even chewing. I'm just about to take a bite of my eggs when Matty taps on the back door and lets himself in.

"Space, remember?" I say.

"Take it easy. I'm just dropping off the revised itinerary and then I'm gone," he says. "I printed an extra copy for your parents, too."

"What a good boy." Mom gives him a hug. Inside, I'm rolling my eyes.

I'm about to say something snarky, but I just can't. With his cropped hair and perpetually flushed cheeks, no matter how old Matty gets, he's still the little boy next door.

"Thanks, Matty," I say instead.

"You're welcome," he says. "It's going to be an adventure."

I don't want an adventure. I want Joey and my old life back. But Mom and Matty are both looking at me, so I give them my best attempt at a sincere smile. I'm tired of letting people down.

The next day, I'm more shocked than anyone when my parents allow me to go to the mall with Lilliana to buy a few things for my trip. Inside, they're softies. Not that I'm gonna point this out or anything. I have to call them from the house phone both before I leave and as soon as I return. I have exactly two hours. Mom takes my cell to work with her. She considered letting Lilliana carry it—the GPS would allow her to track me all day—but she decided against it. My parents are softies, not stupid. Anyway, they don't have anything to worry about. I want to earn back their trust.

"What are you complaining about?" Lilliana asks. We're at Macy's and she's trying on sunglasses. She has an adorable button nose, the kind you'd ask for if you were getting a nose job. All styles of shades look good on her. "Three guys, the open road, Arizona. And time away from that tool. It's like a country song."

"I hate country music."

"The crossover stuff is okay."

I shrug. "I guess, but that straight-up cowboy music gets on my nerves."

"Joey gets on my nerves," Lilliana blurts out before recovering her "happy face" and attempting to put a positive spin on my trip. "Maybe you'll finally go horseback riding. You've always wanted to do that," she says. "Or use the time away to get your head together. Bring a notebook. Write down your thoughts."

Thoughts? Where is this coming from? I'm not one for extra-curricular thinking. Neither is she. At least I read romance novels; Lilliana's reading is restricted to whatever can be viewed on her phone.

"I'm more of an action person," I say. "I need to stay here and straighten things out with Joey."

"That's what you think you need. But let's put your effed-up feel-ings about Joey aside. Aren't you forgetting the bigger issue here?"

"Please don't remind me about the thing."

"Temporary restraining order? I'm just sayin'. You'll go crazy sitting around waiting for your court date. Remember what your attorney told your parents?"

"The farther away the better," I mumble. Actually his exacts words were "out-of-state equals good."

The lawyer's right. Lilliana's right. Everyone's right. And I'm cranky. I need a pick-me-up.

"Let's go to the pet store."

Just Pets sells just that. Hamsters, fish, geckos, birds—small crit-ters. But they also have dog and puppy adoptions, so I stop by when-ever I'm at the mall. I'd love a second dog, but I wouldn't want to upset Pony. He thinks he's my baby. Anyway, I'm in no position to be asking for anything right now.

Just Pets has an adorable fox terrier mix available for adoption. He's got a mostly white face with a black and brown patch over one eye. I want so badly to hold him for a few minutes, but I can't get his hopes up only to send him back. Even at a distance he's got me grinning like a fool and Lilliana has to drag me away from his crate.

"I'm getting hungry," Lilliana whines. "Let's get some shopping done before lunch."

"Okay, okay. I'm coming."

"What are we looking for exactly?" Lilliana asks as we walk toward Nordstrom's.

"Anything that will look cute after sitting in a car for hours."

"Wrinkle free. Check," Lilliana says.

"And light," I say. "Do you know Arizona is, like, a hundred and seven degrees this time of year? Literally. Is that crazy or what?"

"Your parents are sending you to hell. Hell with no ocean." Lilliana then seems to remember she's been trying to make me feel better about this road trip and attempts to smooth over her snarkiness. "But you'll probably get to see the Grand Canyon, right? Or will you? Where exactly are you going, anyway?"

I look at Lilliana and raise my eyebrows. The deeper meaning is not lost on me. On a more literal level, I know where we start and where we finish, but what about that whole middle part? It dawns on me that I have no idea. I'm still in denial that this is happening. I meant to read Matty's updated itinerary, but every time I think about it, it just makes me tired.

The shopping trip is going well; I buy some really cute shorts, tank tops, and sandals. Clothes and accessories make me feel better. I maximize my dollars by picking items that can be mixed and matched easily.

We're about to stop for lunch in the food court when we see him. He's holding hands with that bleached-out thing he calls a girl-friend, and they're standing in line at the new juice bar. Lilliana stops mid-sentence and follows my gaze.

"Rosie," she says, clutching my right arm with both her hands. I'm not sure if she's steadying me or holding me back.

Joey doesn't see me, but the ho does, and when our eyes meet, she gives me this smirk and kisses him right on the lips—for a while. Oh really now? She must mistake me for someone with patience. She shoots me another look, prompting Joey to turn in my direction. Our eyes lock and I hate myself, but I get that hopeful flutter in my chest. He opens his mouth like he's going to say something, then puts his arm around Blondie and drags her away.

"How many feet are between me and that a-hole right now?" I ask. I move to follow them, but Lilliana digs her nails into my arm. In that moment, I am so freaking glad I blew up his car that if I hadn't already done it, I'd be in his driveway with a gas can and a lighter.

"Come on," Lilliana says, and steers me toward the exit. "We're out of here."

Neither of us speaks until we get to the car. I sit in the passenger seat, my heart pumping like a double-kick drum. My skin feels hot.

The rapid rise and fall of emotions makes me dizzy. I go from anger to sadness to resignation. My parents and Matty are right. I can't risk seeing him again before my court date.

"Are you okay?" Lilliana finally asks.

I take a deep breath and wait for my pulse to slow down. My new role as Joey's wild ex-girlfriend is anxiety inducing, depressing, and exhausting.

"I'm not sure if I'm okay, but I will be." I find a good song on the radio and turn it all the way up. "I'm leaving for Arizona in three days and I cannot wait."

Maybe saying it out loud will convince me it's true.

CHAPTER 3

ON SATURDAY MORNING, I FOLLOW MATTY AND EDDIE ONTO the front porch and into the predawn darkness. I'm feeling extra groggy because I had a hard time getting to sleep and wound up taking two teaspoons of Benadryl around two in the morning. It should have knocked me out, but instead I tossed and turned like I had a fever. I even dreamed I wandered around the house looking for my phone and sent Joey a message telling him to meet me in Phoenix on the Fourth of July. Thankfully, when I woke up, my phone was nowhere in sight. My parents probably have it in a lockbox somewhere until it's time to transfer it to Matty. It felt so real, though.

I walk down the steps and cross the lawn. The grass is wet with that annoying early-morning dew, which is making me sorry I wore flipflops. The cicadas are chirping away and, wait . . . is that an owl? My parents follow us. Dad carries my bags; Mom clutches her coffee mug.

She and I share a serious caffeine addiction. This morning, however, my stomach has that sickish first-day-of-school feeling, made worse by my antihistamine hangover. I would have thrown up if I drank or ate anything. Pony was disappointed. He knows I'm the one most likely to share my breakfast with him.

It takes me a second to realize that the burgundy Taurus in Matty's driveway is my ride. Could there be a less cool vehicle? It screams rental, not road trip. I'm still getting over the lame car when a guy gets out of the front seat and walks toward us in a Snoopy T-shirt that says PARTY LIKE A ROCK STAR. Oh, man.

"Hi, I'm Spencer," he says. No kidding.

Matty's mom walks toward us with a thin, dark-haired woman who I'm assuming is Spencer and Logan's mom. I notice a forest-green Jeep at the curb that must belong to her. Now, that's a road-trip-worthy ride. Spencer shakes everyone's hand and Mrs. Davidson introduces herself as well. Except for several lengthy phone conversations between my mom and theirs (and probably a background check performed on the sly by one of my father's state trooper buddies), this is the first time we're all meeting. My parents are all smiles. Oh, I can read their minds all right. They're thinking, *Hallelujah! Rosie is going to Arizona with Matty and a member of the Peanuts gang. What could possibly go wrong?* But then Logan, the answer to my parents' silent, rhetorical question, gets out of the car. He's wearing perfect-fitting jeans and a dark gray V-neck shirt. The short sleeves hug his biceps, which appear perpetually flexed. His torso is twice the size of Spencer's, and he's sporting a sexy five o'clock shadow that would take Matty three weeks to grow. I'm suddenly angry at myself for not bothering with mascara and eyeliner and fumble in my bag for my shades, even though the sun has yet to break the horizon. Thankfully, I did my hair. I always do my hair.

"I'm Logan," he says. *Yes. Yes, you are!* I'm thinking as he shakes everyone's hand.

"Don't worry. We'll take good care of Rosie." Logan smiles at my parents and then me, and I notice that he's taller than all of us, even Matty.

It's like my heart rate and hormones heard the crack of the starting gun, and they're off! *No, no, no,* I tell them. *You two have gotten me in enough trouble already.* But it feels good to temporarily not have Joey in my head.

I look back toward our front door. Pony is watching me through the glass. He wags his tail wildly and gives me his I-need-some-lovin' face.

"Eddie, can you let Pony out? I want to say good-bye one more time."

He grumbles but does it anyway. He'd never admit it, but I know he's going to miss me. The fact that he's even awake right now speaks volumes.

As soon as Eddie opens the door, Pony bolts toward me. I think he's going to jump up on me for one last kiss, but he runs right by and goes to meet Spencer and Logan, twirling his tail like a baton. I should have known. He loves to greet new people, and it's not like he understands he won't be seeing me for a while. I try not to be jealous when Logan crouches down to pet him and Pony practically sits in his lap.

"Come 'ere, boy," I say. He obeys, and when I bend down to give him a squeeze, my chest tightens. "Make sure Eddie remembers to take you on long walks." I turn toward Eddie. "He likes to visit his pal, Suzie. She lives on Cook Road."

I give Dad a kiss on the cheek and he puts his arm around my shoulders for a sideways squeeze. He hands Matty my phone, the sight of which makes my heart double pump as I remember my texting dream. It was a dream, wasn't it?

Mom puts her empty mug down on the steps and envelops me in a big, squishy embrace. No matter how old I am, I never get tired of Mom's hugs, especially ones that leave my shirt with the lingering scent of her Estée Lauder moisturizer.

"Be good. Have fun," she says. I know without looking that she has tears in her eyes. My throat constricts.

"I will, Mom." I want it to be the truth. If not for myself, then at least for her and Dad.

"I love you."

"I love you too, Mom."

"Call us later today," Dad says.

Matty carries my bags to the car and Eddie follows. While Matty loads my stuff in the trunk, Eddie opens the door for me. Before I get in, he gives me a lightning-fast hug and whispers in my ear, "Be safe. Try not to kiss anyone."

I decide to do him a solid. "FYI. Your phone has a GPS," I whisper back. "Don't tell the parents I told you."

Eddie nods slowly as the information seeps in, and then he's gone. Logan and Spencer are already in the front seat. I'm about to sit down when I notice that Matty and I will be traveling with an acoustic guitar between us.

"Can't we put this in the trunk?" I ask.

"Logan says it takes up too much room," Spencer explains.

"So what? We can't crowd the luggage, but it's okay to crowd humans?" I ask.

My backpack is bulging with all my important stuff (e.g., credit card for emergencies, makeup, round brush, *CosmoGirl*, romance novel, Cheez-Its, and tunes) and I was hoping for more space back here.

"Just shut the door," mumbles Matty.

"Matty, can I see my phone for a sec?"

"We're still in the driveway."

"I know. Real quick. Please?" I need to put my fears to rest.

"Here." He slips it to me like it's some illicit substance.

Quickly, I page to my text messages and make sure there are none from last night. Phew. Nothing to Joey about the Fourth of July or anything else. I toss the phone back to Matty.

I wave to my family and the boys wave to their moms. As we pull out of the driveway, I'm surprised by how choked up I get. I've never been away from home before. I mean, sure, I've slept over at friends' houses and at my grandparents', and I've gone down the shore to Lilliana's family beach house, but never this far and with people I just met. My eyes fill with tears. Who gets homesick before they even leave their block? I don't have much time to dwell on this, because as soon as we turn the corner and my house is out of sight, Logan starts laying down ground rules.

"Just so you know, you're not getting any special treatment. We're going to say and do what we want, no apologies for guy behavior," Logan says.

"Fine," I tell Logan as I dig through my bag for a tissue to wipe dried grass clippings off my toes. Stupid dew. "If that includes noxious emissions, open a window. Even my little brother has the decency to do that."

"Only if we feel like it," Spencer pipes up.

Whoa, look at Snoopy growing a set of you-know-whats over there.

"Oh, yeah, and you're on our schedule," Logan continues. "No extra time for whatever girl things you've got going on. If you're not in the car when it's time to leave, we'll go without you."

"No, we won't," Matty says.

"No?" Logan looks at us in the rearview mirror, eyebrows raised. "Watch me."

"Watch me," I mimic. Mr. Tough Guy in a Taurus. My heart rate and hormones stop so fast they kick up a cloud of dust. He's one of those people who announces that he's "type A" as if it gives him permission to call the shots. I'm gonna wind up telling him what that "A" stands for before this trip is over. I can tell.

"That reminds me," Spencer says. "Here's your copy of the itinerary. It will help you stay on schedule." Another one? He hands me a double-pocket folder. Is he serious? There are maps on one side and at least ten typed pages of information on the other. He also has a contact list with all our cell phone numbers. Like we're going to get separated? I can see why he and Matty are such good friends—they're like obsessive-compulsive AAA buddies. I'm too tired to read this right now. Logan is fiddling with the radio and lands on a station that's playing country music. Nooo! Who knew we even had a country music station in the Tri-State Area?

"I don't suppose I get a vote about music," I say.

"Now you're catching on," Logan says.

I want to smack the smirk off that gorgeous face. Instead, I get my own tunes out of my backpack, put on my headphones, and close my eyes. It's my road trip too, and Springsteen is in order. Even though he's not who my friends listen to, I feel a special connection to him—even beyond the whole New Jersey thing—because my parents named me after one of his songs.

I cue up my Bruce playlist, and when the intro to "Girls in Their Summer Clothes" fills my ears, I feel a pang as I realize it's summer and I want to be at the beach, not heading two thousand miles in the wrong direction. I need to sleep. Maybe in a few hundred miles I'll look back on this, and just like it did for the Rosie in the Bruce song, it will all seem funny.

I wake up two hours later, my head against the window, the guitar's neck in my lap, and drool in the corner of my mouth. The car is parked and I'm alone. I look out the window. We're at some place called the Waffle House, and those bastards are going in without me. I push the guitar off me, wipe the spit off my face, and pick through the tangles in my long brown hair. I open the car door, grab my backpack, and stomp into the restaurant.

"Thanks a lot," I say. The three of them are standing inside the door by the sign that says PLEASE WAIT TO BE SEATED.

"We'd have woken you up by the time we were ready to order," Matty says. I'm pissed. He's the one who wanted me here, and now he's trying to starve me so he can impress Logan.

"Speak for yourself," Logan says. "She knows the rules."

Jerk. We follow the hostess to a booth by the window. I roll my eyes at Logan and then take the window seat. Matty slides in next to me. Thankfully, I'm across from Spencer, not Logan. I might have a muscle spasm and "accidentally" kick him.

"I would have brought you a bagel or something," Spencer says. He shrugs and opens the menu.

"Thank you." I give Spencer the best smile I'm capable of without lip gloss and nudge Matty's leg with my foot. "Where are we, anyway?"

"It's on the schedule," Spencer says. "Didn't you read your itinerary?"

Sleeping, duh. But I need Spence on my side if I expect to get fed on this road trip to hell. Besides, there's no reason that Snoopy shirt should keep us from becoming friends.

"You planned all our pit stops?"

"Of course," Spencer says. "We have an aggressive schedule. I want to make sure we get to see everything we want to see."

"What if there's something I want to see?"

"Is there something you want to see, Rosie?" Matty asks.

"I dunno," I say. "I didn't have a chance to think about it."

"I guess launching a full-out vendetta against your ex-boyfriend takes up a lot of free time," Logan says.

"What's your problem?" I say. "Can't you be nice?"

He's smiling, in a cute-ish, not smirky way, and his voice softens. "I thought I was. I let you in my car, didn't I? And I haven't even asked you for gas money yet."

"I guess that begs the question, why did you let me come along, anyway?"

"Because your friend Matty said—"

A waitress in a 1950s-style uniform arrives at our table and renders Logan, and the rest of us, speechless. The woman is older than my mom and has what appears to be a black plastic tarantula in her hair.

"Are you ready to order, or do you need a few minutes?" she asks.

I'd like to order, but my brain is screaming, *Why is there a plastic spider on your head?*

"I think we're ready," Matty says. "Cool hair ornament, by the way."

I can't look at Matty. I'm afraid I'll get the uncontrollable giggles. He's always been good at delivering these witty one-liners without cracking himself up. He does it because he knows what it does to me.

"Thanks. Keeps people on their toes," she says, lightly touching the side of her head. "What can I get you?"

"I'll have a buttermilk waffle, a side of bacon, and orange juice."

"I'll have the chocolate-chip Belgian waffle and coffee," I say.

Logan and Spencer both order Farmer's omelets, English muffins, and orange juice, although I notice Logan requests egg whites. Odd. I didn't think anyone under thirty worried about clogged arteries.

It sounds stupid, I know, but I miss Joey. If we were here together, we both would've ordered grilled cheese sandwiches and fries even though it's breakfast time. We loved grilled cheese dunked in ketchup. We also loved the Yankees, zombie movies, the beach (even in the winter), *That '70s Show* reruns, arcades and skee ball, taking the ferry to New York City, and just doing nothing together—sometimes for hours. I miss all those little things. But mostly, I miss the comfort of knowing I can be myself around a guy. He fell in love with me. The real me.

After the waitress brings our drinks, I go to the ladies' room to fix my hair and apply makeup. The guys haven't gotten their food yet, so I'm feeling confident they won't leave without me. This would be the perfect time to call Lilliana, if only I had my phone.

How did I get here? I think as I stare into the mirror, carefully lining my top and bottom eyelids. My eyes have looked better, but at the moment, nothing seems right.

I'm feeling only slightly more human when I emerge from the bathroom with smoother hair and copper eye shadow, my summer shade. As I walk down the hallway, away from the restrooms, and back toward our table, I pass a pay phone. Aha! That's it. I need to figure out how to use one of those things. Lilliana gave me a prepaid calling card before I left. She vowed to be my eyes and ears back home. Right now, however, my food is probably out, and I don't feel like getting left behind at a Waffle House in—where am I, anyway?

Matty steps out of the booth and lets me slide in toward the window. "So, when's our next stop?" I ask.

"It's in the—" Spencer says.

"I know, I'll read it when we get back in the car. Can you just answer my question for now?"

"Luray, Virginia," Spencer says.

"What's there?"

"Luray Caverns," Matty offers.

"What's Luray Caverns?"

"Only one of the most famous caves in the entire world." Spencer sounds like I've insulted him.

One of? Are others more famous? Spencer is going on and on about crystallized calcite, stalactites, stalagmites, blah, blah, blah. This dude is all about the caverns. It's kind of cute, the way he's getting so excited. I smile and try to listen (okay, maybe not that hard), but all I can think about is what may be lurking amidst those rocks.

"Uh, are there bats in these caverns?"

"I knew it," Logan says. "You can wait in the car."

"Maybe I will," I say. Great comeback.

I silently obsess about creatures of the night during the rest of breakfast, and after three cups of coffee I totally need to pee before we leave. I drag Matty with me, using the excuse that I need to use my phone in private, but the truth is, I'm beginning to think Logan is serious about leaving me behind.

"Uh, I'm not going in, you know that, don't you?" Matty points from me to the ladies' room door.

"You mean you're not going to line the toilet seat with paper for me? Of course I know you're not going in. Just wait here!"

"Relax," Matty says.

"Sorry. Logan is just such a jerk. He's pissing me off."

"Yeah, that's why you'll be in love with him by the time we hit the Pennsylvania-Virginia border," Matty half mumbles.

"What?"

"You heard me; just pee, will ya."

At least I found out I'm in Pennsylvania.

When we get back to the car, Logan is leaning against the driver's door. He looks at us and makes this lasso/whoop-dee-doo motion with his pointer finger before getting in the Taurus. Is that, like, dork code for hurry up? It's very annoying.

Once we're all in the car, Logan lets out a big sigh before he starts the engine. "Notice how you made two trips to the bathroom and we didn't go at all."

"Yeah, well, I heard holding in your pee causes impotence," I snipe.

This gets Spencer's attention. He stops hooking up his tunes to the car stereo and whips his head around.

"That's not true," Spencer says. "Where did you hear that?"

It's not true. At least, I don't think it is. But Matty the peacemaker jumps in and lightens the collective mood. He picks up the guitar and starts strumming, making up his own words to a Black Eyed Peas song.

"I got a feeling," he sings, "there's a plastic tarantula in my hair. I got a feeling, it's a giant arachnid, but I don't care."

"When did you start playing guitar?" I'm shocked.

"Spence's teaching me. I'd be a lot better if I owned my own guitar," he says.

Huh. How did I not know this? He practically lives on our sofa. I pick up my itinerary as Logan drives back toward the highway.

Luray Caverns, here we come.

CHAPTER 4

"WE'RE GOING TO DALLAS? WHY ARE WE GOING TO DALLAS?"
I sputter.

I'm flipping through the folder Spencer gave me as the Taurus makes its way along Skyline Drive—a 105-mile scenic trip through the Blue Ridge Mountains in Shenandoah National Park, according to Spencer's notes. We've passed lots of rolling, green mountains and two wild turkeys. So far, the scenery is underwhelming and the conversation is lacking. After Luray, we'll head to Nashville, then Memphis, and then, for some strange reason, we veer off Interstate 40 and instead head south to Dallas. Why?!

"Booty call," Spencer says to me. He's tuning his guitar in the front seat.

"What?"

"It's not a booty call," Logan insists. "We're stopping by to see a friend."

I wish they'd both quit saying "booty call."

"You don't just 'stop by' Texas," I say.

"I do," Logan says.

"Must be some friend," Matty says. "What's her name?"

"Avery. We hung out all weekend at a prefreshman orientation a few weeks ago. She'll start ASU in the fall too."

I can see Logan in the rearview mirror. He smiles in a way that really pisses me off.

"And we're going to Dallas because . . . ?" I need more here.

"Avery lives there." I can hear the "duh" in Logan's voice and I don't like it. "We've been talking a lot. She said to visit her if I'm ever in Texas."

"But we're not going to Texas, we're going to Arizona, and it doesn't exactly look like it's on the way."

"It is if my brother thinks he's going to get some. . . ." Spencer trails off.

Logan holds the wheel with his left hand and whops Spencer's head with his right.

"Watch the guitar." Spencer's all jammed up in the passenger seat with the acoustic on his lap. Unfortunately, the case is still hogging up the backseat.

"You should be happy," Logan says in my direction. "You'll have some female companionship for a couple of days."

"Days? Whataya mean 'days'?" I ask incredulously. How well does he know this Avery person?

"We're spending two nights at her house," Logan says.

"All four of us?" Is he serious? Maybe she's the kind of person who invites strangers to her house but doesn't really mean it.

"She says there's plenty of room," Logan adds.

"You should have known all this," Spencer says, turning to look at me. "It's in the—"

I hold up my hand to stop him. "Well, if Logan gets to go to Dallas, then I want to go to Dollywood."

"I thought you hated country music," Matty says.

"I do, but I love roller coasters and Dolly Parton. She's Miley's godmother." I have a secret addiction to *Hannah Montana* reruns.

"We don't have time," Spencer says. "From the caverns we're driving straight through to Nashville."

"So?" I say.

"So, Dollywood is near Knoxville, which is before Nashville. We'd have to spend the night there. That's not part of the plan," Logan says.

"Let's change the plan," I say. "We can stay one night in Dallas, which would give us time to spend one night near Dollywood." And then I say, in a singsong voice for effect, "Probably more girls at Dollywood than at Avery's house."

Spencer turns around again and raises his eyebrows. He looks at Matty, who seems equally intrigued by the idea. Aha, I might have a mutiny on my hands. I give Spencer and Matty a knowing smile and let it drop for now. If I work this right . . . Hooray for Dollywood!

An hour later, we pull into the visitors' center at Luray Caverns. I grab my backpack and follow the boys to the rustic-looking main building, where we each shell out eighteen bucks for the tour and proceed to the cavern's entrance.

There's an eerie chill as we begin our slow descent down the smooth stone walkway inside the caves. Goose bumps rise across my arms. If I weren't so anxious all of a sudden, it would feel like I'm on line for the Pirates of the Caribbean ride at Disney World. I wish I were. Where is Orlando Bloom when you need him?

Darren, our tour guide, is going through his spiel about flowstone and dripstone as we walk along the well-worn pathway. He explains formation after formation—like the Great Stalactite pipe organ, these rocks that look like fried eggs—each illuminated with dramatic lighting. Under different circumstances, I might enjoy the beauty of these ancient sculptures, but it's hard to concentrate because (a) I'm terrified of winged creatures with fangs and (b) I'm wearing a tank top and short shorts and it's freezing in here. A guy toward the front with a kid on his shoulders reads my mind and asks about the temperature.

"The caverns remain at a constant fifty-five degrees," Darren says. Hearing that only makes me colder, not to mention hungry. "Remember, at our lowest point we will be one hundred and sixty-four feet below the earth's surface."

Great. Now it feels like the walls are closing in.

"What time is it?" I whisper to Matty. I'm lost without my phone. I need to get a watch. I need to get air. I need to get out of this cave.

"Eleven thirty."

"How long is this tour?"

"About an hour," Matty says.

"If you'll follow me this way," Darren says. "We're approaching Dream Lake. The lake is only about eighteen to twenty inches deep, but the stillness of the water gives you a perfect reflection of the stalactite ceiling. It's an amazing photo op."

I inhale slowly through my nose and exhale through my mouth. I'm trying to appreciate Dream Lake, but my thoughts wander back to the rock formation that looked like giant potato chips, and that reminds me of the Cheez-Its in my bag. Did Darren say anything about eating on the tour? Screw it. I'm cold, starving, and edgy. I move toward the back of the group, pull out my snack bag as discreetly as possible, and sneak some crunchy squares into my mouth. Everyone else is gawking at Dream Lake and taking pictures, but I hang back, munching away and breathing better with each salty bite.

I'm reaching into my pack for bottled water when it happens: Something makes a dive for my head. I stifle the urge to drop the F-bomb as I drop my bag, spilling Cheez-Its onto the cave floor. My heart is about to explode. I turn in circles and start running my fingers through my hair like I'm giving myself a shampoo. *Please don't be a bat. Please don't be a bat.* My silent freak-out is starting to attract some attention. So much for the captivating beauty of Dream Lake. Matty turns around. A snaky smile spreads across his face as he catches my eye and saunters toward the back of the line.

"Ohmygod, ohmygod, ohmygod," I whisper-scream when Matty arrives at my side. "Matty! Something just dive-bombed me. Is it in my hair? Do you see anything?"

I think Matty will know what to do, but he just stands there, smiling and shaking his head. Joey would have saved me from the bloodsucker by now. That's if Joey would have agreed to explore a cave to begin with, which he wouldn't.

"Matty, is it gone?" I say as I grab hold of his arm and watch the cave ceiling. "Was it a bat?"

"Not a bat," Matty says, "Batman."

Matty bends down and picks up a small plastic figure off the floor. By now, we have attracted the attention of our guide and a few random tourists.

"Is everything okay back there?" Darren asks as he peers around the crowd. Then he spots the Cheez-Its on the ground and his eyes bug out. "Miss, I'd like to remind you that food and drink are not allowed inside the caverns."

It's at this point that I see that man with the kid on his shoulders walking toward me. The kid's face lights up when he sees Matty holding the tiny Caped Crusader.

"You found my Batman," the boy exclaims.

I'm too relieved to be angry. Thankfully, Darren is moving on, and the crowd is following.

"You suck," I tell Matty. I don't even want to look at him as I drop to my knees and scoop up the mess I made. Within seconds, Matty is at my side helping.

"Now, that was funny," he says.

I roll my eyes.

And then Matty starts to sing. "I've got a feeling, there's a plastic Batman in my hair. . . ."

I purse my lips and try not to smile, but I can't help it. The next thing I know, I'm laughing so hard I'm doing sleep apnea snorts and I've got to pee. And you know what? It feels pretty damned good.

CHAPTER 5

I CALL MY PARENTS AS WE'RE PULLING AWAY FROM LURAY Caverns. Matty dials for me. He's carrying his responsibility too far. It's so annoying. After what seems like thirty-five-thousand years, he hands me my phone. It's nice to hold my cell again. I miss it. It's like I'm constantly aware of this two-by-three-inch void. After some initial chitchat with Mom about where we are and how I'm feeling, I start to work my magic.

"Guess what?" I say.

"What?" Mom says.

"Logan is taking us all to Dollywood. Can you believe it? I said I wanted to go and he said 'okay.'"

Logan can be a dick if he wants, but now he's a dick on his way to Dollywood.

"You're going to California?"

"No, Ma, Dollywood. In Tennessee."

There's a long pause, and I know it's because Mom is either totally confused by how happy I am to be going to Dollywood or completely dumbfounded by the fact that such a place exists.

"That's great, honey." Mom sounds hesitant. "Have a good time. Let me get Dad. He wants to say hello too."

When Dad finally picks up the kitchen phone, he tells me I need to speak with my lawyer soon.

"His name is Steve Justice."

"Are you kidding me?" I hope this isn't some guy my dad found from a cheesy TV commercial.

"A good friend of mine recommended him. He said Steve knows his way around a restraining order," Dad says. "You're going to have to set up a call with him to answer some questions."

"Okay, will do," I say. "Thanks, Dad."

"Love you," he says, and then he just hangs up. My dad doesn't transition well on the phone. Never has. When the conversation's over, there's no "good-bye" or "talk to you soon." It's nothing but dial tone.

"My dad says admission to Dollywood is on him. I can put it on my emergency credit card." I'm cringing inside at my lie. The karma police are coming for me soon.

What else can I do? If I don't want to spend extra time at some strange girl's house, I need to secure our diversion to Dollywood. Admittedly, I care less about the theme park and more about screwing with Logan's plan. Plus, I don't want them to know I was talking about my lawyer. "Oh, and my mom says to thank Logan for taking such good care of her daughter. Just like you said you would."

Matty raises his eyebrows. He knows when I'm up to something, but I know he wants to go to Dollywood. In my head, I silently promise God I'll pay back my dad.

"Awesome," Spencer says, and pulls out his iPhone. "I'll see if I can get some deets on Dollywood."

Spencer's kid-in-a-candy-store approach to life is very endearing.

My own phone makes the new-text-message noise. I look at Matty. "Am I allowed to read it?"

"Let me see who it's from first."

My stomach does a flippy thing. I don't even want to let myself hope that it's Joey. I'm hurt and mad, but I still want to talk to him. I need closure. It would make me feel so much better if he reached out to me. And then it hits me—can a TRO be violated in reverse?

"Lilliana," Matty says, and hands me the phone. I look at the screen.

yo. got info. call when ya can. later. l.

"Can I call her?"

Matty dials and hands me the phone only after Lilliana picks up. What does he think? I'm devious enough to program Joey's number under Lilliana's name? Okay, I am. I just didn't think of it in time.

"What's up?"

"Joey's been talking shit about you," Lilliana says.

"What kind of shit?"

"He's been telling everyone how you put out on your first date."

"What? How do you know this?" I keep my voice even and turn toward the window. I feel Matty, Logan, and Spencer listening. I don't want to give away how upset I am as the state of Virginia passes by in a blur of blacktop and green.

"My brother's working at ShopRite for the summer. He's worked a few shifts with Joey. Says he brags about all the crazy shit he does with the slut. He's been telling everyone you were easy, but she's better."

In our town, at some point everybody either works at ShopRite or knows someone who does. Sometimes, Eddie hangs out with Lilliana's brother. I hope this disgusting lie doesn't get back to him.

I don't say anything for a few seconds. I'm afraid to talk. I don't want to cry. I am trapped in this car with my anger and I can't do anything about it. What a sleazy thing to do, although I guess I can understand Joey bragging about his exploits with my slutty replacement, but why drag me into it? Is this revenge for his car? I'm shocked he wants to hurt me like this.

"You okay?" Lilliana finally asks.

"I'm good. Call you later."

"Sorry. I thought you'd want to know."

"I did. I do. Thanks."

I disconnect and hand my phone back to Matty without looking at him. I'm helpless. As my life in New Jersey falls apart, I'm hundreds of miles away and relying on Lilliana to tell me what's happening. I'm so confused. Is that all Joey wanted all along? To get in my pants? I thought it was enough for him to be *with* me, not *be* with me.

None of this makes sense. Joey had always been completely respectful. Never tried to push me into anything I didn't want to do. He let me initiate things, and mostly, it was just kissing. He seemed fine with that. On Valentine's Day, after we'd been together for about five months, he worked it so we'd have his house to ourselves for a few uninterrupted hours. He ordered out from my favorite Italian restaurant and bought me gold heart earrings. We messed around on the couch for a while. Joey is the best kisser. He has this way of doing things with his mouth that makes a girl want to do more. So, yeah, it was me who said we should go upstairs. I thought I was ready, but once we were actually in his bed together, on the verge of crossing that line, I pulled the plug on the operation. You don't spend two-and-a-half years in an all-girls Catholic school without developing some sense of guilt.

Joey was wonderful about it. He just wrapped his arms around me, turned my chin so he was looking straight into my eyes, and said: "I love you. I'll wait." Then he added, "Your first time should be special. Even if it's not with me. Remember that, Rosie. You are worth it."

At that moment, he felt like a best friend and a boyfriend. I loved having the excitement of "someday" to hold on to and couldn't imagine my first time being with anybody but him. He would wait for me. I didn't realize he meant until someone willing came along. Maybe if I hadn't put the brakes on, we'd still be together. My head hurts. I close my eyes and lean back against the seat.

I don't know how much time passes before I open my eyes again, but when I do, I meet Logan's gaze in the rearview mirror.

"You aren't getting carsick, are you, Catalano?" Logan asks in his usual, caustic tone. His eyes tell a different story. It's weird, but I can tell he's concerned. Weirder still? The thought of him worrying about me is oddly appealing, making it hard to think of a snarky comeback.

"I'm fine," I say. And leave it at that.

As we're leaving Virginia, we pass a pristine white post fence that seems to go on forever. I try to peer beyond it, looking for an enormous farmhouse or mansion in the distance, and that's when I see them, four gorgeous horses on a ridge near the side of the road. One is black with white around its hooves. Two are a coppery brown, and one is a whitish, silvery color—she looks almost iridescent. And I say "she" because, despite her rippling muscles, she has a girly look about her. The horses make me think of Pony, and home. I wonder if my parents are following me on some website, like the airlines do, charting my progress with the GPS.

We pull into a motel in Pigeon Forge, Tennessee, around seven. Dollywood closes in an hour, so we agree to go first thing in the morning when the gates open. It's obvious this unplanned stop is making Logan uptight, but he thinks we can still be on the road to Nashville by sometime tomorrow afternoon and then push on to Memphis the next morning. He's trying to make up time for the Dollywood stop so we can still spend two nights in Dallas. Either he wants to win as much as I do or he really, really likes this girl.

Or worse, maybe underneath all the nice talk, he's just like Joey and only after one thing. I hope that's not the case, but if it is, that's more incentive to sabotage Logan's Texas side trip.

The motel room has two double beds. It seems like a waste of money for me to get my own room, and truthfully, I'd be scared. I don't do "alone" very well. I'm relieved when Logan says: "Who wants to find out about getting a roll-out bed?" As much as I hate to admit it, I like the way he handles things. Even though he's bossy, I feel safe with Logan leading this trip.

"Me and Spencer can," Matty says.

"Anyone else starving?" Spencer asks.

"Why don't Logan and I make a food run?" Did I just say that? I can't believe I'm offering to spend time alone in the car with Logan, but I don't feel like sticking around here and trying to wrap my brain around the fact that I'll be spending tonight in a motel room with three guys. Boy, I sure know how to make my parents proud.

It stinks to be back in the car so soon—literally. I didn't notice the boys'-locker-room scent while I was immersed in it. Boys are smelly.

"Let's get Wendy's. I like their salads," Logan suggests.

What's up with this guy? Egg whites. Salads. Hasn't he heard of the Baconator? I want to say, *Get a penis.* But I stick to the topic at hand.

"Fine. But I'm getting a burger and fries. I may need a Frosty, too."

"Emotional eating will get you in trouble."

Now I'm angry that I didn't insult his manhood over the salad.

"Listen, Dr. Phil. I'm hungry. I haven't eaten since that waffle hut, which seems like it was yesterday," I only got, like, two Cheez-Its in my mouth before the Batman attack.

"It's just—you seemed pretty upset after you talked to your friend." We're at a red light and he turns to look at me.

"Glad I could provide some added entertainment. What? Tired of listening to your country music station already?"

"I wasn't trying to listen," he says quietly. "Forget it."

He sounds hurt. Maybe that's why I decide to spill.

"My ex is telling people that I'm, ya know, that we—"

"Didn't you?"

My eyes bug and I whack him on the arm.

"Ow. That hurt, Catalano."

"It works both ways. Whataya mean, 'didn't you?'"

"I'm surprised, that's all. I've seen Joey around school . . . and Matty said you were together awhile."

"So you're surprised I'm not slutty?!" Has that been his impression of me from the start? Is it because he knows the kind of girls Joey dates?

Logan actually looks somewhat embarrassed. His cheeks flush and he backpedals. "No. I mean, there's nothing wrong with it, I just figured—"

Thankfully, we're at Wendy's. "Right. I'm glad you've got me all figured out." I open the car door, slam it hard, and leave him sitting there for a few seconds. Eventually, he catches up with me in the fast-food-line maze. I'm looking up at the menu board as if I don't have it memorized. Logan inserts himself into my line of sight and smiles at me. My stomach goes all spacey. I chalk it up to hunger. He's got a small dimple on the right side. I hadn't noticed. Probably because he hardly smiles.

"I don't have you figured out. I'm sorry. Really."

I avert my eyes from him. I want to stay pissed, but I can't. Especially since he said he was sorry. That's more than Joey ever did. Even when we were together and had our little spats, he was never quick to apologize. "Fine. Buy me a blended chocolate Oreo Frosty and we'll call it even."

"Emotional eating," he says.

I get burger combo meals for me, Matty, and Spencer and then turn Logan over to the Wendy's lady. I smile when I hear him tack my blended Frosty onto his order. He wordlessly hands it to me as we head for the car. I pop the straw in and lean it toward his mouth like I used to do for Joey.

Logan raises one eyebrow as he leans toward me to take a sip, holding my gaze longer than expected. "Aren't you afraid I've got cooties?"

"Cooties don't scare me." But the way my heart speeds up when he looks at me with those honey-colored eyes? That's a different story.

CHAPTER 6

IT'S TWO MINUTES AFTER NINE ON SUNDAY MORNING AND I'm in Pigeon Forge, Tennessee, standing inside the front gate of Dollywood. I should be more excited. I would be if I were here with Lilliana and some girlfriends, or even my family. But my reason for this road trip won't exactly win me a spot on Ms. Parton's next TV commercial. "I just got served with a TRO. I'm going to Dollywood!" I wish I were here under happier circumstances. Wait until my dad sees how much admission for four adults costs. I felt light-headed with guilt when I handed over his Visa.

I unfold my park map, and Spencer and Matty peer over my shoulders. Logan stands apart from us, reading the schedule in front of one of the theaters. I guess he really does love country.

"I say we start with the Thunderhead or Tennessee Tornado," Matty says.

"Or Blazing Fury," I say. "That sounds interesting."

Spencer points to the map's attractions list. "Ooh. What about Star Trek Live? I want to leave time for that. It's a Mad Science presentation. Remember Mad Science camp, Matty?"

I don't question how Star Trek fits into a Dolly Parton theme park. I can't argue with the Dollywood logic; so far this place has something for everyone. It's like the Magic Kingdom of the Appalachians.

"Where're we headed?" Logan asks as he rejoins the group. He's in a surprisingly good mood.

"The Thunderhead," I say.

The dark scruff Logan's got going on makes him look very rock star. For a few seconds, my mind slips into hot-guy fantasy mode, but then Logan makes that annoying lasso motion with his index finger and says: "Let's get moving." I can almost hear my dream bubble pop.

We wind our way through the maze for the Thunderhead. There is this girl with ginormous breasts in a spandex tank top about ten people ahead of us. We pass her every time the line moves. If these three morons don't stop gaping, I'm gonna push one of them so hard he'll fall into that cleavage canyon. Finally, we arrive on the platform, where the line splits up and people pair off to wait in cattle chutes for the next coaster to arrive. Spencer and Matty want to ride in the front car. The line for that car is, like, three times as long.

For once, Logan and I agree—we're not waiting. The downside is that I'm now crammed into a tight car with Logan. Our thighs are touching out of necessity, and I try to convince myself that the only reason my heart is yammering away is because I'm anticipating the first big drop. Thankfully, I love roller coasters, so I know I won't go all girly on Logan and grab hold of his arm or anything. The coaster begins its slow ascent, clackety-clacking along the metal tracks. I look off into the distance. The scenery is lush—Tennessee has beautiful rolling green hills. I'm watching some kind of bird with a huge wingspan circle above the treetops when the bottom drops out from under me and we careen straight down, pivoting into a sharp turn at the bottom. Adrenaline rushes through me, and I throw my arms in the air.

"This is awesome!"

"What?" Logan screams.

"This is awe—" But I don't have time to finish before we're falling again.

After a few more fast twists and turns, which press me up against Logan and Logan up against me, the car finally screeches to a halt.

"Looks like Spock and Bones are still waiting for the first car," Logan says. He offers me a hand out of the coaster car. "Bet we have time to ride this one again. You in?"

I try to ignore the tingle when I put my hand in his. "Sure."

After the Thunderhead, we go on the Tennessee Tornado, the Blazing Fury, and the Timber Tower, which looks like a giant circular free fall but falls over like a giant tree, hence the "timber." Spencer shrieks like a thirteen-year-old girl and later explains that he gets vertigo on anything that spins. We end our day at Dollywood with lunch, followed by a show called Dreamland Drive-In, which makes me almost appreciate country music. There's a tell-it-like-it-is raw emotion that I find appealing. It's heartbreak music.

"Three chords and the truth." That's what Logan says when I share my thoughts with him as we leave the show. "Harlan Howard said that."

"Are you sure it wasn't Bono?" I'm being serious.

Logan shakes his head, disappointed. "Let's go. We've got a lot of ground to cover."

Unfortunately, Spencer isn't feeling much better as we leave the park and head for the car. Poor guy, I was hoping food and the air-conditioned theater would help. Spencer is very delicate, I'm learning.

"The only way I'm not going to get carsick is if I drive," Spencer says.

"Knock yourself out, little bro," Logan says. "I'm going to sit in the back and sleep."

"Shotgun!" Matty and I yell in unison like two ten-year-olds. Logan grimaces and takes a quarter out of his pocket.

"Heads or tails." He looks at me.

"Heads."

Logan flips with his right thumb and slaps the coin down on his left forearm. He peeks underneath without revealing the coin.

"Heads."

I wonder if he's being nice and letting me win, or if he doesn't want to be in the backseat with me. Matty scowls. I expect him to demand to see the coin, but he gives in.

"Fine. But if she's sitting up front, we're listening to my tunes. I put a lot of work into Matty's Playlists for the Road, and we haven't listened to them yet."

Then Logan does his lasso finger motion again. He's not going to be happy when I reach over and bend that finger backward.

"What's on here?" Spencer asks as he hands Matty the cord so he can hook up his iPod to the car stereo.

"The tunes range from epic to apropos of location," he says. "Like this one."

Matty taps the screen and cues up a song. Banjo, upright bass. "Country," I mumble.

"Not just any country," Matty says. "Cash." We roll down the windows. The afternoon sun is still blazing, but Spencer claims he needs fresh air so he won't puke up his veggie kabob. Enough said. I'll put my hair in a twist and deal with the aftermath later. We drive in silence as we head toward the interstate. The air smells flowery and the sky is cloudless. I lean my head out the open window and look at my distorted face in the side-view mirror as I listen to the song about love and burning, fire and desire.

I turn and glare at Matty. "What?" he says, all innocent. "Johnny Cash lived near Memphis."

"We're on our way to Nashville," I say.

"A place he helped to define. He was the youngest living person inducted into the Country Music Hall of Fame," Spencer adds.

"Right . . . so this has nothing to do with me?"

"You flambé one car and now you think every song with fire in it is about you," Logan says. "Get over yourself, Catalano."

"Apropos of location," Matty says. "And epic."

Spencer pokes his head into the backseat and looks back and forth between me and Matty as he speaks. His stomach has settled and Logan is driving again. "Here's what we'll do," Spencer says. He flips to the page in his trip itinerary titled Nashville in One Day. Due to our unscheduled stop at Dollywood, he's modifying the plan to fit what's left of today and part of tomorrow and calling it A Taste of Nashville. "As soon as we arrive, we'll head over to Ryman Auditorium to see if we can get tickets for the Grand Ole Opry tonight because we can't be in Nashville and not go to the Grand Ole Opry. Then we can probably make it over to the Wildhorse Saloon for line dance lessons and dinner before heading back for the show. Tomorrow—"

"Okay, bro. We get it," Logan says. "Breathe."

Spencer shoots him a look. He is undeterred. "Tomorrow, we'll hit the Country Music Hall of Fame and Museum, walk around a bit, have lunch at Jack's Bar-B-Que, and be on the road to Graceland by twelve thirty."

"Sounds like a plan," Matty says.

"Sounds like watching paint dry while someone plays a banjo," I say. Spencer looks hurt, and I wish I could take my snottiness back.

Spencer is the last person in the world I'd want to hurt, and I should be thankful we're not spending the evening trying to sneak into nudie bars. A trip with Joey and his friends would have been like a pole dance tour of America. This is a unique bunch I'm traveling with.

Matty gives me a chance to redeem myself. "Jack's Bar-B-Que has ribs. You know you like ribs."

"You're right," I say. "I do love ribs. I'm sorry, Spencer, it was the low blood sugar talking. And the dance lessons sound fun." They don't really, but this is me trying to be more like Matty.

When we arrive in Nashville, we check into a motel before driving over to Ryman Auditorium, where we "luck out" and are able to snag four tickets to the Grand Ole Opry. Whoo. Hoo. Or should I say, yeehaw? From there it's on to the Wildhorse Saloon for country line dancing. I have to admit, Spencer looks pretty good on the dance floor. Matty? Not so much. But watching him try to move his lanky limbs was worth every minute of the hour-long boot-scootin' lessons.

After dinner—I had blazin' wings and a burger—we head to Ryman Auditorium to see a lineup that includes the Charlie Daniels Band ("The Devil Went Down to Georgia" never gets old, apparently), Lee Roy Parnell, Diamond Rio, and some other acts I've never heard of and never, ever want to see again. I know I should be enjoying myself, but I'm homesick. My Jersey Girl soul is shriveling up and dying out here. I'm quiet on the ride back to the motel, and my mood only gets worse when I learn that the pull-out couch is missing a mattress.

"Looks like we're bunking together," Matty says.

"Looks like you're sleeping on the floor, you mean," I snipe. But when I get a good look at the floor, with its faded blue, indoor/outdoor carpeting, I relent.

"Fine," I say. "But if you touch me, I will kill you."

"I was about to say the same thing to you." Matty makes the peace sign and points from his eyes to mine. "I'm watching you."

"Watch away. After I wash my face and brush my teeth, all you're going to see is me sleeping." It's true. I'm exhausted. Both physically and emotionally. I miss Pony curled up on my bed, family dinner at five thirty, day trips to the beach. I want to call Lilliana, but I decide to wait until the morning. I've also got to call my parents for the lawyer's number and then set up a time with his office to discuss my case.

"Matty. Can you text my mom to tell her where we are and that everything is fine?"

"What do I look like?"

"The seven-foot-tall keeper of my phone."

"She's got you there," Spencer says.

"I know, right?" I say. And then I grab a towel and head for the shower. I decide to make it quick. I'll take another one and wash my hair in the morning.

When I come out of the bathroom, Logan and Spencer are sitting at the table by the window and Matty is sitting on the edge of their bed. They're playing cards and half watching a baseball game on TV. I peel away the bedspread and throw it on the floor (I've heard stories about body fluids on those things). Next, I turn up the edges of the fitted sheets and perform my nightly bedbug inspection before I get into the bed on the side closest to the wall. I fold the sheet over the top of the blanket so it won't touch my skin, put an extra pillow in the middle of the bed to keep Matty on his side, then mumble something that sounds like "good night," and before I know it, I'm out.

CHAPTER 7

WHEN I OPEN MY EYES THE NEXT MORNING, MATTY IS STARING down at me, his head propped up on his hand.

"Morning, sunshine," he says. "You fart in your sleep."

"What?!" I'm instantly wide awake. I sit up and smack him with my pillow. "I do not."

"You do," Logan says from the chair by the window. He's reading this thick book with a boring cover. His hair is wet, like he's freshly showered, and he's already dressed. In that instant, he reminds me of my father. "Nothing to be ashamed of. Everybody does it."

I want to die. I don't know if they're telling the truth or teasing me. I kick off the covers, stomp to the bathroom, and open the door. I catch Spencer coming out of the shower mid-stride. He shrieks and it's as if we're on the Timber Tower all over again, only this time, I scream too and slam the door.

I feel trapped. I'm wearing shorts and a T-shirt without a bra, but I don't care. I bolt for the front door, bed head and all. I plop myself into one of the two plastic white chairs under our motel room window and cross my arms over my boobs. The door opens a few seconds later. Matty sits down beside me and hands me my phone.

"I'm sorry," he says. "You don't fart in your sleep."

I don't feel the need to comment further on my flatulence or lack thereof, so I simply take my phone. "Trust me?"

"Yep." Then he gets up and goes back inside the room.

I look at the clock on my phone. Seven fifty-five. Is there a time difference between New Jersey and Tennessee? Either way, it's too early to call Lilliana. She sleeps until noon if she's not working. This doesn't stop me, though. I'm expecting straight to voice mail, but Lilliana answers.

"Hey," says a groggy voice.

"Hey, you answered."

"I've been leaving my phone ringer on just in case you need me." My eyes fill with tears and I'm too choked up to talk. Lilliana is so not the mother hen type. But it confirms what I've always known. She's a great friend. "Everything okay?"

"Define okay. Does it include sitting outside a motel in Nashville with morning breath, bad hair, and nothing to look forward to but a morning at the Country Music Hall of Fame?"

My voice breaks. I'm crying now and not even trying to hide it.

"Don't be such a wuss," Lilliana says. "There's got to be something else you can do. Maybe you can go shopping and meet up with the guys later. Shopping always makes you happy."

"Maybe," I say. Could I? I've never walked around a strange city by myself, and I'm not sure I want to start today. What I really want to do is go home. Not because of Joey. I just want to feel normal again.

"Can you do me a favor and check the bus schedule from Nashville to New Jersey?"

I mull a possible scenario. As my GPS-enabled phone continues to blip westward in the Taurus with Matty, I can take the bus home and stay with Lilliana.

Lilliana sighs. "Ro. Do you really think that's an option? What will you do when you get home? Your parents will freak."

"Please, Lilliana. Please just check."

"Hold on."

Can this work? Will Matty tell on me? Sure, he'll be pissed, but if he blows my cover, he'll be risking the wrath of my father. When did I become an evil schemer?

"There's a Greyhound bus leaving at eleven a.m. today that will get you to Newark, New Jersey, at ten thirty tomorrow morning. That's practically twenty-four hours. Do you really want to spend an entire day traveling on a bus, alone?"

Wow. I didn't realize it would take that long. "How much is the ticket?"

"A hundred and thirty-three dollars."

Oh, man. That's a lot of money to put on my emergency credit card, not to mention the Dollywood tickets I charged. My heart races and there's a pulsing sensation in the back of my skull. Can I pull this off? Should I? What will running home solve?

Lilliana interrupts my thoughts. "Rosie, are you still there?"

"Listen, I'll call you in an hour. Can I stay with you if I decide to do this?"

"Of course. I got your back. But even I think staying away until your court date is a good idea. Stop whining and tough it out. You'll feel better about yourself."

I only hear about half of Lilliana's pep talk. I'm plotting. I'll need to stuff some supplies in my backpack for the bus ride since I won't be able to get my bag out of the trunk once the car is locked. I can tell the guys I don't feel like touring the Hall of Fame. Write Matty a note and leave it on the windshield, under the wiper. Then I'll take a cab and get to the bus station before they're done looking at Kenny Rogers's first pair of cowboy boots. With any luck, I'll board the bus before they notice I'm gone. Logan will probably be happy to be rid of me.

"Ro? Are you listening to me?"

"I am. I am. Let me think about this and call you back."

"Don't do anything you'll regret. You can be very impuls—"

"Yeah, yeah. I know. I'll call ya." I hang up before she can say any more. "Impulsive." That adjective's been attached to my name since I tried to escape the preschool playground when I was four. As the years went on, teachers added "intelligent underachiever" and "determined" to the comments section of my report cards. My mother maintains this is a polite way of saying "stubborn and defiant" but is quick to add that I'm the type of person who is smart enough to do anything she puts her mind to. The problem is, "anything" is rather broad. I'll be the first to admit, I lack focus.

The door opens again, and this time it's Logan. He puts a hand on my shoulder. I'm wound up so tight with thoughts of escape that it's like I melt. His touch feels protective, safe. Can I make the rest of this trip work? Is he a good enough reason to want to?

"We're leaving here in fifteen minutes," he says.

"Fifteen minutes?" So much for giving it a go. "That's barely enough time to shower. How am I supposed to blow-dry my hair?"

"I suggest you bust a move."

Bust a move? Who says that? It's like all Logan's dorkiness is cloaked by that great body. Clark Kent in reverse. I race inside and order the guys out of the room while I shower, change, and toss extra clothes into my backpack. My legs need a shaving, but I have to prioritize. Fourteen minutes later, I step out of the motel room in a brown sundress with my wet hair in a twist, pulling my suitcase on wheels behind me, buoyed by the fact that this may be my last motel checkout with the Geek Squad.

We drive through Starbucks for breakfast and I only get a coffee. Matty asks me if I'm feeling okay. Normally I'd be partaking in a sausage, egg, and cheese sandwich with him and Spencer, but I tell him I'm still digesting my dinner from last night instead of the truth, which is that I'm too nervous to eat. Once again, health-conscious Logan gets some kind of egg-white-wheat-pita-antioxidant something or other. I hold my cup near the air-conditioning vent to cool my coffee as we drive to the Country Music Hall of Fame and Museum. We're supposed to spend an hour or two there before leaving for Memphis.

"I'm going to skip it," I say as the guys get in line to buy tickets. "I'll wait outside."

"Are you sure?" Matty asks. "Want me to stay with you?"

Why does he have to be so nice? It makes me feel extra guilty for what I'm about to do.

"No, no. Go ahead. I'll be fine. I want to get some sun. I'll meet you back here in two hours."

"You shouldn't be all by yourself without a phone." Matty pulls my phone out of his pocket. "Here. Call me if you need me."

"It's okay. You keep it. I don't need it."

Matty raises his eyebrows but doesn't say anything. Can he tell I'm up to no good? If my plan is going to work, the phone needs to stay with him. I guess I could leave it on the windshield with my note, but what if it got stolen? I guess I have no choice.

"Fine, give it."

He plops it in my open hand like it's a hot potato.

"Just remember, no Joey."

I'm so consumed with escape plans that I wasn't even thinking about Joey. Hearing his name triggers the memory of my dream. *Meet me in Phoenix on the Fourth of July.* Inside, I cringe that my subconscious would even think something like that. Thank God it didn't happen. And anyway, my hair is still wet. I would never reach out to Joey looking like this. It sounds stupid, but I'd need perfect hair and makeup to call him. Feeling good, to me at least, starts with looking good. Sadly, I don't have any other real talents, so I stick with what works.

The guys enter the Hall of Fame, and I'm left standing alone on the sidewalk staring at my phone. I should call my mom. I need to talk to her about my lawyer before I leave my phone behind and get on that bus. Poor Matty. He'll be able to cover his ass for a day or so, but after that, I don't know what'll happen. I'm trying to picture how my going home will play out, but I can't, so I don't. I'm getting on the bus and that's that.

"Hi, honey, how was Dollywood?" Mom asks when she answers.

"Great." It really was. No need to mention things haven't been going so well since. "How's Pony? What's he doing?"

"Sleeping in the corner of the kitchen, big surprise. Pony, guess who I'm talking to? It's Rosie."

I hear a couple of quick woofs. "Aw, don't tease him, Ma. What's he doing now?"

"He's looking out the back door for you." That makes my eyes well up.

"Poor guy. I miss him."

"You'll see him soon enough. Hold on a sec, your dad left me the attorney's number. Should I just text it to you?"

"No, no. I've got a pen right here." I hope I don't sound panicked.

"You're supposed to call his secretary, Miranda, to set up a time to talk."

"Miranda? Steve Justice has a secretary named Miranda. Are you kidding me?"

"What can I tell you? That's her name. Is everything else okay? You sound a little off."

How does she do that? Forget the GPS in my phone, it's like Mom planted a chip in my brain. I try to make an excuse.

"Mom, don't make me point out the obvious here. I'm not in a very good place right now."

"I know, sweetie, but things will get better. You'll see. You know what your *abuelita* always says, don't you?"

I sigh. I hope this isn't going to be a long story. "Abuelita says a lot of things, Mom."

"Lo que no te mata de fortaliece."

"Whatever doesn't kill you will make you stronger? Everybody says that, Mom. Is that supposed to help?"

"It sounds better in Spanish."

"No. It doesn't."

"Te amo, mija."

But that does. "Love you too, Ma. I'll talk to you tomorrow."

I may even see you.

My brain feels fuzzy. I need more caffeine, and I'm suddenly hungry. At the museum's restaurant, I get a large coffee and bagel to go. The cashier tells me the bus station is a five-minute cab ride away, so I've got a little time before I need to head over there. I'd rather hang out here awhile longer. I pick up a free brochure about the Hall of Fame and sit outside on a low wall and read up on this place. Hmm. From the sky, the building was designed to look like a bass clef. The windows resemble piano keys and the edge of the building is supposed to be a 1950s Cadillac fin. I decide to step back to get a better view of the piano keys and fin.

I'm standing about fifty yards away from the building facade, cup of coffee in one hand, bagel in the other, when it hits me. WTF? What am I doing? Am I really going to run away? This tingly sensation comes over me and my heart starts racing. I need to buy something. Anything. I walk back toward the museum. There has to be a gift shop in this freaking place. I look at my phone. Forty minutes until my bus leaves. I wander around the gift shop examining the various guitar-shaped souvenirs, then browse the women's apparel. I pass on the black T-shirt that says GOT COUNTRY? in white lettering, but something about the pink tank that says WELL-BEHAVED COWGIRLS RARELY MAKE HISTORY grabs me. I decide the thirty-five-dollar price tag is worth it. After all, it will be my only souvenir of this adventure. I get the shirt and also buy a Hall of Fame postcard for Matty.

After I leave the gift shop, it's time to put my plan in action. I call Lilliana and tell her I'll call from a pay phone when I get to Newark tomorrow. She sounds disappointed that I'm not sticking it out but says she'll come and get me. I rummage through my bag for a pen and flip the postcard to the blank side. I write small so everything I need to say fits and end my note with *I'm really, really sorry. Thanks for trying to help me. Love ya, Rosie.* My chest feels tight as I walk to the car. I put the postcard under the windshield wiper on the driver's side and notice I've lucked out. Spencer left his window open a sliver, probably in anticipation of how hot it's going to be when they leave the Hall of Fame. God bless him. I slide my phone through the crack and it lands on the front seat. Excellent. I take a few steps away, then glance back. My breath catches in my throat as I get a last look at the Taurus before turning away to find a cab.

CHAPTER 8

NO DISRESPECT TO THE COUNTRY MUSIC CAPITAL OF THE world, but I wouldn't want to find myself at the bus station after dark. The terminal is nice enough. Lots of windows. Very blue outside, very white inside. But the neighborhood is a bit sketchy.

As I step through the automatic doors, I immediately get the impression some of the clientele may be too. A man in dirty cargo shorts, worn work boots, and an *American Idol* T-shirt approaches me and holds out his hand.

"Keep hope alive, baby," he says.

I try my best to ignore him and scan the waiting area for an empty seat so I can collect my thoughts for a minute before buying a ticket. A dull ache is forming at the back of my head. I spy an end seat and make a beeline for it. As soon as I plop down, I start rummaging through my bag, pretending to look for something so I don't have to make eye contact with anyone. As I organize the contents of my purse, picking out gum wrapper scraps and old receipts, tattered work boots enter my sight line. I look up to see the man from the door smiling at me with his four good teeth.

"Got a dollar in there, baby? Come on, keep hope alive."

I give him my best northern New Jersey attitude. "How will giving you a dollar keep hope alive?"

He puts a hand to his chest as if he's about to recite the Pledge of Allegiance and says, "Allow me to introduce myself. I'm Hope."

Oh, man. I should have seen that coming. The pain spreads across my forehead. I need Advil. I rub my temples and close my eyes.

"Tell ya what. I'll give you two dollars if you stop following me."

"Deal, baby," Hope says, and I hand him the money, convincing myself as I do that he's going to buy food with it, though his bloodshot eyes tell me a different story. "Have a safe trip, baby, And remember, no matter where you go, there you are."

"Thanks."

I check the time and look over at the maze in front of the Greyhound counter. There's a short line. I take a deep breath. It's time. If I'm going to make that bus home, I've got to buy my ticket now.

I take my place at the end of the line just as a lady at the counter is getting loud with the Greyhound employee. "Try the card again," she says. "I know it's good. I just used it this mornin'."

This is going to take a while. What if I miss my bus? My stomach twists and my heart pounds in my ears. My head may very well explode. Maybe this is a sign that I shouldn't get on that bus. If I leave now, I can get back to the Hall of Fame, retrieve my note, and make up some lie about why my phone is in the car before the boys realize I'm missing. I'm mulling this over as Loud Lady kicks the volume up a notch.

"Maybe it's your machine. Did you ever think of that?"

I peer at the ticket booth as she takes another credit card out of her wallet and slaps it on the counter. "Try that one," she snipes before adding, "jerk." Oh no, she didn't.

Another Greyhound ticket agent steps up behind the counter. He whispers something to his coworker, then opens a second window.

"I can help the next customer," he says.

The line starts moving. He assists two customers while Loud Lady continues her tantrum. Maybe I should try the self-serve ticket kiosk.

"This in UN-believable," she screams. "Someone get me a manager."

And then a horrible thought enters my brain. What if this woman is on my bus and what if she sits next to me? Twenty hours with her instead of the guys—is that what I really want?

If only I had my phone, I could call Lilliana to talk through this. And then I remember the calling card. I scan the room for a pay phone as I simultaneously rummage through my purse to locate my wallet with the card. I spy a phone near the entrance to the ladies' room just as the ticket agent looks at me and says, "I can help you here, young lady."

I step up to the counter.

"Where are you going today?" he says.

Oddly, I hear Hope's voice in my head. *No matter where you go, there you are.* It's the kind of advice one usually finds on a coffee mug, but it's oddly profound.

"Newark, New Jersey?" It comes out like a question. *There I'll be,* I think. *And then what exactly?*

The ticket agent hits some keys on the computer. "That bus will be boarding in five minutes and your total will be one hundred forty dollars and ninety-eight cents with tax. How will you be paying today?"

"Uh, credit card," I say.

I'm about to hand over my emergency credit card when Loud Lady comes unhinged and starts pounding with both fists on the ticket booth glass. I wonder if it's bulletproof. At that moment, a uniformed man who is either a security guard or a real police officer races over and pulls the woman away from the counter. She turns and swipes at the cop's face, but he catches her by the wrist before she can deliver the blow.

"Let go of me," the woman screeches. "You're hurting me." She breaks loose and tries to run toward the door but trips over her suitcase. That's when the law enforcement dude plants a foot on either side of her facedown torso, gently placing one hand between her shoulder blades to carefully hold her on the floor. With his other hand, he talks to someone using a crackling walkie-talkie-type device. I feel sorry for this strange woman with her face pressed against the dirty bus station floor. Who knows what makes people totally lose it? I could be her.

I close my eyes and replay the scene of Joey walking into that party with his arm around that girl. I was beyond pissed. My first instinct was to get in her face. I know it takes two to tango and all that, but I blamed her for going after my boyfriend. When Joey leaned down and tenderly kissed the top of her head, something inside me broke. I bolted from the party as all my hurt and anger bubbled to the surface. I had to do something.

It was just after one in the morning when I pulled up in front of Joey's house. His Mustang was in the driveway, so I knew he was home from the party. I used his Valentine's Day card to start the fire, the one with the surfing penguin on the front that said FOR ONE COOL GIRLFRIEND. It was so satisfying to click the Scripto lighter and send my valentine up in flames. As it burned, I stared as the ocean wave, the yellow surfboard, the penguin's feet, disappeared. Then I dropped the card on my Joey Box and got back in my car. I had no idea things would go so wrong.

The sound of approaching sirens brings me back to the Nashville bus station. My eyes dart from the screaming woman to the pay phone to the door, where Hope is accosting newcomers. That's when I bolt toward the pay phone.

I'm sitting on a bench clutching my bag and sunning my face outside the bus station when the guys pull up to the curb. I couldn't chance a cab getting me back to the Hall of Fame in time. My bus left fifteen minutes ago and I can't imagine being stuck, alone, in Nashville.

Matty jumps out of the rear passenger door. "What the hell is this,

Rosie?" he yells as he climbs out. There's something about hearing my name spoken aloud that underscores the big trouble I'm in. I've never seen him so angry. He's waving the postcard in my face. "How could you? What the—you are something, really something."

Yikes. What's six feet tall and red all over? Let him get it all out. I deserve it. After a few more minutes of his huffing and puffing, I say, "Relax. I didn't go through with it. I called you, didn't I?"

"Do you ever think of anyone except yourself? How do you think I would have felt if I read this card and knew you were gone and there was nothing I could do about it? What was I supposed to tell your parents? What if something happened to you between here and New Jersey?"

I shrug. Because I don't have a good answer. He's right. I didn't want to think it through, so I didn't.

He imitates my lame gesture. "That's it? That's all you've got?" Matty rips my postcard into tiny pieces. He's still yelling, though. "Yeah, well, if you pull a stunt like this again, I'm gonna let you go. Got it?" He throws the handful of postcard confetti in my face. I wince. That I didn't see coming. Tears rise in my eyes.

I shake postcard flakes from the front of my dress. "I'm sorry, okay? What else do you want me to say?"

"You know what? I don't want you to say anything to me for a while. Nothing. Got it? And by 'a while' I mean until we get to Texas. And even then I'm gonna have to think about it." He turns, gets into the backseat, and slams the door.

Spencer gets out of the front seat. "You'd better ride up here,

Rosie," he says. "I'll get in the back with Matty." He and Matty are so much alike, always trying to smooth things over.

Spencer is still talking. "The Hall of Fame was great, ya know. Could have stayed there all day. Too bad you missed it."

I've got to get this boy a life or at least a girlfriend, though to him, the latter would probably equal a life. He doesn't have a half-bad body for a skinny kid. Not that I was checking him out when he got out of the shower or anything. But, well, he was right there in front of me. There's got to be a girl somewhere who will go out with him. Now I am staring at Spencer. *Get in the car, Rosie. Look sheepish and repentant.* "You're right. I probably should have stuck to the itinerary."

"At least you didn't miss Graceland," Spencer says. His sincerity makes me want to keep my sarcasm to myself.

I slip into the front seat and Logan nods toward my bag. "Shopping?" His question puts me at ease. One corner of my mouth turns up.

I take my bad cowgirl shirt out and hold it against my torso to model it.

"Nice. Is there a picture of you in handcuffs on the back?" There's something reassuring about Logan being Logan. He doesn't seem mad, even though I must have thrown off the schedule by at least thirty minutes this time. He catches me off guard when he puts a hand on my shoulder. "You know, if it were my decision, I wouldn't have picked you up, right? I would have let you sweat it out."

"Admit it. You would have missed me."

He smiles and I know I'm right.

"You're a real pain in the ass, you know that?" he says.

"I'd like to think it's part of my charm."

Matty snorts from the backseat and launches my phone into the front, where it lands by my toes. A move that clearly means "Call Joey. See if I care if you screw yourself." Matty and his motherly reverse psychology. Logan, who is either amused or entertained, shakes his head and puts the car in drive while Spencer fires up some old song about going to Graceland.

I lean over to pick up my phone and remember that I'm supposed to call Miranda. First, I send Lilliana a quick text. plan aborted. en route to memphis. hugs, r. Her return text comes quickly. thx for the aneurysm. stay put. promise? I type back. so sorry, my friend. cross my heart. My phone makes the text sound again. But it's not Lilliana, it's Spencer from the backseat. he's only pissed because he cares . . . a lot. I type. i know. you're a good friend. He texts. glad u changed ur mind about leaving. It's hard not to turn around and smile at Spencer. know what? me too. Then I dig out Miranda's number and dial, vowing to make it to Arizona without committing any more misdeeds requiring an apology. Yeah, right.

When Miranda answers, I introduce myself, and she tells me she's been expecting my call. I'll bet. Probably has me down on her calendar as Torch Girl. She asks me to give her a second as she pulls up a fresh Word document, then tells me to start at the beginning and give her a rundown of everything that happened the night of the blowup. Saying it all out loud, again, with an audience (a third of which is very angry at me), makes me feel weird. Out of body. Like I'm talking about some lunatic girl on a TV sitcom. Was this the perspective that my mom was talking about when she tried to convince me this trip was what I needed? I wonder if Mom gets tired of being right.

"Who's she talking to?" Spencer asks Matty.

"Don't know. Don't care," Matty answers. And then he takes out the guitar and starts strumming. I put a finger in my ear so I can block out the background noise and focus on what Miranda is saying.

"Were there any witnesses?" Miranda asks.

"Not that I know of. I went there by myself and I didn't stick around much after I lit the box on fire. But I called Joey from the car and waited until he came outside." I realize how horrible that sounds. I guess it sounds horrible because it is horrible. And hateful, childish, despicable. I decide to keep the part about bringing a Big Gulp along in case the flames got out of control to myself.

"Steve has a guy who does investigations for him. He might want to send him over there. Every neighborhood has a busybody. Maybe someone saw something that can help with your defense."

She's right. I think about Mrs. Friedman who lives across the street from us.

"Do you think maybe it wasn't my fault? The car part, I mean. I know I can't deny that I torched the box." Things are looking up all of a sudden.

"Don't get too excited. There's still the alleged stalking. You haven't had any other contact with the defendant? That is, aside from driving by his house, seeing him at the mall, and the two text messages you sent."

My body gets hot with embarrassment. The trouble I'm in is serious. This can get bad, real bad. I can hear it now. Guys in my town are gonna be like: Rosie the Stalker? Dude, steer clear of that.

"I don't think so."

"You need to know so. Is there anything else Steve needs to be informed of? We don't want to be in court and hear about any surprise phone or computer records."

Why did I say I don't think so? My last night home and the memory of my Benadryl haze has got me totally unsettled, that's why. But there's no way I'm going to tell Miranda about that right now, with the guys listening in. Besides, it wasn't real and I don't want to seem more "off" than I already do.

Miranda's voice interrupts my thoughts. "You still there?"

"Still here."

"So, is there anything else?"

"Nope. That's it."

Before we get off the phone, Miranda sets up a time for me to speak with Steve tomorrow. That should work out fine since we'll be in Dallas by then. I'll be able to talk with him privately.

"What's next?" I ask as I end my call.

"Food," Logan says. "Then Memphis."

"Still planning on getting to Dallas tonight?" I ask. I've made a tight schedule a lot tighter.

"Yep," Logan says.

After a quick, and quiet, lunch at a rest stop, we're back in the Taurus and careening down Interstate 40 toward Memphis and the Tennessee border. I'm in the back with Spencer. Matty rides up front. He still doesn't want to be near me. My phone makes its text sound. Spencer: he'll come around. Me: hope so.

I put in my earbuds. My plan is to retreat into my sonic bubble until we get to Graceland. I select a playlist that will cleanse my ears of country music and my memory of the Nashville bus station and my fight with Matty. I've got on my game face, but my stomach is in knots. I can't stand having him this angry with me.

I close my eyes and adjust my sunglasses. As the miles roll by, I occasionally pause my tunes to listen in on the guys' conversation, partly to make sure it's not about me. Paranoid much? Despite the fact that Matty is still ignoring me, he's been unusually chatty since Nashville. All three of them are.

"The UK has given us iconic bands, but the US only produces iconic solo artists," Matty says the first time I pause my iPod. Elvis's abode no doubt sparked this gripping discussion.

I want to say "Metallica," but I turn up the volume instead. I don't want Matty getting all up in my face about music. He's mad enough already. Anyway, it really is hard to throw any American bands into the same sentence with the Beatles, the Stones, and the Who.

An hour later, during another iPod pause, I hear Logan say: "College football is never going to move to a true playoff system."

"They've got to," Matty exclaims. And here I was hoping to be like a wildlife photographer and get an uncensored glimpse into the male psyche to keep me from making another Joey-like mistake. No dice. I hit play and fish around in my bag for that darned trip itinerary. May as well make good use of my time.

The third debate I have the privilege of overhearing is about superheroes. This one surely initiated by Spencer.

"Green Lantern. No question," Matty states.

"Are you kidding me?" Spencer says. "Are you forgetting the Hulk?!"

I wish I could fly off in my invisible plane like Wonder Woman. Upon my fourth attempt at eavesdropping, I finally think I'm overhearing some real guy talk.

"Check out that rack," says Matty.

Without moving my head, I shift my eyes and try to look at the cars on either side of us.

"Where?" Logan asks.

Yeah, where?

"In the right lane. Two cars up."

Huh? How can he tell from back here?

"Pull up next to the car," Matty directs. When Logan does, I see there are two girls, maybe a little older than me, driving together.

Their cleavage looks pretty much covered up, so now I'm wondering what Matty's seeing that I don't. Matty rolls down his window and begins gesturing. What is that boy doing?

"The rack," he shouts. "Rack!" I can't believe Matty would talk trash to a girl that way, but then I notice he's pointing to the bike rack on the top of their car. It appears one of their expensive-looking mountain bikes is coming loose.

The girl driving the car, who, upon closer inspection, does have a decent rack, misreads the situation like I did at first. Her windows are closed, but it's not hard to read her "F you." Then both girls give Matty the finger before their car tears off down the highway.

"You tried, my brother," Logan says. "Must be her time of the month."

Nice. That's what guys always assume when they can't understand the complex female mind.

A few miles down the road, Logan swerves sharply to avoid what looks like a piece of crumpled metal in the center lane. Not far ahead, pulled off to the shoulder, are the potty mouth girls. Their rack and one bike have slid onto their trunk, and they're both standing on the side of the road looking at what's left of the other bike, stunned.

"That is *so* satisfying," Matty declares.

Logan beeps the horn as we pass and Spencer rolls down the window and yells: "Enjoy your karma, ladies." I laugh hysterically and wish I could reach into the front seat and high-five Matty, but I'm paying the price for my escape attempt.

"That'll teach 'em to drop the F-bomb on Matty," Spencer says.

"Damn right," Matty says.

When the laughter dies down, the conversation picks back up right where it left off.

"Like I was saying," Spencer says, "if the funding doesn't get pulled, they're going to launch a replacement for the Hubble Telescope in 2018, the James Webb Space Telescope. It's an infrared-optimized space telescope and going to be way better than Hubble."

Oh, jeez. I put my headphones back on and pretend to sleep.

CHAPTER 9

LOGAN HANDS ME A CAMERA AS SOON AS WE STEP ONTO the hallowed grounds of Graceland. "Can you take a picture?"

"Sure," I say. "Matty and Spencer, scooch in."

"No way. This one is all me." Logan holds his hands in the air as if he's envisioning a photo caption and says, "Logan at Graceland."

"Okaaay," I say. "Here we go."

I knew he was all about country, but I had no idea he felt some deep connection to the King. I'm almost inspired. After I snap the picture and Logan approves it, I stop a friendly looking couple and ask them to take a picture of me, Matty, Logan, and Spencer in front of Graceland. Although Matty agrees to be in the photo, I stand between Logan and Spencer because Matty refuses to be next to me. I look at the photo when the woman returns Logan's camera. Everyone is smiling except Matty, and even though only Spencer's between us, we look miles apart. I can't last until Dallas.

I sidle up to Matty as we're waiting on line for tickets. "Okay, what's it going to take?"

"Did you hear something?" he asks Spencer.

"Define 'something,'" Spencer replies.

"Forget it. I think it was an annoying mosquito," Matty says.

Clearly, this is going to cost me. I try to think about something Matty really wants.

"A guitar," I say. "When we get back and I get my dog-walking business going, I'll save up money and buy you a guitar. I swear. I'll even work at my dad's factory if I have to. Any kind you want, name it. But please, can you forgive me, Matty? I can't not talk to you until Dallas."

"Wow. Any kind?" Spencer says. "She has no idea how much a good guitar costs, does she?"

"In case you haven't noticed, she has no idea about a lot of things," Matty snaps. "But begging. That's a step in the right direction."

My cheeks burn with anger. I clench my fists to keep from smacking him in the back of the head. I guess this is Matty's way of saying this is going to cost me more than I thought, maybe even more than a guitar. I'm going to be walking lots of dogs. I relax my hands. It's okay. I deserve it. Plus, if it buys Matty's forgiveness and ends the silent treatment, it will be worth it. I'm about to tell him to name his price when he makes an unexpected reversal.

"You don't have to buy me a guitar, Rosie." It's the first time he's looked me in the eye since showering me with postcard confetti at the

Nashville bus station. "How about this? No more escaping and try to have a good time, or at least pretend you're having fun."

I think I'd rather buy him a guitar. "Okay. But it's not like you guys are making it easy for me to have fun. Logan's got his rules and seems perpetually pissed at me. Spencer has his itinerary. You, well, you tease me."

"I always tease you."

"But now I'm outnumbered."

"She is easy prey," Spencer offers.

Matty considers this. "Okay, I can't speak for them, but I'll try if you try."

"Deal." I throw my arms around his skinny middle. "I'm sorry," I say into his T-shirt. He pats my back tentatively.

"You always are, Rosie."

The famed home of Elvis is set back from the main road, behind wrought iron fencing. Graceland is nice, but to be honest, I was expecting a Tara-like, southern mansion. I guess it's the biggest house in the neighborhood, but I've seen better on *House Hunters International*. The fourteen-acre property may be more beautiful than Graceland itself.

We take the audio tour of the house that includes Elvis's living room, music room, dining room, kitchen, TV room, pool room, and infamous Jungle Room. It's like a trip through the seventies. I try to picture normal, family stuff going on here, but it's hard. I mean, just being Elvis is as far from normal as a person can get.

Once outside the house, we visit the family grave site, which is situated beside a circular fountain, and then walk down the long drive to the street. People have written their names and Elvis-centric phrases in chalk and marker on the brick columns of the gate. Logan is at the ready with his Sharpie. The boys pass it between them while I look up and down Elvis Presley Boulevard. Finally, Matty taps me on the shoulder and hands me the black permanent marker. I find space near the gate entrance and write the title of an Elvis tune I know from the Greatest Hits album my parents own: "Hard Headed Woman." Matty peers over my shoulder. "Progress," he says.

At a nearby souvenir shop that sells knockoff, discount Graceland merchandise, I buy an Elvis mug. He's sporting a flamingo-colored jacket with black lapels and standing in front of Graceland beside a pink Cadillac. GRACELAND, HOME OF ELVIS, it says. I get a different Elvis mug for my mom, an Elvis clock that swings its hips for my dad, and an Elvis watch for Eddie that I intend to "borrow" until I get home. I also buy a disposable camera. My parents offered to let me bring their digital, but at the time I was too steeped in bitterness to even envision wanting memories of this journey. At the register, I spot a guitar key chain. I get it for Matty. I slip it into his pocket after we leave the shop.

"Until I get you the real one."

Matty puts a hand on my shoulder and looks me right in the eye. "Ro, forget it, really. It's okay," he says softly.

Even though he lets me off the hook, I know I don't deserve it. Matty, however, deserves a guitar. My family took at least two vacations every year for as long as I can remember, but Matty, he hardly went anywhere. His mom is always working, and they can't afford expensive trips. This is Matty's first official getaway and so far all I've done is, well, be me. And that's hardly good enough for someone like Matty.

For the first time since being served with a TRO—maybe even since Joey cheated on me—I feel like the fog that's been hovering over my brain is finally lifting a little. I think I'm having some kind of spiritual awakening here at Graceland, and I'm not even a fan of Elvis's music. By the time we walk back to the Taurus, I'm determined to make a fresh start on this trip. If only my hair looked better, I think as I catch my reflection in the car door window before getting into the backseat.

Logan merges onto the interstate heading west and we drive across the high-arch bridge that spans the mighty Mississippi River and connects Memphis to Arkansas. The lights dancing on the water look so pretty. Part of me wishes we weren't leaving. It's been a looong day of driving. Originally, we were supposed to stay the night near Graceland, but Logan is determined to get us back on schedule. His schedule, which I messed up. So I guess I have only myself to blame for how tired I am and the way I look right now. I have only me to blame for a lot of things, and that really sucks. Was I really in Nashville this morning? It seems like days since I slipped two bucks into Hope's hand.

I try to fix my hair at a road stop in Arkansas. I'm going to be meeting Logan's girlfriend in a few hours, and I don't want to look like complete and total crap. But it's no use. My locks have suffered a double whammy. I didn't blow-dry my hair with my round brush and I pulled it back in a twist while it was still wet. I give up on my hair and focus on freshening up my makeup. As I exit the bathroom, I stop at the vending machine and get a diet soda. I try to remember what the guys have been drinking. I know Matty likes Gatorade, so I buy him a lemon-lime and settle on two bottled waters for the brothers. I'm sure they won't object. I also buy four bags of chips—baked for the brothers, salt and vinegar for me and Matty.

Logan and Spencer seem surprised when I get to the car and hand them their chips and waters. Matty just says "thanks." He's been around my house long enough to know that it doesn't matter if we're home or away, we like to feed people. It's the Catalano way.

"You look tired," I tell Logan.

"Kinda." He rubs the stubble along his chin.

"Want me to drive? I don't mind. If you'll turn over command of the Taurus, that is."

He hesitates for a moment and then gives me the keys, prompting Spencer and Matty to yell, "Shotgun."

"Forget it," Logan says. Deflated, they retreat to the backseat.

The sun is setting as I drive along Interstate 30. As we near the Arkansas-Texas border, we pass the town of Hope, which immediately calls to mind my bus station buddy. It's the birthplace of former president Bill Clinton—they've even got a highway sign that says so. And not far beyond that sign, I notice some unusual roadkill on the shoulder. I squint, trying to make out what it is.

"Armadillo," Logan says.

"No way."

"Never saw an armadillo before?"

"I'm just a girl from New Jersey," I say without a hint of sarcasm.

"You're living now, Catalano," he says. "See what you would've missed if you got on that bus?"

Spencer and Matty play guitar in the backseat for a while. Spencer is helping Matty learn the chords to "Master of Puppets"—great metal never dies. Eventually, though, they both fall asleep and Logan turns on the radio. I'm surprised when he bypasses the country station and settles on something more alt rock. Now we're talkin'. I'm even more surprised that he knows and likes the song enough to play air drums.

"Can I ask you something?"

"You just did."

I've rolled my eyes so many times on this trip, they're going to get stuck that way. "Why ASU? What made you want to go so far away from home?"

"Wanderlust."

I don't say anything. I'm trying to imagine what it would feel like to want to leave my family to go to college thousands of miles away. I like where I live. All my fantasies about the future involve me, a husband, and my hometown. College has always been this hazy notion in the periphery. Logan must mistake my silence for stupidity.

"'Wanderlust' means—"

"I know what it means. Jeez. I'm not an idiot."

He just raises his eyebrows in a don't-make-me-answer-that face. I push on with my interrogation.

"But Arizona?"

"I visited Tempe and could picture myself living there. The desert was like nothing I'd ever seen before. Plus, ASU has a great sustainability program."

He holds up the book he's been carrying around. I glance at it. "*Sustainability: A Global Approach to . . .*" a big long phrase I don't feel like reading.

"Uh, yeah. Now you've lost me."

"It has to do with the sustainability of environmental resources and how that relates to economics, sociology, politics—"

I hold up my hand and cut him off. "Enough. It's now become clear to me that you, too, are a total nerd."

"I'll take that as a compliment." Logan gives me a half grin and the dimple makes another appearance. My heart does a grand jeté.

"Can I ask you another question?"

"Shoot."

"Why air drums?"

Logan chuckles. In fact, I almost make him full-out laugh. I can tell.

"Probably the same reason you randomly belt out one or two words from whatever song you're listening to on your iPod."

I'm glad it's dark so Logan can't see how red I am. "I don't do that, do I?"

Logan turns toward me and rests his hand on my thigh, which makes it hard to concentrate on the road.

"Yes. Yes, you do."

I scrunch my eyebrows and consider this. I guess I get caught up in my tunes sometimes. "Now I feel stupid." What else is new?

"No worries," he says, then mumbles something that sounds suspiciously like "It's cute."

"What was that?"

"I said it makes me want to puke." He's looking out his window now. I have this urge to touch his thigh. Despite his cranky personality, urges are piling up where Logan is concerned. I'm not happy about that, but it's the truth. So, I keep my hands at ten and two and stare straight ahead at the stretch of highway illuminated by the headlights.

Logan changes the station again. My reprieve from country music is over, apparently. The song is pretty, though. It gives me chills and makes me want to slow dance with a cowboy.

"Who is this?"

"Who is this?" Logan is incredulous. "It's only George Strait. He is country music. Do you know any country singers at all?"

"Keith Urban."

"Because he's hot?"

"Nooo. Because he's a kick-ass guitarist. And he's in *People* magazine a lot."

"I knew it."

"I make no apologies. I like celebrity gossip magazines and hot guys."

"What about college?" Logan asks.

"That was a non sequitur."

"Where are you thinking of applying?"

"You mean *if* I apply. Somewhere in New Jersey. I'll probably wind up commuting."

"How are your grades?"

"B-ish." I pause. "Occasionally more C-ish than B-ish."

"Test scores?"

"You sound like my dad. I'm not telling you my SAT scores!" I say this louder than I intend to and wake up Matty.

"What about SATs?" Matty pipes in from the back. What can I say about a guy who wakes up at the sound of "SAT scores"?

"Logan asked me my scores."

"Logan. You should know better than to ask a lady her SAT scores."

"I didn't ask a lady, I asked Rosie," Logan fires back.

"Ha, ha. How original," I say. "Did you pull that one out of your third-grade joke collection? What's next? A pickle joke?"

"Tell him your scores, Rosie," Matty says. He's chuckling, and we both know why. I kicked butt. Well, not in the traditional Ivy-league-bound kind of way, but in the "Oh, this is Rosie and we're surprised she even took the SATs" kind of way. Low expectations give me the gift of surprise sometimes.

I change the subject. "So, Avery is okay with us getting in tonight? It's pretty late."

"She said it's fine. We'll be staying in the pool house, so it's not like we'll be disturbing anyone."

"Pool house? Who has a pool house?" Country club snobs, that's who, I want to say.

"Your parents?" Matty offers.

"Yeah, it's called 'where I live'! And it's an aboveground pool." This time, my booming voice wakes Spencer. In the rearview mirror, I catch him running his fingers through his hair as he squints out the window. The messy look works for him. I should mention it.

"Where are we?" Spencer says through a yawn.

"Almost to the Texas border," Logan says.

Texas. This will be my sixth state in three days. Seven if you count the drive through West Virginia. I didn't actually set foot in that state so I'm not sure.

We ride on into Texas without speaking until it's time to exit the highway. Then Logan gives me step-by-excruciating-step directions to our destination. Two illegal U-turns later, we arrive.

"Holy shit!" Matty shouts when we finally pull into the driveway of Avery's house, or perhaps the correct word would be "compound."

The half-mile driveway ends in a circle with a fountain in the middle. Graceland has nothing on Avery's digs. The house looks like it belongs in the French countryside, not outside Dallas. I don't know what I was expecting after Logan mentioned a pool house. I guess I was envisioning a big ranch, not a palatial French manor.

"I wonder where the heliport is," Spencer whispers.

"You read my mind," I say as I stare at the imposing mansion. Yet again, I'm totally out of my league.

CHAPTER 10

I PUT THE CAR IN PARK, NOT SURE IF IT'S OKAY FOR US TO leave it here beside the fountain. Then one of the blue double doors opens, and a petite blond girl with glasses peeks her head out. She gives us the one-minute hand signal and then re-emerges in shorts, a T-shirt, and flip-flops. Adorable. Logan steps out of the car and they give each other a friendly but not too, too friendly hug. Still, I realize I'm holding my breath and frowning a little. Logan holds the passenger door open for Avery, then climbs into the back with Matty and Spencer.

"Hey, y'all. I'm Avery," she says, and she turns around and points. "Let me guess, Spencer, Matty."

"Right!" they say in unison like double dorks.

"Rosie," I say.

"Nice to meet you, Rosie. You too, boys." Her smile is genuine, and I think I may like her even though I'm not sure why or if I even want to. "Why don't I show you where to park while you're here?"

We pull around the side of Buckingham Palace, and Avery points to a spot alongside the five-car garage.

"This is good," Avery says. "Grab your things. You can meet my dad and then I'll show you where you'll be staying."

We walk into a kitchen that looks like it belongs on a cable home design show. Tile floors, granite countertops, cherrywood cabinets, and—holy crap, look at that restaurant-size stainless steel refrigerator.

"Daddy? Logan and his friends are here."

An attractive man with salt-and-pepper hair emerges from the family room off the kitchen. He's barefoot and wearing chino shorts with a pull-over green polo.

"Welcome," he says, and shakes all of our hands. "Help yourselves to whatever you need while you're here. My wife is working late, but you'll probably meet her tomorrow."

"Come on, Rosie," Avery says. "I'll take you upstairs to your room and then I'll show the boys to the pool house."

"Why don't I get them set up out there, sweetheart?" Avery's dad offers.

I know I didn't want to come here, but these people are so stinkin' nice, I can't help but like them. Avery and her dad are so warm and down-to-earth. My reservations about feeling uncomfortable melt away.

Avery leads me up this winding staircase in the main entrance hall.

"We have a guest room," she says, looking back over her shoulder, "but I thought it might be fun for you to bunk with me."

Why? I wouldn't think it would be fun to have a sleepover with a complete stranger, especially if that girl is under a TRO and has an impending court date, but what do I know. Maybe this is the way they do things in Texas.

Avery's room is gorgeous—and huge. She has her own bathroom with a vanity and sunken tub, a walk-in closet that's almost as big as my bedroom at home, and a giant flat-screen TV on the wall in front of her bed. "The couch pulls out," she says. "My room is sleepover friendly. It's how my mom compensates for never being around. She lets me have friends stay whenever I want."

"She works a lot?"

"Only all the time. Take my bed. You're the guest."

"No, no. That's okay. I can't take your bed," I say.

"You sure?" she asks. "I want you to be comfortable."

"Believe me, after the motel beds I've been sleeping in, I'll be comfortable. Thank you for letting us all stay here. It's really nice of you," I say. "Are you sure two nights is okay?"

"It's no trouble at all," she says. "It'll be fun."

We stare at each other in silence for a few seconds, not in a bad way or anything, before I begin fumbling with my suitcase. I'm not sure what to say, but Avery is all over the elephant (i.e., me) in the room.

"So," Avery begins. "I know we just met and all, but when Logan called me, he mentioned that you'd gotten into a minor mess and that your parents were making you come along."

"Minor? Did he say I blew up my ex-boyfriend's car?"

Avery is trying to suppress a smile. She's struggling so hard to be polite to this psycho in her bedroom that it makes me laugh.

"I'm not carrying matches or a lighter. Swear. But if you want to change your mind and put me in the guest room, I completely understand."

Avery starts laughing too. "Did he deserve it?"

"He was cheating on me."

"Poop head."

"I know!" I'm so grateful she's on my side, I forgive the fact that she said "poop head." She is just too cute in a nonslutty Barbie kind of way.

"You should have blown up her car too."

I smile. It's funny how a person can go from being a stranger to a friend with just one sentence. "She's not old enough to drive."

Her eyes widen. "Get out. Skank."

"Total skank."

"My boyfriend and I were together for four years when he cheated on me."

"Four years!" I shout, louder than I intended. But I can't imagine what I would have done to Joey if he'd screwed around on me after we'd been together that long. It would have cost him a testicle, I think.

"I wasted my high school years on him. I'm determined not to let it happen again in college," Avery says.

Hmm. Maybe Logan is barking up the wrong tree, then.

"Got a picture?" Avery asks.

"Huh?"

"A picture of the ex? Got one?"

I remember I'm still in possession of both my phone and a few lingering Joey photos that I haven't been able to delete, not yet. I pull up a close-up of him. I remember when I took this. It was October, my favorite time of year next to summer, and we were on our way to the homecoming game. My stomach wrenches when I look at it. I wonder when and if I'm ever going to have these kinds of memories of a guy again. Will taking pictures feel like I'm trying to capture the good stuff before it all goes bad? Right now, it's hard to imagine the exciting part of falling in love. The hurt of the crash landing is still too fresh. I hold up my phone for Avery.

"Hello, blue eyes. I don't blame you for losing it," Avery says.

I can't speak, but the tension goes out of my shoulders. It's nice to have someone understand.

"Feel like going for a swim?" Avery asks.

"Sure."

"Come on, then. The pool is awesome at night. You can kick back in the hot tub, too. Traveling with three guys must be getting old."

"Totally!" I say. Finally. After three days and fifteen hundred miles of nonstop testosterone, a sympathetic face.

The night air is balmy, but the water feels even warmer as I sit on the side of the pool and dangle my feet in the deep end. The boys emerge from the pool house all suited up. Logan has abs and pecs to match his biceps and a sexy trail of hair that begins just above his belly button. But who's looking? Joey had boyish good looks, but Logan is more man, inside and out. I'm relieved when he jumps in the pool and I can wipe the drool off my chin without anyone noticing.

Avery takes off her terry-cloth poolside dress to reveal an adorable halter-style bikini. She has a lean, muscular runner's body. If she's a cheerleader, she's definitely the one who gets put on top of the pyramid. She steps onto the diving board and dives in. Spencer and Matty cannonball after her, but I suddenly feel self-conscious about my ample boobage and don't want to take off my T-shirt just yet. I've been on the road with these guys since Saturday and I thought I was starting to feel like one of them. But right now, the idea of being half naked around them would be too weird. It's stupid, I know. Matty has seen me in my bathing suit hundreds of times. When he's not living in our house, he's living in our aboveground pool.

Matty pops his head up near my toes.

"Why aren't you coming in? You love night swimming."

"Don't rush me."

Matty lightly splashes my legs. He knows I hate that. I retaliate by smacking the water's surface with the bottom of my feet. I anticipate his next move and snatch my legs out of the pool before he can pull me in. But I'm too late. Hands grab my shoulders from behind and push me into the deep end. At least now I have an excuse for keeping my shirt on. I let myself slip underwater and pull the twist out of my hair before I break the surface. It feels good, like I'm cleansing myself of road grime—cheap motel soap, the car's lingering french fry smell, random germs from rest stop bathrooms. I'm so relaxed I forget about being pushed in.

"I can't believe you're not even pissed at Logan," Spencer says.

"It was Logan?" I'm still not angry but play along anyway. "You know what they say about payback. And I've got a strong track record."

Avery starts laughing. "Sleep with one eye open, Logan. One eye open."

This pool is amazing. Its low end has built-in seating, like an underwater shelf, and the heat rising from the hot tub makes me think of witches' brew. I love the lulling sounds of summer bugs chirping and the hum of the pool filter. I float toward the deep end as I watch Logan and Avery in the shallow. He grabs her around the waist and throws her a good three feet into the air. She swims underwater and body checks his feet out from under him. I'm grabbing hold of the side, trying to suppress my jealousy and determine what, if anything, is going on between them when Matty swims up beside me.

"Race ya," he says. "To the low end and back." And just like that, we're kids again.

"One, two—" I don't wait, I push off. But so does Matty; he knows I never wait for three.

I slice through the water as fast as I can, doing my best freestyle. I make a swimmer's turn and kick off from the side of the pool, but despite giving it my all (I'm quite competitive when I want to be), I lose to Matty by a whole body length.

"You beat me bad that time."

"That shirt is weighing you down. Take it off for the second heat."

"Nah, that's okay. I'm ready to get out anyway."

I swim over to the ladder and step out.

"There're towels by the pool house," Avery calls. "Help yourself."

I find a stack of plush, sheet-size towels on a rack outside the pool house door. It's like being at a hotel. I peer in the French doors and am completely blown away by the boys' digs. There's a pool table, several old-school arcade games like Ms. Pac-Man and Donkey Kong, and two sets of sectional leather sofas, which I'm guessing pull out into beds. Even if they don't, they look plenty comfy as is. Holy shit. What does Avery's dad do for a living?

I wrap myself in a plush, blue towel and sit on a stool at the resort-like wet bar, where I left my phone before I got in the pool. I do a quick check for messages. Nothing. I fire off a text to my mom. made it to texas. all good. xoxo. luv u. It's late, but I know she won't sleep until she hears from me.

A few minutes later, Matty, Logan, and Spencer grab towels and join me. Avery scoots behind the bar and opens the mini-fridge. Matty sits on the stool beside me and puts out a hand. Without exchanging a word, I give him my phone for the night. It's just as well. After showing Joey's picture to Avery, I'm feeling vulnerable.

"This thing is stocked, ya know," Avery says. "We've got beer, fruity drinks, wine, soda, water. Who wants a beer?"

"I'll just have a water," I say. Honestly, I don't like the taste of alcohol that much.

"Guys? Beer?"

I can sense Matty hesitating to see what the guys will do. I don't know why, but I'm surprised when Logan says: "I don't drink."

"Not ever?" Avery says. Guess she's surprised too.

"Hardly ever," he says. "Growing up—"

Avery, who is looking at Logan, seems to recall something. She holds up her hand. "Say no more. I remember."

I'm confused. I look back and forth between Logan and Avery as some shared piece of knowledge passes between them. I don't like not knowing what they're talking about. It stings to be left out.

Spencer brings me out of the dark. "I guess you told her we're the spawn of a mean drunk?" He says it matter-of-factly, like it's no big secret, which makes me feel even worse.

Logan answers Spencer with a shrug that confirms he did and remains quiet, but Spencer keeps talking. "Yeah, our dad doesn't know when to say when."

Why didn't Logan tell me? He could have mentioned this during our heart-to-heart in Arkansas. Even though it's not her fault, I don't like Avery knowing something I don't. These are my guys.

A few awkward moments pass before Avery speaks. "Well, I'm the spawn of a renowned cardiologist." She grabs a bottle of white wine and begins to open it with a corkscrew. "And she approves of drinking one glass of wine a day."

"Isn't red wine the one with all the antioxidants?" Spencer asks. No one acknowledges him.

"Does she approve of *you* drinking one glass of wine a day?" Matty asks.

"I don't know. She's not home enough to tell me what she thinks." She doesn't hide her bitterness. "And as long as no one is driving, my dad won't say anything. He knows after I leave for college next month, I can drink whenever I want."

My brain is still running in circles about Logan and Spencer's father. How mean is mean? I wonder. Did that play into Logan's decision to go to college two thousand miles from home? Wanderlust, bullshit. Surely Arizona State isn't the only college in the country to offer a sustainability major. I watch Avery pour herself a glass of wine.

"Can I have one too?" I ask, suddenly wanting to appear more like Avery.

"Of course," says Avery. She hands me the glass and pours herself another. "Matty?"

"I think I'll stick with a beer," Matty says. I promptly shoot him a look. When Avery bends down to look in the mini-fridge, I mouth: "Only one." Matty may think he's in charge of me during this road trip, but I'm still older. Matty never drinks, and I don't want him getting carried away. But at the same time, I don't want to embarrass him in front of a cute girl.

"So, your mom's a cardiologist?" Matty asks. "Do you want to become a doctor too?"

Polite conversation or flirting? It's hard to tell with Matty.

"Me? No. I want to help people in some way, though. My dad is a social worker. I thought about that for a while, but I'm more interested in the big picture. That's what drew me to the sustainability major at ASU. I've also been looking into the Peace Corps for after college. This summer, I'm going to work for Habitat for Humanity."

The Peace Corps? Habitat for Humanity? "Wow," I say. No wonder Logan likes her. They've got a lot in common. I'm slightly envious that Avery knows what she wants to do with her life. I'm slightly envious of Avery, period. I'm starting to feel silly that I never once considered leaving New Jersey. Painful shots, giant insects—not my thing. But what have I done for mankind lately beyond contributing a gift to the Toys for Tots booth at the mall every Christmas?

"What about you?" Avery asks me. I've been quiet, and I can tell she's being nice and trying to bring me into the conversation. "Any ideas about what you wanna be when you grow up?"

Uh, Joey's wife. That would have been my answer a few weeks ago. What do I say here? To be honest, I've thought about applying to the Fashion Institute of Technology in the city. But I haven't told a soul, and I don't want anyone laughing at my dream of designing wedding gowns right now. "I'm not sure," I say.

I sound stupid and immature, and not at all like the kind of girl whom Logan would confide in or drive hundreds of miles out of his way to visit. I'm recognizing how much I want Logan to see me as more than just this impulsive, pain-in-the-ass, emotional overeater. I'm not giving him much to work with, am I? I'd pick Avery too. Suddenly, I feel drained. If I close my eyes, I think I might fall asleep on this bar stool. I push my unfinished wine away. Avery finishes her drink and turns to me. "You 'bout ready for bed? Y'all must be tired."

"Exhausted," I reply.

"Not so much," Matty says.

"Mind if we check out those video games?" Spencer asks.

"Make yourself at home. The pool house is all yours. Me and Rosie will see you at breakfast. Anyone want to go for a morning run?"

She puts her hand on Logan's shoulder as if she already knows his answer.

"Sure," Logan says. Spencer nods.

"Maybe," Matty says. Maybe? That boy doesn't run unless the basketball coach makes him do wind sprints. Is Matty trying to make a move on a girl Logan's into, a girl who also happens to be two years older than him?

"Okay, I'll come by for y'all around seven."

Seven? Ha! That seals the deal. Matty will still be drooling on his pillow.

"What about you, Rosie?"

I'd get winded before I made it to the end of the driveway. "Uh, I don't even own running shoes. But breakfast, I'm there."

"We can get mani-pedis afterward."

"Now you're speaking my language," I say. I give the boys a half wave and feel a pang of separation anxiety. Why? I'm not exactly sure. I should be thrilled to get away from them for a night. I shake it off and follow Avery into the house and up to her room, where, after a shower in her private bathroom, I collapse on the pull-out bed. I'm in that weird state between dreamland and consciousness when Avery's voice pipes up in the darkness.

"We hooked up, ya know."

"Waa?" I mumble. I meant "who," but it didn't come out that way.

"Logan and I. We hooked up."

"Tonight?"

"Back in May. At prefreshman orientation. I let things go a bit too far. I feel kinda bad about it."

Her words blow through my brain like a cold front clearing away heavy humidity. How far is too far? *None of your damned business, Rosie,* says the part of me that wants to be a polite houseguest.

"Anyway, I thought you should know. I see the way he looks at you. Don't get me wrong, I like having Logan as a friend. We're into the same things, he's fun to talk to and text and all that, but like I said, I don't want to start college as someone's girlfriend."

"I don't blame you," I say.

"For hooking up with Logan or wanting to stay single?"

"Both." I appreciate her honesty and want to return the favor.

We're silent for a couple of seconds before I ask, "How does Logan look at me?"

"The same way you look at him, silly," she says. I can hear the smile in her voice. "Night, Rosie."

"Night, Avery." I hope she hears me smiling back.

CHAPTER 11

"JOEY CALLED."

I open my eyes slowly. I'm not sure where I am and if I'm hear-ing properly. A girl's knees come into focus. Avery. Now I remem-ber. I rode into Texas yesterday in a Ford Taurus with Matty, Logan, Spencer, and one guitar.

"What?" I sit up, trying to shake the sleep off.

"Matty told me. Joey called. Mister Blue Eyes. That's him, right?"

My heads swims with a mixture of curiosity and anxiety. "Yes. When? What did he say? Did Matty talk to him? Did Joey leave a voice mail?"

"I don't know the specifics. After our run, Matty was going to tell you himself, but I wasn't sure how you'd feel about him barging in here first thing in the morning. I told him I'd give you the message."

"Thanks, but I'm okay with Matty barging in. That's normal at my house."

I throw off the covers and get out of bed.

"Y'all are pretty close, huh?"

I don't feel like talking about Matty right now. I feel like running downstairs and finding out what the deal is, but I pause for a second and try to be polite. "Close? I guess. Like siblings that don't always get along."

"But you're not siblings. And you don't always fight," Avery says with a knowing smile that I choose to ignore. Is she stalling? Is this about Matty or is this about her not wanting me to find out what the hell Joey said? I'm getting agitated. Who am I kidding? I am agitated. Lately, I'm always agitated.

"Uh, where's Matty?"

"In the kitchen with the boys helping my dad cook breakfast."

"Cool." I'm about to go downstairs, bed head and all, when Avery steps between me and the door. My chest tightens and I'm finding it difficult to take deep breaths.

"Ah, ah, ah," she says. "Hold on. You don't want those three to think you're dying to talk to Joey, do you?"

"But I am. Matty knows that."

I'm resisting the urge to fling her ninety-pound body out of my way and run to the kitchen to find out what Joey said—and call him back. *Breathe, Rosie, breathe.*

"This is the guy that cheated on you and called the police, remember? Before you do anything you'll regret, think about why he's calling you. Does he want to get you in more trouble?"

Why does she care? Would I care what Avery did if the situation were reversed? I look at her face all cute and serious, and still a bit sweaty from that run, I might add. Now I feel guilty, especially for wanting to fling her tiny body across the room.

"Maybe I'll shower first. My hair's a mess."

"Good girl. You can shower in here."

"And shave my legs. That's what I'll do."

"Now you're talkin'. I'll use my parents' bathroom. We'll head down to breakfast together."

Forty minutes later, when I walk into the kitchen with Avery, whatever ridiculous conversation the boys are having while eating their pancakes stops so fast it's like someone hit the mute button. Spencer, Matty, and Logan stare at us. Were they talking about me instead of dissecting all the *Star Wars* episodes again? I walk toward an empty seat at the head of the table, facing the patio. Through the French door, I see Avery's dad watering hanging baskets of petunias. I inhale slowly and look around the table at the boys. I know they must be waiting for me to ask about the Call, but I lock eyes with Avery and the two of us pull out our chairs and sit down. I'm having a *My Fair Lady* moment. I'm the crass Eliza Doolittle and Avery is the gentlemanly Professor Higgins, struggling to turn me into a proper lady with good manners.

Avery passes me a service plate heaped with food.

"Pancakes? Sausage?"

"Thank you," I say, digging in.

"Can you pass that syrup?" Avery says.

"Sure." The tension builds, and I have to bite the inside of my cheek so I don't start laughing. Finally, Spencer breaks.

"Joey drunk dialed you last night!"

I pause. Calm Rosie is leaving the building.

"How would you know?" I'm talking to Spencer but glaring at Matty. "What did you tell them? This is private."

"They overheard me telling your parents."

"Telling my parents? What? Spill it, Matty." I'm so angry, I'm losing my appetite.

"Your parents said if Joey contacted you, I should tell them first. Then I should tell you."

I'm tired of feeling like I'm being handled, like I can't be trusted. I stab a breakfast link with my fork and speak as evenly as possible through clenched teeth. I don't need to make Avery's dad think I'm a freak by throwing a scream fest.

"Matty, if we were home right now, I swear to God I would throw this sausage right at your head." I wave the skewered meat to underscore my point.

A bug-eyed Logan reaches for my wrist and gently guides my fork-clutching hand back to the table.

"Give her the phone," Logan tells Matty.

"She's supposed to call her parents first."

"Give. Her. The. Phone," Logan repeats.

Matty's cheeks flush deeper than usual. Slowly and deliberately, he pushes back his chair, walks toward me, slams the phone down on the table, and exits through the patio door. Avery glances at me sympathetically, then follows Matty. Spencer leaves too. I'm not sure if it's because he's afraid of me or feels bad for Matty. He takes his plate with him, though.

"Joey left you a voice mail," Logan says. "It was three o'clock in the morning New Jersey time. I think Spencer's probably right about it being a drunken call. But Matty didn't play the message for us. Swear."

He's holding up his right hand like he's taking an oath. I nod and stare down at my food. I feel humiliated. Tears sneak out the corners of my eyes and trickle down my jawline. Logan hands me a napkin and I quickly wipe my cheeks. Tentatively, Logan rests his hand on top of mine. His touch calms me down.

"You're lucky. You're getting this over with now. You only fall in love for the first time once."

"That's very Taylor Swift of you," I say. But Logan's right, and I feel better knowing he's trying to make me feel better.

Logan gives me a soft half smile and then he gets up from the table and walks outside. I watch him go and wonder when he first fell in love. Did his heart get broken or did he break some girl's heart? I pick up my phone and dial my voice mail. I punch in my four-digit code: Joey's birthday. How lame am I?

"Yo, Rosie . . ." There's a long pause and I hear music and muffled speaking like he's covering the mouthpiece. "Call me." I play it two more times just to confirm he's being as big of a dick as I thought he was the first time I heard it. Yo, Rosie? I used to be "baby," and what's with the "yo"?

I don't know what I was expecting from Joey, but it was definitely more. The thought of hearing Joey's voice again was so much better than the reality of Joey. At least he didn't mention Phoenix or the Fourth of July. Funny. He finally calls and I've got an excuse to talk to him, but somehow I know if I do, I'll be more of a loser than I already am. I've got to stop messing up. I text Lilliana instead. I tell her about Joey's call and ask if she's heard anything about my skanky ex and his jailbait girlfriend. Then I call my mom. Matty will be proud.

I don't even say hello when she picks up the phone. "He called," I say, and then I start to cry. "He's such a jerk."

"Aw, honey. Don't cry. He's not worth it. You didn't call him back, did you?" Mom says sympathetically.

"No. And I'm not going to, don't worry."

"I believe you. I think you should let the lawyer or his assistant know about this. I don't want that boy getting you in any more trouble. Do you want me to call Steve Justice?"

"It's okay. I'm supposed to talk to him today anyway."

"I miss you, honey. Do you want to come home?"

I wasn't expecting that. Yesterday I would have jumped at the offer. Today, after hearing Joey's voice, I'm not so sure. Lilliana is right. I need to see this trip through to the end. No, I'm right. I want to see this trip through to the end.

"I miss you too, Mom, but Matty would be disappointed. You know how sensitive he can be." *And so do I,* I think, feeling triple the guilt over my sausage-assault threat. "How's Dad? Is Eddie's job going okay?"

"They're both fine, *mija.*"

"Can I talk to Pony? Is he around?"

"Of course he's around, where else would he be?" Mom chuckles. "Hold on. I'll put the phone up to his ear." After some shuffling around, I hear Mom's voice; it sounds as far away as she is. "Go ahead. He's listening."

"Pony? How's my good doggy? It's me, Rosie. I miss you, ya big pooch." As expected, he doesn't say anything. After a few seconds, Mom is back on the phone.

"He looks confused."

"I'll bet. Is Eddie taking him for walks?"

"What do you think? Your father takes him every morning and every night."

"Tell Dad and Eddie I love them."

"I will. Call me after you talk to Steve Justice."

"Okay, Ma. Love you."

"Love you too."

I walk outside and over to the pool house, where I find everyone sitting around watching a show involving catching very big fish. I plop myself on the couch next to Matty. He's got his arms crossed and he won't look at me. I take my phone and put it on his thigh and then I lean my head on his shoulder. He knows that means I'm sorry. I was wrong. But, after pointing a breakfast link at his head, I know I owe him more. I need to say this out loud, in front of everyone.

"I'm really sorry. I shouldn't have threatened you with the sausage."

Still nothing. I get up and stand between him and the television.

"You just did what my parents asked. I was wrong. And selfish."

That last part gets his attention.

"You were what?"

"Wrong! Is that what you want to hear?"

"Yes. And . . ."

"Selfish," I mumble. Matty's always teasing me about that, but I know there's a major grain of truth in his jokes.

We stare at each other for a full five seconds before Avery pipes up. "Okaaay. Well, now that we got that out of the way, Rosie and I are going to get mani-pedis."

"Huh?" says Spencer.

"Nail stuff," Logan says.

"Can you boys manage on your own for a while?" Avery asks.

I jump in here. "Are you kidding? They've got a big day planned. First, the Book Depository where JFK was shot. Next, the ranch where, and I quote, 'they filmed the popular eighties, and recently revived, TV series *Dallas*.' Don't ask me how they even know that. And then it's on to the Museum of the American Railroad . . ."

Spencer is smiling all proud-like because he knows I've finally read his trip itinerary and committed it to memory. Avery is less pleased.

"That's it. We're going out to a club tonight. I want you to tell people y'all had fun when you visited me."

I'm smiling now. I like this girl, which is strange, because aside from Lilliana, I don't usually bond with girls very easily. And to think, I didn't want to spend two nights here. Now I'm so glad we are. But then I think about our line dancing outing in Nashville, and my mood plummets.

"Are we going to a country bar?" I ask.

"I said fun," Avery shouts, making me jump. "I want you to have fun. Not everyone in Texas wears cowboy hats and Wranglers and goes out boot scootin' on Friday nights."

I'm down with her frustration about unfair stereotypes. Not everyone in New Jersey is overly tanned and "stars" in asinine cable reality shows. The view from the New Jersey Turnpike isn't representative of the farms, beaches, and mountains that make up the other ninety-five percent of our state, and we don't all know people in the Mafia.

"I can't wait," I exclaim. Then I add, "Does your salon have that new kind of gel manicure?"

"They do! Cool colors, too," Avery says. "I may get my brows done as well; whataya say?"

"I'm in!"

‿͛ꙮ‿

I call Steve Justice's office while we're en route to the salon. Miranda answers. I fill her in about Joey's message and she puts me on the phone with Steve—that's what he tells me to call him. He's a pretty chill guy. I'm glad, because I probably would have giggled if I had to refer to him as Mr. Justice. It sounds like he's some twenty-first-century superhero. Steve asks me a bunch of questions about the night I torched Joey's car, and he tells me he's going to send an investigator out to talk with Joey's neighbors. This guy really goes the extra mile. I wonder what this is costing my dad. Then he puts Miranda back on the line.

"When are you due back in New Jersey?" she asks.

I can't even remember what day it is. Let me think—it's Tuesday, and I'll be flying home Sunday night on the red-eye.

"Uh, Monday?"

"Okay, I'll set up an appointment for you and your parents to come in and talk to Steve before your court date."

"By the way, you were right," I tell Miranda. "Steve says he's sending an investigator over to Joey's neighborhood."

"He's sending me," Miranda says, and I can tell I've touched a nerve. "He couldn't get his guy, so now I have to do it. I'm the investigator. I'm the paralegal. I'm the secretary. I do everything around here!" She yells that last part, for Steve's benefit, I'm guessing. I start to laugh.

"I'm serious," she says, but I can tell she's just busting Steve.

"I believe you."

"Anyway, it's best to have as much information as possible before your court appearance."

"Thank you," I say, and I really mean it. "Thanks for everything."

"We'll stay in touch."

Avery tells me she's hired a car to take us to a club tonight. At my house, we only use limos when we're going to the airport or prom. "It's picking us up at nine," she says. We're in her room, listening to music, drinking iced green tea, and getting ready to go out. It feels like a holiday.

I'm wandering around her room, looking at framed pictures of Avery's friends and family at various events, when a thick book on her nightstand catches my eye. I pick it up. It's Jimmy Carter's White House memoirs. In what universe would I find myself reading a book like this? In what universe do I read nonfiction books for fun?

"He inspired me to do Habitat for Humanity this summer," Avery says. "He's a great man."

"What will you be doing?"

"Spending a week building housing for families outside El Paso, Texas. Near the Mexican border."

I put the book down and look at Avery. She's wearing a denim mini with a blue halter that really makes her eyes pop, especially now that she's wearing contacts instead of glasses.

"Want me to do your hair?" I ask. I may not be able to build houses, but hair I can handle.

I give her blond locks some Jersey style and also do her makeup before I finish getting ready. It's so nice to be able to take my time. I wear a super-girly minidress with a tiny floral print, spaghetti straps, and a built-in bra that's surprisingly supportive, kind of like Avery turned out to be. And I love how my lavender finger- and toenails look against my olive skin. My hair is cascading past my shoulders and my smoky eyes would make *Seventeen*'s beauty editor proud. A spritz of perfume and I'm all set.

When we step outside, I instantly feel three sets of male eyes on us. We look good. But so do the guys. And they smell good too. Matty always cleans up nicely when he wants to and Spencer, well, his hair could still use some product, but he's not wearing a cartoon T-shirt, so that's a plus. And there's something about Logan in jeans and a snug-fitting tee that makes me want to see Logan without jeans and a snug-fitting tee. . . . I have to stop myself from reaching up and smacking my own head.

I whip out my disposable camera and take a few group shots before asking Matty to take one of just me and Avery in front of the fountain. A minute later, a black stretch limo pulls into the circular drive, and I feel all rock star when the driver gets out and opens the door for us.

"After you, girls," Matty says.

Avery and I link arms and we slide into the cavernous backseat. I'm so psyched to be all dressed up and on my way out. A very girly squeal is threatening to escape my mouth. I can't wait to see this club.

"The driver won't turn back into a mouse at midnight, will he?" I ask.

"Nope. He's ours until dawn." She pauses. "Wasn't the driver a horse?"

"That's right. How could I forget? Cinderella is my favorite princess."

"Me too!"

I'm so glad Avery's not one of those princess bashers. I mean, I know women are supposed to stand on their own and all. I get that. But every once in a while it doesn't hurt to wish for a fairy godmother, a little magic, and a happy ending.

CHAPTER 12

AVERY ASKS THE DRIVER TO DROP US OFF A FEW BLOCKS from the club. She doesn't say why, but I know that hiring a limo was her way of making things easier for her friends, not impressing people, even though she's pretty stinkin' rich. Lilliana would like her. I could see us expanding our twosome to a threesome if Avery lived in New Jersey. As we approach the club, I can hear the thump, thump, thumping of a bass beat and the crash of symbols every time the door swings open. Avery explains they have bands downstairs and a deejay and dance floor upstairs.

"It's all ages. They give out wrist bands if you're over twenty-one, but scoring alcohol is not impossible." Avery smiles. "Especially for us regulars."

I've already decided I'm not drinking. I need to hate Joey for the foreseeable future and I don't want a warm fuzzy buzz to prompt my own drunk dial.

Without making a big deal about it, Logan pays for everyone's cover. Once inside, we negotiate the crowd as Avery leads us to a staircase at the back of the club. Upstairs, Avery, who indeed manages to score herself a light beer, pulls Logan onto the dance floor. It's a fast song and I watch them, wondering if she meant what she said about staying single—or if they'll wind up as a couple once they're both at ASU studying sustainability and saving the world together.

When the music slows, Avery turns toward us, but Logan pulls her back and puts his arm around her waist. My heart constricts for a millisecond and I hold my breath. My good mood is fading fast. I need to turn it around. Matty and Spencer are leaning on the bar drinking sodas. A diet Coke and those two? I love them, but that's not going to cut it. Instead of joining the guys, I head for the ladies' room to fix my lip gloss and regroup.

As I exit the restroom, I spot a pay phone at the end of the hallway. I rummage in my purse for that calling card. I'm not going to do anything crazy. I just need to hear a voice from home so I can shake off my jealousy and lift my spirits. I reread the instructions on the back of the card and dial Lilliana's number. It goes to voice mail. "Hey, it's me. Using the calling card you gave me. Okay. Call me later." She probably didn't recognize the number. No biggie.

I scan the club and find everyone standing together at the bar, where Avery appears to have snagged herself yet another beer. Interesting. But who am I to judge?

I shoulder my way across the crowded room and I'm about to

scooch between these two girls standing near our group when I hear one girl say to the other with disdain: "*El comelibros* has been checking you out since he got here." I follow her gaze. She's looking at Spencer. No effin' way. She just called my Spence a bookworm! Actually, it's even more offensive. *Comelibros* literally means "eats books." Who does she think she is? Her friend answers in Spanish. Roughly translated, she's says Spencer needs to get over himself.

My pulse starts to race and my body gets hot. I can't help it. I lose it. I stick my face in theirs and say: "*No, tú tienes que olvidarlo. Algún dia él va a ser el próximo* Bill Gates. *Y de todas formas, él está conmigo!*" Basically, I tell her to get over herself, that Spencer's going to be the next Bill Gates, and anyway, he's with me. Then I barge between the two of them and join my friends.

"Bitch," one of them mumbles, again in Spanish, as I pass.

I snap my head around and stare. "I heard you!"

She takes a step toward me, but her gal pal grabs her arm. Next thing I know, Logan is at my side. "Everything okay over here?" he asks.

"Fine." Then I take Spencer's hand and pull him to the dance floor. He looks confused as I drag him around, looking for a good spot—I want those girls to see us.

"Why were you arguing about Bill Gates?" Spencer asks.

"Someone's gotta defend Microsoft." I shake my head in mock disbelief. "Apple groupies."

We're finally in a good area and Spencer is bopping to the music.

It's a little like dancing with Elmo, but who cares. He's my friend.

"So, you're fluent in Spanish?"

"Not exactly. My mom is."

Spencer leans in and shouts over the music. "I'm taking Latin." His eyes are wide and innocent, and for the first time I notice that he's got killer lashes.

"That's cool." And I mean it. There is something very cool about the way Spencer knows what he likes and doesn't make any apologies for it. I feel bad for dismissing him and his Snoopy tee when we met and drooling over Logan's biceps. Spencer was there for me when Matty and I weren't speaking. I wish I could be more like Spencer and less like the girls who ragged on him. I'm relieved he didn't know what they said.

Matty, Logan, and Avery join us on the dance floor. Avery cups her hand over my ear. "You're not so selfish."

Avery speaks Spanish? Of course she does. Gotta be bilingual to save the world.

"I shouldn't have lost it like that. It's a pattern with me, in case you haven't noticed."

"You are a wild child," she says. "But you've got a good heart."

Do I? Avery does. That's for sure. I don't blame Logan for wanting to drive all this way to see her. Matty taps me on the shoulder and waves my phone at me.

"Text from Lilliana," he says.

I take my phone and read it. sorry about before. didn't recognize the number. blondie broke up w joey. So that's why he called me. when? why? I type back. A reply comes a few seconds later. yesterday. dumped him for a guy w a convertible. call when u can. luv ya, babe. I guess Joey's crispy 'Stang wasn't cutting it. I wonder what he's driving now. No. I don't wonder what he's driving. Thoughts of Joey are not going to ruin my night.

I hand my phone back to Matty and start shimmying in front of him. Avery comes up and dances suggestively against his backside. He is loving life. I just hope he doesn't do that whoop, whoop thing with his hand and embarrass us all. But then I turn and Spencer's doing the very move I feared and I'm surprised to find I'm not mortified. Not even a little. I sidle up to Spence and bump his hip. He bumps me back. The music fills me from the inside out, making me feel like, well, I'm here with my friends. Deep in the heart of Texas. We dance together for at least five songs and then—

"Look out. Your BFFs. At five o'clock," Avery shouts. She twists my head in their direction. I should have known those girls weren't going to call me a bitch and let it drop. They plow through the crowded dance floor in their skinny jeans and tank tops complete with built-in power padding and head right toward me.

And then it happens. One of them—the one who's wearing entirely too many fuchsia sequins—checks me with her shoulder, hard. They slide over and start dancing with Logan and Matty. As if. I whirl around, about to grab the one who bumped me, but drop my hand to my side instead.

"What am I doing?" I whisper.

Avery comes to my rescue—all five-foot one of her. She hands me her beer (how many does that make?) and muscles her way between Matty and my attacker. Before I can stop her, Avery turns her back to the girl and nudges her with her hip, smiling the whole time. I get the feeling she's not quite sober.

"Yo. I was dancin' here," says the girl.

"That's right, you were," Avery yells over her shoulder.

Uh-oh. Things get positively messy after that. The bedazzled one's friend, who is dancing near Logan, turns to Avery, grabs both her shoulders, and pushes her. I was trying to avoid a fight, but I can't let her treat Avery that way. I put on my game face, walk up to the girls, and scream, "Back off!"

That's when one of them slaps me across the face. My skin stings, and I don't know how I keep it together, but I follow the golden rule of kindergarten and keep my hands to myself. Avery, however, does not. She slaps the girl right back, and that's when someone yells, "Girl fight!"

Out of the corner of my eye, I see two burly bouncers sweeping people out of their paths as they descend on the dance floor and hone in on us. Logan sees them too and at that point, he bends down and flings Avery over his shoulder. Matty sizes me up, hesitates, and grabs my hand instead. We dash toward the stairs, away from the bouncers and the dance floor, while the girls follow, swiping at me like two cats. On the first floor, we pass through the crowd in a blur, crash through the exit, and trip onto the sidewalk. The bouncers stop their pursuit at the door; they've got us where they wanted us anyway, I suppose. The five of us run down the street toward our waiting car. The sparkle sisters curse us up and down, complete with obscene hand gestures, but seem reluctant to pursue us in their stilettos. At least they got thrown out too.

The driver opens the back door as we approach the limo and tumble inside, all of us out of breath. Avery is the first to start giggling. One by one we join in until we're all belly laughing. Logan's eyes are tearing, he's laughing so hard. I didn't know that boy had it in him. It's nice to see. He looks younger.

"I've never been in a bar fight before," Avery gasps. "What an adrenaline rush!" Then she falls over onto Matty's lap. Matty looks surprised, but not unhappy. He lays a hand on her arm and goes with it.

"I'm sorry, everyone," I say. I feel like a shit. I've got smart, classy Avery bitch slapping people in bars. I keep promising myself I'll be a better daughter, a better friend, a better person, but it's not working out so well. "I should have kept my mouth shut."

"Are you kidding? That's the most fun I've ever had," Spencer says. He's so serious, it makes my insides ache.

"Your heart was in the right place," Logan whispers.

He puts his arm around me and gives me a squeeze that sends a warm sensation right down to my toes. I have the urge to fall against him and sink into his side; I want both his arms around me. I want to feel like I'm part of a couple again. But instead, for a reason I don't completely understand, I shrug him off and lean toward the door to look out the window. The Dallas skyline rises sharply out of the flat landscape. *Just like Oz*, I think.

"I was trying to be better." I whisper to myself, but Logan hears.

"Give yourself a break," he says softly. "You're better than you think, Rosalita."

Oh, man, do I love the way my name sounds when Logan says it. In all the time we were together, Joey never said it. Not once. Then Logan takes my hand and gives my fingers a quick squeeze. When he makes a move to let go, I don't let him, and he doesn't seem to mind. By the time we cruise up the long driveway to Avery's estate, I'm feeling better. No, more than that, excited. Tomorrow, when my coach turns into a Taurus, I'll be ready for New Mexico, ready to kick impulsive/angry/reckless Rosie to the curb and own the rest of this road trip.

The sun is barely up and Logan is putting our bags in the trunk of the car. We all could have used more sleep, but Roswell is eight hours from here and the guys want to stop in Amarillo first to see something called Cadillac Ranch, which is going to add at least another hour to today's driving time. Avery's dad got up extra early to make us all a big breakfast. He's the best. I've got to send this family a fruit basket as a thank-you when I get home. We never did meet Avery's mom. I guess being a big-time cardiac surgeon doesn't allow for much time at home. I feel bad for Avery, and for her mom.

When it's time to say good-bye, I can't believe how choked up I get. I hug Avery, holding on to her slight shoulders for a beat too long.

"Thank you. For everything," I say, trying not cry.

"Thank you. For one crazy night. Come see me at ASU," she says. "Anytime."

"I will."

"Who knows? Maybe you'll love it and apply."

I never even considered that I'd be visiting ASU at the end of this trip. I guess because, until now, I didn't have any interest in touring some college campus, especially one that's so far away from New Jersey.

I smile at her. "New Jersey's beaches are the best in the summertime. You may need a break after building all those houses."

"You may just see me," she says.

I hope I do see Avery again—even if it is because she's Logan's girlfriend. Or Matty's. I'll be okay with that. I think. Why couldn't Spencer have shed his nerdiness and swept Avery off her feet? He deserves a girl like her.

I climb into the backseat with Matty. As we pass the fountain, he hands me my phone. "A text from Lilliana. It must be from last night. I guess I didn't notice it during the melee."

I look at the screen. btw, joey knows you're going to arizona.

Oh, shit. I guess I really did text him in my Benadryl haze. The fact that I racked up another TRO violation is nothing compared with my bigger worry. He wouldn't come after me, would he? I don't say a word, but Matty asks the question that's making the pancakes in my stomach feel like they're looking for a quick escape route.

"How did Joey find out about our trip?"

CHAPTER 13

I'M STANDING IN A COW PASTURE ALONG INTERSTATE 40 IN Amarillo, Texas, gaping at ten vintage Cadillacs buried nose down in the brown earth. The cars are covered in spray paint and graffiti. I snap a picture with my cheesy camera in a box.

"Awesome. This looks like Stonehenge," Matty says, shielding his eyes from the glare of the bright white sky as he looks up at the Cadillacs.

"Stonehenge is circular," Spencer says. "This is a straight line."

"It's basically crappy old cars in the dirt," I say. "We took a detour for this? Really?"

"There are no detours on a road trip, Catalano. There is only the road trip itself," Logan says. I'm momentarily bummed that I'm back to Catalano, but then he gives my upper arm a gentle squeeze and my stomach does a back handspring. But my mind reprimands my gut in an attempt to crush the oncoming crush. I throw in some sarcasm for good measure.

"Thank you, Deepak Chopra. What's next, yoga?" I snipe.

"Ha! Rosie doing yoga. An even more improbable sight than Cadillacs in the desert," Matty says. "You do know yoga is a form of exercise, not a cartoon bear, right?"

"Shut up, Matty."

"What? You know I'm right."

He is. He always is. It's like traveling through life with a six-foot Jiminy Cricket looking over my shoulder. Maybe I should think about joining a gym when I get back home. A gym with a pool. I like to swim, and I need to find a better way to deal with stress and my misplaced aggression, as Lilliana would put it. I'm feeling more than a little edgy right now. I've been trying to piece together my last communication with Joey. Did I text him and delete the evidence? Did I e-mail him in my antihistamine delirium? Probably not. I hardly ever use e-mail anymore, but I wish I had used Avery's laptop to check when I had the chance. Maybe it's just a coincidence. Joey could have found out where I'm headed from one of Eddie's friends. But Joey isn't the only thing that's got me all uptight. It's cloudy today, and during the entire ride across Texas, I could not stop scanning the horizon for tornados. Tornados and Wile E. Coyote. I watch those storm-buster shows on cable all the time, and this looks like the perfect place for one to touch down and siphon me, the boys, and the Taurus into its deadly cone.

When some actual tumbleweeds passed in front of the car, I made the mistake of wondering aloud if they come from one particular plant. Spencer, armed with a phone that is even smarter than he is, looked it up for me. Most tumbleweeds are just that, weeds called *Salsola* that were brought to North America in seed shipments from Asia. "So, a tumbleweed is nothing special, just a plant that dries out, disengages from its roots, and rolls away," he said while reading his screen.

A common weed, disengaged from my roots and blowing across America. It's exactly how I feel.

Now Mr. Smarty-pants moves on and is boring us with the details of these junkyard cars. "They are buried at the same angle as the Cheops pyramids," Spencer notes.

"Oh, here we go. Can we be done now, please?" I beg.

"Not before we take some pictures and use these." Matty holds up two cans of spray paint. "Someone must have left them behind."

"So what? We're supposed to decorate the Cadillacs?" I ask.

"Of course," Spencer says. "That's why we're here."

Matty tosses a can to Spencer and starts shaking the other. The metal ball clanks as he walks over to one of the cars and writes his initials. Spencer sprays some ancient-looking design that probably has something to do with the origins of the universe. Logan takes the can from his brother and draws the recycling symbol, then tosses the can to me. I'm impressed they've all resisted any wisecracks about me lighting these babies on fire.

"Whatcha gonna do, Rosie? How're you gonna leave your mark?" Matty asks.

The way Matty says it makes me stop and really think about it. I'll probably never come this way again, honestly, because hello, why would I want to? But how will I leave my mark? I shake the can and mull it over as I walk toward one of the cars. Whatever I decide to paint here might be gone soon anyway. I think about my brick at Graceland, point the can, and spray.

"Hey, Matty! Can you take a picture of me?" I ask.

He walks over with my phone, points, and clicks, capturing Me at Cadillac Ranch standing next to a junk car, on which I've spray painted a big WHY? Those three letters cover a lot of territory for me. Next time I find myself in Amarillo, I intend to have some answers.

Logan walks over and takes a look. "Now who's going all Buddha on us?" And then he turns down the dirt road toward our car, making that round-up motion with his finger. Is it possible I'm getting used to just how annoying he can be?

The bulk of the drive from Amarillo to Roswell is spent on two highways—US 60 and US 70. I am bored and hungry and use my time to make some calls. First, my parents. Steve Justice called them to set up a prehearing meeting. Then Lilliana. No new Joey news, but she digs the photo I send of me at Cadillac Ranch.

I'm still antsy.

"I think I'm gonna call Avery," I announce.

"I texted her a few minutes ago," Matty says.

"You did?" Me and Spencer practically gasp in unison.

"Yeah. She says 'hi, ya'll,'" Matty says, doing his best Avery impersonation.

Logan remains silent, but I see his eyes shift toward Matty in the rearview mirror. Is Logan jealous? Am I? And if I am, is it because Matty likes Avery or is it because Logan is jealous that Avery may like Matty? Then I wonder, if I jump out of this moving Taurus, will I die or simply tumble across the barren landscape like a *Salsola* plant?

I don't feel like calling Avery anymore even though it's possible I'm feeling most possessive of my new connection with her at this moment. I lean my head against the window, look across the endlessly flat landscape, and hope for a twister to take me away.

At some gas station in the middle of Nowheresville, the guys decide it's my turn to pump the gas. People can say all the snarky things they want about New Jersey, but at least we don't pump our own gas. All our stations are full service. It's the law and a good one if you ask me. Consequently, when I step out of the car and approach the pump, I realize I have no freakin' idea how to put gas in this car. I take out my emergency credit card and read the directions on the pump. I decide to get the gas cap off first. I twist and I twist, but it keeps making this awful crunching noise. I peek in the driver's-side window for some help and all three guys are laughing at me.

"I can't get the cap off. It's making funny noises," I whine.

"That usually indicates you're turning it the wrong way," Logan answers.

Spencer offers his contribution: "Lefty loosey, righty tighty."

I roll my eyes at them.

"There it is. The eye roll," Logan says.

"Pay up," Matty hoots. "I bet them five bucks you wouldn't get through this without an eye roll."

I flip them the bird. "What's that worth?" I say, and then sashay back to the pump.

Once I've got the filling process under control, the boys go into the Kwik Mart to buy drinks and snacks.

"Get me a Yoo-hoo! And some Cheez-Its." Nobody answers me. I do miss Avery. I should have called her earlier. I realize how much talking I don't do when I'm with Logan, Matty, and Spencer. I don't get most of their geek-centric pop culture references, and they don't bother to include me in their discussions anyway. It's either that or they all turn on me and it becomes Let's Tease Rosie time. It's getting old. I need to go on the offensive.

When they get back in the car (with Cheese Tidbits, ugh—everyone knows they suck), I take the lead on the conversation and play this game I learned in my high school theater class. It was either that or public speaking, so I picked the nicer teacher who never gives anyone less than a B.

"So, if you were a vegetable, what kind would you be and why?"

Spencer points to himself. "Am I supposed to answer that?" He's sitting in the back with me.

"We all are. It's an acting exercise. We'll take turns. You go first."

"Uh, okay. Let me think."

But Matty doesn't give him a chance. "I'd be an extra-large zucchini. For obvious reasons."

"Really. You see yourself walking around looking like a giant dick?" Logan asks.

"Yep," Matty agrees.

"Guys! Come on. Don't be gross."

"I'd be broccoli," Spencer decides.

"Okay, good. Why?" I ask. I'm happy Spencer is taking this seriously.

"Because I like broccoli."

I look out my window. This is not going the way I hoped.

I try again. "Maybe this would be more interesting if we let everyone else decide what kind of vegetable we are and why."

"Just vegetables?" Matty asks.

"Fine. We can do fruit too," I say. Maybe they'll find that easier. "Okay, so if I were a fruit, what kind would I be?"

Logan doesn't hesitate. "Bananas."

"Why?" I don't know why I'm bothering to ask.

"Uh, lemme think. Oh yeah, restraining order."

I'm not going to let him get to me. "Matty?"

"Um, strawberry."

"Why?"

"Because you were obsessed with Strawberry Shortcake lip gloss when you were in first and second grade. You had that massive collection you kept in a shoe box under your bed."

I can't believe he remembered that. I need a second before I speak again.

"Spencer? What would I be?"

"An orange."

I raise an eyebrow. This I have to hear.

"Because . . . I like oranges?" I offer.

"No. Because you're tough on the outside but sweet on the inside."

Whoa. Caught off guard again. I clear my throat to make those sneaky tears dissolve.

"Did the estrogen level just go up a notch, or am I imagining it?" Logan asks. He starts coughing like he can't breathe. "Open the windows."

Who's the zucchini now? I don't let Logan's teasing bother me. I catch Spencer's eye and mouth "thank you." He winks and smiles. Spencer is neither a fruit nor a vegetable, more like the surprise toy in a box of healthy cereal.

Hours later, after crossing the Texas–New Mexico border at Farwell, I start seeing signs for the Flying Saucer McDonald's in Roswell. It looks awesome. Plus, I'm starving and I'm craving something, anything, dunked in ketchup.

"We are so there!" I nearly poke Spencer on the nose when I lean across him and point to the billboard on his side of the car. Logan just gives me his Logan look.

"What? They've got salads," I tell him.

"Screw the salad. A super-size meal and a shake, that's what I'm talking about," Matty says.

"Thank you!" I shout.

"Fine," Logan says.

We pull into the parking lot a short time later. The restaurant does indeed look like a flying saucer and the play area looks like a spaceship.

"Amazing." I sigh.

"Gee, Catalano," Logan says. "It's nice to see you're finally excited about something. After fifteen hundred miles, I was beginning to think we were boring you."

"Let's see what it looks like inside," I say. I'm the first one out of the car.

I walk through the gleaming silver door and head for the high-ceilinged play area. I smile up at Ronald and Grimace in space suits. If I only had to see fast-food-related kitschy alien stuff while we're in Roswell, I'd be a happy girl. But I know all about Spencer's bigger plans this afternoon.

We grab our food and sit down. I'm a little disappointed that this seating is normal McDonald's style.

"I was hoping this would be more like eating in a spaceship," I say out loud to no one in particular. I dip a fry in one of the five ketchup-filled mini-containers I've lined up on my tray like tequila shots.

"What? You thought we'd enter an antigravitational chamber and float around while we scarfed down burgers and fries?" Spencer asks. Coming from anyone else, this would be sarcasm. But Spencer really wonders if that's what I expected.

"Nah. I just thought the tables and chairs would be cooler."

"Word," Spencer says.

Spencer saying "word" has the same effect on me as my mother wearing my clothes. I take a sip of my milk shake to avoid smiling.

"Let's go," Logan says. "We have time to see the museum before it closes."

"Phew, that's a relief," I say. I buy myself some cookies on the way out. Tours make me hungry. Road trips make me hungry. Restraining orders and ex-boyfriends make me hungry. I think Logan has a point about emotional eating.

The International UFO Museum and Research Center in Roswell has a movie-theater-style marquis out front. THE TRUTH IS HERE, it brags. Doubt it. Inside we are greeted by an alien in chinos holding a sign that says WELCOME . . . PLEASE SIGN IN AND ENJOY YOUR VISIT. Again, I'm gonna have to go with "doubt it." Admission's only five bucks, but one glance around tells me even that is a waste of money. They offer an audio tour, like the kind we did at Graceland, but the museum's really only one big room with bulletin board exhibits like "The Roswell Incident Timeline" or "The Great Cover-up." I don't want to walk around and read yellowed newspaper clips.

"You know what this reminds me of?" Spencer asks.

"The *Deep Space Nine* when Quark, Rom, and Nog travel back in time to a twentieth-century Roswell?" Matty offers.

Spencer and Matty fist bump each other. Nerds of a feather. At least Spencer didn't say "word" this time.

Logan looks at me. "We've got to get those two laid." His conspiratorial smile gives me the shivers. That dimple is going to do me in.

"Don't look at me!" I say. I need air. "I'll be in the gift shop. Come find me when you're done."

After a quick look around at the alien-theme souvenirs, I decide there's absolutely nothing I want to buy—one more bizarre occurrence in Roswell. I never go shopping and come back empty-handed. I leave the poor excuse for a gift shop, find Matty, and ask him for my phone.

"Here," he says. "Why don't you just hold it for the rest of the trip? I won't tell. I can use a break from your parents' incessant communications."

Matty doesn't have anything to worry about. Joey's drunk call extinguished my burning need to communicate with him. I find a spot by the museum entrance and sit down. Something is shifting inside me. My homesickness has abated at the moment; now I'd rather be in New Mexico staring at a plastic alien than on my way back to New Jersey to face what I did.

I pick up a brochure about the museum and leaf through it. Lilliana's text about Joey knowing where I am is still bothering me. Joey wouldn't actually show up in Phoenix, would he? How would he know how to find me? I don't want to talk to the guys about it, especially Logan. He's no longer looking at me like I'm the wild girl crashing his road trip, and I don't want to ruin that.

Finally, I call my parents for my daily check-in (Pony didn't want to come to the phone this time) and text Lilliana. My stomach feels queasy when she texts me about some party at our friend Xavier's. She took Marissa with her. Would I have gone if I were there? Probably not. The last time I went to a party, well—fire, TRO. Enough said. But what about the next party? What's the rest of my summer going to be like when I get back?

A few minutes later I get another text. I figure it's from Lilliana again, but I'm shocked by what I see. can we talk? Here I just got done telling myself that Matty had nothing to worry about. It's from Joey.

The next five minutes is like being on a crash diet with a plate of chocolate brownies in front of me. It's a struggle, but in the end, I dial Avery for support.

"Help me. I just got a text from Joey."

"Be strong, girl. What'd he say?"

"He wants to talk."

"Have his attorney call your attorney," Avery says.

"I wish you were here. We're at the UFO museum."

From where I'm sitting I can see all three boys. They're meandering around sporting dorky headsets—that are no doubt filling their heads with all kinds of fascinating facts—and checking out the uninspired displays. I explain the scene to Avery.

"Did those guys not understand what I meant about having fun?"

"Be glad you missed Matty and Spencer's *Deep Space Nine* discussion."

"Matty asked me for my number."

"We know." I tense up waiting to hear what she says next.

"He's a sweet guy; I would have felt bad saying no. But I don't want to lead him on. Distance and timing are not in his favor."

"I can relate." My muscles relax.

"Ya know, Rosie, sometimes when you don't know what to do, it's okay to do nothing."

I think about that as I delete Joey's text.

Later, at the motel, I tell Matty about the Joey text and give him my phone. "Turn it off. Lock it in your suitcase. I'm tired of looking at it."

"I wish I could, but Mama Catalano would not survive a communications blackout," Matty says.

I sigh and grab my toothbrush. "I'm going to bed." Exhaustion and sheer boredom are overtaking me. We drove such a long way for old cars and little green men. Thank God for the McDonald's spaceship, lackluster seating and all, or today would have been a total bust. It's not that I don't want to have fun on this trip; it's just that this stuff is not my idea of a good time. I feel like I'm on a field trip. A loooong field trip.

I fall into bed with Matty without a fuss. I merely plop a pillow between us, turn on my side, and mutter, "The Grand Canyon better not be the bland canyon. I hope that hole in the ground rocks my world."

"No pun intended?" Matty says.

I open the eye that's not smushed against my pillow. "We've been spending too much time together," I mumble as I shut it again and drift off to sleep.

CHAPTER 14

THE NEXT MORNING I'M AWAKENED BY A BRIGHT LIGHT. MY eyes flutter open and there's a glowing white orb about two inches from my face. Is that the sun? Or . . . oh no. I gingerly feel the back of my head and neck. Phew. No probes. That's a relief. Because obviously, if anyone's getting abducted while we're in Roswell, it's me. That's the kind of luck I have. Reassured, I slowly reach toward the light—and burn myself.

"Sonavabitch!!!" It *is* two inches from my face, and so are the guys.

I sit straight up in bed and grab my sizzling index finger. It better not blister.

"What the hell? Why are you idiots shining the desk lamp in my eyes? A bunch of freakin' weirdos. That's who I'm seeing America with. A bunch of freakin' weirdos."

"There's the Rosie we love," Matty says.

"Don't be mad, Rosie. We have a surprise for you," Spencer says.

"I know, I know. Area 51. More alien crap," I huff.

"Nope. Change of plans. We're going off the itinerary." Spencer sounds so proud of himself.

"Wait, we're not going to Carlsbad Caverns, are we?" I'd seen signs for it on the interstate. "I am so not doing any more caves."

"Better," Logan says. He's already dressed and zipping up his duffel bag.

"You're putting me on the first plane home?"

"It's a surprise," Matty says. He's waving around a brochure that he must have gotten from the table in the lobby. If you can call the Formica counter with the cash register, plastic plant, and Mr. Coffee a lobby.

"Let me see that." I stand on top of the bed and lunge for the brochure. Matty, who is now standing next to me, dangles it two feet above my head. I grab hold of his arm to steady myself and try to launch myself to grab it. It's no use. Jolly Green is too tall.

I'm about to make one more attempt, but as soon as I'm in motion, Matty kicks my legs out from under me. I fall back onto the bed and take him down. Now he's sprawled on top of me, grinning. We've wrestled like this since we were kids, but for some reason, I'm blushing from head to toe. My embarrassment is embarrassing, but my bigger concern is the fact that I didn't sleep in a bra and I'm worried, well . . . let's just leave it at that. I'm worried.

"Get off me, you big oaf." I'm beginning to sweat.

Spencer looks at us with his hands on his hips. "I'd say get a room, but—"

"Enough! Somebody better tell me where we're going today," I demand as Matty rolls over.

"Albuquerque," Logan says.

"To do what?"

"You'll just have to wait," Matty says. He stands up, folds the brochure, and puts it in his back pocket. "This is gonna be so cool."

"Does it involve bathing suits and suntan lotion?" I ask.

"Nope," Logan says. "Jeans and . . . do you even own athletic shoes?"

"Yes. I just don't have running shoes. And what's up with the glasses?" *Thick* glasses, at that. They make his eyes look itty bitty. "I never saw you wear them before."

"Wouldn't you opt for contacts if your glasses looked like that?" Spencer says. "You should have seen him when he was overweight and wore glasses."

"I'd kick your ass, little bro, but we don't have time," Logan jokes.

Discovering Logan was overweight and wears glasses makes something click in my brain. Sure, Logan's got a confident, borderline cocky attitude, but it's more about being smart, and right, than about being hot. Meanwhile, Joey knows exactly how good he looks and works it—flirting with the world is Joey's modus operandi. Logan, on the other hand, knows he's smart, but he doesn't necessarily know how good looking he is. "It explains a lot," I blurt out.

"What?" Logan asks.

"Nothing," I say. "Gotta get ready."

Thankfully he does the guy thing and moves on.

"You've got a half hour, Catalano. Remember, jeans. No shorts."

Forty-five minutes later, we're back in the Taurus. Yes, I took a little longer getting ready today. The round brush was working its magic as I blew my hair dry, and I did not want to rush the process. For once, nobody complains. Logan even lets me ride shotgun.

"You look . . . nice," Logan says softly as he opens the door for me.

I'm not sure whether I should return the compliment or check the back of his neck for probes.

"Thanks," I say. Best to keep it simple.

I click my seat belt and stare out the window. Spencer fires up his tunes. It's his turn to pick the music. I put my shades on, close my eyes, and listen to his first selection. Make that *try* to listen. Classic rock. Better than country, but with Spencer strumming along on the acoustic, it's like being forced to watch someone play Guitar Hero.

"Can we listen to my songs next?" I ask. It's worth a shot.

"That's depends," Matty says.

"On what?"

"If you have an appropriate playlist," Logan says.

"My Bruce mix includes 'Badlands,'" I offer.

"There are no badlands in New Mexico," Spencer explains.

"There is no *Kansas* in New Mexico. And yet that's what I find myself listening to," I say. "'Dust in the Wind'? Does it get any sadder?"

Spencer defends his choice. "I'm learning this guitar part."

I know I'm difficult, I'm aware of that. But these three have no idea how utterly infuriating they can be in their collective passive-aggressive way. I sigh and accept my defeat.

As we pull onto Route 40 west, I look out the window at the caramel-colored landscape. I swear we've passed that same mountain ten times already and we've only been in the car for eleven minutes. My impatience grows with every mile until I blurt out to no one in particular, "If you're not going to tell me where we're going, can you at least tell me how long it's going to take to get there?"

"Three hours," Matty says.

Why do I bother asking? Deflated, I sink down in my seat. Every time we get in this car, it seems like I always spend a minimum of three hours with my butt on these taupe fabric seats until our next destination. I'm getting tired of leaving Somewhere, driving through the Middle of Nowhere, and ending up Somewhere again. I click the heels of my Skechers together. Nothin'. Must only work with ruby slippers. Either that, or my heart knows I don't really want to go home.

We've traveled nearly two hundred miles and for the past hour, no one has said a word. This would never happen in a car full of girls. We'd have endless topics of conversation: movies, boys, music, SATs, celebrity gossip, boys, split ends, gel manicures. Whatever. Girls can fill the silence.

"Why does it take so long to get anywhere?" I finally say.

"It's a big country, Catalano," Logan offers.

"That's why my family sticks to the edges."

"Quit your constant complaining," Matty says. "We're here."

"Really? Where?" I perk up and look out the window.

"I think the sign says it all," Logan says.

"Sandia Stables?" I'm smiling 'cause I know.

"We decided that the only thing better than seeing an alien in New Mexico would be seeing you on horseback," Matty chimes in. "I told them how you've always wanted to ride a horse."

"Seriously?" My eyes and nose burn with happy tears, and for few seconds, that's all I can manage to say. Finally, I clear my throat and speak.

"Thank you, guys. This is awesome."

If I had known, I would have worn the cowgirl tank I bought in Nashville. It seems like that was a month ago. We drive down the long dirt road leading to the horse ranch. Logan parks near the barn and we all get out of the car.

"This one is on me," Logan says, and reaches for his wallet.

I am positively giddy and have to restrain myself from jumping up and down when I see my horse emerge from the barn with the rancher. She is beautiful, just like the copper-colored pair I saw on the ridge in Virginia. She has a diamond-shaped white spot between her deep brown eyes and her mane hangs between her ears like horsey bangs; how adorable.

"Okay now, miss. Why don't you step on over here and I'll show you how to git up on Penny?"

Aw, her name is Penny. It reminds me of Pony. Wait until I tell him about this. As I walk toward Penny and the ranch man, I'm suddenly anxious. Does Penny know I'm nervous? Aren't horses supposed to be really good at sensing human emotion? I've seen *The Horse Whisperer* on AMC. I want her to like me.

"Take a deep breath and relax," the rancher says. "That's my first rule."

In through the nose, out through the mouth. "I'm good."

"Okay now. You're going to stand on the left side of the horse. Take the reins in your left hand, and put that hand up here by the horse's mane."

I follow his directions.

"Good. Now, without letting go of the reins, grab on to her mane."

I'm worried about hurting Penny, but I listen. He's the expert.

"Okay, now you're going to use your right hand to turn the stirrup toward you. Good. That's it. Now put your left foot in there."

Right hand. Left foot. *Okay, pardner, I'm still with you.*

"There ya go. Now grab the back of the saddle, give a little bounce on the ball of your right foot, and pull on her mane and the saddle until you get yourself up in the stirrup on your left."

I never turn around to look at the boys. I just concentrate, bounce, pull, and whoa! Here I am, almost on the horse.

"That a girl. Now swing that right foot over and you're there."

Plop. Houston, I am in the saddle. The stirrups are higher than I expected. I thought my legs would hang down more.

"Whatever you do. Do not let go of the reins. Got it?" Mr. Sandia Stables says.

I give him a toothy smile. I'm quivering inside. "Got it."

Could it be that I'm a natural? That wasn't hard at all. Ha! Look at me. Giddyap. I'm grinning proud. And here's the better part: Logan, Matty, and Spencer all make complete asses of themselves trying to mount their horses. It's beyond me how Matty, who's almost as tall as his horse, can't seem to pull himself up smoothly.

"Grab the back of the saddle, not the horn," the rancher yells. "This isn't a carousel."

I think Matty's horse doesn't like him. It keeps shaking its head and razzing him. It takes Matty at least three tries before his long, skinny leg finally swings up and over. Spencer gets up on the first try but collapses on the horse's neck before getting his right leg in the proper position. Logan's horse keeps taking one step away every time he goes to put his foot in the stirrup. Finally, the ranch guy holds the reins and stirrup for him. I'm surprised he didn't boost Logan up and over too. Now, that would have been priceless.

"All right," says the rancher. "Now that we've got you all in the saddle, I'll teach you basic starting and stopping, and then my son, Lucca, over there is going to take you out on the trail."

I follow the rancher's finger to where he's pointing. Well, would you look at Lucca. That tush was made for Wrangler's. I'm itching to fluff my hair, but it's like the ranch man reads my inner monologue.

"I said it before, but this bears repeating. Never drop the reins," says the father of Lucca. Lucca the god. "Keep your backs straight and your heels down. Eyes up. Don't look at the ground. You look at the ground, you'll be on the ground."

We snap into our best posture and follow directions as the rancher continues.

"Now for some horseback riding one-zero-one. Keep the reins in the center of the saddle, by the horn. Move the reins to the left, and your horse will go left; move them to the right, and the horse will go right. Pull back, slowly, not with a quick jerk, and the horse will stop. To get the horse walking, squeeze with your calves and the horse will go. As you feel more comfortable, I'd like you to try to guide the horse by using that same technique. To move left, apply pressure with your calf to the horse's right side and vice versa."

"Do we have to say giddyap?" Why'd I ask that?

"Only if you think that's going to give you a fuller experience, miss." Rancher sarcasm.

"You'll have to excuse her," Matty says. "She's from New Jersey."

"So are you guys!"

"Yes, but we don't try quite as hard to make it obvious." Logan laughs.

"Yeah, well, maybe I don't think it's something to be ashamed of," I snipe.

That's it. I squeeze with my calves and Penny starts walking. All on her own, she moseys away from the barn toward the nearest trail and I don't try to stop her. That's my girl. Just get me away from these idiots. We understand each other, me and Penny.

"Hold up, little lady," Father of Lucca calls after me. "Don't head down the trail without Lucca."

I wave over my shoulder and play dumb. Let Lucca catch me. Let them all catch me. I can't wait until Penny is galloping. I hear a commotion behind me as the guys attempt to put their horsies in drive.

"Watch it," I hear Logan yell.

"Uh, space, Matty. I need room to turn," Spencer says.

I smile and let Penny take her time as we amble toward the woods. Then comes the cloppity-clop of a horse coming up quickly behind me. I watch the butt of Lucca pass me on the left. His flexed thigh muscles sure look nice as he pulls in front of me and spins his horse around to face Penny. He nods and tips a straw cowboy hat at me. I glance behind me to see the boys have finally achieved forward motion and are closing the gap between us.

"You're a brave one, aren't ya?" Lucca says.

"I'm just excited. This is my first time on a horse."

"Well, I'd say you're doing fine so far."

"Thanks." It feels nice to be spoken to this way by a boy. No taunting. No irony in his voice.

"You like horses?" Lucca asks.

"I do. And I really like Penny. I think she gets me." I stroke her mane and pat her neck. I think I feel her smiling.

"Looks like it," Lucca says.

Oh, man, I love his five o'clock shadow and the way the little indent at the base of his neck provides the perfect cradle for the turquoise and silver charm that hangs from his leather choker. I can't say that I've ever had a cowboy fantasy, but that just changed. I'm mulling over a way to surreptitiously get a pic of Lucca's Wrangler butt on horseback when the guys finally join us.

"We all here?" Lucca asks. "Let's go, then. Why don't you ride behind me, pretty lady? The rest of you follow in single file."

Pretty lady. I know he probably says that to all the girls, but it's something I don't hear very often, and by "very often" I mean ever. I sit taller.

Our horses mosey up the trail a bit as we follow Lucca's instructions and stay in single file. It's already pretty hot—not steamy New Jersey hot, more like standing in an oven hot—and our rides don't appear to be in any rush. Both Penny and I could use another application of deodorant. The view is nice, though, and I'm not just talking about Lucca's gluteus maximus.

We ride in relative silence. I say "relative" because me and Lucca aren't talking and Logan, who is immediately behind me, is not saying a word, but I can hear Matty and Spencer yapping away in the back. Words like "indigenous" and "vegetation" drift my way and I have to roll my eyes. Most of the trees on the trail look like run-of-the-mill evergreen. Nothing too unfamiliar except that I notice when I breathe in, and this is going to sound weird, I can smell them. The air smells so clean. I feel like one of those women in an air freshener commercial. Back home, I'd never give trees or other plants or how they smelled a second thought. Lucca stops and lets me and Penny catch up. I stare beyond the tree line at the jagged tops of the gray mountains. Lucca follows my gaze.

"The Sandia Mountains," he says. He looks older than all of us; around twenty, I'm guessing.

"Thus the name of your stables."

"Correct."

"What kind of trees are these?" For some reason, I care all of a sudden.

"Firs and spruce. A few ponderosa here and there; nothing too special," he says. "You've probably got these in Jersey."

"New Jersey," I say. I can't help it. He's touched a sore spot. In my opinion, you can only call it "Jersey" if you live in Jersey.

"New Jersey," Lucca corrects.

"You don't hear me dropping the 'new' from your state, do you? Where would that get us, huh?"

"Cancún?" Lucca gives me a half smile. "Just like I thought. Feisty."

I smile too. Partly because I'm picturing shirtless Lucca surrounded by sand and turquoise water, the scent of coconut suntan lotion on his skin and . . . I'm going to fall off Penny if I go on. I shake my head to snap out of it. "Well, it's just that I hate when people who aren't from my state do that—especially Philly sports fans."

"I stand corrected."

"Except you're sort of sitting right now," I tease.

I don't know why I'm being so sassy with this complete stranger, who I find wildly attractive. I guess I'm in I've-got-nothing-to-lose mode. He lives in New Mexico, he's too old for me, and I'm never going to see him again.

"Well, since you brought up the position of my rear end, why don't we discuss yours?"

"Excuse me?"

"Take it easy, cowgirl. I'm just wondering what a girl from New Jersey is doing on a horse, in New Mexico, in the middle of summer. Could you have picked a hotter day for a ride?"

I decide to drop the attitude, at least for the moment, and fill him in about how Logan is on his way to ASU, how he'd wanted to bring his car, and the guys decided it would be fun to have a road trip, blah, blah, blah.

"We're leaving him in Tempe with the car and flying home in three days," I explain. Wow. I get a pang when I realize how soon that is. Not to mention, it's almost the Fourth of July. The thought of it makes me feel hollow inside. Partly because I'm still worried about what I may have said to Joey and partly because I'll be missing the fireworks at home. I've never missed the fireworks at Memorial Field before.

"So, I'm guessing one of the three amigos is your boyfriend?" Is he flirting?

"Nope."

Lucca raises his eyebrows. He is flirting. I'm aware that Logan is listening. Matty and Spencer are falling behind, lost in their inane chatter. "So you just decided to go along for the ride?"

"More like was forced to. My parents wanted to keep me away from a guy."

"Ahh."

"My ex. He sort of filed a restraining order against me."

Lucca laughs at that one, but not in a mean way. More like the kind of genuine outburst that occurs when you're caught off guard. His laughter is contagious, and I start giggling too at this wild girl named Rosie who did this absurd thing back in New Jersey. The ludicrousness of the whole thing becomes clearer with every mile of this road trip.

"Why do I suddenly feel like I should be on my best behavior?" Lucca says.

I shrug. "Part of my charm."

He slows his horse down so that it's next to mine and leans toward me. "So, this is your getaway, then? Welcome to the wild west." He puts out his right hand and reaches for my left for a kind of sideways shake. I'm sort of nervous about taking one hand off the reins, but for Lucca, I do. His calloused hand is strong, manlier than I'm used to. I start imagining what it would be like to feel that hand against my cheek, on my shoulder, around my waist. I gotta stop. I'm getting tingly all over. I guess being on horseback can do that to a girl.

So here I am, almost holding hands with a cowboy on horseback—

mountains looming in the distance, the rugged landscape surrounding us—this could be the most romantic thing to happen to me in, well, again, ever. And it would be, if it weren't for the three pairs of eyes I can feel behind me. Maybe I can pretend the three amigos, as Lucca called them, aren't there.

"Is Rosie holding hands with the cowboy?" Spencer shouts.

The blood rushes to my cheeks and even more sweat trickles down the back of my neck.

"What? This darn horse won't move," yells Matty, who has fallen way behind. "What about Rosie and the cowboy?"

I turn around just as a frustrated Matty gives his horse a swift kick with the stirrups. I wince. What is he thinking? He musta put too much somethin'-somethin' in that giddyap because suddenly his horse bolts past Spencer and Logan, picking up steam as he gallops past me and Lucca and down the winding rocky trail before disappearing into the trees. All I hear is the clop, clop, clop of hooves and Matty screaming, "Whoa, horsey, Whoaaaaa!!!"

"Pull back gently on the reins!" Lucca yells. He turns to me, Logan, and Spencer. "Just keep following this trail. The horses know the way. I got this."

Lucca gives his horse a kick, with the correct amount of oomph, and takes off after Matty like a cowboy in a western movie, yelling directions to Matty as he disappears down the trail in a cloud of dust. Hi ho, Lucca; I can watch that guy all day. This is better than *True Grit*.

"There goes your hero," Logan says as his horse walks beside mine. He gazes off down the trail without looking at me. "Did Matty really yell 'horsey'?"

"Poor bastard. I hope he's okay," Spencer says, then asks, "Why were you holding the cowboy's hand anyway, Rosie?"

"Lucca. His name is Lucca, not the cowboy. And I wasn't holding his hand; I was shaking it."

"I thought we got the introductions over with before we started the ride," Logan says.

I scrunch my eyes at him without saying a word. Our eyes lock for a few seconds and then he pulls ahead of me on the trail. He rides pretty well.

"Come on, Rosie," Spencer says. "Let's see if we can catch up to Matty."

Spencer is pretty good with his horse too. He guides his horse around me and gets it to canter down the path. Penny must think this seems like a good idea because she does the same. Once she gets going, it's bumpier than I expected. My butt keeps smacking against the saddle as she picks up speed. Poor gal. I wonder if having a first-timer on her back is uncomfortable for her. She's probably about ready to drop me at the car and return to her shady barn, but I'm not ready for this ride to end.

When we catch up to them, Lucca is standing in the trail, holding two sets of reins as he tightens the saddle on Matty's horse. Matty is sitting on a big gray rock, wiping blood off of his forehead.

"Oh my God, Matty! Are you okay?" I want to get off Penny and run to him, but I'm not exactly sure how to go about accomplishing this. I feel trapped.

"I'm fine. It's just a scratch."

"His horse took him under a branch and sort of scraped him off," Lucca says.

"Dude, you were thrown from your horse? How cool," Spencer says.

"I wouldn't say thrown. It was more of a slow slide." Matty sounds dejected.

Lucca nods in agreement and, to his credit, tries to make Matty feel better. "It's good to fall every once in a while. It means you're learning something. He got right up too. I was impressed."

Lucca finishes adjusting the saddle, and a red-cheeked Matty gets in position to mount up. Like a parent watching her kid take his first swing at Little League, my muscles tighten in anticipation. It only takes him one try to get on the horse this time.

"How 'bout you ride up here with me?" Lucca suggests to Matty. Business before romance, I guess. He doesn't need Matty breaking a bone and suing his father.

Now that I'm a horse away from Lucca, I'm not able to talk to him. In a way, it's better. I'm able to focus on the ride. I'm horseback riding in the Sandia Mountains. When will I be able to say that again? I watch the twitch of Penny's ears, inhale through my nose, and exhale slowly through my mouth. Everything else feels so far away, and I'm surprised to find I'm not thinking about anything, or anyone, as I enjoy the sound of horse hooves clopping along the trail. My hearts sinks as we descend the mountain and I see the ranch in the distance.

When we reach the ranch, we gather in front of the barn, where Lucca and his dad supervise our collective dismounts. Lucca holds Penny's reins and puts a hand in the small of my back as I swing my right leg over my horse and lower it to the ground. I take my left foot out of the stirrup and look up at him. I have the sudden urge to touch the charm around his neck.

"Is this the sun?" I ask, taking the medallion in my hand.

"A glyph."

"Huh?" I'm still holding it in my hand.

"Native American sun symbol. Like hieroglyphics."

"Was it made by Native Americans?" Now that we're not on horseback anymore, I notice he's not that tall—but his chiseled features more than make up for his average height.

"Nah. Some band I saw in Arizona. Bought it off their merch table."

I had almost forgotten my question. *Do not stare directly at Lucca*, I caution myself.

"Nice." I let go of the charm, keeping my eyes fixed on it as I do.

"How long are you in New Mexico for?"

"We're leaving for Arizona from here." Lucca's dark brown eyes search for mine, but I have to look away. Now is not the time to form new attachments.

"Next time you visit, try to do it in the fall. The weather is better, and every October, Albuquerque has its International Balloon Fiesta. Ever been in a hot air balloon?"

"No. But I'd never been on a horse until today either."

"And look how well that turned out. If you decide to do it, look me up. I'll take you for a ride. You'll love floating with the clouds."

My stomach already feels like it is. I know Lucca is just being friendly, but my resistance is fading. Could I make it to Albuquerque in the fall? I'm afraid to look at the guys. I sense they're the ones doing the eye rolling now.

"Call me here when you need to plan your next getaway." Then Lucca leans in and gives me an innocent, but sweet, kiss on my cheek. His scruff gives me chills.

I turn to see Lucca's dad and my three guys staring at us. We stare back at them. It's like a gun duel at the OK Corral. Matty is the first to make a move. He runs a finger along the scrape on his forehead. Logan turns and walks toward the car. Lucca's dad tells him to bring the horses into the barn. Lucca starts to lead Penny away from me, then stops. He takes off his necklace and walks back. In one quick motion, he fastens it around my neck.

"I can't take this," I say.

"How 'bout you give it back next time I see you. You know where to find me." He gives me a crooked, flirty smile, then saunters back to Penny. I think we both know we're never going to see each other again, but I like the idea of having a cowboy in New Mexico to fantasize about whenever I'm in a funk.

Matty waits for me. He puts an arm on my shoulder, buddylike, and leads me toward the car.

"It always starts off well, doesn't it? Let's go before Lucca's horse ends up like Joey's Mustang."

I shrug off his hand and shoot him a cold, hard stare. Matty smiles and throws his arms up in surrender. "Just trying to be helpful."

I give him my give-me-a-break face as he opens the door for me. I'm not really mad; I know he's only joking. As Matty walks around the car to his side, I stand there for a few seconds, my hand on the door, gazing at the barn and the mountains beyond. It's funny, I think as I slip inside and slam the car door shut. It's Penny, not Lucca, who I'm already missing.

CHAPTER 15

THE RIDE FROM NEW MEXICO TO ARIZONA IS THE MOST tedious stretch of the journey thus far. Outside the car, the scenery is flat, brown, and repetitive, while inside, it is ridiculously—no, make that annoyingly—silent. Here we go again. At least girls have actual hormonal shifts that account for their mood swings. It's biology. But these three, what's their excuse?

For the first hour, Logan won't turn on the car stereo. Matty has his earbuds in, Spencer is fingering the strings of his guitar without strumming, and I'm listening to my own tunes. Even though I've got control of my phone (Matty handed it to me when we got in the car), I'm having trouble getting cell reception out here. I keep waiting for someone to say something—anything. I see signs for Historic Route 66, but no one even mentions it. I remember this section of Spencer's itinerary. He called it "The Mother Road."

I'm shocked and disappointed when I yell, "Hey, look, we're coming up to the Continental Divide!" and no one acknowledges that I've spoken. I'm not even sure what it is, just seems like something this crew would be interested in. Why are they mad at me? It's not like I was making out with Lucca. And I'm not the one who kissed him on the cheek. Or gave him jewelry. Fine. If they want to play the silent treatment game, I'm going to win. Honestly, it's like they don't want me to be happy. One step up, two steps back. I am so freakin' sick of this car and them.

I turn up the volume on my music, fold my arms, close my eyes, and plan to sleep until we reach the Grand Canyon. I can't believe I felt wistful about leaving the ranch and this trip coming to an end. I want to see my family and my girlfriends. I want to sleep in my own bed. I want to get my stupid effin' court date over with and get on with my summer routine. This sucks! I am throwing a mental tantrum. I am done with these three. I wonder if I can ignore them for the rest of the trip. It's been days since Dollywood, and I'm ready for this roller-coaster ride to be done.

About thirty minutes later, Matty points a pack of spearmint gum my way. "Want some?" he asks. I pretend to sleep. A few minutes after that, Spencer says, "We're almost to Gallup." I ignore him, too. It's always on their terms. Well, I hope they're catching a breeze right now.

"We'll be stopping for food and gas when we get there," Logan says. "If she wants to sleep, or pretend to sleep, let her."

What I want to do is kick him in the back of the head with my foot, but I keep up my game of possum. Besides, I can eat without talking. A minute later, the car slows to a stop and Logan puts it in park. That was fast. But when Logan starts pounding the steering wheel and yelling, "Shit, shit, shit," I open my eyes and see that we're on the side of the road, not in the parking lot of some fast-food restaurant.

"Flat?" Matty asks.

Spencer leans over to look at the gauges. "Outta gas," he sighs.

This is so not Logan. His personality is definitely lacking in some areas, but I've always felt safe with him. He's like my dad: always in control, always knowing things, like when we're running low on fuel and where we're supposed to be and when. I'm feeling a little sorry for him but quickly push it away.

"Matty and I will walk down the interstate and get some gas. It's only a few miles," Logan says. I look down the road. I can see the next exit from here. It doesn't look that far, but nothing does on the open road. Who knows how long it will take them. And it's disgustingly hot outside. "Spence, you and Rosie stay here with the car."

I pull out a bottle of water from my backpack and hand it to Matty. "Take this. And buy yourself some more at the gas station before you walk back. You need to stay hydrated."

"Thanks, Rosie." He looks less than thrilled to have been enlisted to make the long, sweltering trek with Logan the Grouch.

I watch them walk along the shoulder until their shapes blur in the heat rising off the pavement. Then I join Spencer, who is sitting on the trunk strumming his guitar. He plays a classic rock riff I recognize from Guitar Hero and segues into another song.

"This is my Monsters of Rock Guitar medley."

"You're really good," I say. "How about playing me something I know."

Without even thinking about it, he launches into the chorus of "Rosalita."

"Am I that predictable? A New Jersey girl who likes Bruce?"

"Predictable?" He shakes his head and chuckles. "No."

"Can't deny my love for Bruce."

"Nothing wrong with that. He's a genius. Anyway, I know you're named after the song."

"Matty," I say.

"Talks about you all the time. You know—"

I hold up my hand. I'm feeling embarrassed, for me and Matty. Spencer is about to tell me something that, on some level, I've always known. "I don't think I should hear this."

"Got it. No words. Does that apply to my brother, too? You do know why he's acting this way, right?"

What about Avery? I want to say. But really, I don't want to delve into Logan's or Matty's or even Avery's psyche. I've already made a mess of my love life. No need to enter into a love rhombus. Instead, I take the guitar from Spencer. "Do you think you can teach me to play this thing?"

"For real?"

"Yes, for real. I want you to show me what you showed Matty. I want to be able to play a song."

"Okay, then. Let's start with a G chord."

Spencer puts the guitar on my lap. He takes my left hand and places it on the guitar's neck and drapes my right hand on the body. Then he carefully manipulates my pinkie, middle, and pointer fingers into the correct positions on the nylon strings.

"Push down on these three strings. Careful not to touch the others."

I push down as hard as I can. It's not easy to hold them down, though.

"Good," Spencer tells me. "Now, take your thumb like this—" He grabs my right hand. "And strum." He guides my hand across all five strings.

"That sounded like crap," I say.

"It did. Playing guitar is harder than it looks."

"I can't keep the string down and strum at the same time. This is very uncomfortable."

"I hate to say this. . . ." Spencer trails off.

"What? You don't think you can teach me?"

"You may not want to learn when you hear this: The fingernails must go."

"What?"

"You must suffer for art."

I look down at my hands and the pretty gel manicure I got with

Avery. My nails aren't super long and I don't wear acrylic tips or any-thing, but still. I like the length and how they look with polish. Do I want to sacrifice my happy hands?

I let out a deep breath. "I don't have a nail clipper."

Spencer pulls his keys from his pocket. Of course, he's got one dangling from the ring. Right next to a pocketknife.

"Hand it over," I say. I clip all ten nails extra short and dust the shavings onto the ground.

"I'm proud of you," Spencer says. His face looks so sweet when he smiles. "Ready to try the G again?"

"I'm all yours."

I struggle but keep strumming. Spencer coaches me. "Nice and even. That's it." And then on about my fifteenth try, it sounds like something.

"There's your G!" He's all excited. "Now keep going. Once you master that, I'll teach you the D."

My left hand is getting sweaty, so I wipe it on my shirt and then realize I've forgotten where I'm supposed to put my fingers. Spencer takes my fingers and gently places them where they belong.

"What's it feel like?" Spencer asks.

"Guitar strings?"

"No, being in love. Is it worth it?"

It's an interesting time to ask this. I'm sitting on the trunk of a Taurus, guitar in my hand, taking lessons from a guy who, six days ago, was a complete stranger to me, and why? Joey. Still, I do my best to sift through the bad stuff in my brain and find those golden moments—the ones I hope to feel again someday.

The right corner of my mouth turns up as I remember the rush and excitement of falling in love with Joey. Those first days, weeks, months, were amazing. I thought about him all the time. I had no appetite and dropped seven pounds without dieting. I hardly slept but was never tired and woke up before my alarm most mornings. I couldn't wait to start a new day even though Joey and I didn't go to the same school. That part was hard. We couldn't see each other between classes or at lunch, but every text and phone call gave me a rush. Going to different schools heightened the thrill of seeing his car in my school's parking lot after the dismissal bell. And no matter how often I saw him, it never felt like enough. Back then, I never could've imagined hating him. I never wanted to let him go. I certainly couldn't have predicted the events that led me to this moment in New Mexico.

Spencer, who has been waiting for an answer, misreads my silence. "I'm sorry. I probably shouldn't have brought that up."

"No, it's fine. At first, it was the greatest feeling in the world. The anticipation of seeing him. The buildup to our first date, our first kiss. But then—"

Do I tell him what's it's like when that's over and heartbreak settles into the place where all those good feelings used to live? How the days seemed so, so long and I couldn't sleep at night but I didn't want to get out of bed because nothing felt as good as when I was with Joey?

TV, magazines, even talking to my friends, all seemed tedious. I was uptight and distracted. All I had focused on for the past nine months was Joey, and I wasn't sure what to do once he was gone.

But I don't tell Spencer any of that. He'll have to find out for himself. Not that I wish it on him; I don't. But we all have to go through it at least once, don't we? Instead, I just look at Spencer and say: "Well, you know what happened. Here I am, right?"

"It hasn't been so bad, has it?"

I look at Spencer and wonder if he's ever been kissed. "Can I ask you something?"

"I guess," Spencer says.

"Have you ever—" I stop. I don't want to embarrass him. Not Spencer.

"What?" He nudges me.

I reach for his hair and comb my fingers through his super-straight bangs so they look more tousled and less like his mom cuts his hair. "I was just gonna ask you if you've ever thought of using some product. Here, let me get some gel."

Spencer surprises me and moves his hand up to meet mine. "No, you weren't."

And then I shock myself. I slide my fingers to his cheeks and then, without thinking, I lean my face close, which isn't easy with this guitar in my lap, and kiss him on the lips.

Impulsive. It should be my legal middle name.

I pull back for a second. He's one of the good guys and deserves it. Not that I'm saying he deserves me, but he deserves to be kissed.

And while I'm mulling over all this, Spencer catches me off guard and kisses me back. A real kiss this time. It's soft and sweet and makes me wish I could fall for Spencer, but I can't. When it's over, I realize I'm holding my breath and my knees are shaking. The boy's got some skills.

"You're really good at that," I say.

"*Cosmo*. Great for research." Spencer smiles.

"I'm sorry," I say. "I probably shouldn't have done that. I can't explain why I do anything lately and—"

"Don't take this the wrong way. I'm thrilled to have that first kiss out of the way, and it's not that you aren't pretty, because you are. You totally are. But I can't say I exactly . . ."

"Felt anything?" I offer.

"You either, huh?"

Relief. It passes over both our faces. I can tell.

"Yeah, but that's okay. Save that research for a girl you're really crushing on."

Despite the fact that we're both cool with what transpired, I bite my lip and worry about what I've just done.

"Rosie, relax. He doesn't have to know about this."

"Who?"

He shrugs.

"I don't know what you mean. It doesn't have to be a secret or anything."

But Spencer knows that I know he's got me all figured out. It's nice that I've pretty much exorcised Joey from my heart, but it's getting crowded in there. I think I need to reserve some space near my aorta or something. The last thing I want is to arrive back in New Jersey more confused than when I left. Spencer points to the guitar.

"Back to work," he says. "Two more chords and you'll be able to play 'Free Falling.'"

And then he starts singing about a good girl who loves horses.

I don't know why, maybe it's the sweet sound of Spencer's voice, but my eyes brim with tears.

Spencer stops. "Rosie? Are you okay?"

"Can you teach me something edgier? Maybe something by Pink? 'Free Falling' is too sad." The way Spencer looks at me makes the words pour out. "I used to think I was a good girl. But the truth is, I did a bad thing. I keep trying to justify it by blaming Joey for being a cheating asshole, but he didn't make me feel this bad. I did this. I'm humiliated, mortified, disappointed, and disgusted with myself. I mean, he cheated on me, right? So that's a pretty good indication that he didn't love me anymore. Maybe he never loved me. And what did I do? I could have played it cool. Let him have his jailbait and kept my dignity. But I practically announced to the whole world how badly he hurt me. How much I still loved him. Why did I do that, Spencer, why?"

I jump off the trunk and stand there on the side of the highway and throw my arms in the air in a giant V, the guitar still hanging around my neck. "I shouldn't have lost control," I wail. "And now Joey's telling lies about me, saying I did things with him that I've never done with anyone. Look at where being Rosie has gotten me."

Spencer blinks. "I hope I'm so in love with a girl someday that her breaking up with me would make me want to blow up her car. Well, that sounded bad, but you know what I'm saying. It just means whatever you do, whoever you care about, you're in it all the way. And that's nothing to feel bad, or humiliated, about."

"You really think so?"

"Yes. I do. I think you just need an outlet for all that . . . passion."

"I am passionate, aren't I? That's what I tried to tell Matty."

"And for the record, Joey cheated on you because he found a girl who would do what you wouldn't."

"I'm not so sure." All this time, I figured it was because there's something wrong with me.

"I am. I go to school with him, not that he would know that. I've seen him in action. If Joey wanted a girlfriend, he never would have broken up with you. So don't be surprised."

"About what?"

"If he wants you back."

"I'm tired of surprises. Lately, things aren't turning out the way I planned."

"Good or bad, nothing ever does," Spencer says.

"Fortune cookie?"

"Nah." He shakes his head. "All me."

Logan and Matty finally return, gas can and water bottles in hand. They're both bright red and sweaty. Logan promptly fills the tank and

Matty raises his eyebrows at the guitar. If this surprises him, he should have been here twenty minutes ago. That would have given him an eyeball full.

"Spencer's going to teach me to play 'Free Falling,'" I blurt out.

"Glad you used this time to pursue your latent artistic urges," Matty says.

"Spencer thinks I need to channel my passion," I reply.

"How about you start by driving," Logan says. He tightens the gas cap and walks around to the back of the car to face me.

"He speaks," I say.

"I speak," he says.

Logan lets his hand linger in mine as he gives me the keys, and I wish his touch didn't make every last inch of me want to kiss him, sweaty and all. No more boys. Guitar. I'm going to learn guitar. He looks more relaxed than when he left, and I hate to admit, but I'm relieved he's not ignoring me anymore.

"Feel like driving us to the gas station?"

"Sure." I lift the guitar strap off my shoulder and hand the acoustic to Spencer. "Let's go. I'm starving."

"You're starving?" Matty says. "I just sweat off my last three meals."

Logan pats him on the back. "Thanks for coming, man. Why don't you take shotgun until we get to Arizona?"

Matty eyes him suspiciously. I can't say that I blame him. What happened during that walk to make Logan so nice?

Heatstroke. That must be it. Logan has heatstroke.

CHAPTER 16

MY PHONE RINGS WHEN WE'RE EN ROUTE TO THE GRAND Canyon. I'm driving and have been since we stopped for gas in New Mexico. Matty checks the caller ID. "Lilliana."

"Hold it up to my ear," I say. Matty doesn't move. "Please. Can you please hold the phone up to my ear?"

"Why, yes I can," Matty says. "'Please' and 'thank you' are the magic words."

Lilliana doesn't even wait for me to say hello. "How does Joey know you're going to be in Phoenix on the Fourth of July?" she demands.

I'm so shocked, I forget to censor what I'm saying. "How do you know that Joey knows I'm going to be in Phoenix on the Fourth of July?" It's a good thing I'm driving so I can't see Matty's face, especially since I never answered him when he asked almost the exact same thing in Texas. At the time, I thought it was possible Joey could have found out about my trip from someone else, but Phoenix on the Fourth, that's all me.

"He sent me a message on Facebook last night," she screeches. "He told me you sent him a message on Facebook a week ago, telling him to meet you there. He wanted to know if I thought you were serious. So are you? Serious? Why would you tell him that? Would have been nice of you to tell your best friend that you told your ex-boyfriend to meet you in Arizona."

Ah. Facebook. I'm not usually one for social media. I don't update my status with cryptic messages every twenty minutes. I hardly ever sign on. But that explains it. I don't remember booting up my laptop during my antihistamine haze, but there ya go. Another brilliant move by Rosalita Ariana Catalano. Not to mention another TRO violation. Why didn't I mention it to anybody? Because I was hoping that after all my mortifying and desperate acts in the last few weeks, that one wasn't real. I was doing the guy thing. Ignoring it and hoping it would just go away.

"What did you tell him?" I ask.

"I wanted to talk to you first," Lilliana says. She sounds angry or maybe just annoyed. Either way, it's disconcerting coming from her.

"Why do you think he wants to know if I'm serious?"

Lilliana hesitates, then exhales loudly, clearly exasperated by Joey. Or me. Both, probably. "No clue. Do you think he wants you back?"

At first my heart does a triple salchow at the sound of those words. It would be a small victory of sorts, but the ho and TRO are hard to get past. The person he turned me into that night . . . that's even harder. I don't want to be her anymore. In the past few days, I've come a long way and, well, I've come a long way. Right?

"He's up to something," I conclude.

"Do you think he'll go to Phoenix?"

"I don't know."

"You don't know?! You don't seriously want him back, do you?"

"I need to think."

"What is there to think about? Let me tell him to go eff himself. I can say the Fourth of July message didn't come from you. That someone hacked into your account."

"I'll call you back."

"Whatever. Take your time." Then Lilliana hangs up on me. I don't blame her. I'm fed up with me too.

I know Lilliana is right. But what if Joey contacted her because he does want me back? I think about what Spencer said. It's possible, right? That it could be the answer to all my problems. He could drop the TRO and we could get back together. True, what I'm feeling for him now is close to hate, but I could suck it up, date him for a month, and show him what it's like to be the dumpee. I'd get closure sans a criminal record, squash any rumors about me, and finish out high school without some horrible nickname. What's not to like about that plan?

My mind starts reeling. Do I call my parents and Steve Justice to come clean about the Facebook message to Joey? Do I call Lilliana back and tell her to tell Joey to eff himself? I know she'll be disappointed if I don't. What am I doing? How can I even consider taking him back? What then? We rendezvous in Phoenix and fly home together as a happy couple? Ugh. I hate this! I have this sudden urge to talk to Avery.

"Are you okay there, Rosie?" Spencer is leaning between the front seats.

"Fine. Why?"

"Because you're doing a hundred and one in a seventy-five-mile-per-hour zone," Matty offers.

Yikes! He's right. It's hard to tell out here. A person can drive for miles without seeing another car. "Can we switch drivers soon? I've got some calls I need to make."

"We're stopping in Williams," Logan says. "We'll switch then. In the meantime, ease back off the gas, pardner."

"I gotta say. Traveling with Rosie is like overhearing my mom's soap opera in the next room," Spencer says.

"Overhearing? Who are you kidding?" Matty says. "I've watched *General Hospital* with you on SOAPnet. It's addicting."

"Anything I can do, Rosalita?" Logan asks empathetically.

I make a quick mental list. Kick Joey's ass. Tell Joey off. Take Joey's place. I recognize that last one is not the answer to all my problems. Most likely just the beginning of new ones. Or maybe not. Logan is not Joey.

"I'm good," I say, and keep my eyes straight ahead and don't say another word until I see our exit and pull into the small town that is our destination.

WELCOME TO WILLIAMS, ARIZONA! GATEWAY TO THE GRAND CANYON; that's what the sign said when we arrived fifteen minutes ago.

"More like gateway to the weird," I mumble. I'm not trying to be judgmental, but I'm standing next to a fifty-foot-tall Fred Flintstone, my arm reaching upward as I pretend to hold his hand while Matty and Spencer take my picture. We're at the Yabba-Dabba-Doo camp-site and theme park. Ha! Theme park. For five bucks visitors can walk around the village of Bedrock, where Fred and his buddies lived. This place is as old as the original cartoon. There's a giant dinosaur slide, which looks somewhat tempting, but when I get to the top, it smells like pee and there's no way in hell my tush is touching that thing. I urge the boys to retreat back down the dino-tail steps.

We walk around the rest of Williams, which is kind of quaint. There's lots of Route 66 signage and plenty of stores on Main Street that sell memorabilia from the old Mother Road.

"Williams has the distinction of being the last town on Route 66 to be bypassed by the interstate," Spencer reads from a placard outside one of the shops.

"Aw. Just like that Disney movie with cars," I recall.

"Cars?" Matty says sarcastically.

"That's it!" I say.

We grab a quick lunch at Subway and then walk around some more. I'm procrastinating. I know I should call Lilliana back.

"I'm going to gas up the car," Logan says. We probably only burned a quarter of a tank, but I guess he's not taking any chances.

"We'll get some supplies at that market over there," Spencer says.

"Okay. Let's meet in front of the store in twenty minutes," Logan says.

While Spencer and Matty wander around inside—I told them to get me a snack—I stay outside and make some calls. Just thinking about the sound of my mom's voice gets me all choked up. I can't quite bring myself to reveal my latest Joey transgression. I decide to start with Miranda. It's probably more important that Steve Justice know about this anyway. But when Miranda answers the phone and finds out it's me, she doesn't give me a chance to come clean.

"I'm glad you called. I've got good news," Miranda says.

"How good? Do you think he might drop the whole thing?"

I mean, if what Lilliana suspects is true and Joey wants me back, it wouldn't be a stretch, would it? He'd be out of his mind to think I'd want to be with him again if the TRO's hanging over our heads.

"Don't get your hopes up about that," Miranda says. But we found a neighbor who was home the night of the fire and claims she saw everything. I'm going out to speak with her and record her statement tomorrow."

"Wow. That is good news. Will you let me know what she says?"

"Don't worry. We'll talk about everything during your meeting with Steve, before the hearing. Just pu-lease try to stay out of trouble until then," Miranda says.

She makes it sound so easy, I think as I disconnect my phone. I should call Lilliana back, apologize, and urge her to get in touch with Joey immediately to put the brakes on this thing, but I can't, not yet. First, I want to talk to Avery.

"What am I gonna do?" I ask her. "Do you think he wants me back? Would he actually come to Arizona?"

"First, you're going to breathe," Avery tells me. "Then you're going to check your backpack for the care package I slipped in for you. I can't believe you haven't found it yet."

"It's a mess in there," I admit. I've been stuffing things in without bothering to look or clean up the clutter.

"When's your court date?" Avery asks.

"July ninth. Not until Thursday. I lucked out because of the holiday."

"There you go. Whatever's gonna happen won't happen until then. Make the rest of this trip about you, missy. Got it?"

"But what about Joey; what should I do?"

"Do what you gotta do."

"Uh-huh." That's not very specific. I want to press her for a more definitive answer, but I get the feeling she's not going to offer me one. "Hey, so when do you leave to build houses?" I don't want Avery thinking everything always has to be about me.

"Not until August. I'm waiting until it's good and hot so I can suffer." She laughs. "I'm excited. These houses are going to be totally eco-friendly and sustainable." There we go with that word again. "Don't worry," she says before she hangs up. "I know you know what to do." That silly, sweet girl has apparently already forgotten about the brawl I started less than thirty-six hours ago at the club.

Two minutes after I hang up with Avery, Matty and Spencer come out of the store carrying a Styrofoam cooler. I wonder what Logan will say about the non-eco-friendly material.

"What did you guys get?"

"Drinks and snacks and stuff," Matty says offhandedly.

"We're not that far away from the Grand Canyon, are we?" I'm suddenly tired thinking about another three-hour stretch in the car.

"About an hour, but we may get hungry and thirsty while we're there," Spencer says. "The restaurant in the lodge looks pricey."

Logan pulls up and I expect them to fight for shotgun, but they both get into the backseat without a word. Fine by me. I didn't exactly want to ride with a cooler and a guitar.

"Can you pass me my backpack?" I ask after I'm settled into the front seat.

"Sure thing," Matty says, passing it forward. He doesn't ask for my phone, and I don't offer it up. I know I've got to call Lilliana soon. I unzip my backpack. As I root past my makeup bag, dwindling snack supply, random receipts, napkins, magazines, and two copies of the trip itinerary, I see a Ziploc bag with a Post-it note that says *For your reading and listening pleasure. It's all about the possibilities. XOXO Avery.*

Inside are two brochures, one from ASU and the other from Habitat for Humanity, and a USB flash drive on which Avery has written in tiny pink letters AVERY'S BOYS SUCK, GIRLS RULE MIX. I feel like I'm thirteen again.

"Hey, Spence," I say, waving the USB into the backseat. "Can you help me download these to my iPod the next time we stop?"

No answer.

"Spence?"

When I turn around, Matty and Spencer are shielding their faces behind the Styrofoam cooler lid.

"Are you two sneaking food?" I say. "What's the big deal? Oh my God, you aren't kissing, are you?" This elicits groans of disgust all around.

"They're sneaking beer," Logan says, like a parent who can't be fooled.

"How'd you know?" Spencer asks.

"Did you think I wasn't gonna hear you pop the bottle caps?"

"You got served?" I'm shocked. They both look twelve.

"They were selling beer next to the soda," Matty says. "We just put it on the counter with the other stuff and the kid behind the register never said a word."

"You're okay with this?" I look at Logan.

He shrugs. "As long as they're not driving. And don't get caught." I can tell he's not really cool with it, but he's trying to be.

As we get closer and closer to the entrance to Grand Canyon National Park, the laughter in the backseat gets louder and louder. I'm reading through both of Avery's brochures and learning some interesting facts about both ASU and Habitat for Humanity. I make two very important discoveries.

1. ASU does not allow freshmen to have cars on campus.
2. Jimmy Carter and his wife, Rosalynn, made the first Habitat trip in 1984 and raised the visibility of the organization tremendously.

I was too embarrassed at the time to ask Avery what Jimmy Carter had to do with her inspiration to build houses this summer. I can't wait to listen to Avery's mix to see what other startling revelations I can make. I take out my phone and think about calling Lilliana just as Matty lets out a loud burp.

"I hope they've got railings at the Grand Canyon," I say.

"Not many. We'll keep an eye on them," Logan says. Logan turns to look into the backseat. "We're almost to the entrance, you two. How 'bout you put away those open containers and close the cooler?"

We pay the admission fee at the toll booth and get a map of the various lookout points we can drive to by car, as well as the hiking trails and information about mule and helicopter rides—neither of which I'm interested in. We drive for a few miles before I catch my first glimpse of the canyon near the Desert View observation point.

"Holy Mother of God!" I yell. "Pull the car over!"

Matty lets out another loud burp. "Jeez, Rosie. What is it? Another McDonald's shaped like a flying saucer?"

We clamber out of the car, and it may sound like an exaggeration, but the view literally takes my breath away. The Grand Canyon is its own kind of wonderful. The sheer vastness, the shadows and changing colors, the depth and stillness. I never thought anything except the ocean could silence my thoughts and make me feel so free.

Moments later, a small mishap occurs while Spencer is taking a picture of drunk Matty and me. Matty's in that "I love you, man" kind of mood and wants one of just the two of us for, as he puts it, *Matty's Memoirs*. Our backs are against the lookout railing, and I prop my foot on the lower rung. The vastness of the Grand Canyon stretches behind us. It's so perfect, it almost looks like a photographer's backdrop.

"This one will be a keeper," Matty says, and we put an arm around each other.

Just after Spencer snaps the picture, my foot slides off the railing and I accidentally kick myself in the butt (probably long overdue), which sends my phone flying out of my jean shorts and over the edge. It falls about twenty feet before smashing to pieces on the rocks. It's like the umbilical cord that's been stretching since I left New Jersey finally snaps. Matty and I peer over the railing. My first thought is, I hope I don't get some kind of littering violation. Other than that, I've got nothing.

"Well, as much as that sucks," Matty says, "I am thrilled to be free of your mom's constant barrage of communiqués. I am so tired of my pockets vibrating."

Just then, Matty makes a strange face.

"Your pants are vibrating, aren't they?"

"It's her," Matty says, looking at his cell. "I bet she thinks you're dead. Here, you take it." He hands me the phone like it's a bomb.

I put my hands up. "Oh, no, Mr. Rosie Needs to Get Out of Dodge. This one is all you. And don't let her know you're shit faced."

Matty answers. I hear screaming on the other end. "No, Mrs. Catalano, we're fine. Rosie didn't fall into the Grand Canyon. I know. I know. That's some GPS you had on that phone. Yes, I said 'had.' Uh, here, talk to Rosie."

This time, Matty tosses me the phone like it's on fire. "Hi, Ma. I'm fine. No, no, it wasn't the satellites, either. It was my phone. It fell out of my pocket. That's why you lost the signal." I hold the speaker away from my ear so I don't have to hear her bilingual tirade. Finally, she gives me a chance to speak again. "It's only a couple more days, Ma. We'll just use Matty's phone, but not too much, okay? It's not fair to burn his minutes. Okay, okay. Love you too."

Let's see, Dollywood tickets, a guitar for Matty, and a new phone for me. I'll be working at the lampshade factory, walking dogs, and, ugh, babysitting until Halloween. For some inexplicable reason, I don't care. I feel lighter, like that phone was weighing me down. I'm glad I cut it loose. I'm happy I can't be "watched" anymore. I inhale deeply through my nose. Priceless.

"Hey, have you guys even checked in with your parents once?" I ask the boys. "Why am I the only one with parents who chart my every movement?"

"I told them I'd let them know when we got there," Logan says.

"My mom has a no-news-is-good-news policy. And anyway, she's knows your mom is manning command central next door," Matty replies.

"Hey, don't diss my mom," I warn.

We explore the South Rim for the rest of the afternoon, stopping at various lookout points, before ending up at a spot near the lodge, where we plan to stay until sunset. Spencer is dying to take some more pictures. He and Matty want to hike down a ways into the canyon, and I'm nervous about letting them go too far, but Logan thinks they're both sober again. I find a spot without a railing and dangle my feet over the edge and recline with my arms spread out behind me. Logan sits next to me and assumes a similar position. We watch as Spencer and Matty make their way along a narrow trail below us. Every now and then one of them looks up and waves. At one point, Matty snaps a picture of me and Logan, then he signals their destination ahead: a large white rock that will require them jumping over a two-foot crevice. I'm not going to relax until they make it there safely.

"It's such a long way down," I say.

"A mile." Logan sits up and points down into the canyon. "Do you know at the very base of the canyon, along the river, the rock exposed in that lowest stratum is two thousand million years old?"

"You're making that number up."

"I am not."

"Isn't one thousand million a billion? Can't you just say two billion?"

"Fine. So, the Precambrian rocks at the bottom are two billion years old. The strata near the top are only 250 million years old and from the Paleozoic era."

"It's good to know that when your brother gets trashed, you're here to pick up the factoid slack."

For that, I get a full smile complete with dimple. It's like Logan glows from inside when he drops his guard. When he leans back again, his hand is closer to mine and I can feel the energy between our fingertips.

I try to focus on Logan's paleontology lesson. It's not easy. It doesn't help that I have zero interest in rocks, no matter how pretty they are. "So the deeper you go, it's like going back in time?" I ask.

"Sort of. Exposed rocks closer to three billion years old have been found in Africa, Australia, and the Canadian Shield."

I reply with my own little factoid. "Do you know that ASU does not allow freshmen to have cars on campus?"

Logan doesn't say anything. He just nods.

"So, this whole road trip wasn't about wanting your car out here, was it?"

"It was and it wasn't. I wanted to give Spencer some time away from our town. Our house. Our—"

"Father?"

"Especially him."

"Are things that bad at home?"

Logan sighs. "I can't speak for my mom and Spencer, but things between me and my dad . . . let's just say, I seem to be the target of his anger when he's drunk. But now, well, I'm done."

Logan always seems so in control. Older than the rest of us. But as he talks about his father, it's like I can see Logan as a kid, the bruised little boy who never quite healed.

"I'm so sorry."

"Why? It's not your fault my father's a bastard. I think it will be better for everyone now that I'll be away at college."

Logan clenches his jaw. His cheeks flush with anger. "And if things ever get unbearable for my brother, he can always come out to Arizona and stay with me."

"If I had known . . . I shouldn't have horned in on your time with your brother. I get it now, you know, why you were so mean to me in the beginning."

"Are you kidding? Spencer loves having you around. You make a much better first kiss than Matty."

My face turns the color of the setting sun. "He told you?"

"Blood is thicker than saliva."

"Ew." I bump shoulders with him. "But what about you? You didn't want me around."

He faces me now. "It wasn't that. It's just . . . I spent my entire senior year focused on one thing—getting to Arizona. Part of that preparation meant making no unnecessary attachments. I didn't even go to my prom. And then you stepped out onto the porch that morning and . . ."

I'm flattered and sad all at the same time. "You're not coming back at all, are you?"

Logan doesn't answer me. He stares straight ahead again. I inch toward him until our thighs and shoulders meet. He slides his hand over until our fingertips touch. I don't know how long we stay that way, but we watch the sun go down together. The giant, burnt-orange sphere sinks toward the horizon, coloring the rock layers until it's gone and the canyon is covered in shadow.

When the boys rejoin us, it's time to leave. It's like I'm five years old and leaving Disney World. I don't want to go. I wish I could watch the sun set with Logan again and again. I'd never get tired of it.

We leave the Grand Canyon at twilight. It's quiet in the car, in a good way for once. No words, no music. Silence seems right. I roll down the window and lean my head against the door frame, listening to the wind rush by and smelling the pine trees. I watch the stars materialize, like someone is dimming the switch on the night sky so each shining dot grows brighter and brighter.

Logan is the first one to speak. "Change of plans for the night, Catalano. You can have your own space if you want it."

I'm not sure I like that idea. Even though sharing a room with these three can be a big pain in the ass, as I've said from the start, I don't do "alone" very well.

"What, where? Not that Yabba-Dabba-Doo place." The itinerary is a crumpled mess, complete with powered cheese stains, at the bottom of my bag. I saw it down there when I retrieved Avery's goody bag. I don't feel like digging it out.

"No. That was a dump," Matty says.

"You'll see," Spencer says.

About thirty minutes later, near the park entrance, we arrive at a very rustic-looking campsite.

"Oh, I do not do the camping thing. Absolutely not."

"Come on, Rosie. We'll rent you your own tent. Think of it, your very own place," Spencer croons. Yeah, like that's going to make me jump all over this idea. "They have coin-operated showers."

"Coin-operated showers? Well, now, why didn't you say that to begin with? And just what am I supposed to sleep in?"

"Sleep naked. You'll be alone," Logan says. I hear him smiling.

"You know what I mean. No one said I was supposed to bring a sleeping bag."

"Would you have listened?" Logan asks.

"Probably not."

"No worries. I packed one for you," Matty says.

Sigh. The euphoria from visiting a natural wonder is seeping out of my body. Is the Grand Canyon a natural wonder? If not, it should be.

An hour later, after one too many jokes about "pitching a tent," our campsite is set up. I told the guys I didn't want to stay in my own tent, so we rented a family-size one. I'm trying hard not to think about how many germs are in this thing or what kinds of insects we might encounter tonight.

"Are there scorpions around here?" I've got my hands on my hips and I'm scanning the ground.

"I don't think we have to worry about scorpions this far north," Spencer tells me.

Is he telling the truth or trying to make me feel better? I bite my lower lip and look longingly at the car. If I sleep with the windows open, it won't be that bad, will it?

"Should we get a fire started?" Matty asks.

"For what? It's hot out," I say. "Just pointing out the obvious."

"We need to cook the hot dogs," Spencer says. "Plus just wait, the temp is going to go down tonight."

"We have hot dogs?" I ask.

"Cooler," Logan says.

"I thought we had beer in the cooler."

"That too. We scored the beer when we bought the hot dogs," Matty explains.

"Wait a second." I point from Spencer to Logan. "You two don't eat beef."

"A hot dog once in a while won't kill us," Spencer says. "I generally have two a year."

A weenie roast if there ever was one. "Did you get marshmallows?" I ask.

Matty grins. "Of course. Hershey bars and graham crackers too."

S'mores! Oh, thank you, God. Thank you for sending me on this road trip with guys who would rather sit round the campfire making s'mores than dine at Hooters. Somewhere between dinner and dessert, I get that nagging feeling, like I've still got homework to do. I know I should call Lilliana, but I don't want to deal with home and Joey right now. I'm having too much fun.

I have to admit, precamping rocks. We stay up super late, talking and eating. The boys finish off the beer; even Logan has one. I have a few sips but don't finish mine. I really don't like the taste, and I don't want to have to pee in the woods. With this fear in mind, I hit the public bathroom to empty my bladder and change into sleeping shorts and a T-shirt. By the time I arrive back at the tent, I'm thinking sleep should be no problem at all, except that now, thanks to Spencer, it is.

"I need to sleep by the door," he says. "I get claustrophobic."

"I don't want to be on an end," I say. Selfishly, I'm thinking I'd like to have at least one body between me and whatever wild animal may attack us while we sleep. Inevitably, I end up between Logan and Matty. Is it too late to request my own tent?

Spencer falls asleep right away, but despite feeling absolutely wiped, the minute I climb into my sleeping bag, it's like I've drunk a half pot of coffee. I turn right, and I'm facing Matty. No good. I flip the other way, and I'm facing Logan's back. Better. Logan's head is pointed toward the tent wall, so I can't see if his eyes are closed. His arm is resting on his side, and I'm mesmerized by the ripples in his muscles. I stay in that position for a long time, motionless.

I don't know how much time has passed when I finally peer behind me to see if Matty's eyes are closed. They are. But is he asleep? Too late. My hand is as impulsive as the rest of me. I take my pointer finger and run it the full length of Logan's arm, starting at his bare shoulder and running it along his biceps, inside his forearm, and then into his open palm. He doesn't make a move, so I think he's asleep until his fingers close on top of mine. My heart pounds in my ears. I wonder if he'll turn to face me. I wonder what it is I think I'm doing. Then Matty pops up.

"It's too hot in here," he declares. "I'm sleeping outside." He picks up his bag, unzips the tent, and leaves, without bothering to seal the flap behind him. Spencer doesn't even stir; he must be totally out of it.

I get up on all fours and lean over to close the door. Matty's shaking out his bag beside what's left of the campfire. When I turn back, Logan is half out of his sleeping bag facing me. He's just wearing his boxers. He must've slipped his shorts off at some point. He takes his hand and cups the left side of my face, slipping it under my hair. Oh, man.

"Rosie," he whispers.

I press my forehead against his and close my eyes. "I . . . Sorry."

I scramble outside the tent in my bare feet and walk over to Matty. He's already zipped up like a sausage in his sleeping bag. It's chillier than I thought it would be. Spencer was right. Isn't he always? I ease myself onto one of the logs by the fire and don't say a word.

Finally, Matty speaks. "Spencer told me."

"About what?"

"The kiss."

"Oh." I don't know what else to say. It was Spencer's secret to tell. I can't exactly be angry with him. Matty's his best friend. My throat feels like it's closing. Matty is my best friend too.

"He says it was no big thing."

I try to ignore that Spencer's first kiss with me was "no big thing." I'll chalk it up to Spencer trying to be cool. "He needed to get it out of the way, I think."

"And what about you? Is there anything else you need to get out of the way? I guess I'm the only guy you're not going to kiss on this trip."

"I didn't kiss Logan," I protest.

"But you want to."

"That's not fair. You wanted to kiss Avery."

"But I didn't."

"And I didn't kiss Logan."

He scowls. "Yet."

My chest flutters with excitement at the thought of going back into the tent and finishing what I started. I wrap my arms around myself and wiggle my toes, which are starting to feel slightly numb. "Matty . . ."

"What?"

"Is that what you want? Do you think we should kiss?"

He doesn't look at me. "Do you?"

I don't say anything.

"Rosie?" He turns sideways, sits up in his sleeping bag, and finally makes eye contact.

"I can't risk ruining everything we have between us," I say quietly.

"What exactly do we have between us, Rosie? Because I don't know anymore."

"How can you say that? You are my best friend, Matty. More than that. You're like my brother. We know everything there is to know about each other. I know you better than Lilliana, even. I know that when you were ten, you were so afraid of zombies that you slept with the light on for six months. You remembered my Strawberry Shortcake lip gloss obsession. I know you got that scar above your eyebrow from hanging upside down off the monkey bars and falling off. You know what I looked like when I had zits and braces. You've heard me belch. You've seen me cry. You came to my rescue when I made a complete and utter mess out of my life. I'm so grateful for that, I could kiss you right now for just being you. For always being so good in general, and for being good to me specifically. But if I did, and if things didn't work out between us, it wouldn't be like losing some stupid boyfriend like Joey. I would be losing family."

Matty looks at me for a few seconds before throwing open his sleeping bag and patting the space next to him. "Come 'ere," he says. "You look cold."

I hesitate, but then my brain does a mental shrug and I slide off the log and scooch into Matty's sleeping bag. It's a tight fit, but he moves over and tries to keep from touching me. I pull the sleeping bag across me but don't zip it. Ah, I can feel my feet again.

Matty is flat on his back, arms across his chest, looking up at the sky. Finally, he turns to face me. I can feel him smiling. "You think of me as part of your family?"

"Not just me. My parents, Eddie—you've got to know how much you mean to them. The only reason they let me take this trip is because you were going to be with me. If something were to happen between us, it would have to be the kind of something that lasts for a really long time, because they wouldn't want to lose you either."

"So you haven't ruled it out? Us?"

I don't know how to answer that, but I don't want to hurt him. "No. I haven't. But you know I'd be a terrible girlfriend. I'm more like an icky older sister."

Matty uncrosses his arms and puts one under my head. Then he leans over and kisses me on the forehead. "You will never be my icky sister. Crazy sister, yes. But icky? Rosie Catalano, you are not icky."

"Neither are you, Matthew Ryan Connelly. Now, you're not going to try to grab my boob, are you?"

That gets us giggling like we're kids at our first sleepover. I try to talk, but snorting noises come out of my nose and I can't get a word out. I've forgotten what it's like to laugh like this.

Finally, we settle down and stare up at the endless Arizona sky.

"These stars are amazing. It's like watching a 3-D movie. Some of them really do look close enough to touch." I squint, hold out my hand, and pretend I'm doing just that. I wish someone were taking a picture of me and Matty right now. Curled up together in this sleeping bag. Looking at the universe. Come to think of it, I don't need a picture. Somehow I know, for the rest of my life, no matter where I go or who I end up with, I will never forget this moment.

I turn on my side and close my eyes. Matty drapes his other arm over me, but I don't worry about what it means. Within seconds, he's breathing deep, even breaths. He's asleep. And I'm not far behind. Despite being outside, with no protection from the elements or wild animals, I'm not worried about becoming some coyote's next meal. In fact, I fall into the kind of deep, secure sleep I haven't known since I met Joey all those months ago.

CHAPTER 17

OUR DRIVE SOUTH FROM THE GRAND CANYON IS LIKE something out of a really cool car commercial. We take Dry Creek Scenic Road into Sedona, passing these amazing, giant red rocks that rise above the otherwise flat landscape, dotted with cacti that look like they have thick, waving arms. An hour later, we arrive at Sliding Rock Canyon, a place where people picnic and swim. We all wore bathing suits under our clothes in anticipation of this stop. I changed into mine after my coin-operated shower at the campsite. I brought a fistful of change, not knowing what to expect, but in the end, it wasn't half bad.

I spread out a towel on the rust-colored flat rocks near the water's edge and lather on some suntan lotion that smells like a piña colada. I smile to myself as I think of Lucca and my Cancún fantasy. He was some cowboy.

It doesn't take long before it gets too hot. To avoid getting all sweaty before it's time to get back in the Taurus, I wade into the creek up to my calves to cool my body and take in the canyon around me. Arizona is beautiful, uniquely so. The colors, the cacti, the sky—I think that's one of my favorite parts, the sky, especially at night. But I don't know if a New Jersey girl like me could ever get used to all this desert sand and no ocean.

I'm standing with my arms crossed over my tankini, watching a mom push her toddler around on his SpongeBob tube, when Logan comes up and stands beside me. Neither of us said anything this morning about the tent incident. And neither of us says anything now, but somehow, it's not awkward.

I haven't taken my shorts off yet. I don't plan on swimming, but I'm hoping to get some nice color from the sun reflecting off the water. I can't come all the way to Arizona and return home without a tan—particularly in July! That would be so wrong.

I close my eyes and let the heat warm my entire body. Sedona is hotter than the Grand Canyon. But Spencer says Phoenix is going to be hotter still, which I remember from checking regional average temps when I was packing.

"So," Logan says.

"So," I reply, looking over the top of my sunglasses at him.

"What do you think?"

I choose to assume he's talking about Sliding Rock. "It's beautiful, really. I can see why you fell in love with it here."

"But?"

"But I'm an ocean girl. I like diving under waves and boogie boarding. I like soft, white sand that squishes between my toes."

"You don't think you could get used to all this?"

Why is he asking me that? Is he envisioning a time when I'd have to get used to Arizona? "I didn't say that I couldn't. Anything is possible." I'm starting to believe that.

Logan nods. Then he puts out his hand. "Let's take a walk."

We walk in the water, hand in hand, neither of us bothering to ask why or what it means. When it starts getting deeper, we move to the edge and walk on the rocks. They're so smooth, it's almost like a man-made water park. Then Logan drops my hand. Matty and Spencer are on top of a nearby ledge waiting their turn to dive in. Matty waves to me before making a perfect swan dive in the water, his lean body entering the creek with hardly a splash.

I don't know if years from now something more will ever happen between us, but Matty will always be my Matty, even if he's not destined to be my soul mate. I can't picture my life without him.

I'm so relaxed when we get back in the car. My skin has a nice glow and still smells like suntan lotion. I pull a tank top on over my bathing suit and settle into the backseat. I scrounge around in my bag for a file so I can fix the damage I did cutting my nails for my guitar lesson. Even if my nails are super short now, I still want them to look good. Plus, filing my nails is like meditation—helps me sort things out.

Spencer's driving, and I don't bother asking how long it will take to get to the Phoenix area; we'll get there when we get there. We're spending tonight in a motel near Tempe, where ASU is. Then we'll be there all day tomorrow, the Fourth of July, before spending one last night in Arizona and Matty, Spencer, and I leave on a red-eye. It feels like summer's end, even though it's just getting started. Sigh.

I'm actually looking forward to checking out ASU. I've never been to any college campuses before, not even Montclair State and Seton Hall, which are both under a half hour from my house. From the pictures in the brochure, ASU looks like a cool place to spend four years. The grass is green, the sky is blue, and the students are all sporting shorts, sandals, and lightweight hoodies. Despite having no ocean, the endless summer aspect of Arizona totally adds points in its favor, and I could start fresh as a new and improved Rosie if I came to college here. Only Avery and Logan would know about Joey and the car. But are these good enough reasons to apply? I guess if it makes you happy. But who knows what the next year will bring? I wonder if Logan and Avery will even consider me a friend by then or if memories of this trip will be the only thing we share.

As I round out the nails on my left hand, I work my way through the layers of emotion. My thoughts feel like a ball made out of rubber bands, tight, compact, and overlapping. The trip ending, my court date coming, telling Joey to meet me in Phoenix, not returning Lilliana's call, kissing Spencer, sleeping with Matty, watching the sun set with Logan, losing my phone, losing my mind, losing my heart. What's going to happen when I get back home?

I bite off a hangnail on my ring finger. Avery is right. There's no use looking beyond my court date—whatever's going to happen will happen. That doesn't mean I can't have a plan, though. I've got to stop letting things just "happen" to me.

I'm imagining taking the elastic ball and throwing it into the desert when Matty's phone rings. Poor guy. I know it's for me. He holds up the phone because it's not my mom and he doesn't recognize the number. Unfortunately, I do. The rubber bands in my head all snap simultaneously.

"Joey."

Spencer gasps. Despite my predicament, this makes me smile. "No shit?" he asks.

"No shit," I say. "I can't talk to him, Matty. I promised my mom, and Miranda will kill me. Let it go to voice mail."

Logan sticks his hand out.

"Give it," he says. *I hope Logan talking to Joey doesn't violate my TRO,* I think as Matty hands him the phone.

We listen to Logan's half of the conversation. "Hello? Who's this? Joey. What can I do for you, Joey? Rosie? Now, you of all people should know that talking to you could get her in big trouble. How about you give me the message? Don't worry about who I am. We'll let it remain a mystery for your crack legal team. . . ." Logan covers the phone and talks to us, "This guy is a douche bag." Then he talks back into the phone. "Back at you, man. How about you drop the attitude and just tell me what the frig you want. . . . Tell Rosie you're not going to be in Phoenix on the Fourth of July? What a coincidence; neither is she." There's a pause and I'm not sure what Joey is saying, but then Logan says, "Sorry. Still can't let you talk to her."

"Tell him I'm taking the red-eye home on Sunday. He can contact my attorney after that."

Logan passes along the message, then simply hangs up.

"What an a-hole," Logan says as he tosses the phone back to Matty.

"He wasn't always," I mumble. "That was not the Joey I dated."

"No offense," Spencer says, "but no one seems to know the Joey you dated."

"Word," Matty agrees.

Silenced by the truth, my lame defense stays lodged in my throat. Joey hasn't dropped the TRO. He knows contacting me is trouble, and he's only calling me because his girl dumped him and he wants something. How the hell did he get Matty's number? Lilliana? Maybe. I don't blame her. It's my problem, not hers. What does all this say about me, exactly? Why am I the kind of girl who would date a guy like Joey?

I can't answer that, but I should explain to the guys why Joey's calling. "It's my fault. I told him to meet me in Phoenix on the Fourth of July."

"What?! When?" Matty is incredulous.

"Relax. It was the night before we left. I couldn't sleep. I took some Benadryl. I messaged him on Facebook. It's all a blur at this point."

This last bit of information gets Spencer all excited. "Imagine if he had shown up."

"Yeah, well, that's not happening. Like Joey said, he won't be in Phoenix for the Fourth of July."

"And like I said, neither will we," Logan repeats.

"Sure we will," Spencer says. "We'll be there in an hour."

"Change of plans, bro," Logan says. "Stay on this highway through Phoenix toward Tucson. When we get to Interstate 8, we're going west."

The trip along Interstate 8 brings us through a desert of a different sort. As we approach Yuma, Arizona, and the California border, the sand changes to actual, well, sand. The white, dune kind like we have along the New Jersey shore. It's beautiful. The late afternoon sun makes me think of Christmas cards depicting the three wise men on camels, traveling along the pristine sand with a brilliant, golden star to guide their way. And then I do see the brilliant golden star, like a halo, up ahead.

"Mickey D's!" Matty shouts.

It's not the Star of Bethlehem, but after a long drive, it's practically the next-best thing.

Logan rushes us through our super-size meals. "Come on," he urges. He's piling crumpled napkins and his empty salad container on his tray. "You can eat your fries in the car. I want to cross the mountains before it gets dark."

I know what's coming next. Yep, there it is: the finger round-up motion. It hasn't made an appearance since Texas, but it's back in full force. Oh, how I've missed it.

෨

The drive over the mountains from Yuma to San Diego is more dangerous than it looks. The mountains are steep, and there are water stations every so often—for overheated cars—along with signs reminding drivers to carry jugs of water to cool their engines while crossing these mountains and the desert.

I'm happy there's some daylight left when we cross over to the California side and drive toward San Diego. It's like the whole world springs into Technicolor. Green trees and lawns, petunias, impatiens, pretty yellow flowers I don't know the name of. Ruddy earth tones had dominated so much of our trip since Texas. It makes the contrast more spectacular. Like that first taste of sugar after you've been on a diet.

It's getting late, but Logan drives until we reach Mission Beach. After we park, I'm the first one out of the car. Matty is right behind me. We both kick off our shoes as soon as our feet touch sand. I look at Matty and don't even have to say it. We both take off running, like Dorothy and the Scarecrow through the poppy field. I know he'll get there before me. In a pool, I have a chance, but on land, there's no way I'll catch him.

I pull off my top at the edge of the dry sand but don't bother with my shorts before I dive in. I've lost count of how many times in my life I've run into crashing waves, but tonight is different. This is the Pacific Ocean. I've just driven across the entire country.

I stand with my back to the waves and look toward the shore, beyond Logan and Spencer, the parking lot, the car, the road. I inhale deeply, and it's like I can feel the distance, every single mile I traveled from New Jersey to this point, right here. The cold water doesn't bother me. I close my eyes and savor the smell of the ocean, the quiet in my mind, the intensity of the moment. When I open them again, the world snaps back into focus. I hear the sound of the waves, and Matty's laughter, right before he grabs my shoulders and pushes me under.

I lick the salt water off my lips as I sit, wrapped in a towel, on the hood of the Taurus watching the ocean and listening to the whoosh of the surf. Even though my bathing suit and shorts are still wet, inside I am warm.

"Wait until tomorrow, Rosie," Spencer says. "You'll see how blue it is."

"Are you dissing the East Coast?" I ask.

"Not at all. But the Atlantic is green. This is the Pacific. We're talking blue, blue. You'll see," Spencer says.

"So, I guess you guys have been to California before?"

"We drove the coastal highway from San Francisco to San Diego. I was eight and Logan was ten." Spencer pauses. "Our family was more of a family back then."

"Let's find someplace to stay," Logan interjects, before Spencer travels too far down memory lane.

"Thank you," I say when my eyes meet Logan's.

"You're buying your own boogie board tomorrow, Catalano," Logan says. "And don't get my car seats wet." He turns toward the driver's door and is about to put his index finger in the air when I gently grab his wrist with one hand and push his finger down with the other. "It's okay. We're right behind you."

The Fourth of July. We're walking back to the hotel after watching the fireworks over Mission Bay when we pass a restaurant with an outdoor café. There's a small stage beyond the bar, and a band is doing a sound check. I look at the poster draped behind the drum kit. It's a sun symbol—the same one that's on the necklace from my cowboy.

"Hey, I think that's the band Lucca was talking about! Holy crap. What are the chances? We've got to check them out," I say. I don't want tonight to end. It's my last night away and our last night all together, if not forever, then for a long time.

"What kind of music do they play?" Spencer asks.

"No clue."

"Who cares?" Matty says. "It beats hanging around the hotel. Who knows when I'll ever be in San Diego again, or anywhere else for that matter."

As Logan and Spencer walk toward the outdoor café, I stop Matty and throw my arms around his middle. It takes him a moment to recover from my spontaneous display of affection before he hugs me back.

"Uh, Rosie? What's this for?"

"Everything," I say into his shirt.

"Are we done now?"

I pull away and look up at him. "Yeah. I think we're good."

I'm pleasantly surprised that the band plays a mixture of power pop and rock—Bruce-like storytelling with smart-ass, Weezer-type lyrics. Matty and Spencer, the music snobs, stand close to the stage to judge "the chops" of the band, as they put it. I sit on a bar stool, sipping a Diet Coke and accepting the ebb and flow of euphoria and melancholy as both emotions wash over me. Logan sits next to me, and I'm slightly irritated by this girl in a bikini top who's talking to him while she waits for her drink, but I watch the band and revel in the fact that I don't really want to talk to anyone at the moment. I don't have a phone anymore, but even if I did, I don't want to reach out to anyone on the "outside" right now. Tonight belongs to me and my guys.

I finish my drink, and since Logan is still yapping to this girl about ASU, I make my way toward the stage to hang with Spencer and Matty. As I squish through the crowd, the band launches into a power ballad, evoking a few whoops and some applause from fans obviously familiar with their music. I'm eyeing up my next move to cut through the throng of people when I feel hands on my hips. I hope to God it's someone I know. I gingerly turn sideways. Logan. Phew. Or maybe not. He presses against my back and sways me slowly back and forth to the music, dancing, but not really dancing. Goose bumps spread from the back of my neck across every inch of my skin. He gently lowers his chin onto the top of my head and wraps one arm across the front of me while keeping his other hand on my hip. I rest my cheek on his forearm and inhale the scent of his cologne, the scent of him. As we sway back and forth to the music, it takes every ounce of self-control I have to not turn around, put my hands on his shoulders, and—

Logan moves his lips to my ear. "I want to do so much more than kiss you, Rosie."

I know what he means. My own x-rated thoughts start with a kiss, then progress to me running my hands under his shirt and down toward the button of his jeans. I spin around and touch the tip of my nose to his. Our lips are about a centimeter apart. Either I stop right now or not at all.

"What are you thinking?" I ask.

"That I'm going to be in Arizona and, after tomorrow, you're not. You?"

"I'm thinking about something Avery said and . . . I've still got a lot of things I need to work out." I stand on my tiptoes. This time I'm the one whispering in his ear. "To be continued," I say. "I hope."

When I pull back, he looks confused or hurt or both. But he doesn't press me. Unlike Joey, Logan is not the kind of guy who would start something he couldn't finish, and maybe for the first time ever, neither am I. When the song ends, so does our moment. Sometimes, it really is best to do nothing.

CHAPTER 18

FOR AS LONG AS I CAN REMEMBER, OUR FAMILY HAS BEEN renting the same beach house at the New Jersey shore. Rentals begin and end on Saturdays, with the standard "checkout" time being eleven in the morning. It doesn't matter if we're there for a week or a month, come Saturday, no one ever wants to leave. So every year, for as long as I can remember, we kid ourselves. We say: "Even though we have to be out of the house by eleven, we can still spend the rest of the day on the beach. Right?" But guess what? That never happens. Because once we've packed the car with bedding to boogie boards and vacuumed up sand from the hardwood floors, the vacation is over. Stretching it a few more hours wouldn't feel right. Our time at the beach ends when we turn in our key.

That's how I feel when we arrive in Tempe on Sunday. We're taking a red-eye home, so we still have the entire day to look around, check out the ASU campus and Logan's dorm, and grab some dinner. But the collective mood of our little foursome makes me realize our road trip ended when we crossed the mountains, out of California back into Arizona.

It's nearly dark when Logan pulls up curbside at Sky Harbor Airport. On the ride over, I obsessed about how I was going to say good-bye. Should I kiss him on the cheek? Tell him I'll call him when I get home? Ask him when we'll see each other again? In the end, it turns out to be none of the above. Logan gets out of the driver's seat, walks around the back, and pops the trunk. I stand on the sidewalk, fiddling with my hair, as he helps the boys unload our bags before shaking Matty's hand and giving Spencer a brotherly hug. Then he turns to me, opens his arms to bear-hug width, and says, "Rosie." I step toward him and give him an awkward squeeze with my backpack slung over one shoulder. When I look into his eyes, I want to cry. I get it; there's too much to say, so we aren't saying anything. Almost. I do, however, manage to whisper, "Thanks for the ride."

Twenty-five minutes later, we've made it through security and I'm standing at a newsstand, deciding on snacks and reading material for the five-hour plane ride home. It's an overnight flight, but I know I'm not going to be able to sleep. I push away the image of Logan pulling away from the curb in the Taurus and the overwhelming sensation that my home for the past nine days has left me. I shake it off. I have to. This trip put me back together, and I refuse to get all torn apart again. So there, Logan Davidson. Enjoy your 120-degree Rosie-free Arizona summer. I'm just about to reach for one of the magazines listing the one hundred best college deals when Matty practically tackles me and pulls me into the aisle with the paperbacks.

"Get your hands off me, you big goon," I say. By now, he knows I mean "big goon" in the best-possible way.

"Joey's here," Spencer says.

"Oh, *Dios mío*!" Apparently emergencies turn me into my mother. "How can that be? He said he wasn't coming."

"He lied," Matty says. "Big surprise."

"Okay, here's what we're going to do. Spencer, follow him and try to find out what flight he's on. If he's on our plane, we'll simply change our tickets and take the next flight home. No need to panic, right?" I take a deep breath. "Spencer, what are you doing? Get going."

Spencer shrugs. "He's not here." Then he high-fives Matty, who's all pressed up against the bestsellers with me.

Matty grins, releasing me. "I couldn't resist."

I expel all the air from my lungs and am reminded of Batman dive bombing my hair at the caverns—too relieved to even be angry. "Come on. We'd better get to our gate."

Matty raises his eyebrows. "That's it?" He sounds disappointed.

"Not exactly the reaction we were going for," Spencer agrees.

"Maybe it's time you started expecting the unexpected. At least where I'm concerned," I say.

On the plane, Matty, Spence, and I sit three across in an emergency exit row, the kind with all the extra leg room. Sweet karma. I remember why Spencer wanted Matty along to begin with and I offer to hold his hand during takeoff.

"It's okay, Rosie. I don't think I'm afraid to fly anymore."

I grab his and Matty's hands anyway. *Neither am I,* I think.

The flight seems excruciatingly long, and when they finally allow us to deplane, I want to sprint down the aisle, which, of course, isn't possible. Instead, I watch the other passengers search through the overhead bins and wait as one row of people at a time make their way toward the exit.

Inside the terminal, we head for baggage claim on the lower level. I stand by the automatic doors while Matty and Spencer go and pick up our luggage and Spencer's guitar, which required special cargo instructions. I keep peeking through the doors to see if I can spot my dad's car. Outside, the sun is rising. I'm considering waiting by the curb and trusting Matty and Spencer will know where to find me when I see the boys coming toward me with all our bags and the guitar. Hooray for me, positive energy continues. Except—"That's not my bag." My heart sinks. My favorite sandals are in there. And the dress I wore the night we all went out in Dallas, and the Elvis stuff for my family, and the necklace from my cowboy. What if somebody took my bag by mistake?

"Stay right here," I say, grabbing my suitcase's doppelgänger from Matty. "I'll find it."

"We'll go back," Matty offers.

"It's okay, really." Matty's handled too much for me already. "I'll be quick. See if you can spot my dad."

I dash back to the baggage carousel. I don't want the person whose luggage got switched with mine to leave. I arrive at carousel 2, which only has a few bags left, including mine. I see it turning the bend on the conveyor belt. As fast as I can, I throw the strange bag back and head for mine. *Come to Mama.* I'm jogging alongside my suitcase and am about to snatch it before it goes around another turn when I hear—

"Rosie!"

Joey.

Slowly, I turn as my bag continues along on its merry way.

He's on the other side of the carousel and partially blocked from view by the chute where the bags come out.

"What are you doing here?" I look back over my shoulder to see if I can spot Matty or Spencer. I feel trapped.

"I've been trying to talk to you."

Me and my big mouth. Why'd I go and tell him I'd be on the red-eye today? I keep moving along the belt. I just want to get my bag and sprint toward the door. Joey follows my gaze and grabs my suitcase before I can.

"Drop the suitcase, Joey," I say. I don't want to get any closer. I'm probably already within TRO violation territory. "You know I can't talk to you. Whatever you need to say, tell it to my lawyer."

"Come on, Rosie. I miss you."

He's lying. I know it. He's up to something; I just don't know what it is.

"Maybe we can work things out without going to court."

Hmm. Why does Joey want to stay out of court? "So drop the TRO, why don't you," I snap. "You're the one who filed for court protection from big, bad Rosie."

I want my suitcase. I'm not going to lose all my special memories because of Joey. I take a few steps backward, keeping Joey in sight while glancing around for any sign of Matty and Spencer. Joey starts moving toward me. "Come on, Rosie. Let me hand this to you."

"Just leave it right there, Joey. You're going to get me in more trouble."

The internal struggle is becoming too much. I'm about to say screw it and just get the hell out of there when, out of nowhere, Spencer comes up behind Joey and screams: "Drop the bag."

Startled, Joey whips his head around and that's when it happens, Bam! His face smashes into the guitar case Spencer has slung over his shoulder. I didn't think Joey hit it that hard, but he obviously hit it the wrong way because blood spurts everywhere. Holy mother of God! I'm ashamed to admit this, but my first reaction is to run toward Joey so I can grab my suitcase and sprint for the exit.

And that's exactly what I do.

CHAPTER 19

SO MUCH CAN HAPPEN IN NINE DAYS. I SIT ON MY BED, laptop on my knees, paging through all the photos from our trip. Matty brought them over on a flash drive this morning. He probably could've just e-mailed them, but he said he also wanted to wish me luck. Me and my parents are meeting with Steve Justice later today. Anyway, I'm glad he stopped by.

It's so weird, I think as the photos slide by. During the school year, the weeks can sometimes blur together like one colorless, uneventful day. But in just over a week, I'd been from Chestnutville, New Jersey, to the Pacific Ocean and back again: 3,165 miles of driving. Spencer tracked it.

I thought it would feel good to wake up in my own bed this morning, but honestly, it was strange. Despite the fact that Pony was plastered against me, his head on my pillow with one paw draped over my shoulder, I felt lonely.

Yesterday morning, after I recovered from my initial reaction to the Joey bloodbath at Newark Liberty Airport, I returned to carousel 2 with my dad to find Spencer, Matty, and Joey's brother all gathered around him. Spencer, who of course is certified in CPR and first aid, was applying a makeshift compress to Joey's nose. It looked like someone's T-shirt, but I really didn't want to ask. I just stood beside my dad until airport security arrived with one of those golf-cart-type vehicles to help Joey to his brother's car. All this time I wondered how it would feel to talk to Joey again, but as I watched him drive away, I didn't feel love or like or even hate. All I felt was sorry. For everything.

When Miranda called early this morning to confirm our meeting, she said she heard from Joey's counsel that his nose is, in fact, broken. But technically, since it was no one's fault, no one is in trouble. Yet. My court date is Thursday, so we'll see.

I called Avery last night to fill her in on everything from San Diego to the guitar-case attack on Joey's nose. I also wanted to run an idea by her. Regardless of what happens Thursday, I know I've got a karmic debt to repay (seeing my dad's shocked, pale face at the airport when he saw Joey's nose really brought that point home), and I've got a two-part plan for how to do it. Avery loved what I came up with, and she even offered to fly in for my court appearance. It was sweet of her to offer, but I didn't want her to spend that kind of money. She just laughed and said, "In case you haven't noticed, my family is loaded." I told her to save the trip to New Jersey for a happier occasion.

Mom knocks on my door just as I click on a photo of me and

Logan—the one Matty took of the two of us sitting on the edge of the Grand Canyon.

"Come in," I say.

She comes over to my bed and peers at the screen. I consider closing the photo before she sits down but don't.

"Nice picture," she says. It is.

I can tell she's worried that I've fallen wildly in love again. I haven't. Even if I had, I'm determined not to contact Logan until I work out some things or he contacts me, whichever comes first. In the words of both Spencer and Yoda, "Stalk no more, I will not."

I push my laptop aside and throw my arms around my mom. She's nothing short of stunned. "I'm so sorry, Mom. For everything I put you and Dad through."

"Sweetheart, it's okay. We love you . . . just don't do it again."

She laughs, but I know she means it. If she didn't see my hug coming, this is going to knock her flip-flops off.

"Mom?"

"Yes?"

"I think I might like to go into fashion design. I'm going to take drawing as my elective this year, and I want to learn how to sew."

"I think that's a great idea, *mija*," Mom says. "Abuelita would love to show you, and you know your father has some machines at the factory, for small detail work. You can practice there."

Now I'm the one who's shocked. "I thought you would laugh at me."

Mom puts her hands on my shoulders and leans back to look at me. "What? You don't think I remember Rosie Couture?"

I tilt my head and smile. "You were my best client."

"And biggest fan." Mom cups my face in her hands like I'm six again.

"Well, as long as that didn't surprise you, I've got something else I want to talk to you about." This time I put my hands on her shoulders.

"I'm listening."

"It can wait until after we see Steve Justice today. I want Dad to be there too."

She kisses the top of my head. "More coffee?"

"Definitely."

"I'll put a pot on. Meet me in the kitchen."

"I'm going to be better, Mom. Wait and see."

"We don't want you to be better, Rosie. Just happy."

Steve Justice opens a bottle of Tums and shakes four into his palm. He's a thin guy, fortyish, with a friendly, elflike face. He started off all smiles, but I think I'm giving him agita. I've just finished running down the chain of events leading up to Joey's arrival at the airport and Spencer's guitar accidentally breaking my ex's nose. Poor Steve. I'm too much for him. I wonder if this will cost my dad more money.

Miranda is seated at the conference table with us in Steve's office. She's younger than I thought she'd be, early twenties maybe, with greenish-blue eyes and pretty auburn hair that she's wearing in a neat French braid.

"The good news is," Miranda says, "we've found an eyewitness. The neighbor I told you about? Lucky for us, she's a big fan of the *Late Late Show*. She saw Joey on the night of the fire."

Miranda goes on to explain that the neighbor watched Joey walk over to the burning box and attempt to snuff out the fire with his baseball cap. According to the neighbor, when flames engulfed his cap, Joey looked panicked and flung it. She said it sailed through the open car window and landed on the driver's seat of Joey's Mustang. The faux fur seat covers ignited instantly.

"And get this," Miranda continues. "The neighbor lady said he retrieved a fire extinguisher from the house, but then, instead of using it immediately, he stood there and watched the car burn for a while. The neighbor said she was getting nervous about the flames reaching the gas tank and was about to dial 911 when he finally put the fire out."

That bastard!

"So I wasn't responsible for totaling his car. How cool is that?" I'm all excited.

"It would be a lot cooler if you hadn't also continued to stalk him," Steve says drily.

Stalk, schmalk. Joey is such a wuss. I did what most kids my age do when they break up. It's not all that easy to let go.

"So you think Joey wanted his car totaled?" Dad asks. "Does this qualify as insurance fraud?"

"It's possible," Steve says. "We're certainly going to bring the matter up with his attorney. I have a call in to her already."

"That is awesome!" I say. "Do you think he'll drop everything?"

"Don't get too excited," Steve says. "You still might be looking at community service for the TRO violations."

I kinda figured that might be the case. That's why I came up with my two-part plan.

"I just hope they don't press any charges against Spencer. The nose wasn't his fault."

"So far, no news is good news," Miranda says.

I'm still nervous. Joey tried to pin the torched car on me, so it's possible his mommy is looking for someone to blame for breaking his nose. Especially if he needs plastic surgery.

"Now then," Steve says. "Let's talk about Thursday."

Steve reviews court procedure so I'll know what to expect, and after he answers all our questions, we say our good-byes.

"I don't know about anybody else," Dad says as we leave Steve's office, "but I could go for pizza."

Emotional eating. No mystery where I get it from.

"Let's get takeout," I say. "I've got something I want to run by you both, and I want Matty to be there."

Matty and my brother are sitting on our back deck when we pull into the driveway. I help Dad carry the food, and Mom walks toward the kitchen door.

"It's a nice night," she says. "I'll grab some paper plates and napkins and we can eat out here."

The five of us sit around the glass-top patio table, making short work of the pizzas, antipasto, and bread sticks. Pony is at my feet waiting for me to slip him my crust, and if I didn't have to make an appearance in court in thirty-six hours, all would feel right with the world.

"So, Dad," I say as we're finishing dinner and Mom breaks out the ice cream. "I've been thinking about what Steve said about community service. Maybe . . . well, could you use some help at the factory?"

My dad questions me with his eyebrows. "You're saying you want to work for me, for free? It's a nice gesture, but I don't think that counts as community service."

"No, no, this is more of an idea I had. I'd like to start a class."

"Class? What kind of class?" Dad asks.

"Not a class, really. More like a group. An English conversation group. You know, so nonnative speakers can practice their skills? I know I'm not a teacher or anything, but I'm almost bilingual. Do you think some of your employees would be interested?"

Eddie looks dumbfounded. "Hey, Matty, what'd you do with Rosie? Did you leave her in New Mexico? Nice job finding a replacement, though. Looks just like her."

Mom shakes her head at Eddie and puts her hand on mine. "That's a great idea, honey. Your grandparents would have loved to have something like that when they came here. English can be so confusing."

I nod in agreement, then stick out my tongue at Eddie, just to make sure he knows it's me and not my angelic twin. "I was thinking I could start with some practical phrases like ordering from a menu or going to the bank. Then maybe some small talk, like about celebrities and pop culture? I did a little research online. There are actually lesson plans out there, and I found out the library runs a similar eight-week course. I'm gonna stop by there tomorrow. Get some tips."

"Do you even know where the library is?" Eddie asks in fake awe.

"Enough," Dad says. "Tell you what. Put together a plan and I'll see if anyone is interested. But it will have to be on their time. Lunch breaks or after hours."

"Got it," I say.

"Good." Dad's not letting on how proud he is that I came up with this idea, but I can see it in his eyes, and that's all that matters.

"Hey, maybe me and Spencer could help out too? We're looking for a community service project to do for our junior year," Matty says.

"That would be great, Matty," I say. "Thank you. I know I don't say it enough, but you are the best."

Matty's cheeks go red, and Mom raises her Diet Coke. "To Matty." We all click plastic cups.

Even though I didn't get to work at the bridal shop, and the dog-walking business fell by the wayside, I'm excited about the summer that's emerging from the ashes. I wasn't always the kind of girl who wakes up early on a summer day and heads to the library to gather information on how to teach an ESL class. But tomorrow, that's exactly what I'm going to do. First, I've got explain to everyone that my plan includes a part two.

CHAPTER 20

THURSDAY, JULY 9. MY MUCH-DREADED COURT DATE HAS arrived. I'm seated in the front row of the courtroom. Steve Justice is to my right, by the aisle. Mom, Dad, Eddie, Matty, Spencer, and Lilliana are to my left—we take up the entire first row. We're turning a TRO appearance into an afternoon at the theater.

We wait for the judge to take the bench, and each time someone new comes into the courtroom, the doors swings open and bangs dramatically against the wall. They could really use a stopper or a heavier door.

Aside from rattling my nerves, the noise also makes me glance nervously over my shoulder to see who's arriving. Part of me hopes I won't see Joey or anyone in his family (so far, so good), and part of me keeps expecting Logan, although I don't know why. We just left him in Arizona. Plane tickets are expensive, and his classes have started. I know Spencer has been in touch with his brother about the whole "airport incident," but I haven't heard a word from him. Not one. Granted, I haven't gotten a new cell phone yet, but he's a smart guy; if he wanted to reach me, he could. It's okay, though. I didn't have time this week to let it bother me. I spent most of yesterday working on my lesson plans.

Finally, the judge enters the courtroom and we all stand.

"Please be seated," she says. She puts on her reading glasses and opens a file. I'm not the only one in court today: There are numerous traffic violations and another TRO appearance, which is the first case on the docket. When the judge calls the defendant in that case, the complaining witness decides to drop the allegations, saying she was mistaken when she said her husband had hit her and threatened to kill her. I'm afraid for her. The judge looks doubtful and disappointed but adjourns the case nonetheless. After sitting through appearances on DUIs, speeding tickets, and parking violations, it's finally my turn.

My underarms are sweaty and I can feel the redness starting in my face and spreading all over my body as the bailiff announces my case. *State of New Jersey v. Rosalita Ariana Catalano.* The judge is the first to speak.

"We are here today to decide if this temporary restraining order will become permanent. The defendant, Ms. Catalano, will have a chance to dispute the allegations. After that, I will make my decision. I've read your evidence in this case, Mr. Justice," Judge Tomlinson says. "I understand you're prepared to call a witness."

"Yes, Your Honor, we are."

I turn around and see Joey's elderly neighbor in the back row. She's all dressed up and rocking a nice shade of pink lipstick. She waves at Steve when he glances her way.

I'm relieved Joey and his parents didn't show. Steve explained beforehand that they weren't required to be here. Joey's probably not making any public appearances until his nose heals. No one ever said he wasn't vain.

Anyway, this is my day in court, an opportunity for me to answer the allegations in the temporary restraining order. I hope the judge appreciates my honesty and sincerity and goes easy on me. I don't know what I'll do if the temporary order becomes permanent. Staying away from Joey won't be the hard part, since we go to different schools, but it might get awkward for Eddie, Matty, and Spencer. Come September, they'll see Joey every day. Not to mention, being a girl under a restraining order won't garner me any votes for prom queen this year. I'll be lucky to get a date.

"Well, then, Mr. Justice," the judge says. "Shall we hear from your witness?"

That's when the prosecutor, an attractive older woman, stands up.

My palms are sweating and my entire body feels hot as I stare at the judge and wonder how this is all going to play out. I'm on the edge of losing it when the prosecutor speaks. "Your Honor, that won't be necessary. We have approved a request made by Mr. Marconi's attorney that the allegations against Ms. Catalano be dropped."

At that moment, it seems like my entire row lets out a collective sigh of relief. I turn to Steve, who's grinning big, like the Cheshire cat. I have the urge to high-five him, but I keep my glee in check.

This is exactly what we were hoping for! Steve contacted Joey's attorney and informed her that he was reaching out to the insurance company responsible for paying the claim submitted by Joey's parents for the totaled car. Steve also said once our eyewitness had testified, he would make the claims adjuster aware of her testimony as well. If Joey's mom had been attempting to commit fraud, Steve figured that would be enough to make them drop their petition for a permanent restraining order, and Steve was right.

The courtroom goes quiet again as the judge is about to speak. "Well, then, as much as I'd like to adjourn this case and grab an early lunch today, I for one am not willing to excuse Ms. Catalano's clear violations of the TRO while it was in place. Violations, I might add, that Mr. Marconi made the court aware of through counsel." She's looking at Joey's attorney when she says that last part.

The judge picks up a piece of paper and reads. "Let's see, two text messages, one message through a social networking website, a phone conversation between Mr. Marconi and an unnamed associate of Ms. Catalano, and, the granddaddy of them all, Ms. Catalano's violation of space restrictions at Newark Liberty Airport on July sixth."

Huh? The granddaddy of them all? I came to court today completely prepared to pay for my mistakes. I never wanted to weasel out of my TRO violations, and I can accept my much-deserved punishment for the things I did wrong, but that last one's not fair. Joey was the one who came to meet *me*. I'm squirming in my seat, itching to say something, but Steve shoots me a look that says: *Zip it.* At least the judge didn't mention Joey's broken nose. I guess he's not blaming me for that, too. Again, this speaks to Joey's vanity, not his sense of decency. How would it look if people found out that Spencer's guitar case had kicked Joey's ass? Or, in this instance, face.

The courtroom door swings open again with a bang. I hold my breath and close my eyes as I prepare to turn around and see who walked in. I'm convinced it's Joey or his parents.

"Avery!" Matty yelps.

She flutters in like Tinkerbell, looks at the judge, and gives her a smile and small wave. "Sorry, ma'am," she says with her cute Texas accent, then scurries up the aisle and sits in the second row, right behind me. My throat feels tight. I turn and mouth, *Thank you.* Avery gives me a thumbs-up. After I told her it wasn't necessary to come today, I didn't expect her to show up! I may have lost Joey and some self-respect, but I made three new friends—great friends—as a result of this whole mess. I'm including Logan in that count even though I'm not sure where we stand.

"Mr. Justice," Judge Tomlison says, "would you like to address your client's alleged violations of the TRO?"

I'm not happy that Joey showing up at the airport got lumped in there, but I'm prepared to accept my punishment. I told Steve I didn't want to make any excuses. All my friends and family have been ridiculously supportive even when I haven't deserved it. I owe it to myself to face what I did, admit I was wrong, and recover my dignity. Not only that, but I feel I owe it to the universe. People have given me so much these last few weeks, and I've got to start giving back—and I mean by doing more than court-ordered community service.

In fact, I'm starting this afternoon. My hair is all washed and pulled back in a neat ponytail, not only because it's a conservative look for my court appearance, but because I'm going to see my hair-stylist, Jimmi Gerard, so we can chop my hair off into a nice bob with a wedge and donate my hair to Locks of Love for kids with cancer. It's not saving the world or anything, but anyone who knows me knows it's a sacrifice. One small step for Rosie.

Steve answers the judge's question about my TRO violations. "That won't be necessary, Your Honor. Ms. Catalano is not contesting those allegations."

Judge Tomlinson writes something down and shuffles some pages before speaking again. "Okay, then, that will conclude your appearance on the TRO today, Ms. Catalano. We will set a date for your sentencing, and at that time I will determine how you will make amends for your transgressions. But let me say this: I do not appreciate your taking that TRO lightly, and I would anticipate probation and some community service in your future," she says. "Being named in a TRO at the tender age of seventeen is nothing to be proud of, and I intend to make sure you learn a lesson. After your sentencing, I do not want to see you in my court again. Is that understood?"

"Yes, Your Honor. It is," I say.

Then I lean over and whisper in Steve's ear, reminding him about my two-part plan. I discussed it with him when we arrived at the courthouse this morning.

He clears his throat. "Your Honor, if I may. My client and I are wondering if that anticipated community service needs to be served in its entirety within Essex County and, more exactly, New Jersey."

The judge raises her eyebrows. "Approach the bench, Mr. Justice."

I clench my fists in anticipation as Steve converses with the judge in hushed tones.

"In August?!" the judge exclaims. "It's going to be hotter than Hades." Then she looks over at me and I give her a sheepish grin. "I like it!" she says. "I think it will be a good experience for Ms. Catalano."

When I turn around to face Avery, she's all smiles.

CHAPTER 21

THE TEXAS SUN BEATS DOWN ON ME, CAUSING SWEAT TO pour down the entire length of my face, starting above my hairline, somewhere under my white hard hat. The top of my head is easily ten degrees hotter than the rest of my body.

The coordinators for Habitat for Humanity have had a radio playing all morning, but it's hard to hear over the staccato hammering and the constant buzz of power saws and drills. Anyway, this close to the Mexican border, the musical options seem limited to country and Tejano. I'm still wearing goggles from a morning holding the ends of two-by-fours while one of the supervisors ran them through a circular saw. My face may feel cooler if I take them off, but judging from the white paint speckles, I'm doing a service to my eyes while painting this six-foot fence at one of the nearly completed homes. El Paso in August. There's nothing like it.

"What kind of guitar did you wind up getting Matty?" Avery is painting alongside me.

"A Yamaha. I went for the more expensive model, even though Matty said I didn't have to. He deserves it."

"What about your class? Are y'all gonna keep teaching it in the fall?"

"Yeah, about that. It didn't exactly turn out to be my class. My neighbor, Mrs. Friedman, is a retired English teacher. She wound up running the class while Matty, Spence, and I helped out."

"Still, it was your idea," she says. "You should feel proud."

"I do, but with Mrs. Friedman doing most of the work, I wanted to find some other way to serve the New Jersey part of my community service. Mrs. Friedman helped with that, too. She got me a gig doing makeovers at the senior center."

Avery laughs. "Sounds like a better match for your skill set."

"Hey, I'm good. Those older gals looked ten years younger when I was done with them!"

This summer has been super busy. I've learned that hard work sure does keep a girl out of trouble. In addition to the English conversation class, my dad wound up employing me, Matty, and Spencer at the lampshade factory. I worked in the office, and my dad taught the guys to run the stitching and cutting machines. I used my lunch hour to practice sewing. I even made two sundresses, designed entirely by yours truly. The boys are still working at the factory and will be until Labor Day. I'll be here in Texas until then, building houses with Avery and paying off the balance on my debt to society. The New Jersey chapter of Habitat for Humanity would have been happy to have me, but it's nice to be able to experience this with a friend.

"I sure wish we were on that beach of yours right now," Avery says. "Tell me about it."

My vacation at Lilliana's family beach house never happened. I was too busy. But after surprising me in court that day, Avery stayed in New Jersey for a week and we took some day trips to the beach. It was a blast. She got along fabulously with Lilliana and Marissa, and us girls hung out with Matty and Spencer the entire time. It was more fun than I deserved to have. By the end of the week, it was clear that Avery and Matty are into each other, but who knows if anything will ever come of that. Like Avery said, time and distance (not to mention age) are not in their favor now. Still, life's all about the possibilities.

Avery and I have been painting this fence for an hour now. I cannot wait until it's time to break for lunch. I look like crap. I'm not wearing any makeup, my short hair is no doubt a matted mess under this hard hat, and my white Habitat for Humanity T-shirt is soaked through around my neck, down my back, and under my armpits.

"Have you heard from him?" she asks. This is the first time Avery's mentioned Logan. I clutch my paintbrush tighter.

"No. But I'm sure he's real busy sustaining things," I say. Too bad one of those things wasn't a connection with me. I'm so stupid. I thought we'd at least come out of all this friends. *Live and learn, Rosie.* It's time to work on me.

I'm proud of the steps I've been taking. I've been gathering college applications, and my parents said they'll take me to visit FIT in

September. I'm even trying to talk them into letting me go to public school this fall—to save on my Catholic school tuition—but they don't think it's a good idea for me and Joey to be in the same building, even though I know I can handle it. It's just as well; I'd miss being with Lilliana and Marissa, but somehow, if I wind up staying at Sacred Heart, I'm going to miss Matty more. I've grown majorly attached to him this summer. Not in a boyfriend-girlfriend way. It's more about sharing an experience that only the two of us, and Spencer and Logan of course, can understand.

I think back to my first day home. I felt so lost in my own town. The houses were all so much smaller and closer together than I remembered. And there was the traffic and the crowds; there was no breathing room. That's the way it is, living in a suburb so close to New York City, but after my road trip, nothing felt right. Nothing felt the same. I know Matty felt it too. Still does. He would have given anything to come here with me to build houses, see Avery, look up at the big night sky.

Avery bends down and uses a screwdriver to pry open another can of paint.

"So, do you think you're gonna call him?"

"Call who?" I play dumb.

She sighs. "Logan."

"Logan? Why on earth would I want to call Logan?" It comes out much louder and angrier than I expect.

"Because you haven't spoken to him in over a month," a familiar male voice says from behind me. I drop my paintbrush on my work boot.

Logan.

He's standing about ten feet away from me, wearing a hard hat, a Habitat T-shirt, and jeans that are baggier than I'm used to seeing on him, but that doesn't stop him from looking good. Slowly, I walk toward him until I'm right up in his face—eyeball to plastic goggles. I want to make sure I'm not imagining this.

"What are you doing here?" I say softly.

"Building houses, what else?"

"You drove six hours in that blasted maroon Taurus to build houses?"

He doesn't ask how I know it's six hours from Tempe to El Paso and I don't ask him if there's a local chapter of Habitat for Humanity in Tempe. Instead, we stare at each other. He reaches over and takes off my goggles and lets them drop to the ground. Then he grabs my hips, pulls me close, and kisses me.

We only separate when one of the supervisors whistles loudly at us through his teeth. "This isn't a high school dance," he says.

"He's right," I say. "I've still got a lot of work to do." I pick up my goggles and walk toward my unfinished fence and Avery, who's pretending she's been painting this whole time. I glance over my shoulder, raise my index finger in the air, and make a lasso motion.

I turn back toward the fence and smile when I hear Logan jogging toward me.

Acknowledgments

It's difficult to express the deep sense of gratitude I feel for all those who helped make my dream a reality, but I will try my best to name everyone before the music is cued up and I'm ushered off the stage.

Thanks to Kerry Sparks, my amazing agent, for rescuing me from the slush pile, believing in my writing, and working so hard to make me a published author. You rock!

To my editor extraordinaire, Annette Pollert, for her unwavering enthusiasm in championing and editing this novel. Thank you for making every sentence, on every page, better and for understanding Rosie's charms and a cowboy's allure. I am so lucky to have had the opportunity to work with you!

And to all the amazing people at Simon Pulse, especially Bethany Buck, Mara Anastas, Katherine Devendorf, Karina Granda, Carolyn Swerdloff, Siena Koncsol, Karen Taschek, and Lara Stelmaszyk.

To Sarah Cloots and Rekha Radhakrishnan, editorial consultants, for reading early drafts of this novel and providing the perfect road map for revision.

To the Rutgers Council on Children's Literature and the New Jersey chapter of SCBWI, for providing writers with the opportunity to make connections and perfect their craft.

To my writer friends who so generously give of their time and talents and push me to become a better writer: Melissa Eisen Azarian,

L. P. Chase, Karen Cleveland, James Gelsey, Sharon Biggs Waller, and especially Lisa Anne Reiss, without whom I never would have finished that very first draft. I am blessed to have you all in my corner.

To Jorge Miranda and Magaly Barzola, for their excellent Spanish translation. Thank you.

To Michael Justice, Esq., for his legal advice and humor, both of which made this novel better.

To my book clubbers, Sheryl Citro, Jen Post, Lori Mido, and Francine Ruzich, for reading my drafts and listening patiently as I shared each milestone on the road to publication.

To my *comadre*, Adriana Calderon, for believing in me when I sent that first query letter to *Cosmo* all those years ago and for reading more drafts of my work than anyone should ever have to. And to her husband, Steven O'Donnell.

To my wonderful friends, for years of antics, adventures, and road trips—the kind worth writing about!—Diana and Joe Barbour, Jeff Davis, Jennifer Johnston, Esther Northrup, Lisa Paccio, Dean Potter, and Tracy Sharkey.

To my grandmothers, Theresa Juliano and Columbia Salvato, for their respective love of words and storytelling, and to my grandfathers, James Juliano and George Salvato, my first fans.

To Dolores and John Doktorski, who make me feel like their daughter.

To my sister, Melissa Collucci, for always being the voice that tells me I can, especially when the one inside says I can't. And to her family, Anthony (more brother than in-law), Anthony James, and Cassie. I love you all.

Most important, I must thank the other two-thirds of my power trio, who put up with me on a daily basis. To my husband, Mike Doktorski, without whose constant love, support, understanding, and patience (lots and *lots* of patience), I'd be lost, and to our daughter, Carley—our greatest gift—who, when she was only six years old, said to me upon my completion of the first draft of my first novel: "Mommy, even if no one buys your book, you're still an author." God bless her. Thank you for allowing me the time and space to pursue my dreams. I love you both so much!

Finally, to the Power Trio I give thanks to every day for all that is good.

Anna Michels worked as a Norwegian language tutor, historical interpreter, farmhand, and waitress before building a career in books. She lives in the Chicago area with her husband. Visit her at annamichels.com or on Twitter @AnnaKMichels.

Jennifer Salvato Doktorski once took a cross-country road trip in a celery-green Oldsmobile. She's a freelance writer who has written articles and essays for national publications, including *Cosmopolitan*. She lives in New Jersey with her family and their dog, Buffy (The Squeaky Toy Slayer). *How My Summer Went Up in Flames* is her debut novel. Visit her at jendoktorski.com.